# THE DANDY
# VIGILANTE

## KEVIN DALEY

ANAPHORA LITERARY PRESS

TUCSON, ARIZONA

ANAPHORA LITERARY PRESS
5755 E. River Rd., #2201
Tucson, AZ 85750
http://anaphoraliterary.com

**Book design by Anna Faktorovich, Ph.D.**

M
Daley

Cover Image: "Two well-dressed men standing, one holding newspaper and eyeglasses, the other holding a book." 1897. Items in High Demand: Library of Congress Prints and Photographs Division Washington, D.C.

Edited by: Courtney Carroll

Published in 2014 by Anaphora Literary Press

The Dandy Vigilante
Kevin Daley—1st edition.

ISBN-13: 978-1-937536-64-0
ISBN-10: 1-937536-64-5

Library of Congress Control Number: 2014934999

# THE DANDY VIGILANTE

## KEVIN DALEY

For my students; and for Lu Lingzi and my brother Tommy, two curious souls who loved to cross borders to learn—one gone in an instant, one faded away in many months, both too soon.

# CHAPTER 1

## Sunday, 2:20 p.m.

As I revolved through the brass door, into the hotel, I knew I'd lost her. I'd hung back too far on Tremont Street and the shortcut through the Parker House was a bad idea. Conferences had let out, and the lobby was chock-full of people as aimless as amoebae. I squeezed and bumped my way through them with their bags, pamphlets, and smart phones.

Exiting onto School Street, I turned right and hustled down the sidewalk. My wooden cane clicked among the Bostonians and visitors out on this late Sunday afternoon. My pace was fast, considering my attire— worn out, droopy brown pants, a matching vast, and a dress shirt, all that were picked up from the Salvation Army yesterday.

Debbie Stapleton was her name. I looked down a sliver of an alley, but couldn't see her; checked a dim side street, not there either. I veered onto Washington Street. On a vendor's grill to my left, sausages sizzled, incongruously close to the Irish Famine Memorial: a starving couple embracing their dead child, cast forever in bronze. I paused and stared; maybe never having a child was better than having a dead child.

On my right was a bookstore, its façade a wall of windows. I adjusted my bowtie and scanned the people inside for a flash of blonde hair, but didn't spot her, so I walked into the heart of Downtown Crossing. Wide sidewalks hosted carts of souvenirs and snacks being hawked between retail store entrances. Bargain hunters with shopping bags shuffled along the cobblestones and tinted pavers.

A block ahead, a woman looked both ways before crossing the sun-drenched intersection at Winter Street. It was Debbie. You don't often see a dress like hers; vivid red with a broad white stripe running diagonally across her chest, taut against her body, but fluttering along the knees like a sail's luff—and this feminine craft, she had great lines.

Head down, I concentrated on my movement, just some old man in a hurry. The edge-worn wingtip shoes affected my gait, but my cane barely touched the ground as I picked up speed, anxious to see where she was going. All I knew was that she wasn't where she was supposed to be.

I looked up to keep her in sight—and sucked in my breath. She was right in front of me, twenty yards and closing; she'd turned around. I coughed and turned to face a boutique's display window with tight-clothed mannequins standing on high. I pretended to search my pockets as my heart thudded away.

In the reflection, Debbie appeared and looked my way.

Then she passed behind me, her face as blank as the female mannequin in front of me; the bony hips and shoulders of the mannequin posing like a question, to which I answered, *No, plastic anorexia doesn't look good on you.*

I followed Debbie out of Downtown Crossing. She turned onto Bromfield, where foot traffic died off. Old buildings faced each other across the street's narrow longitude, their edifices in shadow. I tossed a look to the side, just a pedestrian catching his reflection—in my case, a gray-white head of hair, a white mustache, and a posture properly stooped. Several buildings ahead, she slowed, slipped her cell phone from her purse, and looked at it—an address for a private rendezvous?

As I stopped, a motion to my left in an alley distracted me. Teenagers at the other end faced a white-haired lady standing near a dumpster. She wrapped her purse strap around her arm and clutched it to her chest.

Up the street, Debbie slowed, slightly turned to the wind channeled by the buildings. She checked her phone again.

In the dusky alley, the elderly lady shook her head and stepped back. The tallest kid, in a studded leather jacket, pushed her shoulder and held out his hand. No one else was around.

I growled in frustration and turned down the alley. My cane clicked loudly as several times I glanced up to them and down to the ground. Surely, they wouldn't want a witness. One spotted me, pointed me out. The tall one backed off; the other three did nothing. But then he was nodding at me, smiling like it was a two-for-one day at Macy's, with misguided youths receiving senior citizen discounts. I dug my nails into my palms. Crime was one thing. Picking on the weak was an entirely different animal. I was a victim once.

"Yo, yo, yo, what we got?" Head tilted, he pointed his thumb at her. "This your old lady?"

The lady pursed her lips, looking ghostly in the dim light. She sported a daisy brooch on her pastel blouse over an ivory-colored silky skirt. Her pink skin glowed through white hair thin enough to blow off like the head of a dandelion gone to seed.

I scrutinized the four guys from twenty yards away, watching for hidden hands, bulging pockets, glints of sharp metal. A skinny kid, about seventeen, wore a spiked bracelet around his wrist. I hoped it was just to draw attention away from his acne scars. He moved behind the tall guy.

The other two guys looked older and heavier; they stepped to the side—to stand off or to jump me? One was dressed in faded Old Navy-like clothes, but the other resembled an escaped P.O.W. behind enemy lines with his filthy clothes, tangled hair, and mean face. Altogether, they could do me damage.

"Yo, grandpa, this lady owes us some money, courtesy pay for walking her across the street. You know," he checked his friends, "like Boy Scouts." They laughed on cue. He reached out and they bumped fists. He appeared to be the oldest, about nineteen. I knew he was the one to concentrate on.

"That's-that's a fib, a fib," the elderly lady blurted.

"I'm here to pick her up," I said, trying to ignore the palpitations in my chest. "We're late."

The woman opened her mouth briefly.

"Hey, prince charming." The tall guy grabbed the lapels of his jacket, head cocked. "She ain't gonna make it to the ball, man."

"Why don't you guys leave her alone? I mean, really, come on." Guilt him out of it. "She's a lady, an elderly lady."

He hesitated, checked his guys, who appeared undecided.

"Mind your own business, old man," he said.

"I will if you will. Let's all leave." I stepped closer and straightened my posture. He was a wise guy; we'd see if he was wise enough to recognize determination. "Okay?"

"Fuck you." He grabbed at the purse, causing the lady to stagger.

"She's coming with me," I shouted as I lifted my cane and shook it.

This was getting absurd.

He started laughing. His accomplices joined in, and he reached for my cane. He was a bit taller than me, about six-two. He pulled, but I held on. He tilted his head, eyeballing me. "Better let go, papa."

I stepped in and twisted the cane away. He was surprised, thought it was luck, and didn't notice that my slate-blue eyes weren't blurred with age. The P.O.W. look-alike circled behind me, but the tall one shook his head to call him off, then he grabbed my cane again. "Come here, geezer. You wanna mess with me?"

I let him get a good grip. He tugged hard. I twisted it away again, same technique, against the thumb, stance firm, controlling my center of gravity. He was flabbergasted.

"Check it out," skinny kid said, leaning side to side. "He crazy."

The tall guy's face darkened. Adrenalin hit my bloodline—he was coming. I didn't need this.

"I'll fucking—" He lunged.

I stepped right, my left foot stayed, and he tripped over it.

"Oh," the lady gasped, stepping back. "Please! Let's just go, get my skirt and go!"

The skinny kid guffawed, and the other two mustered a laugh at their fallen comrade, which only pissed him off more. I kept my eyes on them, but the lady's comment about her skirt confused me. Maybe one of them had her shopping bag.

He leapt to his feet.

I checked the other punks and dropped the cane behind me, hoping to diffuse the situation.

He lunged. I dodged wider, whipped out my corncob pipe, and as his arm grazed at my chest, I jabbed the pipe tip at the nerve by his carotid artery.

"Ah. What the fuck?" Sitting on the ground, he rubbed his neck. I knew the pain.

He pulled out a knife—I didn't know that pain. Didn't intend to, but I couldn't abandon this lady. I stepped back into a fighting stance, my hands and arms loose in front of me.

"Come on, Johnnie," the Old Navy kid said and glanced down the alley.

I snatched my cane from the ground and nodded to the lady to move behind me.

"My skirt," she pleaded.

Stepping backward, Old Navy crushed a soda can. "Uh-uh." He leaned toward Johnnie and whispered, "Let's get out of here."

Johnnie glared at me.

The Johnnie-whisperer tugged his arm. "Forget it, man. We ain't looking for that. We got shit to do."

Bad-boy Johnnie pulled away, scanned the area, then he jumped at me, thrusting the blade in front. I dodged and smashed his wrist with my oak cane. The knife flew out of his hand as he cried out.

"Oh fuck, man, look at your arm," urban P.O.W. guy said.

Johnnie held it up. His wrist was fine—I must've missed it—but his forearm was noticeably bent. Well, I had swung hard, but - suspected that he was vitamin-D deficient. He tried to straighten his arm, winced, and went pale.

"Fuck that." P.O.W. lunged closer to me, his grimy hair swinging, grinning wildly. "We ain't taking that, muthafucka—you dead." He rolled up his sleeves to display the grim reaper and skull tattoos on thick forearms. He pulled up his pant leg; no tattoo, but tucked into his boot, a sheathed hunting knife that he whipped out.

Skinny boy moved behind me and grabbed the old lady by the neck. She cried out.

"Kid," I said, "you better let her go. No one else needs to get hurt."

He laughed. "You the one gonna get hurt on, man."

*Knife be damned.* I turned, grabbed his scrawny neck, and squeezed for all I was worth. He twisted and pushed the lady against the wall. She went down. He slammed his wrist spikes into my shoulder.

P.O.W. guy hovered, waving his hunting knife.

And that was when I saw it, the lady's blue skirt on the ground. The silky garment she wore wasn't a skirt; it was a slip. Near the skirt was her plain white underwear, messed with alley dirt, or worse. Rage flooded into me.

I spun skinny kid by the arm and shoulder, smashing him face-first into the brick wall and a lifetime of dental issues.

Then I turned to the last contender, the fake P.O.W. with a long blade and short temper. His heightened posture belied his lack of training. His belt buckle jangled. Fists raised, he ran at me, which I countered with a leg sweep. It landed him on his ass, but as I moved in for the finish, he scrambled up and slashed my shin with the knife.

His expression was less confident, but then he came at me, slashing diagonally left and right, left and right. I moved backward. This was where Indiana Jones would whip out his pistol and shoot the attacker; alas, no gun on me.

He lunged with an overhead stab. I blocked, moving sideways, and used both hands to continue his downward stab, completing the arc of his attack all the way into his own abdomen.

He froze. The moan and big "O" of his mouth weren't gratifying enough; with an upper elbow strike, I shut him up, and he slid to the ground.

I stood over him, blood dripping down my shin, wanting to do him more damage, *wanting to kill him.*

Johnnie ran off, unsteadily, cradling his arm. Skinny was out cold.

The elderly lady whimpered. "Please. Help me."

I helped her up and tried to calm her. She had cheek abrasions and was unsteady. Otherwise, she seemed all right. My shin had a one-inch cut; not too bad, but weird to see the white of my shinbone.

"*Oh my,*" she said. "They're all gone?" She glanced at the last one, who'd moved to the wooden fence and was trying to climb it.

I retrieved her skirt and helped her step into it. Neither of us mentioned her underwear. Images popped into my mind that I shoved aside. I straightened my gray wig then gave her my arm, in keeping with my character. When we reached the street, I checked behind. Several tracks of blood were on the fence, but P.O.W. punk was gone.

She was steady now, and flush; excited, I assumed, from my surprising chivalry. I never imagined what a thrill it could be to cause such a glow on an elderly lady's face.

"Thank you," she gushed. "Thank you, I never—"

"You're welcome," I said, turning to leave. "And yes, I never either."

Walking up Winter Street, I smiled, until realizing that I'd lost Debbie and the bleeding reached my ankle.

A memory surfaced, of high school. I'd been attacked and abused by a guy named Paul Arena, a name and a face I'd never forget.

Prickles rose on the back of my neck.

I quickened my pace, checked left, and took a right. At the corner of Boston Common, I passed the brick-and-wood Park Street Church, scanning pedestrians, and hurried up Beacon Hill toward the golden-domed State House. My sock was bloody. My quarry wasn't in sight, and I might not get a chance to tail her for a few days. Debbie might have found whatever building she'd sought.

I should have checked the city hall area, but couldn't delay any longer. I had to get an article in before the deadline. I straightened my posture and tossed the cane and corncob pipe into a trash barrel.

Funny, what suddenly maddened me was the hot dress Debbie was wearing, the red one with the white stripe. I'd bought it for her for our sixth anniversary.

# CHAPTER 2

# Monday, 7:30 a.m.

The dusky confinement made it hard to focus.

*Block the punch, attacker's wrist to my hip, forearm to the back of his elbow. Twist torso, bend him at the waist, then push down on the elbow to break it or force submission, depending on intent.*

It was tight quarters in my barn's second floor practicing *go shina kata*, but little room was needed for these Japanese close-in techniques. Yesterday, some punks; this morning, I defend my head against roofing nails penetrating the age-blackened wood. Cuts would easily show through my pate's stubble veneer, and my shin would definitely scar, but it was wrapped in a butterfly bandage.

At each end of the barn, windows relieved the claustrophobic feeling; one was filled with blue sky, the other with colorful foliage against the glistening backdrop of Sunset Lake. It was a good place to forget one's troubles or to imagine beating some guy's ass. I felt uneasy about inflicting serious injuries in the alley, but those punks got what they deserved.

It was easier to exercise without the gray wig and worn-out shoes. I was in my thirties, not seventies. My left knee hurt, but the stratified heat should be good for ligaments and my lofty goal of staying in form. My eighty-pound punching bag and speed bag were on the ground level. I'd hit those for fine-tuning. I was back to my ideal weight range, around two hundred, complete with resurfaced stomach muscles wrought with hundreds of sit-ups, crunches, and planks weekly, plus snacks of raw green beans and carrots alternating with bananas.

I climbed down the steep, open-plank stairs with a glance at the old dog leash hanging on the wall. I toweled my face and neck then started on the speed bag establishing a rhythm. My enterprise piece on a spat of liquor store robberies came to mind; due today and still choppy. I switched to my right fist.

A shout came from outside. I peeked through the barn door and saw my wife leaning over the deck rail.

"Dax, we have to go," Debbie called out.

Her smooth, light-brown skin, a gift from her Trinidadian grandmother, contrasted with her blonde hair, soft and frizzy. Her body was oh-so toned, and as she turned and brought all those nice features inside I couldn't help but wonder, if she had also brought them to another man yesterday.

I smashed the speed bag, which stuttered to a diminishing bobble. "Okay."

Leaving the barn, I passed the paint cans and brushes I'd use for the house trim. Inside, I rushed through my shower and put on cologne as olfactory insurance. Debbie slapped my bare butt as she passed me exiting the bathroom. I was conditioned to smile, knowing her grin was for the loving tease.

"No time to shave, huh?" she said. "I'll be in the Jeep, hon."

I nodded. "Be right there."

She had an appointment this morning with the local OBGYN, who referred us to the fertility doctor last spring. Debbie told me she may have an issue, and my sperm count was a little low, but there was no clear answer. She was taking my Jeep Wrangler 4x4. It wasn't her style, but her Lexus was getting detailed. The only problem was, she wouldn't drive the Jeep on the highway. She'd watched a program on deadly SUV rollovers, and now getting her into my Jeep for a highway trip was like getting her to swim to Martha's Vineyard after watching a *Jaws* marathon in an IMAX theater.

Sore from yesterday, I stretched out in the driveway. She had the soft top up, windows zipped, and A/C on against the muggy September morning. I hopped into the passenger side, and we left. She appeared well rested, but wore unnecessary makeup, like the shading around her nose she applies to make it look smaller.

"Oh, by the way, don't let anyone snatch your iPod in the subway. On Channel 7 news—" She turned left onto Central Avenue.

I glanced at her. "What?"

"According to the Boston Police, there's a rash of that going on," Debbie said.

As if I cared about that now. "Don't worry, honey. I'd give the guy a lot more than a rash if he tried that with me."

She shook her head. "Violence begets violence. Besides, people get shot for much less these days."

"So we just roll over?"

"Report it, of course." She glanced at me, not rolling her eyes but her tone implied it. "Let the system handle it. You can't single-handedly stamp out the urban culture of guns and gangs and so forth, can you?"

Debbie was a thirty-nine-year-old psychologist. We'd joked that I was her number-one patient, but in the last year, there seemed to be an element of truth to it when at times she'd hit a nerve with her spontaneous analyses. I'd told her my black belt in karate was nothing to her black headband in psychology.

"I suppose the system works at times, but some lessons are better learned the hard way." As we drove past Tremont Street, I glanced at the elm trees fronting French's Common. "It's like that Smashing Pumpkins line about having to be there until your kid's old enough to get laid. If they haven't learned their lesson, they should."

"Dax. How can you say that?"

"You mean, how can I say that to you, knowing how much you empathize with urban youth and—"

"It's—"

"I know, I know," I said, "but people should be able to stick up for their rights."

She wagged her finger. "That's not how the police commissioner says to deal with it."

I made a face. "He says whatever the mayor tells him to say."

"Of course; the mayor's a leader. He might even become governor."

I watched her. "Up on your politics, are you?"

"I do read the *Boston Times*, you know." She smirked. "Governor Leno escaped that old campaign finance scandal and might run for president, so—"

"The point is," I said, "that even if the police arrest kids they get sucked into the system, and—"

"And that's what the district attorney is for, Dax, prosecution. But there's the prevention side, too, which is more important," she said, tapping her thigh.

"Of course, you're right, but if you make street crime more *immediately* risky you'll have a larger impact. Maybe they'll stay clear of trouble in the first place and not end up doing worse. Slap their hand right away, or whatever it takes."

She pulled into the parking lot of the train station. I unbuckled and shifted in my seat, the image of flowers in my head—a bouquet that I hadn't given her, but that I'd seen on the floor of her car recently; flowers that never made it into the house, but disappeared for some reason, a reason I'd like to know.

"Well, look." My heart beat faster. "If something is risky, you know, if you risked getting caught with immediate consequences, wouldn't you think twice?"

"What?" Debbie faced forward. I couldn't read her.

Her cell phone rang. A car behind us beeped.

She checked the rear-view mirror. "Well, bye."

"Okay then. Bye." I hopped out and waved at her through the window.

She waved back by releasing a few fingers from her cell phone—a microwave, I supposed. I wondered if she could recall when our greeting and parting consistently mandated a kiss.

A romantic dinner was probably overdue; a romantic dinner that'd be productive, I hoped, assuming she wasn't screwing around, which was something my inner investigative reporter would determine, one way or the other.

Of course, I didn't believe she was unfaithful. I'd been performing an exercise in investigative journalism. I had to pick someone to follow, and it made sense to follow someone I knew. I could cross-check surveillance information with my own knowledge or what I could easily find out. That way, I could double check myself.

Still, just the thought of...

From a window seat, I stared out at a train on an adjacent track. It appeared to inch forward until a tug from our train showed it was us departing Braintree. Passengers had their faces in books, monitors, or windows. None appeared to be the type to snatch another's property. I pulled out my cell phone.

The issue of crime and injury was broader than my debate with Debbie, and simpler. If something was going to hurt you, and the police or the school or whatever authority couldn't protect you, then you protected yourself. Sometimes, you had to take things into your own hands.

Still, I regretted our clash and that I hadn't curtailed it with a compliment to her which would have made us both feel good.

After scanning our newspaper's online edition, I plugged in my earphones and tried to relax to Jean Michel Jarre's *Oxygene*. I was late for work and hoped that I wouldn't get assigned to a distant story today and have to rent a car.

At the JFK station, I got out and walked to the *Boston Times*, a brick and glass structure sprawled between Morrissey Boulevard and an ocean inlet. Dark-green box trucks loaded newspapers at the docks near the massive, high-speed presses. The second floor held scores of offices with employees in circulation, advertising, accounting, and personnel.

On the third floor, I looked out over a sea of information, waves of desks with people, paper, and electrons circulating until coalescing into stories in print or on the web. Reporters, researchers, editors, clerks, and secretaries all worked in the sports, art, national, and foreign divisions. At the center was the local news operation, my area. Walking briskly, I avoided eye contact. About to duck into my cubicle, I sensed a figure looming.

"Grantham. Dax Grantham. I thought I recognized you."

Too late, Leo Kravitz spotted me. I straightened up, so he wouldn't misinterpret my stooped posture as cowering rather than the lingering disguise affectation it was.

"Glad to see you recognize your office," Kravitz said. "It's been too long. What, a vacation you forgot to mention? Hit the lottery?" He'd been city news editor here since before I started my career seven years ago. Like me, he was a little over six feet tall; unlike me, he had a thick mid-section and a weathered face.

"Good morning, Your Excellency," I said, checking out his paisley tie from an uncertain era.

"Knock it off. You think I'm a prick? Just tell me and we can have a nice intellectual discussion about my being Lou Grant on steroids and Prozac, but tougher, because this ain't—I said *ain't*—a TV sitcom. Is that what you want, Mary?"

I shook my head.

"And you can tell me how hard you work out there gathering information to spread to the populace as part of your First Amendment-in-action life."

I smiled. He was tough, but a straight shooter. "Okay, I gotcha."

He pulled off his thick-rimmed eyeglasses. "Gotcha? *Gotcha?* Please tell me you know why I'm upset. This is not my usual mini-tirade. You're slipping, Batman." He jutted his head forward and waited.

I shrugged.

"You missed the meeting."

"The meeting? Oh, fu—" I almost swore. "Damn, Kravitz, I'm sorry. I totally blanked on that. My wife needed my car and I was sidetracked."

"I don't care if your wife was on the train tracks. Pick her up on the way back—twice if you have to."

I twisted my lips. "Not funny."

"I'm an editor, not a comedian," Kravitz said.

As city editor, he chose which local and regional news stories ran where, especially the half-dozen or so on page one and Metro Front. A good guy to keep happy.

"Get here on time for meetings, especially ones like that. I give you leeway, so work with me, won't you?" He shifted on his feet. "Listen, go to police headquarters and get statements on recent crime prevention developments. And take Cinderella here with you."

He nodded toward Jimmy's cubicle and marched off. Too late to tell him I'd worked overtime at home last night; I wouldn't get his sympathy anyway.

Leo Kravitz's friends in city hall thought crime might worsen since high school would start again soon, adding new sources of youth conflict. The police department's Youth Violence Strike Force and School Police

Unit were ramping up. They approached Kravitz for him to oversee story coverage with a sense of civic responsibility. Not compromise journalistic integrity, of course, they'd said to him, but to rally the teams, encourage solutions without raising a vigilante counter wave—or bad press. That was my take on it, anyway, a tad cynical. I haven't covered crime and politics long enough to develop many contacts in those areas, but I didn't need them to know such was the way of the world.

Yesterday, Kravitz told me I was to take a couple of newer journalists to cover the purported increase of crime in Boston. With 100 to 150 gangs, there were 1,100 to 1,400 youth actively involved in violence. Incredibly, only one percent of them committed over fifty percent of the violence. I had to find a way to get close to some of them, as safely as reasonably possible, for my story. I'd work my police contacts for an in, maybe starting with my friend Sunny.

In my cubicle, I checked online how the Red Sox were doing. Catching up to the Yankees; not unusual, but I had to have faith the Sox would come out on top. Next, I reviewed the crime material I'd gathered. It suggested a possible record crime rate in Boston, with violent offenders on top. Mayor Grasso was taking a lot of heat and passing it on to Police Commissioner Weston and others down the line. To their credit, they were reaching out to inner-city areas, where the most crime was occurring.

I stuck my folder in my backpack. Exit stage right. Forget "Cinderella"—Jimmy, that is. Let him take the pumpkin. I stepped out into the breeze easing in from Dorchester Bay. My cell phone rang. It was Kravitz, so I answered.

"Listen, Grantham, skip police headquarters for now. Get over to Downtown Crossing, a little alley off Bromfield Street. Some crazy old guy saved an elderly lady from a mugging by hoodlums yesterday. See if you can get witness statements, then—"

I hung up, stunned, already trying to think of an excuse for having done so. I powered off my phone. What the heck? He'd just assigned me to cover the story of what I'd done.

# CHAPTER 3

# Monday, Noon

I arrived in Roxbury at the muster point of an anti-crime march, which was long, but nothing compared to the five, ten, or twenty kilometer walks for hunger, cancer, and other things that could kill you. The crowd was dense. I flashed my reporter ID around, asking questions; the ordinary but outraged citizen angle. A woman in her thirties was flattered by my request to photograph her. I jotted her responses on my pad. Two men in their forties said no thanks. Actually, the second one said, "Whoa, no thanks," and waved me off like I was about to take his mug shot.

Kravitz came to mind. I could be scouring Downtown Crossing for witnesses, pulling a police report, and getting the old lady's address, but no way was I going near that alley or the story to get caught in a news photo or video. God forbid the old lady or one of the punks recognized me and tipped off the police or the media. What if I got charged with assault and battery or assault with a deadly weapon, or worse, attempted murder? Besides, it would be unethical, even creepy, to cover the story of my own actions. I certainly couldn't report that it was me there, incognito, *and* that I'd been following my wife—that could be a double play, damaging a marriage and a career.

I turned on my cell phone, having conjured the best excuse for disobeying Kravitz's instruction.

My phone rang—Jimmy. I answered.

Jimmy said, "Kravitz was asking me about—"

"Hello? Jimmy? Are you there? I—" Pause. "Kxszssh." I hung up and turned off my phone again, planting the seed of my excuse so Kravitz wouldn't skin my ass.

A Hispanic state representative stood on the platform. We made eye contact, and I saluted her. She accentuated her smile and waved. I'd interviewed her by phone already. It was a good example to my boss that I worked effectively, but a good example I couldn't share until he saw results from the crime story series and was open to my self-praise. Perhaps I should show more initiative, like requesting an interview with Mayor Grasso to discuss his possible bid for governor. If I spotted any city councilors here, I'd corral them into decipherable opinions and see if they differed from the mayor. Street crime was a hot issue in several elections.

On the platform, a dark-skinned man in his late-twenties wearing a maroon beret wielded a megaphone, getting the crowd riled about the safety of our streets, our homes, and our schools. People waved, shouted, and raised arms or fists. Some held personalized placards for dead loved ones or bobbed their messages for peace and justice or against crime. I photographed the area to verify my written descriptions later.

The man spoke about integrating ex-convicts to prevent recidivism and insulating youth from those who fell back into crime. I jotted notes with a blank line for attribution. Volunteers in teal-blue T-shirts handed out flyers. I took one and was surprised. I knew the speaker; Terry Mc-Call, a/k/a Terry X, T-bone, and Father Time. The latter name earned during his bad days, fighting for survival in high school and on the streets, at one time homeless. A few years ago, I wrote an article about kids missing the transition from high school to higher education; he was a featured example. He'd made good, which made me feel good.

If you put aside the crime cycle's repetitiveness, the energy here was great. Eventually, the anti-crime march started, and I had enough material to cover my butt. Heading back to the train station, I entered an area of two-story brick buildings, a mix of retail and service shops. I crossed to the shady side of the street.

A block ahead, a guy sprinted my way. He was thin, olive-skinned, and held a box. A middle-aged guy followed, limbs pumping, stomach-stretched shirt heaving with each step, flashing crescent moons of underbelly. They certainly weren't coach and competitor, unless you counted the young man as competing with other thieves and the older man as trying to coach him out of it.

The older guy flagged pedestrians ahead by raising one arm higher than the other as they pumped. He kept yelling, "Stop him," between huffs and puffs.

Pedestrians stepped deftly aside, letting the young man fly by with his box of trophies. It seemed this competition was over.

I stopped and stared. Why should I risk my life for a few goods? Maybe he had a starving baby at home or this was the only time he stole before being hired by someone who wouldn't discriminate but would pay him a fair wage—or was that just Debbie's voice in the back of my head?

The young man spotted me and read my face and posture for intervention. He checked behind and then smiled for having outrun the shopkeeper and passed through the faux gauntlet of citizens.

I noticed that the logo on the box he carried matched the shopkeeper's shirt logo. It irked me, and my left leg shot out as quickly as the thought that brought it out. The thief tripped. The box flew out of his hands. Dozens of sparkly metal lighters flew onto the cement and tar.

He rolled, cursed, and jumped up, glaring at me with hunched shoulders, clawed fingers, and destruction in his eyes. He resembled the Hulk, except for the lack of bulk and green skin. His clothes were so baggy, though, they'd probably fit upon metamorphosis.

I shrugged. The shopkeeper was almost here. Hulk growled at me as if sending me a message. I should interview him: *So, tell me, what are the latest punk communication techniques?* But he took off.

The shopkeeper arrived, breathing hard. Exertion boosted his complexion to that of a Mediterranean sunbather slathered with rouge.

Standing beside me, he watched the thief fade into the city. "Thank you... Thank you so... much."

"It was an accident," I said, thinking this was messed up—two crimes in progress I'd stumbled upon in two days. "Besides, I needed a light."

"Ha." The shopkeeper picked up a lighter and handed it to me.

"No thanks," I said. "I don't smoke." I noticed his swelling cheek and red eye. I bet the punk had clocked him.

"I don't care, sir. I'm sick of them," Shopkeeper said. "I just want to thank you."

What could I say? Tell Debbie I had a guy here in favor of citizen intervention? "You're welcome."

I pocketed the lighter and continued my journalistic journey like a vignette in the inner-city version of the *Canterbury Tales*. What was the moral here? Don't run with sharp scissors or hot lighters?

*** 

I stopped at a pub to have a celebratory bite—alone. I certainly couldn't share this do-gooder deed with anyone back at the office, and I needed to think, to figure out Debbie.

I hoped for a good old Irish draft. With the looks of this dingy place, though, I should be ordering Schlitz or Old Milwaukee. I didn't even see a Guinness tap. No Guinness? Someone should shut this place down.

"Could I get a draft beer, please," I said from a stool.

The bartender, adorned with a Rastafarian cap, asked what kind.

"Anything cold and fresh."

He went for the Pabst Blue Ribbon and served it up.

"Thanks," I said.

He nodded and walked to the other two-thirds of his crowd—that is, the two other patrons sitting a half-dozen stools away. I combined my first sips into a chug; the beer was good, cold. Pabst and I hadn't met in a long time.

Dropping my forearm and mug onto the bar, I exhaled an, "Ahhhh."

They looked over at me.

I lifted my mug. "Fresh draft."

The elderly guy nodded, and they all turned away.

I appreciated the novelty of the ancient black and white television overhead. Its thick metal wall-mount looked like it could secure a safe. The news reporter of color—or of tint, for this television—was Bella French. She was covering the anti-crime march live, interviewing people and regurgitating politicians' sound bites; the same thing I did. The only difference was she had sound and color, and my words were collected into coherence later—hardly "live." Forget "Extra, extra, read all about it!" That was long gone. Now it was simply "turn on CNN" or just check your smart phone.

What happened to those punks who'd mugged the old lady in that alley? I hadn't been in a real fight since high school, if losing in an attack like that counted. Two seniors had cornered me alone after school, one of them an especially twisted bastard. So... bad. But I'd survived. I stared at the scarred wooden bar. The punks I hurt in the alley? Yeah, I shared a bit of my pain with them. That was justice, for once.

I noticed my tight grip on the mug. My appetite disappeared. I dropped a few bills onto the bar.

"Downtown, crime is increasing," the TV reporter said. He introduced a pre-recorded interview by reporter Brad Seitz. They showed the victim—and I nearly spilled my beer.

She still had that glow about her; or maybe I had to face the fact that brushed on blush had caused it, not my rescuing her. One cheek was bandaged. She was chastising the camera and wagging her finger as if that tall young hoodlum was watching. At least she wasn't holding a parasol.

I laughed. The bartender and patrons looked at me, then at the TV, and laughed a bit. I laughed harder, knowing that they weren't thinking what I was thinking. They went back to guarded expressions and stared at me, as if I might be going off the deep end, which they might have experience spotting. Alas, I left without the benefit of their feedback.

On the sidewalk, my face flushed at the thought of those punks victimizing an old lady like that. It was cruel. I hoped it wasn't also a sexual assault. No word on the cops catching them yet. I could've killed one of them, literally, which made me nervous, but defense of another was legal to the extent the other person could use self-defense. If I was an old lady, and could bust his bones, what the hell, why not put him out of commission for a while, like I did to Johnnie. Or like P.O.W. man, whom I helped stab himself. Yes, I had exceeded Guardian Angel guidelines. So what?

I turned on my phone and retrieved a message, Kravitz asking if I'd hung up on him. Demanding to know where the hell I was. If I had any interest in still working for the *Boston Times*, he'd said, I will cover the city hall press conference tomorrow and see if I could write up the mayor's anti-crime efforts in a decent light. He left a press release from the mayor's office on my desk to "give me a head start."

I didn't like that.

And there was another thing I didn't like, about the mayor's office, something personal. While leaving the driveway the other day, I saw flowers on Debbie's car seat. They didn't come from our garden. They didn't appear later so I could ask her about them, either. I slipped out to check her car. No flowers. On the floor mat I found a note saying that she was a beautiful woman, he liked the way she thought, and he looked forward to spending time with her. No signature, but it had letterhead: Office of the Mayor, City of Boston.

I'd get to the bottom of that political stationery, but first I had to play my office politics right by facing Kravitz. I needed his help in more than one way.

# CHAPTER 4

## Monday, 2:45 p.m.

Along sun-embossed Morrissey Boulevard came an onshore breeze carrying that salty-Atlantic scent. A nice day to do not-so-nice things, like telling Kravitz to shove it because my ambition was to give our *Boston Times* trucks something to deliver instead of newspaper for kindling fires or for puppy waste targets. Instead, I'd claim cell phone trouble and hadn't heard him say to go to Downtown Crossing for the elderly mugging story.

Kravitz promoted fast and accurate reporters to national or foreign desks, and if stylish, to Living/Arts or the Sunday magazine. The alternative was to linger too long, like me, in the Metro Section, which had less status despite its importance. My goal was an assignment to the I-Team, our prestigious group of investigative journalists, digging for the facts and motives. I planned to apply to a certificate program at the New England Center for Investigative Reporting, which required a letter from the applicant's media employer. I was pinning my hopes on Kravitz writing that letter and I needed it soon.

I waved to the security guard as I entered the building and then made my way to our cafeteria, since they didn't deliver to cubicles. I picked up a slice of pizza and a diet soda. Earlier today, I was watching television and the old lady told the reporter that her anonymous rescuer was "dandy," but the anchor coined the phrase "dandy vigilante" and asked the public for any information.

And I could give him some, but I was not interested. I had enough to deal with already, personally and professionally.

Among other things, Kravitz had been calling me superhero names. Perhaps it had sunk in, so I helped that old lady, and then the shopkeeper. It was that thought that made me laugh in the Roxbury bar. "My hero," said she, hands pressed against her tilted cheek. Replied he, kicking the dirt with his boot, "Aw shucks, ma'am, it wudn't but nuthin'." She hadn't actually said that, but it didn't block the kick I got from her interview.

As soon as I set the pizza on my desk, Jimmy, came out of his castle, which was what I now liked to call his cubicle.

Jimmy was wiry and athletic, second-generation Vietnamese. As he was the youngest and latest staff addition, I'd shown him around. He probably thought I was jaded, but I just liked to mess with him a bit.

"Hey. Could you check this out?" Jimmy handed me his draft article about Mayor Grasso's million-dollar investment in a Community Learning program, working with the public schools and the Boston Center for Youth and Families.

Grasso's face came to mind. I didn't like it. I'd first seen it in an election pamphlet during his campaign; handsome, maybe, but he resembled that of Paul Arena, my high school nemesis. I shoved all that out of mind.

I read the article; it was good. "Maybe cut the part with the mayor preening about the Camp Harbor View summer project."

"But, it received a Crown Community Award," Jimmy said.

"Yeah, and we're proud, but it dilutes the story about Community Learning. Besides, it might be edited down or turned into a sidebar."

Jimmy nodded, but didn't appear to agree. He was ambitious. He'd even tried getting an interview with the mayor for his article.

"And hey," I added, "if you do reach Grasso or his chief of staff, don't waste the opportunity. Ask whether he has the support to run for governor."

"Is he definitely in the race?" Jimmy tilted his head. "He'd be going against Governor Leno, wouldn't he?"

"Governor Leno will probably be making a presidential bid. Leno won't announce it, of course, until he's sure. He won't endorse Grasso before then."

Jimmy fingered his chin. "Even though Grasso's running out of time? Maybe he's putting Grasso under pressure, for some reason."

I nodded. "Good point."

Jimmy reminded me of when I'd been a younger reporter at a newspaper in Cambridge. Before that, once upon a time, I was on the Braintree High School newspaper, when I'd dressed as a girl to do an article on the female perspective. It was an eye opener. I was treated badly. I wasn't a great-looking girl, but it still hurt. My article was an indictment of male expectations.

I flicked on my computer.

I got a playful whooping on the school bus, but later I got cornered in the locker room by a couple upper-classmen on the wrestling team, Paul Arena and another creep. I should have expected something, but not that. I'd always remember that attack, especially that way, although I tried to forget. After high school, I learned karate, had a growth spurt, and never wore drag again, which, years later, Debbie said was healthy to avoid anyway.

Jimmy said, "Mr. Kravitz said he wants you to go with me on an interview assignment today."

I'd planned on leaving early to follow Debbie. Initially, I'd thought this field exercise would give me something for my application to the investigative journalism training center, but it gave me something unexpected, and I couldn't just let it sit. I had to know if something was really going on with her. But I also had to get back on the boss's good side, so I better help break in the new guy. "Sure."

"Some store clerk or rack jobber got robbed near the march in Roxbury. Some idiot pedestrian tripped up the perp." Jimmy shook his head. "Who does that?"

My heart dropped. That shopkeeper guy would ID me for sure; I hadn't been incognito. What was going on with my karma? If Kravitz found out, it would piss him off, and above him, the executives would freak out about liability issues in my stopping a crime while on assignment.

"Wait," I said. "Was it a box of lighters?"

"Huh? Yeah," he said. "It just happened. How'd you know?"

"Cultivated sources," I said.

"Who? It'll help me get a good start."

"Jimmy, you need to discover for yourself. Cultivate your sources, as part of your career development here."

"I am. I'm cultivating you."

"Thanks, but I'm over-cultivated at the moment." I smiled. "Interview the guy alone for the experience; get all the angles. Gotta run. Have fun."

"What? Where're you going? Let's do this together and we can stop in Dorchester for *pho*. You said you like Vietnamese soup."

"Going to my destiny, of course, and I don't like *pho* on this day of the week." I grabbed my backpack.

He bit his lip. "But, you know, Mr. Kravitz wants you to go with me."

Over my shoulder, I said, "You really don't want me to come along and hold your hand now, little Jimmy, do you?"

He squinted and waved me off. "Fine."

I called out, "This is just between me and you, buckaroo, okay?"

***

On the Red Line to Central Square, I felt buoyant. Part of me was certain Debbie wasn't doing anything wrong, and the sooner I realized that, or confirmed it, the sooner I'd stop burning brain cells with worry. I'd told her I was working late, so a good sign now would be her simply going home from work.

The train doors flew open like horse-racing gates. Backpack shouldered, I strode forth in the lead and took the stairs by twos to street level. On Mass Avenue, I hung a right into the 1369 café, got the key off the counter, and went to the men's room via the narrow aisle, an obstacle course of bags, feet, and laptop cords. Minutes later, I opened the door as an old man, *sans* cane. I wore the same baggy brown trousers, but this time belted high above my waist, which should enhance my sexy shuffle down at the nursing home—someday, that is. I wore the same pants and gray-white wig, but no bowtie or vest.

I left the key in the door and exited the back of the café. At Cambridge College, I stood by the clinking flag posts, staking out her office across Mass Avenue. I toyed with the idea of a tin can as an accoutrement.

Across the street, Debbie came out but turned toward Harvard Square instead of the Central Square train station. Among a pedestrian spectrum of varying ethnicities and sizes, I shuffled along three car lengths behind her, as close as I dared. She paused at a storefront; I hesitated then tied my shoe—a junior investigator move, but at least it separated the timing of my action from hers. She went in and soon exited with one hand holding the twine handles of two shopping bags. It was a bit unusual that she'd shop on a weekday, a bit unusual that she'd shop right after work, perhaps, and a bit unusual that she'd bought clothes at an over-priced store.

In front of the Harvard Inn, she sat on a bench in a small garden. Soon, a man in a tan blazer and blue jeans smiled as he took her hand with both of his and gently shook them. She smiled generously, too, and I didn't like it. The situation graduated to suspicious.

A ten-minute walk led to the Charles River. This man wasn't her patient, unless she'd claim it was a field exercise for therapy. Of course, I could still claim this was a field exercise for me, toward becoming an investigative journalist. They only shook hands, but his hands enveloped her hand for an extended time. That wasn't professional, unless you were selling caskets.

I paced the sidewalk across from the river, stealing intermittent glances at that man, with his trimmed brown hair, sleek blazer, and leather shoes stepping in close proximity to my wife. He looked like someone who worked in an office, say, the office of the mayor. Or some other office—the note to her on that city stationery could be a red herring, for all I knew. There was no sign he worked in city hall, but what could I expect, a city badge or armband?

He hadn't put his arm around her or pulled her close while they laughed as if they were shooting the remake of *Love Story* here. I didn't know whether I wanted to see something that overt, but it would end this ignorance, and I could bust them and maybe bust him in the nose. If not, there was still hope, because I did love her. I considered bumping into them to test their reaction until I realized her reaction would be: "Dax, what are you doing, dressed as an old man?" And I'd say what? "Um, I'm doing an undercover news story. And what under-covers work are you doing, Debbie?"

They climbed to the arch of the footbridge. Tanned, decent physique, blond-highlighted hair, he looked like one of those guys about fifty-years-old who could pass for forty. Midway, they leaned against the concrete railing. Below, the river's brown water coursed through the grassy banks. The sky loomed here. She gesticulated, talking passionately about something. Still, no touch that was clearly romantic rather than familiar—cautious, or were they new to each other? Or was I paranoid? What a time to ask that, masquerading as an old man down by the banks of the River Charles—"love that dirty water." But not the dirty laundry.

I sauntered by trees alongside Memorial Drive, recalling the year after I'd transferred to Suffolk University. Debbie and I had met and slept together within a month of the semester's start. It wasn't her usual *modus operandi*, I believed, but we had a blast right from the get-go. For months, we drove around in my large, beat-up Chevy Impala with a suicide knob on the steering wheel.

I'd taped a desk bell to the dashboard, and we cruised away the college-era blues. Whenever one of us said something funny or had a good idea, we'd slammed that desk bell with our hand. I'd say, "Hey baby, let's hit the beach." Ding! She loved the beach.

Or she'd say, "Hon, you wanna… you know." And her smoky, hazel eyes made me know. Ding-ding-ding! I slammed my hand on the bell. If I could have driven a-buck-eighty straight to her home and pulled up into her bedroom, I would have, but her room was on the top floor of a triple-decker in Winthrop, and her roommates wouldn't have appreciated it. Sometimes we just made do in the car. We were soon in love, in deep, and free—except for one significant interruption, but that was another story.

The sun was getting low. They left the footbridge and waited for the crossing signal. Traffic slowing, they poised on the curb, checking both directions. Their hands tangled in each other's arms—traffic anxiety or calculated intimacy? The white-lit stick figure signaled them, and he escorted her across.

When they stopped at Baskin Robbins, I stood behind a pole across the street. How many therapists have ice cream as treatment? None. "Ice cream and I scream therapy." No. They licked, talked, licked, and talked. My face was hot. The guy was lapping in front of my wife. As he tilted his head back and laughed, a cold dab clung to his lip. She pointed, but he missed it, so she blotted the ice cream off with her napkin. It gave me an icy jolt to the heart. I could have gotten that for him—with a baseball bat. Then he could check in his hands for cavities.

# CHAPTER 5

# Monday, 5:50 p.m.

Debbie was cornered, in a sense, as I stood at the head of the stairs. Below, her heels clicked on the kitchen tiles. I'd arrived home first and changed in the bedroom, several times dashing to the window to look for her and checking the mirror for the same old me rather than some old man. She couldn't come upstairs to integrate her shopping into her wardrobe or hide it without running into me. The bags would invite questions she'd want to avoid. If I questioned her too much, though, it could raise her suspicion of my suspicions, and I'd lose the advantage. Besides, it was better that she not discover the lengths to which I was going to reassure myself of our marital foundation. It was my insecurity; why trouble her with it?

A wonderful rationalization.

I bounded down the carpeted stairs to feign a good mood. She was drinking a glass of water, holding the bag behind our granite-topped island counter.

"Hi, honey." I smiled.

If only she had a little ice cream by her lip.

She put the glass down quickly. "Hi! I didn't know you were coming home so soon."

"Just came from the library," I said. "Research. Boring. How was your day? Extraordinary, I hope."

"Oh. No. Daily grind, you know." She nodded. "How's your grind? I thought you were going to be late tonight. You've been putting in a lot of hours lately."

"I got lucky at the library. Found what I needed right off the bat."

"Hey, could you check the mail for me, hon? Thanks. I'll see what's for dinner."

Drat. She could hide those bags.

"Sure. In a bit."

"Do you mind? I'm expecting the mortgage statement and the—what do you call it—like, scarecrow?" She laughed. "The escrow. It's driving me bonkers trying to figure out the balance before and after the refinancing. Thanks, hon." She had a nice smile.

**29**

"Oh." I returned the smile, for real; it would mean more if she hid the bags than if she didn't; much more. "Sure."

"I can get it." She took a half step.

"No, no, I'll get it. Don't wait up for me. If I'm not back in thirty minutes, send for help." I winked.

I checked the mailbox at the end of the driveway. No mortgage statement. I glanced back at our house, an antique colonial on a large lot on Sunset Lake. It'd been love at first sight, and we'd bought it. At Debbie's urging, we refinanced to renovate it. I still liked it despite the extensive changes. It gave me a warm feeling of being grounded, of being part of a history, from when it was built in 1850 through my childhood, even though my being adopted meant that it was a history I'd never had. Who knew if my ancestors were even in America in the nineteenth century? Perhaps I'd bought my roots with this house in some small measure.

Back inside, I tossed the envelopes, which fanned out on the counter.

She put something into the microwave. "Did you see anything from UPS? I ordered Climbing Rhode Island Reds, three of them to start."

"What are they?"

"A hybrid tea rose, a climber. They bloom prolifically." She beamed. "I'm going to plant it beside the barn."

"Nope, nothing from UPS. So, is the mortgage even due now? The statement isn't here."

She eyed me, then entered the defrost settings.

"When's it due, anyway?"

She paused. I was putting her on the spot.

"You know that I know. That's why I pay the bills as one of my domestic blessings—I remember, you don't. But that's cool, right, Dax?"

Whoa, stepped in it again. I once tried to wrestle control of the bills away from her. Part of my best defense was a good offense thing in our Sharing-Domestic-Duties-Fairly-Conflict, as we'd jokingly referred to it later.

"I'm gonna go shower now," I conceded.

She grinned her victory grin. I headed upstairs.

"Wait. Come here."

I walked back part of the way. "What?"

"Closer."

I moved nearer, noticing how perfectly applied her rose-colored lipstick was. "Yes?"

"Could you take these upstairs for me? Thanks." She reached behind the counter and handed me the shopping bags.

I looked into her hazel eyes, surprised. Or was I? She was a psychologist, with a mental grasp like a steel trap, in which I got caught occasionally. "Sure. What are they?"

"Just stuff I had my eye on that I finally got."

"Uh-huh. Anything special?"

"Not yet," she said, crinkling her eyes.

"What do you mean?"

"Don't remember that, either? Jeez."

"Um."

"It's not special until I wear it. Right?"

I'd told her that before, when I was the Sweetest-Man-She-Ever-Knew. Did I still hold that title? "Of course, baby."

In the bedroom upstairs, I poked through the bags, trying not to rattle the paper. I undressed while checking them, tugging my arm out here, examining the merchandise, stepping out of my underwear there, catching my balance.

Nothing but clothes inside. No lingerie. No condoms. No Cat Woman or adult-sized schoolgirl outfits. No sex toys, which definitely wouldn't be denominated marital aids in this instance. Not a single no-no.

Relief lasted only a moment because there was a lack of evidence of wrongdoing, but not evidence of right doing. Also, she'd been working late and going out more often these past couple months. These clothes may soon be special, but they revealed nothing of my wife's intentions or actions. I could check her purse when she wasn't looking, but that felt too invasive.

Showering, I contemplated death, marital in this case, the emotional equivalent of nighttime skydiving in foreign terrain. People get caught cheating all the time and surely not all were openly denounced, so getting caught likely happened more often than people knew. However, here I was trying to find out the truth, but coming up empty. I wished I could trust her. I closed my eyes and tilted my head back. Steaming water scalded my scalp. Damn. I should just bite the bullet and ask her about the flowers, ask who wrote that note.

Instead, as she showered, I combed through her pocket book for some sign of city hall, a note, a letter, a receipt, a business card. Then the shower turned off. I hastily put everything back, feeling like a louse.

Nude, Debbie came out toweling her hair. She turned on the porcelain lamp on the bedside table and hummed as she powdered herself in front of her bureau. I admired her beauty behind, and in front, via the bureau mirror. I lay on our king-sized bed with a towel around my waist. The scene was like a bookmark in an old chapter of ours, when next she'd be kissing her way up my legs to start something. That book might stay shelved tonight, though. Lately, our efforts to get pregnant were less frequent.

She put on close-fitting charcoal slacks and a beige open-neck blouse that pulled naturally and revealingly with her moves. Her female exec look was sexy to those prone to being in the mood, i.e., men. One cold night she'd come home late and didn't want to get undressed for bed, and I'd shown her how much I liked it. Eventually, that female exec look lost favor. She didn't seem to care for it, perhaps recalling her patients' hangups, and doing it for me wasn't the same as doing it with me. It lacked the turn-on of turning-on your mate, that juicy mutuality.

Her books were piled on the nightstand. If it wasn't a nookie-night, she'd read, usually biographies or non-fiction. But now I was confused—she was putting on a necklace and new shoes.

"You're trying to match the jewelry to your new outfit?"

"Sure," she said. "I have to look smart."

"For?"

"Tonight. Did you forget?"

"Forget what?" I was ready to hop off the bed and dress in a hurry.

"Ah. You did forget."

"It seems so," I admitted. "Sorry, I'm on a roll. Guess I'm tired."

She appeared disappointed, but perhaps her best defense was a good offense. You didn't have to be a psychologist to master that one; just a sports fan.

"I'm going out, Dax."

"Oh?" *Damn it.* "I thought you were just trying it on."

She perfumed her neck and wrists. "No."

"Sorry, where're you going again?"

"I mentioned last week that I had this scheduled for tonight in case you wanted to make plans without me, work late, or whatever."

I hadn't paid such close attention last week. And she wasn't telling me; a little price to pay for forgetting, as if I didn't care where she went. If only she knew how much I cared and the proof thereof, she'd be surprised.

"Come on, where are you going?"

"Somewhere." She checked the fit of her blouse. "You'll remember."

"Well, it's not like I have a staff to rely on, like a mayor or something."

She leaned toward the mirror to put in earrings, expression unchanged.

"You know?"

"And?" she said.

"And? And nothing. I've been busy, my mind on go, like wondering, since you mentioned Mayor Grasso's gubernatorial run earlier, whether he has the support. Finance, endorsements, campaign staff." I shrugged.

"Uh-huh. Anyway, the chicken masala is defrosted. Just heat it up. I'm going, bye-bye." She kissed my cheek and went downstairs. "If I'm not back in three hours, send for help."

Her repartee meant I was forgiven for forgetting. Or was that just sarcasm? She still didn't tell me where she was going. Boy, she sure knew where to place a ball so I had trouble fielding it.

"Bye, hon," I called out.

Time for Super Dax! My God, what a joke I was. But I had to go. Maybe she hadn't told me where she was going, and I forgot often enough to doubt myself, and she was relying on my faulty memory to keep me off balance. I grabbed my disguise from a bottom drawer, just in case. I'd wait to leave so she wouldn't recognize the Jeep.

"Dax?" she called out. "Just so you know, I'm taking the Jeep."

The front door slammed.

*Shit.* I dressed in a flash and ran downstairs. In the kitchen a vase held a yellow rose that matched our garden variety. I flew out the door and opened the barn. Her Lexus wasn't there. They were supposed to detail it and drop it off.

Jealousy and suspicion sank like a lead diaphragm into the pit of my stomach. I was so worked up that I'd follow her in a snowmobile—if I had a snowmobile and it was winter. But I did have a motorcycle, which was overdue for maintenance and inspection. I grabbed my silver helmet from the cabinet. Keys were in the ignition of my Harley Davidson, which was also silver. While rolling it backwards, I snatched tan-colored wood glue off a shelf. Driving away, I popped the clutch, accidentally popping a wheelie. I stopped, took a deep breath, and took it down a notch—I was dying to know, not to die.

I took the split to I-93 North. After a mile, I still didn't see her, and I'd gotten here fast; too late to turn around for another tack. Then again, why would I think she took the highway? I could kick myself, if I weren't on two wheels. What would make her drive my trail-rated Jeep on the highway after all her railings against dangerous SUVs?

*A rendezvous.*

In Cambridge, I headed toward her office, which was near where she'd seen him. I punched the throttle, passing cars left and right, weaving through traffic on Memorial Drive. Then I thought I saw her. I slowed to pace myself with the suspect vehicle, my very own dark-blue Jeep.

# CHAPTER 6

## Monday, 7:00 p.m.

A black-suited man opened the buzzing door across the street. Upstairs was the office of Debra Stapleton, Ph.D.; she'd kept her surname and left "Debbie" behind to tailor her professional image. In the window, her silhouette moved away from her desk.

To my left, a slim, young guy in jeans and sneakers loitered in front of a closed real estate office, looking inside. He was alone, no bus stop nearby. His hoodie hid his face well. Hiding the face was inherently suspect, hence laws against wearing masks in public places. Even medieval knights lifted their visors to show their face as if to talk rather than fight. My disguise had the opposite effect; no need to lift the wig to allay others' concern. But who was under any hood? It could be anyone from Red Riding Hood to the evil Galactic Emperor.

I was more aware of crime these days. I felt it was a civic responsibility to take action, although I'd taken this action-hero image, meant to amuse me, to an unhealthy degree. What else could I have expected, lurking in the shadows that my wife passed? It was the best position from which to spot crime, and my grubby-old appearance was certainly no deterrent.

At first, my motivation to track Debbie's activities was to experiment with journalistic surveillance and investigation. Now I wondered. Had I picked her as a practice target because I'd unconsciously suspected something? Also, journalists were highly observant and attracted to action. I was aware of physical danger, too, being a martial artist. That was all part of why I was here. I wasn't crazy. There was logic to it. I could be instant justice, and had to admit that I liked it.

Across the street, the guy in the hood grabbed a young woman. Affectionately, they kissed and walked away. So maybe his looking into the real estate offices wasn't so furtive after all. He was probably just bored waiting for his girlfriend.

An hour later, the man left Debbie's office. Dark shiny hair, down to his collar, early thirties; I didn't recognize him. I would keep an eye out for him at the mayor's press conference tomorrow. I matched his pace for a block and a half. Then he crossed the street toward me. He appeared upset. Had Debbie turned him down or broke it off?

Nope. That wasn't it. An alarm chirped in a black BMW 700 series sedan, its deep sheen reflecting me in contoured detail. It was definitely not a city government vehicle. I recalled that she was, in fact, working late. She'd mentioned having to accommodate someone's schedule, a rich dot-com guy contemplating divorce. This must be him. Boy, what a way to have your memory jogged—*idiot.* Debbie's private counseling practice, which she felt ambiguous about, was struggling. I'd suggested alternatives, but she didn't respond, except for expressing her interest in adolescent issues.

I walked back to my Harley.

To be fair, she was a great psychologist. With me, she was always empathetic, understanding my foibles and fears starting from our college days. Except for the limited success of one child therapist, she was the only person to get me to really talk.

Once, Debbie and I were in Salem for Halloween. The carnival atmosphere included the dark Fun House of Fear. I avoided entering it—nothing to do with Halloween. She'd dragged me to the entrance, pleading that we weren't too old. Hiding my fear, I assumed she had no clue about it. However, she sensed my true reluctance when anyone else would have missed it.

After ably deflecting my defenses, she'd said, "It's fine to admit. It's something about it that bothers you. Something that wouldn't bother most people." She didn't even add, "Right?" She knew.

I paused, and then told her, "I don't like... closed-in spaces."

Debbie leaned her face toward me, open, non-judgmental, but she was going to wait me out, not let me off. I balked, but then recognized her patience, her genuine concern.

Finally, I said, "Oh, some guys put me inside a plastic bin one time. And took off. Problem was, it, ah, it locked, and I couldn't get out for hours."

She nodded.

"I tried banging, kicking. Made me hotter. Dizzy. Don't know if I passed out or fell asleep."

That was about all I shared. She would not press me for more details than I was comfortable giving. She revealed herself to me that day, more than I'd revealed myself to her.

I put my helmet on and started my bike. So, she wasn't messing around with some guy at her office. Good. The guy had come out after an hour, the usual length of her sessions, and he hadn't been glowing or disheveled in the least. Maybe I'd been overreacting lately.

Of course, I'd been overreacting.

I decided to have more faith and go home. I waited for the sidewalk to be clear of pedestrians. They didn't need to witness this dumpy old man getting onto this Harley Davidson. I smiled, imagining a walker bungee-corded to my sissy bar.

I could focus on my job now, like generating questions for the mayor's press conference tomorrow in case he announced his candidacy for governor. He almost had to because it was so late. Pundits said he first must clear it with Governor Leno, though. Just three years ago, Leno's endorsement had pushed the relatively unknown Grasso over the edge to win his mayoral election. Apparently, there was an old connection to Grasso's grandfather, who had run a printing business in the governor's Western Mass town back in the day.

Debbie came outside. She got into the Jeep, checked for traffic—by mirror *and* by direct view, as I'd stressed to her—and made a U-turn for Mass Avenue south. Why didn't she take the same way home? I followed, curious, through Central Square. Then we passed MIT and the bridge across the Charles River. A half mile past Boston Medical Center the area was downtrodden, and I was alarmed.

*Debbie, Debbie, Debbie, where are you going?*

Off the main street, she stopped in an area with dilapidated houses and short scrappy yards. She leaned to look at one house before continuing to a part of the South End that was better but bordered a high-crime area. She pulled into the well-lit valet corral of a restaurant, a trendy one I'd heard about. The valet took the keys, smiling at the well-dressed woman exiting a slightly beat trail-rated vehicle. I wondered what to do. Give my motorcycle to the valet? The absurdity was appealing.

I passed and turned right onto a side street jammed with parked vehicles. A hundred yards down, I settled for a space on the sidewalk in front of a small tree set in a grated planter. No one was around. After slipping off my helmet, I had to retrieve my wig from inside it and plant the gray cover back onto my head.

I headed back to the main street. A couple was ahead, so I deepened my slouch to enter character. Adding a sway to my walk was easy with the shoes' outer edges worn down, as if Charlie Chaplin had owned them. The guy ahead, mid-twenties, held the young woman's forearms. She seemed to plead. Closer, she appeared little over nineteen, even with makeup, and African-American. I tried to catch her eye, but she focused on him. He stared over her head, waiting for me to pass.

Why should I assume he was endangering her? They didn't seem strangers to each other. Besides, I had to make sure Debbie didn't duck out of the restaurant. She could be picking up food or have the wrong place or the person she was meeting couldn't come. I didn't want Debbie around this area unescorted, no matter what she might be doing. With her blonde hair up in a bun and dressed in fine clothes and accoutrements, muggers could see Debbie as such an ideal candidate that she could pass for a police decoy.

I smelled food before I turned left, toward the restaurant. Patrons passed in and out; the valet hung around the curb.

But it bothered me, that girl's possible situation back there. At least an older couple sat in chairs on a porch a few buildings down. Besides, maybe the chick was hitting him, and he was just protecting himself. It could happen.

I shuffled to the window, but the reflections were obscured. Then I shifted and saw her, smiling, in her new outfit, elegant—*Debbie*. She sipped water across from a man. A lamp shade blocked his face from my view. I clenched my teeth and heat flooded my body. Under his dark suit coat, his shirt was so white that it seemed to glow; a ubiquitous uniform in certain circles, but he could be anyone. She was engaged in the conversation. Did she think his suit was nice? Was it special once he put it on? We were in Boston; did he work for the city?

"Excuse me," someone said sharply.

I turned around. The valet, average height and thin build, in his twenties, leaned closer. "No loitering."

On the other side of the window, my wife clinked glasses with the man.

"Leave now, please."

I spun on him and glared; he stepped back.

"Whoa, look, if you're hungry or something, hit the Pine Street Inn, okay?" A Mercedes sedan pulled up, and he called out, "Be right with you, sir."

I stomped past him, under his watchful eyes, until he drove the patron's car out of sight.

Call me crazy, but I entered the restaurant. In the dining room, the man pushed his chair back and stood, taller than I'd thought. Two glasses of wine were on the table, and appetizers. As he eased by her chair, she said something, and he turned. His face in profile was poorly lit.

He touched her arm and kissed her cheek—a slow peck as excessively long as its duration, as far as I was concerned. She glanced each way as she stood. He put his arm around her waist and escorted her from the table toward the restrooms.

I moved toward the exit, but waited. I couldn't believe this. A good part of me never expected to find something. Denial? Hope? Or was it entertainment for an arguably sick man—me? I leaned against the wall, pressing my hand to my chest. My face was burning. This was too much.

I wanted to confront them; verify the information like a competent journalist, then kick him in the balls. Then walk away from everything, for good. But I didn't want to be that crazed, jealous husband. I had to retain control and my dignity. Besides, what had I really seen that proved anything?

From behind a wide-leafed palm plant, I saw them at the table again, fifteen yards away. I was afraid to misinterpret the scene, afraid to be accurate. The manager I'd noticed earlier paused at their table and greeted them, patting the man on the shoulder. Approaching now, the manager spotted me and tilted his head.

"Ah." He nodded. "Dining with us this evening?" His smile faltered as he took in my appearance.

"Thanks, no, I'm on my way out," I said. "Just stopped by to meet someone for a sec. Say, who's that man you just said hello to? I think I know him." I pointed him out.

"Ah, him, the mayor's new chief of staff, Bradley Swanson. He's a regular. Seems his city salary doesn't mind, so we don't either, of course." He smiled.

"What the hell?" I muttered, staring.

"Pardon?"

"Sorry. Thought he was someone else."

# CHAPTER 7

## Monday, 8:30 p.m.

Debbie was dining with Bradley Swanson, the mayor's chief of staff. *Why?*

From the restaurant, I walked around the corner, toward my motorcycle. The young couple was now just off the sidewalk, on the cement pathway to the apartment building. The area was desolate. The guy, a Caucasian, had his back to me. He jerked her by one arm to grab the other.

The girl winced and pulled away, staggering on her high heels. "Stop it!"

I caught a whiff of tangy perfume or cologne.

He got her other arm, too. "You agreed. I've had it, so get inside. Now."

I clenched my fists. This wasn't a fight; it was damage control. He was way too big for her. She tried to pull away.

His face contorted in anger. "Get the fuck inside. You know the deal, knew it when you came here, bitch."

She shook her head, her hair scarcely moving. "No, not that, I didn't."

I coughed, but they still scuffled. I had no choice.

*Enter the Old Man.*

I was ready for some old-fashioned transference anyway, unfortunately for him. My heart thudded away.

"What's going on here?" I used my grumpy voice.

She barely looked at me, frustrated, probably at my apparent uselessness.

"None of your business, asshole," he said. "Keep moving."

To think, I could've been like most people and not notice or get involved.

"You move it, vulgar man," I said evenly, but perhaps it wasn't fair. I looked like an old man and he had no clue what I was holding back inside.

"What'd you say to me, old muthafucka?" His hand moved to my throat. "Wanna try saying that again?"

The guy used both hands and squeezed, but I tucked my chin and turned my head to protect my airway. Situation escalating—fine.

Huskily, I said, "Leave—her—alone."

He whipped his head around to yell at her, "Don't you fucking move."

I tried to stay in control, but it was hard to handle the adrenalin. I brought my fists up through his arms, my forearms breaking his hold on my throat. I stepped back. "You swear more than a bad comedian."

"Unbelievable. I'll give you something to laugh about. Fuck you."

He stepped in with a punch straight toward my face, with good hip rotation, I noticed, as I ducked low and punched him in the groin. I then jerked his arm down as I stood, slamming my head into his jaw. This was not your father's *go shina kata*; it was improv.

The girl screamed. He dropped in a heap.

"No, fuck you," I whispered, feeling every bit Clint Eastwood as I stood over him.

Movement caught my eye. The people on the porch stood to see where the guy fell into a heap.

"You all right?" I asked her.

She nodded. "I'm just a dancer, that's it. I'm just a dancer. A real college student, really, and someone said it's easy money, even fun. It was, a few times, but—Oh my God. I—"

"Look, I'm in a hurry. Can you get home by yourself?"

"Yeah." She stared at him, then at me, disbelievingly. "Yes."

"All right," I said. "Get going, before your audience wakes up."

We looked down at him. Her feet moved up and down, high heels clicking in place, hands shaking, and then she ran away. From around the corner, I heard, "Thank you!"

Mr. Heap remained so. I followed the girl toward the restaurant. She was gone. Passing the restaurant on my left, I couldn't see Debbie inside. The valet, out front again, tried to stare me down—jeez, give a guy a little power.

I crossed the street and reversed direction for another pass.

Then Debbie exited the restaurant. The man escorted her down the stairs. Was he the one she'd met in Harvard Square? I had to take a chance if I was to follow her or him—or both, if they left in the same vehicle. My stomach turned. They stood at the valet corral as the man flagged a cab.

My Harley was farther down and across the intersection, at which Mr. Heap now appeared, unsteady and bleeding from the mouth. With him were three guys in their twenties, wearing white tank tops and baggy jeans. Shoulders hunched, they scanned the area intently.

I stuffed my wig under my shirt and rolled up my sleeves. Now Debbie could recognize me, but it'd be easier to explain why I was here than explain why I was here waiting for an ambulance.

Nerves stifled, head down, I walked to the intersection and glanced up casually as if my heart weren't beating 120 beats per minute. One guy was now by the restaurant, and one was across from it. Mr. Heap lingered at the opposite corner and another guy was directly in my path. As I crossed and reached the sidewalk, this goon of Mr. Heap gave me a hard stare. I faced front and kept going around him, just another guy—not old.

Farther down on the left, the couple in their sixties or so was standing behind their chairs on the porch. She tried to reach for his cell phone.

He pulled it away. "No. You saw that older guy take care of him; it's all over. It was great."

"But it *ain't* over, I'm telling ya. Look at those lunatics walking around, one with a bat. They're nothing but trouble, bad trouble."

"That old guy was something." He chuckled. "It's dark, but he knew what he was doing," he said. "Knocked him out flat."

*No, not flat. In a heap.*

"Yeah, yeah," the woman said, "but he's not staying; they are. You call the police, if you won't let me. Think you have to be on a neighborhood watch or something? You—"

"No, that old man served him right, and he doesn't want trouble with the cops. Wait, here comes one of 'em now. Get inside. I'm gonna get a picture." He tapped at his smart phone as she muttered and went inside.

I kept walking, past my motorcycle. When I reached a downtrodden area, I put my wig back on. My head was sore from head butting Mr. Heap.

On a building stairway ahead, a group of young guys hung out, most in T-shirts and baggy, low-hanging, dark pants. They sounded and appeared Hispanic. A couple of them had nylon hairnets. Turning around could draw them to me. I slumped and took out the blanket from my backpack to look like an old bum rather than a grandpa with pockets to empty.

As one guy came off the porch, I left the sidewalk, but he came toward me in the middle of the street. I stopped.

His gaze shifted to an approaching car behind me as he asked, "'Sup, man?"

I heard the car accelerate fast, so I dashed past the kid and to the side, and looked back.

The kid was thrown upward with a loud bang and rolled over the roof of the Camry, which had low-rider suspension, racetrack wheels. He landed behind the car, arms and legs splayed.

"*Conio*," someone screamed.

"Get him," another shouted.

The driver skidded then gunned it forward.

I stepped back into the road, but the driver didn't hesitate. I threw my blanket over the windshield as I dodged between parked cars and then whipped out my note pad.

The car accelerated and swerved to get the blanket off. The wipers came on. The car's front end caught a parked car and spun until its back end crashed into a car on the opposite side, blocking the street. Its wipers pushed the blanket down.

A passenger fled. It was Mr. Heap.

The driver tried forward and reverse, smashing back and forth to free the car, then took off. I wrote down the plate number.

The other guys were running to their injured friend, shooting looks at me and the car. Some chased Mr. Heap, who had run in the direction of the car—good. Someone sprinted past me with a handgun and fired several shots at the car. *Time to go.*

I ran down an alley then circled back toward my motorcycle. After several minutes, I turned the last corner.

It brought me face-to-face with Mr. Heap in flight.

He skidded, but punched, catching my head as I ducked. I lost my balance, and he punched under my rib cage, knocking the wind out of me, and I fell. He lifted his shirt and pulled a semi-automatic pistol from his waistband.

I crouched to spring, but he was too far away; so was the gun. His eyes jerked around for pursuers or witnesses, then glared down at me as he gripped the gun sideways, raising it.

My insides clenched. I stared into the gun barrel and into his eyes, all shadows, hoping to see a sign that I'd live.

Sirens sounded. His face didn't change. He sighted the gun, aiming at me.

Then he tucked his pistol behind as he turned and ran. The relief was incredible.

After several steps, he skidded and spun with a distorted face and raised his arm, gun in hand. *He'd changed his mind.* I fell back to shrink my profile.

He fired. Then took off running.

I should get up, I thought, but suddenly my limbs felt like liquid, and I sprawled. Then I got up and ran like hell. My ribs hurt as I got back to my motorcycle and tried to catch my breath. I didn't feel blood trickling on me anywhere, as if shot. I tucked the wig under my shirt and put my helmet on.

I made a full stop at the intersection like a good two-wheeled motorist, legs shaking. Another police siren sounded.

I hurried to get home first so I wouldn't have to explain to Debbie why I wore old Salvation Army clothes and had a heap of gray-white hair on my belly, the wig that I'd stuffed under my shirt. I'd rather quiz her about politics: Boston politics.

I reached home. No Jeep in the driveway. In the living room, I fixed a scotch on the rocks. Tonight was surreal, like in the movie *After Hours.* I sipped, added more ice, and sipped, thinking that my bloodline, my unknown, adoptive bloodline, that is, almost ended tonight. *I almost died, childless.* Debbie and I had been trying to have a child, and it was deeply important that I be there for that child, be available, healthy, dedicated, and alive; ways in which my biological parents, unfortunately, had been deficient.

I washed up in the master bathroom and changed the bandage on my shin. I worried about the kid hit by the car, but had no assumptions about his life. It was a crazy freaking world. He could have been a drug dealer or a kid minding his neighborhood. I tried not to be judgmental about appearance. I used to not care much what people thought of my clothes or hair style. It was part of my freedom. I later concluded that others expect you to play the role you dress for.

Like a hooded Treyvon Martin? That was unjust for a hoodie to factor into the analysis of that citizens-watch guy who shot Treyvon. Hoodies were too common to reasonably derive a negative inference, and adding the wearer's race shouldn't change that. Yup, I knew about the risks of appearance more than ever now, but I'd first learned that very lesson the hard way long ago, once upon a time in high school. If you dress like someone you're not, you might get treated like someone you're not.

I set out Debbie's toothbrush with toothpaste on it, and then got an ice pack for my ribs. At my desktop computer, I typed:

*car hit kid july 16 at 9pm +- in south end. MA license plate = 36HD34.*

I thought for a second, then added a signature:

*s/ the Dandy Vigilante*

Headlights flashed on the cedar tree outside my window. I put on medical gloves to print the note and an envelope addressed to the Boston Police Department headquarters. I didn't want to risk a trace or voice recording with the anonymous tip lines.

I heard her come in the front door. I stuffed the note and envelope into my backpack. I dimmed the light, stripped, and slid into bed. As Debbie entered the bedroom, I closed my eyes.

*I could've died tonight, honey.*

She finished in the bathroom, shut off the light, and got into bed. I sensed her looking at me, then felt her pull the covers over my shoulders.

I peeked through the slits of my eyelids as she slid down and rested her head on the pillow. She'd stripped down to her underwear. Usually, she slept in the nude if not too tired or cold. At least she didn't take her morning shower tonight. I was too shaken to question her. She exhaled the scent of garlic in my direction. I'd probably dream of Roman legions doing nasty things or of me getting shot—in the heart.

# CHAPTER 8

# Tuesday, 10:40 a.m.

City editor was an exhausting position, and Kravitz had held it longer than anyone. Back in the day, he was a foreign correspondent and, subsequently, the Washington Bureau Chief, always with his wife's support, despite his often being away from her and their daughter. Now his daughter was in Los Angeles, and his wife was with the angels. He hung on, overseeing beat reporters, feature writers, and the general assignment reporters. I assumed his political skills helped his longevity, too. Scratch my back and we'll delay certain questions to get you a clean press conference this close to the elections and any campaign announcement, Mr. Mayor. Then we get the juice later, the insider info.

That didn't mean I had to like it.

I emailed Jimmy to meet me at the press conference. I didn't want to talk to him after reading his small piece in today's paper about the guy, me, stopping the thief yesterday. Jimmy quoted two witnesses; neither called what I did brave or a public service, and one called it stupid. That the witnesses had stepped aside for the thief wasn't mentioned. And the shopkeeper's appreciation was conspicuously absent. Between Jimmy's writing and Kravitz's editing, the article blew.

About to hit send, Jimmy called out, "Hey, Dax, press conference at two. You ready? Dax?"

"I heard you," I said. "That's right. Kravitz and I discussed it and agreed that I should take along the greenest reporter, which happens to be you, you lucky leprechaun. Make yourself appear there, and I'll meet you."

"Uh-huh." He stood at my cubicle with a peculiar look.

"What is it?" I said.

"Um, Mr. Kravitz's note."

"What?"

"He said I was going with you," Jimmy said.

"Yeah, so?"

"It also said to call him if you try to ditch me."

\*\*\*

Boston, a beautiful, cultured city with architecture mixed of old-world Europe and modern structures. In Government Center, our Boston City Hall was, thankfully, in a class by itself. Situated by the JFK federal building, it looks strikingly similar to a parking garage.

City hall was all cement and flat lines. Stale. Its architectural inspiration seemed derived from behind the pre-fall Iron Curtain. At least the Berlin Wall had interesting graffiti back then, and even tightly controlled Prague had a wall of recurring graffiti of colorful protests against communism. Boston City Hall had a lot of color, all of it gray; more like a jail than a building representing a great city in the land of the free.

But I'm not complaining.

If I saw the mayor's chief of staff, Bradley Swanson, at the press conference, I might end up in jail, the way I was feeling. I'd planned to visit the mayoral suite of offices, alone, and track down Swanson for off-the-record questioning. I needed to see if he recognized me or my name, and anything else I could fish out of him, but Kravitz had messed that up by telling me to take Jimmy.

Kravitz added for me not to ask about the alleged police brutality recently on Blue Hill Avenue. "It keeps our focus, and the story's all played out anyway," he'd said. As we passed through the metal detectors, Jimmy got beeped. A guard cleared him with a wand while I scanned for signs of Bradley Swanson. I couldn't believe I hadn't searched for a press release on him to find a photo. *Dummy*—not something an I-Team member would miss.

The eighth floor conference room was crowded. On the platform police and several well-dressed civilians were gathering as quickly as my perspiration. The glass wall had two wooden doors, one at the front for VIPs and one at the back for regular Ps like me.

We squeezed through the door, no empty seats in sight, no wall space; not cool. I tapped my foot. No sign of Swanson. If this press conference ended soon, I could get back to Cambridge in time to catch Debbie leaving her office. Discovering that she was faithful would be a balm; otherwise, the itch to find out was a growing cancer of the skin, enveloping my soul in death.

At least, my license for inner melodrama hadn't expired.

Still, I noticed I'd been digging my thumbnails into my palms; the anxiety and pain I felt were real, and were paradoxically both enervating and energizing.

Someone touched my shoulder. "Dax Grantham?" The guy was leaning through the doorway.

"The one and only, most likely," I answered.

"I'm from the mayor's office. Follow me, please."

I scrutinized him—perfect teeth, a tasteful tie, but in his late-twenties; not Swanson. He escorted us out then through the VIP entrance. At two vacant seats, the guy removed reserved signs.

"There you go." His smile was a flash, too brief to warrant its magnitude.

"Gee, thanks," Jimmy said.

"Roger that, sit."

Jimmy gleamed like he was about to throw his graduation cap into the air. I felt like I was flunking out. Despite all the risk last night, I hadn't learned much about Debbie's doings.

News cameras lined the wall. Microphones lined the conference table. The chatter crested as the camera lights came on, then quieted as a uniformed cop opened the door. In came Mayor Grasso, who appeared stockier in person. He had large brown eyes and buzz-cut black hair. Following him were men in dark suits holding papers. None were Swanson, and I let out a breath. This was getting to me.

The mayor took the podium, six others flanking him. He gestured, they sat, and he detached the microphone.

"Good afternoon, ladies and gentlemen." He was an ex-Marine known for directness. He preferred no introduction; just get to the point, him and what he had to say, like too many politicians.

"Suffolk County District Attorney Cohoon, Police Commissioner Weston, and I, are working closely to address a persistent flaw in our society—crime. Each crime is an affront to the pact that we have, to protect each other. By crime prevention and law enforcement."

The mayor indicated the police commissioner, Richard Weston, who nodded, iron-faced.

"But it takes more. We need prosecution." The mayor turned to the D.A., Charles Cohoon III, a big-headed man with a tall nose between dark, deep-set eyes.

"And we need community cooperation, especially from those affected and those with information to report. Our neighborhood watches are active, a presence on the streets that can deter crime or spot it and report it—just report it. I've invited community leaders here, too, as a show of unity." He pointed out a dozen men and women behind him in a line of chairs wearing everything from suits to ethno-garb like colorful, draping African and Indian clothing. Several smiled or nodded.

The lights dimmed, and a screen came down. The mayor showed two dashboard-cam clips, policemen arresting muggers. He called two policemen up, handed them plaques, and started the audience clapping as they stepped down.

"Thank you," he concluded. "I'll take questions."

Reporters raised their hands and called out. The mayor looked at me, but I hadn't formed anything close to a question. Jimmy watched me. The mayor called on a *Herald Tribune* reporter.

"Mayor Grasso, to prevent virtually all reasonably preventable crime, what do you think it would take?"

The mayor nodded. "Realistically, we're not going to eliminate all crime. But we will use everything we have. If this was the jungle with a clear enemy, well, that would be one thing. But we have civilians, and criminals of all kinds. Information is vital for our new initiative."

"So what's the action plan and who's its architect?" the *Herald* reporter asked. "Was it someone working on your campaign?"

"It's a combined effort, different elements of the government and the public. Other areas, like education, have to be in excellent shape. It's simple in a way, but don't underestimate the basics. Step by step."

I didn't have a fix on this first-term mayor. He had some popularity, but we'd see how much at the polls soon. He had a business background, but some questioned whether his empathy was real and would translate into help. Like those thugs in the South End last night, they would cause trouble again, so how, Mr. Mayor, could we prevent that without risking our own lives?

The mayor stopped his scan on me and then took a question on vigilantism, dodged it, and turned back to me with a flicker of expression that I couldn't decipher. It was as if he recognized me, but we were never introduced.

I felt writer's block descending, oddly enough. Then images flashed in my mind, images of all I'd done to follow Debbie and of who might have bedded her.

Jimmy nudged me, whispered, "Dax, ask him a question."

The mayor called on a female reporter from Channel 4 News. "Do you plan to hire more police or put more out on the streets for this crime wave?"

The mayor put his hand on the microphone and turned to the police chief.

Jimmy tapped my forearm. "Dax, what's up?"

I waved him off. "It's timing."

The mayor turned back to the reporter. "First of all, we don't have a crime wave. There's a normal ebb and flow of crime—how much, what kind, etcetera."

"This isn't white-collar crime we're talking about now, right? Or is that part of your focus."

"Well, you know." The mayor appeared irritated. "There are all kinds, and crimes, violent or not, should be punished accordingly. The different sentences and judicial discretion and the D.A.'s office, they will address that."

She said, "But that's after they're caught, and if a conviction is secured, right?"

"Right." The mayor pointed at her. "That's why we're dealing with it preventatively."

"What's different?" she said.

"The fact is we have potential criminals among us all the time. We have to keep them from stepping onto that slippery slope. Youth programs, for example. Community involvement, family involvement; they all count. It says all of this in the press release, and I direct your attention to that. Thank you."

The mayor smiled in dismissal and made eye contact with me, and I figured the reserved seats were likely provided as a favor to Kravitz.

Jimmy nudged me. "Ask him about citizen watch groups or vigilantism."

"No." I was the last person who should bring up vigilantism.

Wait, his new chief of staff; I could ask who on his staff was working on these crime issues.

Other reporters called out to the mayor, who glanced around then faced us again.

Jimmy looked at the mayor, at me, at the mayor, and then raised his finger. "Uh, Mr. Mayor?"

*Uh-oh.*

"Yes?" The mayor's eyebrows lifted as if amused.

"What about vigilantism?" Jimmy asked.

I didn't know if I should reel in Jimmy, or even how.

The mayor shrugged. "What about it? It's a crime, of course, to take the law into your own hands."

"But there have been reports of vigilante activities in response to this, ah, this flow of crime." Jimmy blushed.

I heard people whispering.

The mayor tensed; his strong features showed through the extra weight he carried. "There's nothing legal about it, and I want to discourage people from blowing this out of proportion or getting agitated by vigilantes. Report what you see, use the neighborhood crime watch groups, but don't put yourself in danger or attempt to arrest or punish anyone. That's what the police and D.A.'s office are for."

District Attorney Cohoon cleared his throat. In the angled lighting, his skin texture was like tapioca. He leaned toward the microphone. "I can tell you this. 'Law is order in liberty, and without order, liberty is social chaos.' Archbishop Ireland said that about a century ago, and it can only hold true more so now." After an awkward pause, he pushed a lock of ginger-colored hair off his forehead and straightened.

The mayor pointed to another reporter. "Yes?"

"There are reports of an old man who has intervened in several crimes. The description appears to be the same. Can you comment on that?"

"Sure," the mayor said. "It's a recipe for disaster, especially if either one is armed. The perpetrator might not value the old man's life, or the old man feels vulnerable or scared or wants to 'stand his ground,' then what? There are too many variables."

Julia, a local talk radio reporter, asked, "Sir, do believe that self-defense is an ancient, inherent right, and if so, who should carry guns? Fight or flight, Mr. Mayor?"

He shook his head. "Putting aside the Second Amendment for the moment, let's look at the first rule of survival—get away, alive. Otherwise, someone's likely to get hurt. Vigilantism will enflame people and more will get burned. So let's nip this in the bud, folks. Forget it. Don't do it. Let the police do their job. They're doing a fine job. Anyway, the story about this old man could be a fable for all I know."

Chief Donovan leaned forward to speak into the mayor's ear. Police Commissioner Weston was appointed despite antagonism with Donavan.

The mayor said, "Chief Donovan can address that question."

Commissioner Weston watched Donovan step up to the microphone. "Some reports are being verified—being checked out, I mean," Chief Donovan said, "but it's probably a hoax or a mentally ill man or something. He should be caught and examined."

"Right," the mayor added. "Don't get sidetracked by a loony."

Julia asked, "Are you saying this old man is a 'loony'?"

Mayor Grasso tugged at his tie. "Now, wait, I didn't mean it like that. Don't let me see you quote me on that. It's just a safety issue, for him, even if he exists, and for innocent civilians."

Julia tucked her hair behind her ear. "Even if those civilians are victims of violence and this older man intervenes?"

"He should have called on his cell phone, got a video—I mean, taken a picture. He could have at least yelled out." The mayor shrugged.

The thought of cell phone cameras made my heart skip a beat. It was easy for *my* image to get captured, too.

"Not head-butt the guy in the jaw because he thinks he's judge and jury," the mayor said. "Hey, maybe he thinks he is all those people, I don't know." He glared at Julia with a tight smile.

My head was still tender from slamming into Mr. Heap's jaw—if

Grasso only knew. I held up my hand, a question half-formed in my mind, the other half on order, but I had to get something to show Kravitz.

"An old man did that, too, head-butted someone?" Julia said.

The mayor frowned. "Look. I cannot comment on an ongoing investigation. However, if we catch anyone taking the law into their own hands, they'll be dealt with harshly."

"So there is an investigation—one—meaning it's only one old man? And in your example, what if he doesn't have a cell phone or camera?"

"We're done with that. Okay?" The mayor shook his head as he turned to the other reporters. He stood straight. "I have an announcement."

Another reporter called out, "What do you think of what they've nicknamed the old man, 'Dandy Vigilante'?"

Mayor Grasso paused. His face reddened. "No further comment on that, thank you."

Too late? I stood. "But, Mr. Mayor, excuse me, didn't he do good, this vigilante?"

Chief Donovan leaned forward. "There are some—"

The mayor snapped his head toward Donovan before glaring at me, shaking his head.

Donovan noticed. "That's all, no comment, thank you. Except don't audio-video record police. It can interfere."

"Now, one last thing," the mayor said. "There's been a rumor lately. That is, that I'm going to make a bid for governor. Well." He paused, a serious expression sinking into his face. "I'd like to put that to rest once and for all." He scanned the reporters as if admonishing them. Then his lips eased into a smile. "At this time, I am announcing my intention to run for governor."

A tremor rippled through the press corps. This was unexpected. Despite rumors, Governor Leno didn't openly speak of his plan to leave office, whether for his anticipated bid for U.S. President or otherwise. It almost smacked of bad form. Then again, he announced his "intention" to run, not his candidacy—sounded like a lawyer had scripted that.

"We have an election committee putting things together, so details will come. For now, I wanted to put that rumor to rest—in my own way, of course."

A few reporters laughed, but hands shot up, others stood and called out.

I shouted, "Mr. Mayor," which drew Grasso's eye. "Does this mean Governor Leno will be running for President?"

The mayor looked himself over. "Do I look like Governor Leno? I'll have to accept that as flattery, under the circumstances."

That drew a few laughs, especially as the governor was a dozen years older.

"And if so," I continued, "will he endorse your bid for the corner office as he pursues the Oval Office?"

"Mr. Grantham, so poetical. I'll consult your creativity when it comes time to redecorate. Well," he announced, "that's all for now, folks." He headed off the podium.

"Mr. Mayor, do you believe the Boston crime rate will be made an issue in your campaign?" I said.

Mid-stride, the mayor paused and squinted, but thought better of responding and continued out the VIP door.

I exhaled, wondering if it was wise to question Grasso like that, raising the very issue they were obviously trying to pre-empt for his campaign. Kravitz wouldn't like it.

\*\*\*

Jimmy and I filed out with others onto the red bricks of City Hall Plaza. The Big Apple Circus was taking down its huge tent, which was here for several weeks each summer. Emblazoned on flags and tents were the words "Big Apple." Meanwhile, in the background, "Boston City Hall" was merely an indent in its cement façade. I wrote to the previous mayor a few years ago that juxtaposition of such New York City and Boston images was hurtful to Bostonians, and asked that the city spend a little money on gold embossed lettering, at least. He never responded. It was probably too low a task for him to tackle, but the devil was in the details.

"We'll take the Red Line back." I was pissed off. No Swanson, no material, the mayor's enmity earned; Jimmy off the leash. Jimmy was ready, but Kravitz liked to ease in new reporters, perhaps to set up an expectation of control.

Jimmy lowered his gaze as we walked up Tremont Street.

"Flow of crime?" I said. "What the hell?"

"Yeah." He pursed his lips. "The mayor had that analogy of ebb and flow, and I knew he was staying away from the phrase 'crime wave' or the word 'increase', so I was stuck."

I stopped outside Park Street Station. "You have gumption. I'll give you that, but don't jump over me like that."

He nodded.

"All righty then." I started walking. "Come, my poet."

"Ha, he thinks you're the poet," Jimmy countered.

As the train began to sway, Jimmy said, "Boy, I want to nail that story, though, the vigilante angle."

"Get an election angle, if you can."

"No, no," he said, waving his slight hand. "Did you see the mayor? He was upset. Everyone else will cover his election, but this stuff will surface."

"Jimmy, he was angry because he lost control of his message. As he's quoted before, any battle plan doesn't survive the first encounter with the enemy."

"Come on. The mayor is the law and order type," Jimmy said. "Follow the rules."

I shook my head. "Maybe I'm cynical, but he is playing the rules. Appear strong, in control. It means more votes."

Jimmy shrugged. "Kravitz pointed out that Mayor Grasso helped co-ordinate the local Marine's Toys-for-Tots program."

I made a face. "Grasso did that for a while—just before running for election a few years ago. It's good politics. Just like the photo a few months ago of him and his dogs in front of his house. It's branding."

We strode into the *Boston Times*, me with a sense of renewed purpose. I soon grabbed the keys to my Jeep and left for a South Boston coffee shop with my laptop to write in privacy, an article on the mayor and crime—a preemptive one.

# CHAPTER 9

## Tuesday, 11:35 p.m.

The vast city room of the *Boston Times* was dimmed and empty. I wouldn't be surprised to find a reporter or two snoozing among the rows of desks piled with books, computers, reports, and flags of paper. Hacker Reynolds, an assistant city editor, dozed at the U-shaped city desk. On the other side of the elevators, a maintenance man operated a floor buffer.

As I walked to my cubicle, police scanners emitted voices of dispatchers and cops, their Boston accents literally English. We'd inherited the accent from the non-rhotic, as in drop the "r" unless followed by a vowel, speech of seventeenth century Eastern England. Outside my window, touch-and-go showers moved northeast across the murky sky in fast, narrow trains.

My desk lamp created a photonic pool of brilliance. My computer screen remained blurry, despite sucking down another coffee. I leaned back in my chair recalling how in the spring Debbie had complained about me working late. I put in even more time now—ironically, because of my marital investigations—but without further complaint. Did she wonder if I was screwing around?

"There you are."

I leapt out of my chair, half karate stance, half gun shooter, and wholly off guard. "Jesus, Kravitz."

"I'm the latter, not the former," my boss said.

"What are you doing here?" He was here to come down on me because of the article I submitted earlier.

"At this hour, I mean."

He crossed his arms tight. "Why didn't you get to Downtown Crossing for that vigilante story?"

I said, "My cell phone was—"

"Whatever. I found out Jimmy went to interview that shopkeeper—alone." His face crumpled. "You used to be so good. You've fallen on hard times, huh?"

"Look, I'm sorry. I really am, Kravitz, but—"

"So what is it, leukemia got you down? Your grandmother die for the third time? What?" He jutted his chin.

"I was going to finish and get over there, but I—" All excuses, real or imagined, felt lame. I could offer my material on the anti-crime march. Instead, I set my forehead down on my desk, closed my eyes, and moaned in frustration.

"Look, don't cry for me, Argentina," he said, straightening. "Cry for Boston, the people you failed to edify with what was surely to be an award-winning piece that would place their lives in context and solidify meaning in the fragmented perceptions of their worlds. Instead, you wrote this crappy article on the mayor's press conference."

I lifted my head.

"Look, come down to my office."

I followed him. Three interior glass walls enclosed windowed offices for senior editors and columnists. He often manned the large desk outside his office, where interns filtered out phone calls from crazies and fact-less fanatics and screened in calls from those on high or offering the down low.

Inside, he paced in the space behind his desk. I sat in a chair across from him, knowing what pissed him off—my article's idea of a higher order, a larger responsibility in crime fighting in which the police and the state apparatus were "important." What I hadn't written, however, was that they were "the" answer and dismissed vigilantism.

He stuck his hands on his hips. "What will it take? Threats? You know what they are, so why do I have to voice them? You're a great writer, Dax. You might have a spot on the investigative reporting team, someday—I know that's where you want to go. Just do your job, the way you're supposed to, and on time." He raised his brow. "You let Jimmy ask the mayor questions. You didn't ask any—or any that elicited a useful response." He apparently learned what I'd asked the mayor. "The article you wrote, it's a waste of ink."

I shrugged. "It's not so bad, is it?"

"Not when you look at it through thirty years of journalistic experience."

I tilted my head up. "And a certain component of that being political experience, right?"

Kravitz gazed out the window before dropping into his chair. "Welcome to the big leagues, son, when editorial is so subtle it develops a fan base that buys papers and supports the advertisers who support us." He paused then nodded. "Anyway, it's our right to shape the stories in legitimate ways."

I wrote that defense of a loved one calls for action, that defense of home and of others had roots in the law. A crime might not happen to you or in front of you, yet people needed to be proactive. As a safety, I'd quoted a Boston Police officer about neighborhood crime watches, good locks on doors and windows, and keeping areas well-lit.

"Well?" Kravitz said.

"So, is asking friendly questions of a mayor running for higher office a legitimate way? Or is that just getting along?"

"What are you talking about?"

"The mayor, I believe. He expected me to ask questions," I said.

"How the hell should I know? Besides, you're a reporter, aren't you? Of course he's going to expect questions from you."

I nodded. Good point. I had to be clearer, or cleverer.

My article concluded with something positive for the mayor: "This ex-Marine's war on crime is active." However, I implied that real citizen action was in joining the war, which hinted at vigilantism; an implied hint. I'd thought it safe enough to write. I was wrong.

"We're going with Jimmy's article tomorrow," he said. "Unless you come up with something stunning. Given your recent track record, I'm not encouraged."

"What?" He knew I could have something ready. "Well, how does it look, his article?"

"Not bad," he said. "Check it out and see how this story is done. You can give him some tips, if you have some." He picked up his phone, my cue to leave.

Back at my cubicle—if it had a door, I would've slammed it—I picked off the dated papers pinned to my cubi-wall and trashed them. At least my cubicle had a window, which made it feel open. So, Jimmy would get his first by-line. I'd congratulate him, maybe, but first I read his article on the "board," the electronic workspace we shared for some projects. His article was what Kravitz wanted all right. Call me defensive, but I didn't want to be preempted by a journalist who played his office politics right. *Li'l pip squeak.*

Jimmy got quotes from Mayor Grasso, probably via email or from Kravitz. The mayor had labeled the so-called Dandy Vigilante as an example of danger, of what not to do. That wasn't from the press conference. And, news to me, the driver who had run down that kid near the restaurant had also run down an innocent pedestrian afterward, a middle-aged man. The blanket was viewed as a contributing factor, by making the driver panic. That pedestrian was still in the hospital, while the kid had sustained minor injuries only. The driver was on the loose, and the passenger, my so-called Mr. Heap, was nowhere.

"I was going to send you an email, but some things are better off not in writing."

I spun in my chair; Kravitz again. "Like what, my article?"

A line deepened between his eyebrows. "Hey, look, Robin, I do my job. You do yours."

"So I've been demoted? What happened to Batman?"

"Dax. From now on, I'll approve your articles before they go to production. Just like I do with the others."

A perk canceled, my face slapped. It was rare for me to receive and for him to give. "What, no detention?"

He crossed his arms, but his face softened.

"For how long?" I asked, shuffling papers on my desk.

"For now," he grumbled.

Usually, as long as anyone I chose proofread my article, it went direct to production instead of to the copy desk. "It better be temporary. I earned some freedom here, didn't I?"

"For better or worse. And guess what. You'll cover the vigilante angle. Surprised? However, you'll do it conservatively. Call it penance for your article."

Against my better judgment, I said, "Or call it the pendulum of my article."

"Don't get smart, Agent 86." Kravitz didn't smile, but didn't scowl, and calling me a character name again was a sign of normalcy for him.

"Fine. So tell me how this works."

"Unless you obtain superb corroboration of a vigilante, dandy or otherwise," he said, "you point out the weaknesses in the possibility to discredit rumors. If no hard proof, we infer there's no vigilante wave to counter the alleged crime wave." He shrugged. "After all, there is no crime wave, right? Not a proven one. So it's no surprise that there wouldn't be a counter to it. That's the idea for now; preempt the story. We shut it down so as not to encourage that kind of activity. It's civic responsibility."

"But—"

"You have forty-eight hours. That's it."

My mouth opened, but he cut me off with a wave of his hand.

"I'm not changing everything. In fact, I'm not really changing anything, because notwithstanding all I've said, the story is still the story, whatever it is." Kravitz pointed his finger at me. "That will never change, no matter what." With that reassurance, as much for him as for me, I believed, he walked away.

Sometimes I walked a fine line, writing under my byline, by choice of diction, quotes, and angles. It was amazing how semantics could color perception, especially over time. Just compare liberal press with conservative press on straight news stories. That was why the *Christian Science Monitor* was so respected; it was neutral. I wouldn't want a column, though, because of the constant pressure to come up with something witty or wise or entertaining or poignant. Our well-reputed team of investigative journalists was a better fit for my aspirations. Now Kravitz made the fine line I walked a tight rope, and I suspected city politicians of holding one end.

The less freedom you had to write, the more creative you could be, necessarily. It was the default position when your freedom had been limited, of course, and it worked better in fiction. In truth, it was frustrating.

Then it hit me. I got assigned to the story of the secret vigilante— but *I'm* that vigilante. If found out, I'd be fired for a blatant violation of editorial policy. My career would nosedive.

I left the office, wondering what to do, other than write in third-person perspective. In the lot, I hopped into my Jeep, thoughts churning.

Then I got it.

With the Jeep's soft-top down, I drove away. Down-shifting into second gear, I turned right onto Tremont Street where brick buildings lined each side. The tepid wind bathed me.

So it was time to get the "real story;" fine. I'd make the most of it, knowing just where to scoop one. Kravitz was right, the story was the story. It was also a journalistic ethics nightmare. It jeopardized my career, and it could incriminate me in multiple crimes as a vigilante. *Wonderful.*

But screw it. I hadn't wanted to do this, but now I would get interviews and write a story like never before, assisted by the ultimate insider witness—me. I'd blow past Jimmy and blow Kravitz away. *Pulitzer or prison, here I come.*

# CHAPTER 10

# Wednesday, 12:15 a.m.

**M**y cell phone rang. *Kravitz.*

I turned off the B52s just when I was starting to feel normal, sort of, listening to *Private Idaho.* At least, I felt as normal as one could when disguised as an old man on the prowl again. The torque of my 4.0 liter engine responded as I punched the accelerator and released the clutch.

Damn. I answered his call.

"Look, Grantham, out in those wood-paneled offices, I'm held accountable," Kravitz yelled. He then demanded a better article about the mayor's plans for keeping Boston safe and threatened a written warning. "The article wasn't well-received, especially in Government Center," he said. "Some possible mayoral candidates even used it to criticize the incumbent."

Obviously, the mayor or his staff was pressuring Kravitz.

"Everything's connected, Dax."

Of course it was, like the mayor's connection to the governor, as well as Kravitz's connection to the mayor—and to my career, which could be disconnected.

He hung up. I was being reeled in further.

Next second, Debbie called.

"Yeah?" I should have calmed down before taking the call.

"Hey, you're late."

"Yeah. Stuff going on." I mentioned the written warning—a mistake.

"Dax." She sighed. "My practice isn't bringing in enough if you lose your job. It was stupid to write in support of vigilantism anyway."

It suddenly popped into my head that it could be someone else in the mayor's office who'd given Debbie the flowers and note, not Swanson. Could be the mayor himself for all I knew.

Then we argued about crap, like my first marriage, which was so brief I called it my starter marriage. She brought that up to throw me off because I'd implied—only implied—I might have an issue with trust. After we hung up, I was pissed off all over again.

Cornering onto Columbia Street, I was going too fast when a mutt dashed into the street. I swerved. The left wheels lifted, and I braked too late. The Jeep landed on its side. Sparks flew as it slid toward parked cars. I ducked, and stopped, inches away.

*Fuck.*

Hanging from my seat belt, a death grip on the wheel, I shut my eyes, feeling like an idiot. Was this why we hadn't been able to conceive; she'd gotten tired of trying or she wanted to try someone else for fun, or worse, she considered getting pregnant by another man?

"Don't worry, sir! I called 911."

I opened my eyes to a man crouched on chubby knees. I unbuckled and slid to the ground, feeling numb. My neck and shoulder felt raw. The windshield was cracked.

"Wow," he said. "You all right?"

I glared. "Dandy."

He shrugged. "Sorry."

Beside the roll bar, I said, "Help me."

The man rocked the Jeep with me, metal grating, and then it bounced hard onto its wheels. I stood back and examined the side, noting the whitish lines of bare metal in the scrapes. The damage wasn't deep, but the black trim over the wheel wells was gone.

His expression probably indicated wonder at my old-man strength. I said thanks and drove away, feeling dazed, but the Jeep felt steady and I picked up speed.

I couldn't believe Debbie had brought up my first marriage like that. When we first started dating, we didn't have an overt understanding that we were exclusive. A couple of times I met up with a different woman whom I'd been seeing off and on, casually. Meanwhile, Debbie let her feelings flow freely, which I freely accepted—and returned with interest, which, in retrospect, I shouldn't have done because it implied exclusivity. When she learned about that other woman, she was upset. Hell, I had to admit, in that sense, the blame was mine. But we clarified that and moved on, or so I thought. One day, I'd mentioned that I was still married. Debbie took exception to that basic fact and deleted me from her list of humans she knew. I'd expected that she'd give me a chance to explain.

Approaching a red light, I downshifted.

Ellen. What a blast—that is, we'd ignited and burned out fast. We did the first love thing, both falling fast, holding each other tight, like parachuting in tandem into a beautiful la-la land. Then *bang*, the missed period. *Bang*, the guilt and fear, the inner and outer debates, then the romantic union, *que sera sera*. And finally, *bang*, the proposal—three strikes you're out. We'd planned a small wedding, cheap instantly becoming romantic.

She got her period; we got married anyway to prove our love. Twenty was freaking young for nuptials, unless you came over on the Mayflower. We moved to a dumpy apartment above a fish shop in Plymouth Center. It turned out nice to be near the water, but not near each other. Her entire family was landlocked in Vermont, then she was, too; she went back. Yup, that was my first wife.

In my senior year of college, I got a letter from Ellen explaining that she'd divorced me in Vermont the year before even though I hadn't shown up at court, because she was getting married again. Huh. I called to congratulate her and said I hoped she had a nice annullable ceremony. She said, "Huh?"

Not that I'd cared.

Later, I saw Debbie at an off-campus party and told her that I'd "lied," accidentally; that I had been divorced before but hadn't known. She was more open to understanding, and we got to know each other better, dated on and off, banging that desk bell on my dashboard at our leisure.

I rubbed my neck and shoulder where the seat belt had locked-up. On Mass Avenue, I headed north and the long bridge over the Charles took me toward MIT, but then made an illegal U-turn. I had to think. After several turns, I parked on a side street, got out, and walked the Fiedler foot bridge over Storrow Drive to the Boston-side riverfront. Not always a pleasant place late at night. I'd covered muggings and rapes here.

On a bench by the Community Boating building, I sat in shadow, staring at the docked sail boats. A mess of light danced haphazardly in the choppy river. My breaths were shallow. Water slapped and sloshed between bumping sail boats. I was hurting, tied up in so many knots, but hadn't cried. I hoped Debbie's infidelity was imaginary, that I could trust her.

Or at least trust that I could take whatever came.

I'd survived a broken childhood. My last foster parents, as old as my grandmother, the only surviving relative I knew, had adopted me. In the back of my mind, or my heart, I probably didn't want to give in to their efforts, their love, which frustrated them. Then they were gone, too.

"Now. Just give it," I heard; a quiet, male voice in the dark.

I stood and zeroed in on moving shadows and scuffling sounds about forty yards away. A large man stepped into a pool of dim light, holding another man's arm away from him, like a fencing posture. We were near the Hatch Shell, but the boat house area was darker. I felt to call out, but my breath depleted at the thought.

The other man was medium-sized, thin, but moving forward. I saw a glint of something in his hand. A bottle, a knife?

"No." The larger man leaned forward, arms extended.

Could be just a watch or keys. Maybe they knew each other.

"Shut up and give me your money. Now."

I walked away from the water, perpendicular to them. My heart wasn't into intervening. My impulses were skewed. No more being a vigilante. It made me feel bad, for everyone and everything.

*Just give it to him, dude.*

I kept going, toward the Hatch Shell. He was a big guy. He could handle himself. So I was leaving, so what? Just hand over the money and call the cops. The mayor would be happy about that. In fact, I'd better call the cops. But I patted my pockets—nothing. My cell phone was in my Jeep, or maybe it had flown out and landed on the street.

I was angry with myself. *It's transference, Dax*—Debbie's voice echoed in my head.

Debra.

Looking up at the sky, I held out my arms and blurted out loud, "What do you want from me?"

Under a light pole ahead, a couple on a bench stared at me. I kept moving and heard a whisper, "Crazy old man."

They got that right. I sprinted flat out along the river for as long as I could.

Eventually, I drove to a Chinese restaurant in Braintree. I drank Tsing Tao and gazed at TV pixels. Recalling the mugging, I realized it was too late to contact the police about it; the perpetrator would be gone, and the victim probably reported it already.

The restaurant closed, and when I reached home, Debbie was asleep. In my home office, I locked the door, put on headphones, and went to YouTube. It took several songs, but one finally drew tears—*Can We Still Be Friends*, Todd Lundgren.

Later, I crawled into bed. She was on her back. The small space between us might as well have been a canyon.

\*\*\*

Morning sunlight, coffee, and motorcycle riding woke me enough to feel the pain, but not enough to clear my mind. I'd resubmitted my article to Kravitz. Our good working relationship seemed 700-kilometers south of Pluto. I knew what he'd meant about treating the mayor well, being a "good citizen," but like he said, the story was still the story. This one would put him to the test.

I stopped staring out my cubicle window and got back to work, head aching, neck and shoulder strained. I shot a paper ball at the trash can, missed, and considered taking a second ibuprofen. Last night, I was too upset and conflicted to do anything. This morning, I'd left Debbie's frizzy blonde hair covering her eyes rather than waking her.

I went to pick up the ball of paper and noticed Kravitz approaching, looking hurried, not harried. "I passed it through for publishing," he said. "Just shortened it first."

Surprise, surprise, surprise. I'd expected him to trash it, and me. Normally, he'd let me review his edits. "Good."

"We're going to run it with Jimmy's companion piece," he added.

"What?" Jimmy's article had better be shorter than mine.

"It's about a homicide last night, by the river," Kravitz said. "Where were you, in the South End?"

"Yes," I said. "Talking to that restaurant manager."

"How'd you miss this one? No scanner? Not checking your text alerts?"

My cell reception actually was sketchy. "I'm sorry."

"It's all right; Jimmy got it."

Jimmy popped his head above the cubicle divider. "Yup," he said and disappeared.

*Little gopher.*

"How was he killed?" I asked, scared to know.

"Well, it was a man, as you assumed, an insurance actuary. Murdered during a mugging at the Hatch Shell."

*Oh, shit.* I pictured the victim, and it felt like a punch in the stomach.

"And get this—because the *Herald* didn't know about it until this morning, it's not even on their website, so it's our scoop—an old man fitting the Vigilante's description was spotted there, and he failed to intervene. Actually shouted and ran off."

"Really?"

He shrugged. "Unless the batty old man was yelling at himself."

I had to ask. "Did the victim die at the scene? Was it a knife?"

"Yes. Too bad your instincts weren't turned on last night. Tell you what. See what you can come up with about citizen reaction: 'The DV Retires'—no, that's too camp. 'DV has a change of heart, listens to the mayor?' Something like that." He stepped closer and lowered his voice. "If it's better than Jimmy's, we'll go with yours. He's pretty good, you know."

I frowned, stung. "Maybe. But don't let the cub out too far from the den. What else did he write?" I watched for Jimmy's head to pop up.

"Read all about it in the news, Flash." Kravitz slapped me on the back as he headed to Jimmy's cubicle.

He was gloating over the Vigilante's apparent change of heart. But what the young couple had witnessed at the Hatch Shell was my break of heart, from contemplating a possible infidelity on top of my screwed up early life. And it was a bad rap for the Dandy Vigilante, criticizing him when he does something *and* when he doesn't; now Kravitz wanted to rap the vigilante harder, and with my help. True, I'd passed up being the Dandy Vigilante last night, but maybe I shouldn't have. *I could have saved that man's life.*

A movie came to mind, *End of Violence*; satellite cameras zooming in on violent urban crime, and criminals being summarily shot from a remote device or police being called in. Was that the answer? If so, who watched the watchers? Good intentions can always go bad. Had mine gone askew?

The punks assaulting and robbing that elderly lady are what got me started on this path. But how could I not help her? And what if they'd ganged up on me? Then the thief with the lighters—what if my speculation was right, that the thief's need was extreme and his action rare? Would jailing him be the best answer in the overall scheme of things? Mr. Heap, though, he got what he deserved for trying to force that girl into his apartment for sex. Although, I was lucky his crew hadn't caught me. Then, after the teenager was run down, I was almost shot by Mr. Heap himself.

I felt unsure of myself, but I was certain that I should have helped the Hatch Shell victim. The police couldn't be everywhere. Would "Big Brother" watching have saved this man? The truth was that I could have been one of the little brothers, who accepted the mantra "power to the people," and saved him.

Kravitz came back, smiling. "Oh, and ironically, the one time he backs down, we get a better description of him. Again, assuming it's him. We're going to print that, too."

"Print what?" Jimmy joined us.

Kravitz gave him a thumbs-up. "The description of the Dandy Vigilante."

"See? I knew there was something to this guy." Jimmy faced me. "But wait, there's more!" he said, imitating a Ginsu knife commercial.

Kravitz looked at me.

I hated them both. "Well, don't get carried away, little britches."

Kravitz smirked, either at the John Wayne quote or the competition brewing in his staff.

"Watch out for copycat vigilantes," I added.

"Whatever." Jimmy practically skipped back to his little castle. "It sells copies," he said over the partition, parroting the powers that be. "And the beauty of it is we don't risk a slander charge," he said. "The Vigilante can't come out of his cave, or closet or whatever, to defend himself." He ducked down into his cubicle.

   I went into the bathroom and locked the stall, trying to catch my breath. Not the best place, but I couldn't show how wrecked I was. I eyed the roll of tissue, willing myself to loosen tears or puke, but everything stayed inside.

# CHAPTER 11

## Wednesday, 9:25 a.m.

Jimmy left for a snack. I left for "humintel," easing over to his cubicle. Displayed were photos of his Vietnamese family and one of him and a cute redhead holding snowboards. I peeked at his work in progress. It described the Vigilante, per the young couple at the Hatch Shell, as in his late sixties, initially, but when he walked under the light, around fifty. They were still over a decade off.

I checked over my shoulder.

The couple hadn't noticed a stooped posture, but the Vigilante stood about six-feet and wore a ring. When the man shouted and sprinted off, the couple figured he wasn't some old guy, but the Dandy Vigilante.

My wedding ring—I should have taken it off.

I opened Jimmy's previous document, a draft of an article about Governor Leno's anticipated run for U.S. President. I closed that and checked his email; whoa, one from Bradley Swanson.

Someone called out my name. I kept my head down and sorted email by name and saw more. So Jimmy was cultivating his sources all right— the new chief of staff. Apparently, Swanson got Jimmy the interview with the mayor. It wasn't canned material after all.

"What're you doing?" Jimmy was coming around the corner.

I closed his email, shuffled papers, and swiveled around. "I can't find my note. I didn't think I dropped it off yet, but I can't find it in my cubicle. Did you get my note today?"

"What note? About what?" He appeared dubious.

I folded my arms. Technically, I was still lead journalist on this series. "About process. You're still supposed to give me drafts of your articles on the crime series." The best defense, yada-yada-yada.

"Oh, that. I mean no, I didn't get your note."

"You didn't get my note. Fine." I feigned irritation and headed to my cubicle.

"Well, Dax, I ah—"

I turned around. "Yes, James?"

"I guess I can do that. I just thought we hadn't finalized that. With Mr. Kravitz stepping in and all, I thought I was all set, on my own now, you know?"

"Well, get it straightened out. See if it's too much to 'cc' me an email of your articles before publication."

In my cubicle, I looked out at BC High, then visited the Channel 7 News website. I was rewarded with Marguerite Ordoñez; almond eyes, generous lips, smooth tan skin. She had the subtly husky, feminine voice of an early-morning girl, like Demi Moore. She was fiery at her job and hot on the screen—even hotter in person, nearly browning me in her intimate glow once, something I'd continued to imagine. Marguerite was the sexiest reporter I knew and among the most competent; the old one-two that would make me swoon.

Still lost in reverie I turned on her video clip.

Marguerite interviewed the mayor, who talked about the Dandy Vigilante using unkind appellations and adjectives. I'd like to rewind the mayor, erase him. This was grossly unfair. The Vigilante needed to redeem his reputation before there was a public outcry for his/my head.

Ironically, if the Hatch Shell victim had been a kid or a woman or an elderly or handicapped, I'd have intervened. It was on the man's strength that I'd hung my excuse not to. And where there was death, there were family and friends, and a funeral. They'd try to make sense of his death, and I couldn't help. I felt so horrible, and in an odd cerebral way, as if too stunned to feel it fully right now.

My professional and personal lives were intertwined in a downward spiral. It was time to do something about one or the other. Bradley Swanson was trespassing, as far as I was concerned, by getting close to, and maybe even intimate with Debbie. I had to do something about that, at least.

\*\*\*

The rain thinned to mist, leaving dark wet streaks that cut through city hall's concrete façade. I leaned against a column outside the entrance, watching for Mr. Bradley Swanson, Chief of Staff to the Office of the Mayor in the City of Boston, and possible sleaze extraordinaire. I tugged down my new Boston Bruins cap, which contrasted with my latest old-man persona. No wig this time. A little different than the description the police had.

"Spare change?" I held out a paper cup to another exec-type striding by. He ignored me like the rest. Oh-for-ten.

Canceling my afternoon meeting with Kravitz was a good idea—if only I'd actually done it. Instead, I'd rushed up Route 1 to the Salvation Army for more "new" clothes and got my Jeep from the auto body mechanic, who'd get the estimate approved by the insurance company before the repairs. In a Faneuil Hall bathroom, I'd put on used shoes, faded tan pants, and a slightly stained light-blue cardigan. Adding smudges of dirt, I tugged threads to hang, and smeared a touch of tan wood glue to my cheeks.

Several police cars fronted Cambridge Street. A patrolwoman walked the brick plaza. More police were in and around city hall. A text alert from Channel 7 News—ahhh, Marguerite, what arcs shape your body—said police were being reallocated to reinforce city streets, which the mayor denied.

I moved closer to city hall's recessed glass wall at the entrance, but stayed out of the line-of-sight with the security station inside. Lunchtime meant more people for me to scan. I hoped to follow Swanson, see both sides of the circuit. He might even go to Debbie today. Her new voicemail greeting said she was either in session or at lunch.

"Spare change?"

I stuck out my grimy paper cup again, making passersby avert their eyes. I examined anyone within thirty yards of the revolving doors. After forty tedious minutes, I was more anxious about being late for my meeting with Kravitz.

Blindly pushing out my paper cup again, I asked, "Spare change?"

"Excuse me?" A woman's voice; it made me cough.

I turned halfway before I realized it was Debbie. I dipped my head and rattled the few coins in the cup.

"Dax?"

I tucked my head further to the left.

"Dax, is that you?"

"Spare change?" I said in a gravelly voice, turning to the right.

Something was waved in my face; a twenty-dollar bill. She stepped in front of me and lifted my cap. "Is this what it takes? What the heck are you doing here? What are you, doing?"

I grunted and turned away.

"Surprised to see me? Well, the news isn't always pretty, is it?"

"What?" I made eye contact. "Don't know you, lady."

"I don't know what kind of—"

"Shhh. I can't tell you here."

"Oh." She straightened. "Well, fine, I'm late anyway," she whispered, looking away. "Sorry. Look, I didn't get a chance to email you. I have an appointment tonight."

I kept my head down. "That's a lot of night work lately."

"That's the way it is. I have to."

"You mean you want to," I said.

"What are you saying?"

"Look, I'm working an undercover story, as you've undoubtedly figured out. You're gonna blow my cover."

"What story? It's the Dandy Vigilante story, isn't it?"

I hesitated. "What? No, why would—"

"Because you're dressed like that, of course."

"I'm more of a bum, a panhandler, you know? Cops do it all the time."

"I certainly hope so," she said. "I saw Jimmy's article and thought you might be trying to get a better story on him. And if you were that vigilante character, I'd say you had better get some help, pronto."

"Don't be silly," I said lightly.

"Did you know the vigilante killed that guy, the one who mugged the elderly lady downtown?" She watched me. "He apparently stabbed him in the stomach."

I lowered my cup of change. "But he didn't—"

"He had blood loss and an infection, never went to the hospital. Just heard it on the radio. Police say the elderly lady identified him from photos."

"Oh." The news shocked me. P.O.W. punk was dead. "Wow."

"The Jeep's damaged. You're out all hours. I don't know." She threw up her hands.

I had to keep talking. "So what's your meeting tonight?"

"Another patient. Flexible appointments build my practice."

"Uh-huh." I wondered why she wasn't trying to buzz off.

I felt queasy. The mugger died, too. And I'd caused it, kind of. Idiot should have gone to the hospital.

"At least I don't have to fly around like a crazy reporter, sometimes dressed to kill and sometimes dressed to look like your smell would kill."

"So you saw my article clipped down to a sidebar to Jimmy's story? He compares Boston Regional Intelligence Center's crime statistics favorably with other cities." I squinted. "That's not news, that's politics, and I'm pissed. Statistics can be tricky. They easily pull out favorable views for the mayor."

"Look, I gotta go, all right? Thanks. Tell me more about it later."

"Sure. See you later." *Or sooner.*

Walking away, shaken, I cursed under my breath with all sincerity. Half a minute later, I looked back. She was gone. I hadn't asked where she was going, but that was part of my revised plan.

I took my bag of clothes back to Faneuil Hall, changed into my normal clothes and washed my face. Then I backtracked and entered city hall, eyes peeled for her or Swanson.

*The mugger, stabbed with his own knife, mouth agape*—I swept the image aside.

Debbie had recognized me; couldn't believe it. So the first end of the circle showed up instead. She must be here to see Swanson.

At city tax records, I typed his name into the computer and got a couple of addresses, but only one matched his middle initial. Brad, do you have a secret visitor coming? Well, how about a second visitor, also secret? What, three's a crowd? Too bad.

In fact, if Debbie had to see him this afternoon and again tonight, it indicated a full-blown affair. Hell, what if it was from this afternoon *through* to tonight, all hot and heavy? And about that I'd have something to say—or do, like diminish the volume of his cranium.

I breathed in deeply, and then exhaled slowly. No gun, nothing crazy. Nothing was confirmed, I told myself, nothing confirmed; don't freak out in city hall.

Damn it, I had my chance with another woman, too; several chances, in fact. I should have gone to bed with Marguerite, that field reporter from Channel 7 News. The bed was right there. Right there! My God, she was a goddess: glamorous, exotic. Maybe I'd have another opportunity, the way this marriage was looking; but then Marguerite wouldn't want me, I supposed, the way things go.

On my cell was an email from Kravitz: "Where the hell are you? I have news. Answer your cell phone, for crying out loud."

Screw it. I had better things to do than get banged up by my boss. My wife covered that area pretty well, even if I contributed by driving close to the edge of the mental highway. A new disguise was in order; back to my resource of pseudo-salvation, the Salvation Army, to gather my one-man army—*Zatoichi*. I stifled a laugh.

I got on the elevator figuring I'd first take a gander around the Office of the la-ti-freaking-da Mayor. Swanson might have written that note to Debra, but I wondered who else could have written it on "Office of the Mayor" stationery. Many people staff that office, with multiple suites, some using that stationery.

Then again, if I'd incorrectly assumed Swanson wrote the note, may-be I was wrong about Debbie possibly screwing around on me at all.

*Ding.* I arrived at the mayor's floor. The doors opened, and a large state cop blocked my way. He looked in. A half-dozen well-dressed men and women stood behind him, Mayor Grasso at the center.

"Well, well, well. If it isn't the ombudsman for the vigilante crowd."

"Mr. Mayor," I said, trying not to look surprised.

"You recognize me, grand, but why don't you ID the Dandy Vigilante you so admire, huh? Your article was a piece of trash, Grantham."

*Piece of trash*—same phrase Kravitz used. "Well—"

"Don't you think the man's a menace? Or don't you think?"

Okay, gloves off. "You needn't be insulting, Mr. Mayor. After all, per-haps the vigilante wouldn't be popular if the administration had done a better job of reducing violent crime." *Touché*. He had no instant come-back. "Hope it's not a liability for getting Governor Leno's endorsement," I added sarcastically.

The mayor stepped toward me quickly and the state cop, startled, stepped between us. I paused for the requisite moment, then walked around them and took the stairs.

# CHAPTER 12

## Wednesday, 12:30 p.m.

Riding past the Prudential Center, my mind felt uncomfortably imbalanced. Trespassing was trouble, but going inside Bradley Swanson's condo for an "investigative" burglary was tremendous trouble.

Instead of the oak walking stick, bought to use like an Irish fighting stick, I'd opted for this fold-up white cane and trench coat from the Salvation Army. *Zatoichi*. I was unsure how to feel about the way I'd felt when the idea came to me. Adventurous mental distress, I supposed. To pose as a blind man, like the famous Japanese swordsman, superior and just. Maybe the protagonist's blindness made me feel I didn't have to see unpleasant things, but could still fight them—*huh, something Debbie would say.*

I parked around the corner from Bradley Swanson's condo. He lived on the first floor of a ten-story building off Huntington Avenue. As I set my cell phone to silent, I saw that Jimmy had emailed a draft of his story, in which the mayor had acknowledged putting more police on streets for community contact, not because of any increase in crime. Yeah, right. It was to preempt a growing perceived need for people like the DV. One of my cop sources said that pressure to find the DV and stop vigilantes increased since a state representative announced her candidacy for governor and criticized Grasso on street crime.

After changing behind a dumpster, I put on my "silencer," a rubber tip for the cane. I donned cheap sunglasses and passed the corner, tapping the cane, surprise and justice on my side.

Two scruffy guys in their twenties approached in a bouncy yet slouching way that bespoke habitually suspect activity. Something in the air was bad; Spidy-senses tingling or the enhanced senses of the blind? No, it was their red-tinged eyes and the way one guy nudged the other as they spotted me and crossed to my side of the street. They were looking for fun or for money.

And I wasn't in the mood.

Ahead, the shorter guy stopped at the curb, gestured to the other one to stand in a doorway, and then waited for me to pass between them, which I did, tapping my white cane. I sensed him, for real now, moving in from behind, and I spun on him. "Don't you fucking try it, mister," I yelled, cane cocked like a baseball bat.

He leapt back, open-mouthed, and scrambled, falling into a trash barrel—right at home.

*Cane, $5; used shoes, $2. Your assailant stays ass-planted on the ground, hands out behind him, staring at you in shock—priceless.*

I faced the taller guy, who was also shocked, but laughing and holding out his palms at me. He grabbed his homey by the arm, rapid-fired some Portuguese-like language, and shoved his accomplice ahead, laughing harder. The shorter one glanced back, angry and stunned, as they rounded the corner.

Exemplary crime prevention, if I did say so myself. Maybe they thought I was undercover police. But the eyes deceive, for they'd be only half right.

*Focus.* I had to be vigilant to spot criminals or police. If someone discovered me as the DV, my career wouldn't survive; and if I discovered what I thought I might, my marriage wouldn't survive. If charged with manslaughter of that knife-wielding punk? Well, I had a shot at proving self-defense, but beyond that it was anybody's guess.

Out front, there was no sign of Swanson or Debbie. No recognizable vehicles, no police. No pedestrians either, so time to get "lost" in the alley beside Swanson's 1,250 square-feet condominium, minding adjacent units. Then I froze—Debbie's voice coming through a window. They talked about his condo and the real estate market. He mentioned the importance of his role in the mayor's staff, subtly, but then dropped not-so-subtle names. Then silence for several minutes.

"I love the fresh tulips." I heard flatware being gathered.

"No, please, relax, Debra darling, I'll get it later. Let's adjourn to the den."

He said something else, but I couldn't hear what. Darling? It sounded like Swanson was trying to be cute, probably trying to get into my wife's pants. What else would she be here for at this hour? I toed the dead leaves at my feet, observing the dirt patterns on their once-bright surfaces.

"More wine?"

"Gosh, there's daylight out there, but yes, please, it's exceptional. I haven't been struck by a fine wine in so long. Please write it down for me—unless it costs more than thirty dollars."

"I'll do better than that," he said. "I get it by the case and will spare you a few bottles."

"Well." She giggled. "If you must."

"Nice to see you let your hair down—literally. You know where I discovered—"

I missed the end of what he was saying. I stretched up by the window for a second, but couldn't see them.

"Wow," she said, "your two weeks in Europe?"

"No—I confess, different trip. I'm a travel-aholic."

She laughed. "You certainly are. And you still have time to find some public property to make private."

"Yes, unearthed for you; to have and to hold, privately."

"Well, not exactly," she said.

I shook my head. *What?*

A bell rang. Swanson said, "Fresh baked cookies for dessert. You like?"

"I like."

Baked her cookies, too. That bastard. Through the lace curtain, I saw her stand, heard the sound of an oven opening. My heart was pounding.

"I'm a little tipsy. Definitely too much for a weekday."

"Oh relax, have some fun; you deserve it," he said.

"Don't worry. I am."

I heard a switch flick. Darker now, I saw his silhouette near hers. They stood together, then moved to the side—an embrace?

I heard a sound from her. "Mmm."

"Mmm hmm." Swanson.

Cookies or kisses?

I couldn't see through the curtain liner and wanted to grab that crate, stand on it, and push aside the curtain, the lace, rip the screen if I had to. But they'd discover me. And being a blind man on a crate looking into people's windows? No one believed a peeping Zatoichi.

My legs felt weak. This was no office "appointment." Debbie lied.

Then footsteps sounded up the alley.

***

Standing near my cubicle, exhausted on every level, I wondered if I'd even have this dubitable refuge for much longer. I just couldn't stay at Swanson's condo, emotionally, and someone had entered the alley. I wished I'd waited around for something definitive on their rendezvous, but I felt ill wondering about types of evidence—evidence to the senses and the mind. I had a gut feel, and there was a lot of guilty contact with incriminating rendezvous. I punched my palm. I should have stayed.

How did I get here? Running around like a lunatic incognito helping victims of violent crime, while my wife, the one person to count on, even grow a family with, was running around. How long had it been going on? How far had it gotten? Had I been too trusting? The roots of that trust went deep into her intuitiveness and understanding, which reached back to before she even knew me, back to formative events in high school.

True, as our marital relationship evolved, I thought her intuition became invasive, and I'd accuse her of psychoanalyzing me—"I'm not your patient." Those moments passed, but perhaps my reactions did some damage. I'd long wanted to talk about whether she thought I ultimately chose journalism as a counter to my traumatic experience in tenth grade. Debbie knew a few details, but not the cruelest part.

It was my first solo assignment for the high school newspaper. I'd dressed as a girl to get an insider's view of being female. Other students had seniority over me on the newspaper, and I'd been on the shy side. It was to be my bold move, my coming out—out of my shell. However, some guys did not so understand. They took it the wrong way, and took it too far. Debbie and I probably wouldn't have that conversation now.

"*Hey.*"

I moved into a stance two feet back as I turned.

"Oh, yeah, that's right, you know karate." Kravitz yawned. "Well, look, Kato, I'm on my way out."

"What is it, Leo?" My voice sounded shell-shocked.

"I'm reassigning you."

"*What?* To what?" Some kind of demotion.

"Not a big deal, really. It's white-collar crime. It'll dovetail nicely with the street crime series, which will run its course. We need you to be ready, see?"

He sounded too optimistic. "Do I see? See what? Jimmy riding my coattails into Grasso's election campaign?"

He frowned. "Hey, there's no need for that."

I took a deep breath. "If it's my articles, I'm sure—"

"No, no, no, Dax." He waved his hands at me. "I knew you might think something like that, which is why I preferred explaining in person instead of an email that can't look you in the eye. That's not it. I need you to get a lead on that area and be ready. We can't just focus on street crime. That wouldn't be fair."

*Fair?* "I—ah." I shrugged.

"If you're not keen on Jimmy working with you, think of someone else. We'll talk later, sketch out ideas on how to tackle it."

Kravitz paused. I thought of his deceased wife, the memory of whom probably caused that flicker across his face—or I was projecting. They'd had a great relationship, from what I could tell. He left.

It was time. Something had to give. I was more worried, more lost. More dammed up inside. Time to confront Debbie.

# CHAPTER 13

# Wednesday, 2:50 p.m.

Debbie entered Cambridge Common from the Harvard Square side. I'd texted her that it was urgent to meet me, but then hadn't answered her calls. She was halfway down the path, and I was I tapping my foot. She passed the plaque that avowed that General Washington had taken control of the revolutionary troops here.

Closer, she glimpsed the sunlit foliage before beaming a smile at me. "Hi—"

"I just want to know if this is the first time or if there were others," I said, in as matter-of-fact a tone as I could muster. I stood from the bench and crossed my arms.

"Excuse me?" She stopped. Her eyes darted around for pedestrians within earshot.

"You heard me," I said.

Face lined, she stepped closer. "No, actually, I don't think I did."

"I said, is the first time, or were there others." A rapid bass-beat of blood pulsed in my ears. My lips compressed.

"I heard you," she said softly. Tree-filtered light played upon her frizzy blonde hair. "I can't believe it. Are you saying what I think you're saying? That's why you asked me here?"

At least she was smart enough not to try playing dumb. I looked her in the eyes. "Yes."

"Wait. Others what? What do—?"

"You've been seeing someone," I blurted.

Debbie stared. "Seeing someone romantically?" She frowned—fear, maybe hurt. "What makes you say that?"

"BS," I said.

She shook her head and shrugged. "Bullshit? What's BS?"

"Come on, Debbie. Just tell me."

"Sorry, hon—I mean sorry I don't understand. You tell me, so I can tell you, okay?"

"Brad?"

"Brad?" She glanced away thoughtfully, but then gasped. "Bradley Swanson? BS? Oh, Dax, what are you been thinking?"

"You know what I've been thinking. You could say I got it second hand, in part." Second hand from the DV, if that counted as a separate person. "And my right to self-defense includes you, baby, because you're a part of me, right?"

"Are you, what, thinking of hurting him or something?"

"Maybe I have a right to. Anyone who trespasses in certain ways should expect some repercussion."

"No." She exhaled, and her shoulders fell slack. "I don't believe this. You're scaring me, Dax. No, no, no. Not in a million years. Don't you know he works for the city?"

"I do know, and I'm sure the mayor would not be impressed with him."

"There's nothing going on with him. We've met to review possibilities for a youth counseling center. That's all."

She sounded genuine. It could make sense. My mouth opened a crack, but my heart froze as hope, and tentative embarrassment, flooded through me. "A youth center," I said, not a concession or an accusation. "A youth center?"

"Yes, hon."

She touched my chest. I stepped back. She wasn't closing the deal on this one; not yet, not without me knowing. I recalled what I'd witnessed.

"Remember when we discussed it? About six months ago. I mentioned it when I was despondent. About my practice being a business and a struggle, and not a help to young people. I've always been interested in the teen transition years. From Margaret Meade to urban rap and so on. My own teen years were somewhat puzzling to me."

"So suddenly you're off meeting with the chief of staff of a major U.S. city, talking about getting some land?" Oh—shouldn't have mentioned land. "Did you know him before?"

"No. This is recent. I did research first. Boston Public Library, government offices, non-profits. Some online research, telephone work." As she touched my shoulders, sunlight caught her hazel eyes. "And it's looking good. However, it seems you and I have been too busy lately."

"Well." I kicked myself for not sticking around Swanson's condo or bugging it or hacking her office email or something. I could have hired a private investigator for that, but I'd become masochistic, apparently.

"So what happened? Some nasty rumor, somebody saw me out with him? Of course, we had dinner. We checked out possible sites in Boston." She cupped my face with her hand. "But that's all, Dax," she said softly. "That's all."

I was in retreat, but still had ammunition. And I demanded satisfaction. "So, you're saying—you're saying there's nothing going on between you two?" I wiggled my index finger between her and an imaginary him. Was I imagining this situation?

"Right," she said. "Come, sit down." She stepped over to a wooden bench and patted a spot for me.

I went to her. "And there never was?"

"Never was, Dax. Oh, honey."

I sat. She leaned toward me and pecked my cheek. I was softening. I'd gotten myself all riled and convinced. Now what? There were still difficult questions, but even putting aside embarrassment, pursuing this would leave my flank exposed.

But I had to do it. I didn't want to suffer anymore. I couldn't. This smoke had to clear before I fell into an emotional hole I couldn't crawl out of. I was still in a bad place.

"Debbie. You met him for dinner, several times?"

"Yes. We met. Business, that's it," she said tenderly.

I shook my head. "So why didn't you tell me?"

"I don't know. I think I wanted to hold back until I had something definite. I was going to tell you about it."

I said, "Tell me about it? But not about him."

"About it and him, hon. He's helping me, in a big way. I should be thankful. I am thankful."

"So why the chief of staff? How do you know he's not leading you on?"

She didn't answer. I thought I had the offensive again, but she covered with a feigned?—look of indignation.

"Look, if it would make you feel better you could meet him."

"When?" I challenged.

"When? When?" Her hazel eyes got hot, and she tossed her hands up. "When we have a ground breaking or whatever. There might not have to be a ground breaking, though, because we might get a lot with an existing building."

"Why not now? Take me along to your next meeting. Share the happy venture with your devoted husband."

"Oh, Dax. Is this going to be a problem?" She stood. "When it's appropriate, that's when you should meet. Anyway, it should be soon. He has the locations narrowed down."

I needed my best volley, but confronting her with everything was too damning of me. She'd question my stability; bad enough that I questioned it. So what would it be? Door number one: the cozy restaurant dinner, making toasts, his arm low around her waist? Door number two: Her swiping the ice cream off his lip? The kiss on the cheek?

I stared at my feet. "I see."

No, it was door number three: the night at the condo. I hadn't stuck around for the ninth inning that night, but losing something that important was hard to face. To be fair, I didn't even see him get to second base. My heart filled with adrenalin and dread. She'd be pissed off, but she'd have explaining to do. Besides, she wouldn't know I'd left early, so I could bluff more out of her.

"Look, Debbie." I stood. "About dinner at Swanson's."

"When? I mean. It was only once, so I guess I know when. How did you know?"

I shrugged. "Well—"

"No, really, Dax. How do you know? You also knew about the restaurant, right? What else?"

I was ready to challenge her cover story. "First, one thing I don't know. Why you said you were with a patient that night."

"Because my patient canceled. I called Brad and we met. We were to meet a property owner about acquiring a small parcel of land that, if added to a city-owned parcel, would make a buildable lot." She put her hands on her hips. "That's why."

"Has the mayor even signed off on this?" I said. "Isn't he worried about perceived favoritism during his campaign?"

"And you, what have you been doing?"

"Me? Working. Problems with work. That I haven't mentioned yet."

"So what were you doing in City Hall Plaza in disguise? You were just following me, weren't you?"

"Me? No. I was shocked to see you. You could see it in my face, I'm sure."

"If you showed me your face. I can see it now, though, and I tell you—" She shook her head. Shadows under her eyes and fine lines made her look tired, but I bet I looked worse.

"I was under cover. Some punks have been rolling pan handlers." This, I'd come up with earlier—lame, but functional. "It's for the crime series I'm reporting on. Kravitz has me running around like crazy, and kind of leading a couple of reporters on it. If I excel, there's a good chance of promotion."

"All right." She nodded. "There. See, we find out, we move on. That wasn't so hard, was it? However, I don't want you following me around— or him. It's creepy and invades my privacy. If you want to know something, ask me. And we should talk more."

"Yes, right, talk so I can ask you a question like, did you kiss Swanson?"

She pulled her head back. "You're asking me this? No, I didn't."

"Hug him?"

Debbie glanced at a man about my age in a suit approaching. He passed by.

"I don't know," she said. "Yes, I suppose, but not in a meaningful way—not the way you mean it. Just friendly, celebrating progress. He was interested in youth also, before he met me."

I knew the answer to this one. "So, did he kiss you?"

"Jesus, Dax. Do you—"

A couple of backpack-laden students were coming down the path. One stopped to take a cell phone call and jabbered on. Debbie and I avoided eye contact. We waited. She walked onto the grass and I followed.

"What do you think?" She shook her head. "Yes, he did. I remember. So what? It was on the cheek. It's European, but it's done here, too, especially among certain people."

"Certain people?"

"Remember, you encouraged me to do something about my career. My ambitions, my hopes. Well, I did. If someone paid me a little extra attention along the way, it's no big deal. I didn't cross the line. Maybe I did keep the entertainment value or interest or even a little flirtation to myself."

"So he's just a guy? A man with power who takes you out to dinner, to his house, other places, too, right? And flirts with you. And you said nothing happened. I'm supposed to be comfortable with that? To hell with that."

I moved away, determined to shut her out.

"Wait, Dax. There's something you should know."

This could be it. I swallowed and turned. She came to me.

And I couldn't read her for the life of me.

After a moment, she said, "About Bradley Swanson."

I cleared my throat. "Yes?"

"Bradley is gay."

I got those dueling feelings again, relief and embarrassment. "He's... gay?"

"Well, I thought he was gay, but I think I missed some signals and took it as the sweet side of his personality. I think he's actually bisexual." She looked at the ground then at me again. "He has a lover. He doesn't talk about him, but he has one. What he does talk about is getting a dirt-cheap lot from the city next to an available small parcel. He talks about making things happen. You should be happy for me."

"Whoa. Okay, so I buy that you're not doing him illicit favors, but is he doing you any?"

"I'll ignore the implied insult. Do you even know what you just said?"

"Oh, illicit favors? No, didn't mean it like that. Sorry."

She closed her eyes, head down. "He said it wasn't a problem as long as there is a bid process or it's for approved purposes." She looked up. "I don't owe him and he doesn't owe me, and the mayor approves of it. When this is over, it'll be a great city resource, and it'll give me a base to secure funding for a non-profit teen-counseling center. It's my dream, Dax. Bradley paid attention to me—well, it was welcomed. Even when I came to believe he was bisexual. So what?"

I sucked my lip.

"Besides," she said, "crossing that line is what bothers me most about people. I see it in my patients. They meet someone new and off they go. I saw it with the man I was once with, and thought might have had a future with, once. I never told you that, but at one point I did see it going in that direction. And—"

"And what?"

She stared hard. Maybe she was about to let something slip.

"What?" I gave a nod.

"And I saw it in you."

My heart fluttered. "What?"

She looked down. "You heard me."

My mind fell into the depths of her accusing eyes. "Saw it in me?"

"I knew you thought she was attractive."

"Who?"

"Marguerite."

I hesitated. "Marguerite who?"

She said loudly, "Do I have to find the channel for you and spell it out?"

"The woman from Channel 7 News? So what? That's not hard to admit; many men are," I said. "I'm sure you're attracted to other men, too. I mean, it's a fact, right?"

"Is it hard for you to admit more?"

"What are you saying?"

"I'm saying…" She tilted her head to look me in the eyes. "What you think I'm saying."

"What does this have to do with where we are now," I said, "either way?"

"Everything."

"How."

"How?" she said, looking disgusted. "This is how; apparently, she does more on her field work than what we see on TV."

"Like? What's your point? We can discuss it."

"Ha. 'So we can discuss it.' You're so full of crap. I saw you in traffic and waved, but you didn't see me. I turned around, but you were ahead by a traffic light, and I couldn't squeeze into the right lane to catch up. I thought I'd lost you and was going to leave, but the light turned green, and you—" She pursed her lips. "You turned into the hotel. But not to bang a U-turn."

"Debbie."

"Save it, Dax."

*That day at the hotel.* "No, Debbie, it wasn't like that."

"Wasn't like that? You're right. It was more like seeing you go up stairs to the outside balcony and walk into that room. I really *hoped* it had something to do with a story you were working on. But it wasn't a news story. It was our own little tragedy. Any doubt was erased when she squeezed your butt."

I said quickly, "Oh my God, I'm only going to say this once because it's so lame. And it's not an excuse or an explanation—or maybe it's part of that. But it is the truth. I wanted her, she wanted me, I'm quite sure, but we couldn't start. I realized that, from my side, all the fantasy was just that. I don't know if it was guilt or the fact that I thought of myself as a better person or—"

Debbie's mouth opened as if to say *ha*, but she closed it and glared.

"Or what, but it didn't feel right. She sensed it, too, I think, and didn't try anything either. We talked a bit until knowing that it wasn't the best idea to be there. That's it. I was stupid. I'm sorry. Nothing happened then, nothing before or after. The only thing satiated was our egos, I suppose. You of all people should understand that."

Debbie sucked in her breath. "Fuck you."

"Huh?"

"I should understand that of all people? Go to hell," she shouted. "Don't put that on me. Don't load my role as an independent professional onto my personal shoulders. It doesn't work that way. If it did, I'd have said you're a reporter and should have reported to me what you did—or what you allegedly didn't do. Bastard. " She violently shook her head. Her hair clip fell to the ground.

"I'm sorry," I whispered and tried to push frizzy blonde strands from her eyes.

She batted my hand away. "So was I seduced by Brad at some point? Or was I reduced by you? Did I get my revenge, or simply have pleasure? Whatever it is, I've heard it all. I feel quite good and normal, comparatively speaking. After all the stuff clients tell me they do and have been through, and put people through, whether they realize it or not, and now you."

"Well?"

"Well? Well? The answers?" She jutted her face out for a moment.

"Stay tuned. I'll get back to you. On a different channel, then you can tell me why you work so late."

She spun away, hair bouncing across her shoulders as if brushing me off. She strode toward the square. I stared until she crossed the street, mixed with pedestrians, and disappeared.

I kept staring.

Good God. Too many unanswered questions and following her would be more difficult now.

I wondered about my marriage, my career, my—then something clicked. Not lipstick on the collar, but white-collar crime. Bid *or* approved purposes?—or not. What if Swanson had been sneaking little parcels of unused city land to his favorites and covering up the paper trail? Were there irregularities in the process? Short cuts for the politically connected? Outright theft? I'd just been assigned to white collar crime. Getting something dirty on Swanson would get my footing back with Debbie and be a huge scoop for the paper. Not often did one hope a person was bad, but this was such a case. And with politics in general and Swanson's two-way libido, it was possible.

Debbie wouldn't be in the middle of anything as untoward as improper city real estate transactions, but she must be kept clear of whatever I discover. Meanwhile, I'd take her word, all of those words, and believe that she was ultimately faithful. I'd just do my job. Maybe it was a leap of faith, maybe a leap of logic; maybe both.

# CHAPTER 14

# Wednesday, 3:25 p.m.

On Mass Avenue, by Harvard's law school, my Jeep's windshield was adorned with a dazzling orange notice of my contribution to city coffers, i.e., another parking ticket. I snatched it and hopped in, imagining a confrontation with Swanson. I couldn't wait for a breakthrough with Debbie, my investigation, or anything. I had to do it today and see Swanson's reaction, maybe get information about Debbie or the real estate that he deals with. I raised the soft-top and zipped the windows before pulling out.

The lights atop Boston's "old" John Hancock building indicated the weather: steady blue, clear view; flashing blue, clouds due; steady red, rain ahead; flashing red, snow or, in the summer, the Red Sox game was canceled. And if my Jeep's soft-top was up, I was feeling blue; if the soft-top was down, I was feeling sunny. For various moods, I could adjust windows, remove doors, or even latch the windshield to the hood. Right now, if this Jeep was more adept at my self-expression, the paint would be peeling off. I was disgusted with life and sad at what had become of Debbie and me, regardless of who did what. I'd just never seen it coming.

As I turned toward Kendall Square, my phone vibrated. A text message from Debbie: "Answers are no of course but I didn't say I believe you that nothing happened."

Answers were "no," but what exactly had been the questions? If she'd stuck around, maybe we would have talked it out, and live answers were more reliable. Had she left to escape the indignity or escape the element of surprise?

She always blew me away. Beautiful, smart, and she knew how to love; much better than me. I wished I wasn't determined to verify her story, but it just might be bullshit after all, and not knowing one way or the other was the worst part. Yeah, I had an issue with trust, one that had long tied me up inside. But it wasn't with her; it was with the world, a world full of crime, of abandonment, a world ripe with hurt. I had to find a way to tell her that. I had assumed that she'd known, but I hadn't consciously realized that until recently. Why had I expected her to realize it and deal with it?

Meanwhile, I had to deal with things my way.

I'd investigate Swanson's side, his relationship with Debbie and his real estate dealings, and how they overlapped, if they did. Kravitz didn't trust me to write in favor of the mayor, so now he wanted white-collar crime stories? Fine. That would include government corruption. It would be sweet, oh-so-sweet to find something ugly on this law and order administration, and on the chief of staff, no less.

Over the Longfellow Bridge, I passed through Government Center traffic and parked at the city hall look-alike garage. Inside the New Chardon Street courthouse, I passed through the metal detector and the court officer handed me my backpack. Being clean and not asking for spare change surely helped me get through without a pat down. All sorts came through for matters of juveniles, land, housing, district court, and family and probate court. I fit in here on multiple levels at this point.

My cell phone rang: Jimmy. I answered.

"Hey, Dax." He sounded chipper.

"What's up?"

"Ah, sorry, I hope you didn't mind, you know, Kravitz going with my story. I feel—"

"Look, don't flatter yourself by feeling bad. If you want, you can do me a favor, though."

"Yeah? Okay—wait, what is it?"

"Something you can handle, don't worry. Write an article about the Guardian Angels."

"The what? Like, the angels who watch over us or the angels who helped the Bruins bring back the Stanley Cup?" He laughed.

"Hey, watch it, mister. That wasn't divine intervention. That was God-given hockey talent. And no, I'm talking about the old citizen patrol group that helped reduce street crime years ago. If Kravitz and company don't want vigilantes running amuck, and who would, better have some effective neighborhood watch groups helping out the police."

Jimmy agreed to do it, and I was glad to keep vigilantism alive in the press. Coming from another person, Kravitz might be more open to the subject.

The Suffolk County Registry of Deeds was on the courthouse's lower level. I tried one computer terminal, but the monitor flickered so I switched to another one. I searched for Bradley Swanson in the records of real estate ownership. Even with combinations of names, spellings, and initials, I only got several other addresses—his in Boston and a couple in Revere and Winthrop with a different middle initial. So I targeted specific areas. You never knew how a database would respond. I could get lucky, but after a while, no dice. I threw down my pen, rubbed my neck, and stood to stretch. I'd searched using other database fields, even if unfamiliar. Nothing.

There was another option. I checked a box to include in the search all readable text in the documents themselves, even though in pdf format. Bradley Swanson, multiple hits. *Yes.* However, they appeared to be his notarizations of others' signatures on deeds. I suppose that was common for a notary, especially one associated with real estate work. However, all were dated within the last six months. He didn't have any apparent interest in these, and it may be nothing, but it was a start. I printed the deeds, all forty-six of them.

Time to introduce myself to Swanson.

After leaving the registry, I turned right, but envisioned Channel 7 ahead, next to the post office. *Marguerite.* So I banged a U-turn—no, let's say, I turned around and went by way of TD Garden to Faneuil Hall for a quick cup of chowder. Afterward, I walked up State Street to approach Government Center from the west. I passed beneath the iconic, huge steaming teakettle by Starbucks, which would probably call it a coffee pot. The Boston Tea Party had happened nearby, though, so a teapot it was.

I entered a coffee shop, close to city hall's main exit. I bought a coffee and sipped at the counter along the glass wall. The dying sunlight slanted onto the red bricks; lengthening shadows reached for the heart of City Hall Plaza. I took the deeds out of my backpack. Most were of city real estate. Several appeared legitimate; others were more interesting. Forty-two of them deeded parcels to a name I didn't recognize: Karen Hickey. Maybe I'd get information or an admission from Swanson, unless Debbie had already warned him. Still, I was going to lie in wait for a certain notary public.

A Registry of Motor Vehicles search earlier had shown that Swanson didn't own a vehicle; it seemed he was a taxi-and-train kind of guy. He could have a city vehicle, but I was unsure how to find out discreetly. I watched closely, as the train station nearby drew a lot of foot traffic. People would be getting out of work soon. I opened my web browser and skimmed the *Boston Times* between visual scans for Swanson. One article caught my eye; "Mayor Paul D. Grasso will travel to Washington, D.C. next week to join mayors from 20 states at the national summit of Mayors Against Illegal Guns." Of course, mayors were against illegal guns, and I was on their side. I supported First Amendment freedom of the press, but not aggressive gun lobbyists' version of the Second Amendment. Then again, karate "empty hand" versus a handgun? No contest; bullets trumped bones. Even I had a license to carry; I just hadn't bought anything to carry, yet.

A *Hub News* article showed polls with Grasso losing a few points in the governor's race as crime continued to be an issue. It cited the semi-popular but controversial Dandy Vigilante as an example. *Ha.* Some saw the mayoral coattail getting caught in a door, which made it harder for Swanson to ride.

I called Swanson's office and claimed to be waiting for him at "the meeting," figuring he was always going to meetings—the assumptive approach. His assistant said he was just leaving, that he'd be there soon, as if buying time for a harried boss. I asked in a huff to confirm the meeting place so there'd be "no further miscommunication." She told me the A-1 police station. I hung up abruptly to stem questions, and to punctuate the ill will.

On the edge of City Hall Plaza, at the pergola by the JFK federal building, I sat at a bench, worried that I might miss him. Ten minutes later, though, I saw a good candidate, ice cream lip man, carrying a heavy briefcase so briskly his gait was arrhythmic. So it'd be now, face-to-face.

Ahead of Swanson, I took my stand while he checked his briefcase clasp and switched hands. He was a big guy; not sporty, just thick limbed. Steps away, he lifted his head. I was in his path. He adjusted, and I blocked him.

He slowed. "Excuse me."

"Excuse you?" I said, eye to eye.

His expression betrayed his opinion that I was a lunatic. "I'm in a hurry." His public relations skills apparently quit for the day.

I stepped back and extended my arm to corral him then pointed past the gladiolas to the seats under the pergola. "Could you step over here a moment?"

"I don't want any, whatever you're selling." Brows furrowed, he tried to go around me by the pergola, but I stepped into his path. He straightened, becoming an inch or so taller. "Do you know who I am? I said I don't have time."

I pointed to my palm. "First of all, you didn't say 'I don't have time.' You said, 'I'm in a hurry.'"

He shifted on his feet. "I—"

"Uh, uh, ah." I wagged my finger. "I'm not finished. Second..." I jabbed my palm. "I do know who you are. The question is, do you know who I am?"

A practiced diplomatic smile crossed his face—a voter, a community leader? However, I was too rude and odd for that profile so his face flashed anger. "What the hell—who are you?"

"I'm Debra's husband."

He froze—not from recognition, but for a response. There was a chance he had something to hide. A smile popped up onto his face, as genuine as a mannequin. "Oh. I'm so sorry. I, I didn't know. I'm Bradley—"

"I just want to tell you to lay off her."

"But I'm only—"

"I know, she said you're trying to help her. But there's more there, especially on your end."

He considered this, appeared confused—as to the facts or a response?

"What makes you think that? I assure you, we're only colleagues. Maybe I've taken her under my wing a bit, but she is charming. And we—"

"Save it. Just a warning. The 'extra-curricular' attention you give her is inappropriate."

"A warning." He huffed. "I can't believe this. To accuse me and her, of—" He leaned forward, red in the face, and glanced at a man passing under the pergola staring at us.

The man wore a white shirt and striped tie. "Mr. Swanson, everything all right?"

"All right?" He smiled. "Yes. Good night, Troy."

The man waved and kept going.

"It's not an accusation, per se," I added. "Just a collegial caution. I know you're trying to help her, and I'll accept that you have a common professional interest. I'm just a bit concerned, okay? I don't want to sabotage your assistance." Doubt nibbled at my anger. I bit my lip, until I realized it. "I mean, as long as the mayor is okay with it."

Swanson nodded. "Don't worry. This is my thing, and the mayor trusts me. He's behind us all the way." His posture relaxed. "Debra's a treasure, but I've already got mine. I'm doing her and the city a favor. She'll be a good director when we get this together." He checked his cell phone.

I nodded. "Okay, then."

"Okay," he replied.

I turned to walk away, but he added, "Just don't let this happen again."

Cheap shot. I kept going. If Swanson had a professional interest in Debbie's objective, then this scene shouldn't affect it. If he pulled the rug out from under her, it would mean his personal interest in her, and in being petty, outweighed his interest in the youth of Boston. So be it, either way.

At the Kinsale on Cambridge Street, I sat at the bar. Rows of liquor bottles pointed up at dangling ellipses, the rims of hanging glasses catching the afternoon light. The well-dressed after-work crowd filled the place. I'd probably hear something from Debbie any second now and that would be uncomfortable. My Guinness diminished as I tried to sort my thoughts and feelings and distinguish between the two. After a second Guinness, it hadn't worked, and it was getting noisy inside. I paid my tab and left.

It was getting dark, especially with building shadows. When I got to my Jeep inside the garage, my cell phone rang—Kravitz. It went to voicemail, and I retrieved it. He wanted to see me in person ASAP. I drove to 93 South, aiming for the JFK exit to the *Boston Times*. My cell phone beeped—an email. Someday, junk mail might kill me, inducing me to read my way into a guardrail. It was Debbie, though, and what she wrote was unbelievable.

I looked up and swerved back into my lane. The Boston Police were reviewing a video purportedly showing the Dandy Vigilante at the Hatch Shell. *Damn it.* Why would she send me this? And my facial disguise was merely a patina of glue to mottle my skin. In fact, I hadn't even put that on. Those videos could be grainy, but it depended on the system's quality and the distance. The police might be able to ID me.

Phone ringing—Debbie. Time to think would be nice. As I parked, it rang again. I took a deep breath and answered.

"It's me," she said.

I hoped she was tipping me off as a reporter and not projecting any suspicion of me as the DV. "What's up? I got your email."

"Yeah, interesting, don't you think?" she said.

"Yup, I do think. It's on the news?"

She paused. "No."

"Really?"

"Really. Just so you know, Bradley Swanson called earlier. He mentioned the video. I thought you could use the lead." She cleared her throat. "And I have good news."

How the hell could there be good news or anything distantly related to good news? "Yeah, what is it?"

"Bradley found the final candidate for the property. For the youth center."

I nodded, wishing I could see her face. "Excellent, Deb. Hope it's what you need."

"I think it is. I do. It even has a building in decent shape. So no tough renovation or construction issues to deal with."

"Good," I said. "Great. I'm glad."

"He's going to show me which one and tell me all about it. Tonight. At eight o'clock. And I want to go see it."

I figured she was telling me and asking me. "I see. Well, tell me how it goes."

"Thanks," she said. "I'll see you at home."

"Okay then, bye," I said.

*What can I do?* I wondered.

The answer: what I must. I didn't like that I had to do it; there were things I didn't like about myself, but tonight, maybe tonight, I could lay the foundation for a stronger inner security and peace.

I turned around. My boss could wait. Somehow, I knew this was going to be it. My burning questions would be answered, for better or for worse.

# CHAPTER 15

# Wednesday, 8:25 p.m.

D riving past the high wall of the South Bay correctional facility, I hoped, for good reason, never to see the other side. My cell phone rang. It was a cop, "Sunny" Toni Brown, a friend, and my best contact on the BPD.

"Well, if it isn't my favorite woman in uniform, Officer Brown. How are ya?"

"Worse than before I met you, Grantham. But you gotta be alive to complain, ya know what I'm saying?"

"I do. What else you saying? You there yet?"

"Yyyyup."

"Me, too. I'm pulling in now. Dark blue limo, a/k/a my Jeep."

I pulled into McDonald's, which was sandwiched between Mass Avenue going one way and a street behind going the other. I pulled over next to her squad car, and we got out.

I said, "What's going down, Jackie Brown?" I liked to tease her with that eponymously named movie, in which the sexy Pam Grier starred as the action heroine.

"What, no kisses first, Dax? Good with those thin lips—ha." She grinned a moment, then said in a low voice, "It was a cell phone video from someone on scene."

"Oh yeah?" Cell phone video could be high quality, but was preferable to capturing me on a professional surveillance system. "Thanks for the info. I appreciate it."

"I know you appreciate it, which is why I don't mind so much that you don't show it."

I gave her a pretend lovelorn look. "Oh, Jackie. You're the best."

She put her hand on her hip. "That's enough."

"Aren't you going to confiscate that cell phone, arrest the person for audio-recording the DV without his knowledge?"

"What are you yapping about? You're the guy who wrote against cops using the wiretapping law to arrest people using cell phones to record people."

"Yeah, particularly police, but—" Arguing a new position on this might be suspicious. Besides, the police would use the video of the DV since they had it; a convenient replacement for their dashboard cam, this time. "Whatever."

She said, "And how do you know the DV hadn't *known* about being taped, making it legal? We don't know that. However, I'll certainly ask him when we catch him."

"*If* you catch him, officer," I added.

"We will, sugar. Anyway, that's all I got, and you didn't get it from me. I see my name in your article and—"

"I know, I know, something about my rectum exchanging thermal energy with your gun barrel. Well, I thank you, sunshine."

Static came from her radio. She grumbled something and said she had to go. We touched hands as she slid by me to get into her car. She waved as she pulled out, lights flashing.

On Monday night, I'd seen Debbie pull over on the way to the restaurant, apparently to look at a property, so she might exit the highway near here. I got a coffee and re-parked my Jeep near the exit to the street. I cautioned myself not to slam it into gear when I saw her and scald my lap and vicinity. I was hurting enough on the inside.

Too bad Debbie hadn't mentioned the address. Fortunately, more Jeeps were on the road than Lexuses—or would that be Lexi? In the artificial light, several cars had hues nearly indistinguishable from hers. Where had they all come from? When you buy a car, you notice that make and model everywhere, but it was worse when actively seeking one. It took an hour and two of false alarms, including chasing down one Lexus, but there she was. I crouched, eyes above the dashboard.

After a few cars passed, I followed. With turns, in less than a mile, she reached a house near the one she stopped at before. It was a two-story, single-family house. No cars were parked by it or in the adjacent vacant lot. Although the porch light and two inside lights were on, the house appeared empty.

She went in the front door. A potential youth center location? This wasn't a lovely lovers' lair, but if they were romantically involved, it would show. Passionate sex could be had just about anywhere, and an unusual place could even add to the thrill. I could listen for intimate conversation, but without curtains, I might not need to—a kiss, caress, or embrace could easily be revealed. Sitting in my Jeep down the block, I had to reign in my imagination. Tonight could prove there was nothing to worry about or that there was everything to worry about.

After Debbie and I first met, we dated on and off. During our longest off interval, over six years, she graduated with a doctorate in psychology from Boston University and almost married a business grad student, but she never talked about him. That was fine with me. We got married, eventually, almost seven years ago. Now she might be cheating on me and that was not fine with me. Seven years ago—that rang a bell, the "seven-year itch." Was someone else scratching my wife's itch?

I tried to be Zen and meditate, yet remain wary. It was hard to do, but I needed to pass the time without screaming. Finally, heart in my throat, I decided this would have to be Zen-to-go.

I hopped out and scrambled to the dark, vacant lot, which was full of brush and mounds of rubble. Several rats, I think, squealed and scurried as I made my way. The windows were closed; the interior walls were bare. I heard heels pacing the floor. After a half hour, other than glimpses of her, nothing happened. She finally left.

Well, maybe the real estate thing was legitimate and Swanson was only trying to help a good cause. And he was right; Debbie was charming. But I was confused. Swanson hadn't shown. Maybe Debbie spotted me, or maybe he had. I waited in case he showed up, she returned, or both.

***

Thursday morning, at my desk, bleary-eyed, I handwrote Kravitz a note to apologize for not getting back to him yesterday. It would also show that I came in extra early this morning. I pushed his office door open. He was in.

"Well, look who showed up." He put down his pen.

"Huh? What's up?"

Kravitz leaned back in his leather chair and cradled his head. He gave a single-syllable laugh. "You are."

I sat and we had a surprising little chat. It was good news.

Later, at my desk, Jimmy stopped by.

"Ah, another dedicated reporter," Jimmy said.

"Sure." I rubbed my eyes. "How're your articles coming along?"

"Good. I mean, I'm working with Bella. She's up on the state-level of things. I'm thinking of looking at past crime legislation that failed, why it failed, and how it would have affected today had it passed. Know what I mean? What do you think?"

"Hmm," I said. "I think you're making me think too early in the morning. But seriously, not a bad idea. A lot of work, but it could pay off. Go for it."

"Thanks. I will." He nodded. "Hey, Bella's pretty cool, isn't she?"

"Yes, 'pretty cool'. First two words I'd put together to describe her. And you're in good hands. Speaking of hands, why don't you use yours to get me some coffee?"

Jimmy laughed, and he actually got us coffee.

"Oh and congratulations," he said. "I just heard about the award."

"Thanks."

The New England Journalism Award committee had picked me as an award recipient this year. In a story I wrote in the spring, people's right to openly audio-video record police was pitted against police use of an old anti-wiretapping statute to arrest, too often wrongfully, those recording the action.

"But I think there's another Dax Grantham around here," I said. "I didn't write that crap."

"Yeah, sure." Jimmy shook his head with a grin and dipped into his cubicle.

I kicked my feet up onto the desk and stared out my window. A train of puffy clouds skirted the horizon. I yawned. When I left this morning, Debbie was still in bed. She hadn't slept well, which I knew because I hadn't either. And our truce hadn't included cuddling to fall back asleep.

While I worked on articles-in-progress, Debbie popped into my mind again. I pushed back from the keyboard. I sent her a test-the-waters email: "Hi there, great news about the property. Are you free? Did you have dinner yet? We can celebrate. I have good news, too."

A minute later: "Sure. Dinner at Pho Pasteur in the theater district? At 6:00, or I can do earlier. What's your good news? D."

*Yes.* I passed that hurdle. She was "talking" to me now. Given our argument in the park, I supposed she was entitled to this emotional leverage. These marital ups and downs and flat lines were hard to endure. I confirmed, but said I'd tell her the news there.

***

Rain sprinkled the restaurant's front windows. Patrons came and went as I sipped a Viet beer at the bar, which was cute with its six small stools, low ceiling, and bamboo motif. I was a tad excited; it felt like going a date, except we'd definitely go home together afterward and the consummation of our making up would be an excellent option.

Debbie came inside and shook water from her jacket. She leaned over and shook beads of rain from her frizzy blonde hair. She looked up at me and smiled. It felt good. *You are my sunshine.*

I stood and returned the smile, pushing away the reasons to restrain it. When I kissed her cheek, I caught a whiff of rain-on-frangipani scent. We were led to a table. She faced the front door, which I usually liked to do in the spirit of the *Wild Wild West.* At first, we hid behind the menus and small talk.

"So what's your good news?" she said, enthusiastically. I loved it.

"Nothing much," I replied. "I got this regional journalism award. Kravitz gave me the word this morning. There'll be a little celebration later, don't know when."

"That's super, Dax, that's great!" She touched my arm, but pulled back to switch hands on the menu.

"Thanks." For some reason, I didn't want to share that Kravitz also had agreed to write the letter for my application to the investigative reporting program.

"Problem is," I said, "I copied part of the article from another writer."

Debbie looked up, serious, but then said, "Oh. Nice try."

I grinned. A server filled our water glasses. My appetite was growing.

She asked, "So what was the article?"

"That First Amendment one, people getting arrested for recording police."

"Ah, my guess would've been the one about inner-city youth missing the transition to college. Did you know more young black men are in jail than in college? I don't know if that's a national or local statistic, but it's so crazy I should double-check it. I refuse to believe it, and if it's true, I refuse to accept it. Besides, it can cost fifty-grand annually to incarcerate someone—a lot more than college costs." Her face was flush. "And it's mostly preventable. Provide effective education so they grow up to be good citizens in the first place. Shouldn't we care for them while they're young and innocent instead of as adults with recalcitrant problems?"

"Preaching to the choir, my dear," I said.

"Ah, sorry, there I go again. I'm just excited about helping youth now."

"Clearly." I scanned the dining room for the server.

"I'm not sure I remember that article, though. Did you tell me about it?"

"Busy as hell, then, I suppose," I said.

"You know, it was your other article that started me re-thinking my career, to involve youth. In fact, in a way, it led to this—the youth counseling center. The idea is to get referrals from the Boston Centers for Youth & Families. They identify them, we help them."

The server came by and took an order of Chardonnay for her. It was time she and I toasted.

"Wow. Congratulations on your award." She nodded, smiling.

"The award? I don't know. It's often arbitrary anyway." I leaned back.

She smiled softly. "And I say don't be modest. Congratulations, hon."

*Hon.* Seemed my demotion to Dax was over. "Thank you, thank you. So tell me about the property. That's a big score, getting one with a building on it."

"Yes. It is." She sat up, her blouse tightening over her small breasts.

"Although." She fingered her chin. "I looked at it last night. There're superficial issues, but if structural issues too, it means paperwork, hurdles, and inspectors."

Here was the elephant. I hesitated, but asked, "Does Swanson think it needs reconstruction? I mean, he knows about that stuff, somewhat, doesn't he?"

She took out a black-lacquered clasp and bound her hair. "I'm not sure, but we'll have it inspected to see where we're at. I'd like to go when they do. And you can come along and finally meet Brad," she said.

Whoa—Swanson hadn't mentioned he already met me?

She furrowed her brow. "I hoped to ask him about an inspection, at least to get a tentative answer, but he didn't show up at the property last night."

Ah, honesty, verifiable honesty. The relief felt wonderful. With a little more, I could probably build back my trust and put it all behind me; get our lives back on track and build the family I'd longed for. Focus on my career again, too, like a sane, non-vigilante-freak.

"Oh?" I said. "Too bad, but you got to see the place, right? What's it like inside?"

She swirled her wine and then eyed the door. I couldn't tell what she was thinking. "Well. Some of it," she said.

If Swanson hadn't shown up, the front door must have been unlocked. I changed tack. "Is the outside—in what kind of shape is the outside?"

Looking over my shoulder, she gave a curious expression. "Dax?"

I turned around to follow her line of sight. My heart plummeted. Police, one uniformed, one plain clothed; their eyes were on us.

*Oh God.* I faced her again.

She touched my forearm on the table. "Something going on? I think they're looking at us."

I couldn't believe all this was coming down on me now, here. After all this: my life had been fractured, then seemed to be coming back together, especially with Debbie. Maybe I'd turn around and the cops would be leaving.

But Debbie looked up, over my head.

In the window reflection, the detective loomed, badge in hand. "Excuse me."

I was ready to stand. The uniformed cop was by the door. The glints on his belt were handcuffs, which I pictured on my wrists, then I'd be led out, the dark Crown Victoria door open—"Duck your head." Ding dong, the Dandy Vigilante was dead.

But wait. He wasn't looking at me. He was looking at her.

"Sergeant Detective Jim Flaherty, Homicide Unit," he said, displaying his gold badge. "Are you Debra Stapleton?"

# CHAPTER 16

# Thursday, 6: 50 p.m.

We were buzzed in past the bulletproof partition at the police station. Sergeant Detective Flaherty pointed to a bench and told me to wait. He opened a door for Debbie.

"Hey, wait," I said. "I want to go with her. You haven't even told us what this is about. Maybe she wants a lawyer. Debbie?"

She shrugged, looking confused.

Flaherty's crows-feet eyes radiated white meridians through his tan. "Look, this is the way it goes. Blow money on a lawyer if you want, but we're only going to ask a few questions." He spoke in low, measured tones. "Your turn will come."

"Is this a homicide issue? Who is dead? At least tell me that," I said.

He ran his hand over his hair, which was combed back into jelled, gray-black lines. "Yes, it's related to a homicide issue."

The door closed behind them.

Was one of her patients a murderer or was it a questionable suicide? They wanted to talk to me, too, perhaps to verify things she'd tell them, but if I was free to go, maybe I'd get her a lawyer. Then again, they hadn't arrested her, and she didn't have anything to hide, of course.

Better get a lawyer. On my cell phone, I looked up a criminal lawyer I'd once interviewed, Claude DeLay. His office was nearby at One Center Plaza. I had to leave a voicemail.

Ten minutes later, a man in short sleeves came out, introduced himself as Lieutenant Detective Reynolds, and apologized for the inconvenience. He had a medium build, thick arms, and brown, freckled skin. I stood and shook his hand.

Instead of taking me into an interrogation room, he offered me coffee.

What a good cop.

"So, what'd ya do last night?" Lieutenant Detective Reynolds said.

Then it hit me—they could be after me, but were using Debbie as a decoy to get me to talk more freely. And she was innocent, so she'd talk to defend herself. Smart.

"Me?" I cleared my throat. "Not much. How about you?"

"Yeah. Me neither." He paused. "So where were you? Who were you with?"

And any inconsistencies in our statements were cracks to pry at.

"At home, I believe. Why?"

"Here. Let's sit down. Who were you with?"

We sat on the bench. He gave me the eyes and a shrug, but I refused to be rushed. I folded my arms. "I was at home and I was at work. I had a late meeting with my boss at the *Boston Times*, Mr. Kravitz."

"And your wife, she can verify this?"

"That I was at home? Sure."

"You're saying she was home with you?"

"Yes."

"She was home all night? But you weren't?"

"I said she can verify I was home. I can verify she was home. That's all. I had a meeting with my boss, around, I don't know, late evening. So what's this about?"

"What time was your meeting?"

I dropped my hands. "Hey, I told you. Now you tell me. What's going on? Who the hell died? Detective Flaherty said there was a homicide."

"He said that? Well, yeah. There was. You know. We're just doing our jobs. I've read some of your articles. You know how this stuff works." He scratched his head. "Even if you sometimes don't like how it works."

"Oh, come on."

"Fine, Mr. Grantham. I'll cut to the chase, as they say. Is there any reason to think your wife is screwing around?"

My stomach did a flip. I'd stalked both her and Swanson. *Oh my God—it was Swanson.* "I don't think so."

"Sorry I have to ask. Do you know who she met last night?"

"Well. She had a meeting." I swallowed. "Something about—wait, are you accusing her of something?"

"She's a person of interest, that's all. Who did she meet?"

"I'm not sure."

Reynolds gave an upward nod. "Name Swanson ring a bell?"

"Sure. He's chief of staff for Grasso."

He said, "You like the guy?"

"I don't know. I suppose. I mean, I don't know him well."

"Uh-huh. And?"

"And that's it," I said. "Is he dead?"

"That's what we're trying to work on."

"Huh?"

He paused, apparently deliberating. "Yes. Doesn't look good for natural death either. The papers—I suppose you, too—will be all over this story." Looking at the floor, he mumbled, "The chief of staff."

"So why Debbie?"

"It's possible she was supposed to meet Swanson. We're tracking his whereabouts in recent days, yesterday especially, of course. Anything you two can tell us will help out, okay? We really need your help. So when did she leave the house?"

The old civic responsibility gambit; "We don't suspect you; we just need a little information, citizen," but not your Fifth Amendment rights, they mean, because helping yourself into prison was okay with them.

"I didn't say she did leave the house. And I'd like to see her now."

He sighed. "Sorry. She might be a little while, but let me see. I'll be back."

After ten minutes of pacing, asking to see her, and no call back from the lawyer, the door opened. Sergeant Detective Flaherty came through, followed by Debbie.

"We'll be in touch," Flaherty said. "Have your lawyer contact us ASAP so we can finish."

"As soon as I find one," she murmured, taking my arm. "It's Bradley Swanson. He's dead."

"I know. Shhh." I pulled her close.

"Killed." Her face showed distraught; her eyes were red-rimmed. I escorted her out the door.

"Let's go home," I said.

On the sidewalk, I asked if she was all right. Before she could answer, Detective Reynolds rushed out.

"Wait," he said.

Detective Flaherty followed and stood by me while Reynolds pulled Debbie away.

"What are you doing?" I yelled, moving toward her.

Flaherty grabbed my arm.

"Ms. Stapleton," Lieutenant Detective Reynolds said, "you have the right to remain silent." He read her the rest of her Miranda Rights as I gaped.

I moved closer, but Flaherty held on. "Sorry, Dax. We ran the prints on the weapon."

His words ran through my heart like so many stabs.

# CHAPTER 17

## Friday, 8:00 a.m.

I stared over the attorney's desk at a bare spot on the wall, which seemed higher than it was given the low couch. Life as I knew it would be over. Debbie, jailed, yet she couldn't have murdered Swanson. *No way.* If she had somehow caused his death, there must be proof that it was accidental or in self-defense. At worst, I could only imagine unintentional manslaughter, which, under extenuating circumstances, could bring probation or a shorter sentence. However, theoretically, if she'd murdered him, for whatever reason, our marriage was over, wasn't it? Her arms couldn't embrace me with the arms of the state gripping her, which also meant no kids, no family. No home.

My throat constricted. I'd lost my father, then my mother. I couldn't remember how much time had elapsed between their deaths, anywhere from a month to a year, maybe more. After my grandmother died, I was adopted, so I'd lost my brother, too. Nothing could comfort that kind of pain. You lived with it. Period. You lived with it like a presence, a void forever unfilled.

After consulting with the attorney, he stepped away to make a few "sensitive calls," i.e., he didn't want to reveal his sources, especially to a reporter.

Framed photos with VIPs, diplomas, and awards covered his "wall of fame." The hardwood door was tall enough to belong to a wizard or someone of similar ego, and the light-green tint to his walls reminded me of dollar bills. It was a favor for him to see me without an appointment this morning, or so the secretary implied after I'd knocked on the door to this Emerald City. I knew any lawyer would be all over this case just for the publicity.

Attorney DeLay dropped into his high-back leather chair, scanned his notes, and removed his glasses. "It's as you said. Bradley Swanson was killed last night. His body was found, anyway. A neighbor presumably reported lights on inside and an open front door."

"Okay, so why was Debbie arrested? An accessory? Murder? Manslaughter?"

I listened for "No, no, not that," then he'd tell me a tolerable story.

But he said, "Yup. It's murder—kitchen knife below the solar plexus. That's all they'd tell me for now."

I hung my head. "Is it true, her prints? On what? The house? That's nothing. She was there, walking around." But Flaherty had said the prints were on the weapon, I recalled. "Swanson didn't even show up. He must have come later, and someone else, too—the murderer."

"She said that? Wait—look, this is getting odd, ethically speaking. You're hiring me, but she's my client. Understand? I haven't even spoken with her yet, but tell me what you know. How do you know that's all she did or that someone else was or was not there? Anything you can tell me that will help her."

"She went for a meeting. I think, yes, she told me later he was a no-show. So she waited around and left. She, she—" I stared at my shoes, my head pounding. I didn't want to incriminate myself. "She couldn't have done something like that. She's just not that kind."

"Mr. Grantham. I've met many of the 'not-that-kind.'"

I raised my head.

"Sorry, nothing implied there," he said. "Another thing, I have to warn you, as you are not my client, you have no attorney-client privilege to invoke should you tell me you were involved in any way."

"I—"

He held up his hand and stood. "I'm going to the police station. This is a serious case, Mr. Grantham. Remain here, and my office manager will discuss the fees with you. We'll talk again."

"Don't wait to call me if you find out more." I stood. "And I didn't do it, by the way. And I want to see her. When can I see her?"

"Hold off," he said. "Better to avoid conversations with her while she's in lockup. If overheard, we can't claim the spousal privilege to exclude it from evidence, if it comes to that. I'll try to arrange bail."

"How much will we need?"

"Don't worry, I'll let you know."

***

News of Debbie's arrest got out. I'd taken refuge in the North Shore, inside the Reading Public Library. When Attorney DeLay finally called me, I stepped outside.

"The police based their initial questioning on a simple idea," DeLay said. "Swanson and your wife arranged a meeting at that house, which is the murder scene. And it was done by text message, which is a common method for illicit lovers to communicate because they're often unable to speak. No motive was apparent, besides the pro forma possibility of an illicit romance gone bad, especially with the cake and champagne they'd found on scene. She denies the implication, of course."

They were seen together elsewhere, he added, but nothing definitive. Hell, I knew that much.

"They'd asked her about politics, about promises—particularly any reneged upon. The nature of her relationship with him, what they were working on. She wisely asked for a lawyer, but fingerprints on the knife clinched it for the arrest. By the way, have you signed the fee agreement and arranged the retainer?"

"Yeah." *And sorry I don't have a first-born to offer you.* The retainer was huge and didn't even include a trial.

"Good. By the way, as a matter of law, fingerprints on a murder weapon alone cannot sustain a conviction. They must establish that she was there at the time of death. Theoretically, her prints on the knife could've been made at a different time or a different place than the murder." He said he'd look into everything and we'd talk again then hung up before I could question him.

I retrieved my backpack and threw it into my car. Everyone had been trying to reach me, mostly colleagues who knew Debbie's last name was Stapleton, not Grantham. Some calls expressed personal concern, but many sought the story. It would be a silent "no comment" from me.

Driving on 93 South toward the Registry of Deeds in Boston, I wondered if I should try to visit Debbie despite DeLay's warning, and if I should have brought the extra $10,000 cash I'd withdrawn from my retirement account for a possible bail bond.

This was crazy. I was her only exculpatory witness. I'd seen her at the vacant house, and Swanson hadn't shown up while we were there, as far as I knew. Disclosing that would implicate me in a number of ways.

I was at the murder scene, too; that would look like the jealous husband stalking her—shit, and wasn't that the truth? Maybe not the whole truth, but the cops wouldn't care.

I rolled down my window. Cool, dry air filled the Jeep.

Could Swanson have already been there? The upstairs had been dark, yet I doubted that she had a flashlight. Was there evidence of a candle upstairs? He could have been in a room on the opposite side from my vantage point.

She'd only paced up and down, I thought. And there were no suspicious sounds. Then again, they'd say the knife didn't make much sound going through his torso, now, did it? And they'd be right. A quick stab in the stomach wouldn't spray blood on her like other wounds could, either.

I entered the parking garage and cruised for a space. This conclusively ended any suspicion of Debbie having an affair with Swanson—

prospectively, that is. On the other hand, the police would investigate and probably find out more than I knew, perhaps more than I wanted to know. I was so happy being reconciled with Debbie.

Maybe something was on the cusp of happening between them, but divine intervention or fate stopped them—or a decision not to do anything, like mine in the hotel room with the reporter, Marguerite. I'd almost messed up with her. It had started as breakfast, colleagues, but Marguerite's interest in me was flattering and overt, so I responded in kind, and it escalated.

This was insane. Helping Debbie could implicate me. And my exposure not only included my jealous confrontation with Swanson, it included his goal of catching the Dandy Vigilante—me.

Back inside the registry, I searched deeds under variations of Debbie's name. If I found other real estate in her name, it could implicate her in something, or it could lead to someone else, an alternate suspect for Swanson's murder.

Her name didn't come up, but I checked Swanson's name again and was blown away. Those deeds were no longer in the woman's name, the woman whose signatures Bradley Swanson had notarized. All forty-two deeds transferred the real estate to a trust, The Good House Trust, yesterday; the same day he was killed. And someone else notarized them, an undecipherable name. I tried looking up The Good House Trust itself to see if it was recorded; no dice. I couldn't check the trust's schedule of the beneficiaries, which lists the real owner or owners. What the hell could I do with a non-existing or unrecorded trust? This was worse than a blind real estate trust, where beneficiaries' names weren't recorded, but the trust and trustee names would be. Here, I had nothing.

Then I noticed the lower left corner of every deed had a return address. The registry required it to return original deeds to owners after recording. However, it wasn't an individual; it was a law firm. Worse, it was out of state. The original deeds were mailed back to the new owner's attorney in Rhode Island. The deeds would be in the attorney's client file with the trust document and schedule of beneficiaries. I needed the name or names of the beneficiaries, the true owners. The murder and deeding of those properties on the same day was too much of a coincidence.

What could this have to do with Debbie? Swanson was to get her real estate for her youth counseling center and had supposedly just locked in on a lot. Maybe Swanson betrayed her some way, reneged on the real estate or a promise of the youth center directorship.

*My God, what if I set off a chain reaction?* I confronted Swanson, he reneged on her? He seemed egotistical enough. He could have provoked Debbie at the house, perhaps misleading her with faux-celebration cake and champagne for the youth program house. That was the only way I could imagine she'd knife him, in an emotional outburst caused by the crushing of her aspirations.

By the time I'd crouched in the vacant lot, I heard her pacing inside. Was she waiting for him or was she in shock at what she'd just done to him? She didn't show any sign of being overwrought that night, though. Swanson probably hadn't shown up, like she said.

I could help her. *Somehow.*

An idea came to me, a risky one. I left the registry.

At home, a car was parked across the street at the corner of Azel Road. I got my binoculars and saw two men in a car with extra antennae—an unmarked cruiser. Maybe the police were interested in me, too, but based on what? Did Debbie say anything about me confronting Swanson? That would open up everything. I'd be screwed.

But I started a document, one that wouldn't be saved on my computer, but could save Debbie. I typed a note to the police as a witness who'd seen Debbie walk inside the house, but hadn't seen nor heard Swanson. She just paced for a half hour, then left and didn't go back. I hesitated, and then signed as "the Dandy Vigilante" That might be more credible than an anonymous note. Getting it to the police was another matter.

I looked out at the black gleam of the unmarked police car. What if they were waiting on a search warrant?

In the kitchen, I saw that the wood block holding our kitchen knife set was full, and I searched the drawers, but couldn't tell if any of the miscellaneous knives were missing.

Getting ready to go I thought to myself, *This might be the dumbest thing I've ever done.*

# CHAPTER 18

# Friday, 1:30 p.m.

Sunshine warmed my black, Cuban-styled shirt, which fluttered in the open Jeep. I was returning to the scene of the crimes; the hit-and-run of the teenager then the middle-aged pedestrian, and the gunshot at me. I'd dressed corporate casual and left my motorcycle home, unlike the Vigilante that night. If I lost my anonymity, I'd find the mayor's enmity aimed at me, and get fired, then get jailed. Safer to lie low and suppress the spirit of vigilantism arising within. It conflicted with my old sensei's sense of non-violence. It could also get me killed, another good reason for non-violence.

I parked on Huntington Avenue, thinking that I shouldn't embrace the chance to kick someone's ass, even if the person deserved it. Better to concentrate on my career and salvage my personal life now. First priority, write a superior article, which would get Kravitz off my back. With my insider knowledge of several incidents, that shouldn't be hard.

I walked to Northeastern University and entered the quad, seeking the young woman that Mr. Heap had assaulted. She danced to help pay for college, she'd said, and this was the campus closest to the scene.

In both directions, foot traffic from academic buildings and environs passed me. For over an hour, many college women passed by. *En mass*, it struck me how young they looked. When in college, I certainly didn't think of us as kids. In fact, I was with Debbie for a while in college, and the things we did, and where we did them; wow.

After checking the student center and around campus, I hopped back into my Jeep and drove up and down Huntington Avenue, keeping an eye out for the girl. Even with my attuned peripheral vision, it was difficult. Anyway, she could be a night student or at a different college. Too bad, she'd make a great interviewee, and I'd like to know that she was safe. The consolation was that now I didn't risk explaining—to her, my boss, my readers, and possibly the police—how I, the reporter, found her and got the inside scoop.

As the Dandy Vigilante, I could be charged with malicious destruction of private property, reckless endangerment, and assault; also, assault and battery for, perhaps, unnecessarily knocking out Mr. Heap. Trespass, interference with police work, etc. I didn't forget the punks in the downtown alley at the start of all this—several counts of aggravated assault and battery, and oh yeah, homicide.

Maybe the powers that be would eventually drop the charges if assured that I'd stop my vigilante activities and believed my self-defense and justifications. If they didn't, I'd have to place my faith in a jury not to convict me. However, one "maybe" with the police and D.A., and one "faith" in an anonymous jury were uncomfortably weak barriers between prison and me. Better not get caught, period. I recalled an old adage: for every way you thought of not getting caught, ten ways would escape your thought.

I stopped at the South End restaurant. On my cell phone was an interesting news feed: Governor Leno expects to run for U.S. President, but won't endorse anyone for Massachusetts's governor yet.

The main dining room was nearly empty. "Hello?"

In the back room, a dark-haired young man was setting up a station. "Excuse me, where's the manager?"

He pointed and made a curve with his hands. I backtracked around the wall. Left of the kitchen, a door to a small office was open. The desk chair was empty, but something stopped me in my tracks. The *Herald Tribune* on the desk was folded out to a page of an article, "Vigilante or Menace?"

Noises came from the kitchen on the right. I pushed open the swinging door; cooks doing prep work, so I went back to look at the news article.

"Ahhh!" Behind the office door, a man leaned against a filing cabinet, green eyes wide with well-defined eyebrows and hand pressed to his thin chest. "My goodness. Please do *not* do that to me."

"Sorry." I took a deep breath. He was the manager I'd seen the night I came into the restaurant as an old man. "You scared me, too."

He straightened up and patted his styled blond hair. He resembled one of the Gibb brothers, maybe Barry. "Me, scare you? I doubt that. Although my partner claims it's possible." His suit fit perfectly, his tie knot GQ-cover qualified. "I'm Brian, the manager. And you are? The gentleman who forgot his D&G glasses last night?"

"No, no, I—"

"Ah ha!"

"What?"

"You have that sly look of detective all about you." He waved his arms in a big arc. "Miami Vice in Boston, right? Just look at that shirt. Someone picked that out for you? So this is about that hit-and-run Monday night?"

"Whoa, slow down," I said. "Sorry, not police. I'm just a lowly reporter."

"Here to scoop the story? Sorry, too late. I already gave an interview." He twirled his head slightly and stepped into the hall.

"The *Herald*? Is it in here, your interview?" I picked up the paper. The article was complete with quotes at the right points from the right people. The police chief said the neighborhood was relatively crime-free. *Not*. The mayor called for cooperation and witnesses. The *Boston Times* failed to indicate that the one who threw the blanket onto the windshield was the DV. "I see the valet was interviewed, too."

Brian made a face of distaste. "Ricky couldn't stop talking about himself. And that elderly gent he shooed away. He's insufferable; Ricky, that is."

"I'm sure he is," I said. "Valets these days, huh? Ricky kicked out an old man?"

"Yes, and the old man took a nutty on those tough guys around the corner, or on one of them, I mean."

"Took a nutty? Is that what Ricky said?"

"No, that's my phrase for the crazed violence, but frankly, I'm glad he did it. They've been rude to me before, calling me fagot, being threatening."

"Huh. Sounds like the guy got what he deserved."

"Thank you! We all think so around here."

I followed Brian toward the front door. "Did anyone else get injured or was it just the one assaulting the young woman?"

"That girl. Poor thing. An old couple down there saw it happen and walked up the street later. That's when Ricky talked to them."

"So what do you think of the mayor's crime-fighting agenda?"

Brian smiled. "Paul Grasso? Oh, he's on my agenda." He grimaced. "Don't quote me on that!"

We stopped at the front door.

"Bradley Swanson was a regular here, wasn't he?"

"Oh." Brian's face fell into despair. "The poor lad. I—" He choked up.

I nodded. "Yeah. Know anyone who would do that to him?"

"Absolutely not. He was so nice. It's so tragic. Tipped well, not a bit of trouble, always polite, engaging."

"Thanks, Brian. I guess that's about all. Hey, do you know anything else about what happened with him or with the girl?"

His eyebrows arched in the center. "Not other than what you see in the news. Sorry, ah, what's your name?"

"Grantham." I stuck out my hand. "Dax."

He cleared his throat. "Dax Grantham? Well, that's funny."

"It is? Why?"

"Because I knew something about you when I looked at you, I sensed it."

My mind raced. "What do you mean?"

"Your initials, D and G. That must be why I thought of the D&G glasses left here yesterday. Well, that plus you resemble him, actually, the guy who left them here. He checked for his glasses last night, but we hadn't found them yet, so I hoped he'd come back. Anyway, I'm good like that."

I nodded. "Yes, I can see that. Thank you for your time." I turned to leave.

"Anytime, Dolce—or is it Gabbana?" He laughed, hands clasped.

I pictured Brian enlivening a piano bar in Ogunquit and smiled. As I drove away, I didn't see any cops tailing me, but if so, they'd only see a working journalist. I could visit Debbie later.

# CHAPTER 19

# Friday, 4:20 p.m.

August hit me in the open Jeep as I passed the Brigham and Women's Hospital entrance. Not only was a parking spot open out front, but the meter had time left. Behind the information desk, a white-uniformed security guard sat on a tall chair. Gray locks peeked out from under his cap as if to point out the liver spots. He was tall and wide, although thin-limbed and hunched. He asked if he could help me.

"I think so. My aunt told me the room number, but I forgot. Paris Savard?"

I needed this interview, provided I got the right kind of material.

"Let's see here," he said. "Are you a relative?"

"Yes. Cousin."

"Had to think about that one, huh? I guess we're all related, if you go as far back as Africa. Mr. Savard is black." He eased back in the high chair. "And the nurse said no more press."

"But—"

"I've been around, son. I know how things work. *Boston Times?*"

"How'd you—?"

"Lucky guess. I can tell you he's listed in stable condition. Try tomorrow."

My cell phone vibrated. I ignored it. "Well, I guess if anyone knows how things work, it's you. And if you can give this to my cousin later, I'd appreciate it." I folded a $20 bill into my palm; then slid it forward on the counter while looking down the hall. "Just want to give him a card, you know? I won't be long."

He tilted back his head. I hoped his cap would fall off. "Hey," he said, "take your twenty bucks and hit the road, Jack."

"It's Dax, not Jack."

He made a nasty face. "I don't care if it's Ajax. It's the road for you, chum."

Out front, I made for the intersecting street without looking back. Yeah, I was done here—except for the emergency entrance, that is. Mr. Savard was an innocent pedestrian who hailed from Haiti. I'd have to get his room number by snooping. I hustled through the ER and down the hall.

Ten feet ahead, the same elderly guard stepped out from an alcove, nightstick in hand, tapping his leg. His head was appropriately tilted for someone who'd internalized all the cop movies of last century and had the benefit of surveillance cameras.

"Step into my office." He indicated the stairwell.

"You kidding me?"

"Nope." He pointed the nightstick at my side. "Go."

I swatted it aside as I stepped into the stairwell.

"I don't think twenty bucks is enough for your cousin's needs. He has retirement to consider."

I couldn't believe this, being shaken down by Barney Fife's older brother. "Well. Why didn't you say so? Thirty. The rest is for my mother."

"What a good boy." His hand opened. "But I told you to leave, revoking your implied license to be on the premises. You know what that means? It's a hundred to me or two policemen to you."

"A hundred? You want a hundred from me? What the hell, you gonna blow me too for that much? I'm a journalist, for crying out loud."

"Your choice. The way I understand it, they'll arrest you. Maybe they'll let you off, eventually." He shrugged. "Choose."

I shook my head.

He pushed the radio button on his shoulder and checked in, probably with a fellow extortionist.

"Unbelievable." I opened my wallet, counted out fifty-seven dollars and showed him the empty wallet. "I'm not going to the ATM for you so don't get any ideas. Now it's your choice."

He eyed the money, then me. After a moment, he snatched the cash. "Aw. Your lucky day, we're having a special. Have a nice day." He pocketed the cash as he left through the stairwell door.

"Shaken down by a geriatric, Nazi, rent-a-cop piece of crap," I growled.

The guard opened the door, leaned in, and eyeballed me. "I heard that."

I grimaced and put away my wallet.

He grinned. "Room 631."

I took the stairs to the fifth floor and checked room 531's position. A nurse asked if she could help me. Wrong floor, I replied, and took the elevator. I got out at six and strode past the nurses' station to Room 631. I knocked on the open door. Nothing. I knocked again.

"Yes? Enter." An accent.

The first bed was empty. Sun lit the curtain screening the far bed. As I approached, the man in the bed followed me with his eyes. Casts confined his left leg and arm. His right arm was in a sling on his chest. All that white contrasted with his rich ebony skin. The security guard was right. We're all related, even rent-a-cop himself, in which case, he shouldn't have charged me, the blackmailing jerk.

I nodded and introduced myself. "Paris Savard?"

"Yes. I already talked to the reporters."

"Sorry you got hurt." I shook my head. "Can you tell me in your words what happened?"

Usually, after open-ended questions, I didn't let on what I was looking for until the interviewee had committed to surrounding or partial facts, then I'd push for answers.

He gazed at the wall. "I talked to the police."

I stayed quiet, letting the momentum of his thoughts keep him on track. It also implied it was his turn to speak, but he seemed too emotional. Finally, in a kind tone, I said, "Actually, sir, I know the basics of what happened. I'm sorry. Maybe it's better if I just ask a few questions. Okay?"

Mr. Savard weighed that; he nodded.

"Did you get a look at the driver? Can you describe him?"

Mr. Savard shook his head. "I hear the car, turn my head, see the headlights. It hit me. I spin. Don't wake up there."

"Where were you going?"

He hesitated. "I don't remember."

I thought he did. "Where were you coming from?"

He shrugged slightly. His eyes watered. "I see my daughter. At my apartment."

"Who was she with?"

"My wife."

I was unsure if this was a language barrier. "Do you live with them?"

"Yes." He paused. "No. I don't know. I was going to stay with a friend. Look for a job. But I miss them." He faced the window, but I could see that his eyes were closed.

"I'm sorry," I said. "Have they been here? Did you talk to them yet?"

He frowned, appeared pained. "I don't know."

I nodded with pro forma commiseration posted on my face; then it hit me for real—him missing his wife and child, his near-death experience.

I held up my finger. "Excuse me a moment." I checked with the nurse at the station. She said his wife and daughter had come in after he was transferred to this room, but that he'd been sleeping.

I went back to Mr. Savard and let him know.

A tear crossed the border of his lower eyelid. "Thank you," he said throatily.

I nodded, feeling choked up, too.

"There's one thing I can ask you."

"Anything," he said.

"Did someone tell you what happened before that car hit you? The driver hit a teenager, and someone tried to stop the car by throwing a blanket on the windshield."

He nodded.

"What do you think of that?"

He rolled his eyes. "Everyone should try to do something to stop people from hurting other people. He tried."

"And you're okay with that?"

He gave a weak smile. "It's in God's hands."

"Yet God helps those who help themselves—or maybe those who help others?"

"*Oui!*"

I returned the smile. "Thank you, Mr. Savard."

He closed his eyes. I touched his shoulder and left, grateful to be alive and healthy, and hopeful about healing relationships.

I was also thankful for the quote.

Maybe Grasso was right. The DV—I—was a nut, intervening in crimes. I got Paris hurt and nearly got myself killed. The Dandy Vigilante was getting old. It was time he retired, especially since the decedent Swanson had been trying to catch him.

I went home. DeLay had left a message for me not to try visiting Debbie tonight. I called his office, but got no answer. Asshole.

# CHAPTER 20

## Friday, 7:15 p.m.

The night screamed for motorcycles and rider gear to be fire-engine red or rain-slicker yellow. Low clouds, wet roads, and reduced visibility were something to avoid on a silver bike that blended into the shiny blacktop like a splash of water. My blue jeans flapped. I still hadn't eaten and verged on dizzy. I got off I-93 at the Chinatown exit.

The DV needed one definitive rescue to redeem him before he hung up his cape or, in this case, his wig, and get on with life. I felt trapped inside and unable to talk to Debbie about these things. I had to put her aside for the moment, though. Making mistakes wouldn't help either of us. I had to consider my future, too. Who was I? What was right? I needed my balance back.

Watching for bad drivers, and bad pedestrians, I made my way toward the Roxbury side of the South End. The public's curiosity about the Dandy Vigilante was piqued by TV and newspaper reports of his heroics, or antics, depending on the person's perspective. The mayor condemning him merely heightened public interest.

A female reporter had said to the mayor, "About the man run down by the car. Do you think the old man who intervened is the same one, the Dandy—?"

"Look," Grasso interjected, "I cannot comment on an ongoing investigation."

"He's being investigated?" she said.

"Look, it's simple," Grasso said. "If the old man caused an accident with his blanket, and his panic hurt an innocent civilian, then that's bad, right?"

"Hispanic?" she said. "Do you have information that the driver was Hispanic?"

Grasso looked around in disbelief. "Panic. I said his panic caused him to run down an innocent civilian."

Thus, her line of questioning ended.

I turned into the neighborhood of the hit-and-run. I'd tracked down two adults who were on the porch that night, eighteen-year-old Jose Peňa and twenty-year-old Jose Perez. After parking my Harley, I sauntered to the porch, eyeing doorways and windows for potential interviewees. I was anxious to get this done.

It hit me hard again how bad I'd screwed up. A man died. I was there at the Hatch Shell and could have saved him. Maybe I would've been successful, or maybe I'd have gotten killed, but that was a theoretical solace. I needed to redeem myself in the public eye, if not my own. However, no opportunities had appeared since to rescue anyone, stop a crime, or even walk an old lady across the street.

I was back at reporting with a vengeance; well, with determination. The pen was mightier than the sword, and if I couldn't use one, I'd use the other to get the story and uncover criminals.

I whipped out my press ID from inside my jersey and hung it out on my chest. Inside the foyer, I jotted down the mailbox names on my notepad. At a unit upstairs, a teenager answered the door. I held up my ID to him. "*Yo journalista.*" The kid told me that Jose and Jose were cousins from Santo Domingo and lived in the next apartment on this floor.

Next door, I knocked beside the peep hole. Someone came and paused; then a young Hispanic man opened the door. He had a broad nose and short black hair. I could hear something sizzling on the stove. The scent of cilantro wafted my way.

I introduced myself, showed him my ID, and he confirmed that he was Jose Perez, and that he'd been at the scene with Jose Peña.

"The other Jose is here, too." He called out, "Hey, Peña."

"*Que?*"

"*Un journalista,*" Perez said.

The rapid-fire reply was in Spanish.

I asked, "What did he say?"

"He said he's expecting El Duke in his white Hummer, not a journalist, and to—well, he swore at me."

I leaned into the doorway and called out, "*Por favor?*"

I heard bedsprings, someone apparently getting dressed in a hurry. Jose Peña appeared in the hallway, tall, thick-bodied, and sporting a close-cut goatee. He ducked into the kitchen and shut off the range, then came to the door, looking serious. He asked the other Jose, "*Policia?*"

"No," Perez responded.

"Sorry," he said, allowing a smile. "My cousin is always playing tricks on me." He stuck out his hand. "Jose Peña." He had dark-brown eyes.

"I'm Dax Grantham of the *Boston Times.* Glad you speak English. I haven't used Spanish in too long."

"I came here for college. I'm at U-Mass."

"Good school. What's your major?"

"Undeclared."

"Wise choice. I still don't know what I want to do." I smiled. "So the night the victim got ran down, you were there?"

"Yeah," he said. "It was my friend. I told the police it must be a mistake of identity. There's a turf war the police gang unit know about, but we aren't part of it. We want to move out of here."

Perez described the incident.

"It happened fast, didn't it?" I said.

He nodded. "We almost had him because this old man stood in the street. They try to run him down too, but he waited to step out of the way then threw his blanket to the windshield, so they crashed. One guy got out, and we chase him. The car got away."

I made a note on my pad. "The car smashed its way out, too?"

"That's right," Peña chipped in, punching his hand. "Or we would've killed him. Oh, hey, don't put that down. They'll kill me, man." He gave a nervous laugh. "Seriously."

"I get it. It stays out." I said. "So what do you think of the old man?"

"He like a freaky old matador." Peña held out an imaginary cape. "But didn't wave the blanket like that. Anyway, he's a brave man, that Dandy Vigilante—if that was him. Maybe loco." He pointed to his head.

*More than you know, perhaps.* "Didn't you guys see him walking down the street with a backpack before the car showed up?"

Peña stared at me. "You know that?"

I hesitated. "From another witness."

They asked who the witness was, but I wouldn't divulge my source—me. They answered another couple of questions. "Well, I gotta wrap this up. If you could tell him something, the old man, what would you say?"

Perez glanced at the floor. "Well, I don't know where he came from and don't know where he going, but I'd say thanks."

Peña appeared sincere. "*Si, gracias.* The DJ on radio, he said a thank to the old man. I mean, he—"

"Mira, you don't speak English *or* Spanish well." Perez punched the arm of Peña, whose mock groans of pain were so exaggerated it turned into laughter, and Perez joined in.

I couldn't help but smile. They seemed like brothers. I wondered how it would've been to have had my brother around growing up.

"Some people said this is the same old man who helped other victims of crime. What do you think?"

"Unbelievable, man," Peña said. "I can't wait to see what he's gonna do next."

Me either.

I was thrilled that they appreciated my help and my method. I thanked them and left my card then got back to my Harley. Adding what I knew,

I had a great story. I knew exactly who to interview and what questions to ask because I was there when it happened. What supreme journalistic confidence, but I was unsure whether I'd shaped it unfairly or unethically. Asking questions with the actual images in my head was unprecedented. My story had to be better than Jimmy's, but I couldn't exhibit one iota of slant or Kravitz would nix my story and my DV redemption. I also had to be careful not to get caught as the DV, as described in the Greater Boston media. Sightings had been coming in.

I started my bike. Once, my brother Tommy and I were in our room, under the covers, when he told me that a grizzly bear had attacked our dad. He said that was why I couldn't go to the funeral. I think it was a car accident, though. I heard my mom on the phone, drunk and crying. They used to fight about her drinking, but her drinking became really bad after he died.

We lost the apartment, Tommy and I got placed in separate foster homes, although I went to my grandmother for a time. My mom had gotten worse, and then she supposedly got real sick and died, which was what my adopted parents told me much later. Maybe they were trying to be kind, saying that so I wouldn't feel impossibly drawn away from them, but I believed it.

I pulled out, and soon the unmarked Crown Victoria sedan was at a discrete distance behind me. The boys were back on the job.

# CHAPTER 21

# Friday, 8:25 p.m.

At home, I printed my D.V. note about Debbie's innocence to the police. I called major hotels until finding one in Cambridge that would work for my plan. From there, I'd go meet a suburban beauty for a tête-á-tête, although she didn't know it. And the detectives in the Crown Vic weren't invited.

Next, I finished my article on the hit-and-run, adding the Paris Savard's perspective that God helps those who help themselves and others. Regarding the criticism of the DV, Mr. Savard believed everyone should try helping each other—his words, not mine. I wrote about Jose and Jose and the girl dancing to pay for college but who'd been attacked by Mr. Heap, leaving out that appellation, of course. I submitted the story online to Kravitz, believing it was too solid for him to edit it away.

I left in my Jeep and drove to Cambridge. On Memorial Drive, alongside the glimmering Charles River, I spotted the detectives several cars behind, as expected. After passing some MIT buildings, I turned into the Hyatt Regency Hotel and entered its garage. The detectives pulled over before the valet area, which was busy. One detective got out and walked into the garage.

I parked, grabbed my backpack, and headed toward the pedestrian exit. I ran up several stairs and along the glass-enclosed walkway. Behind me I heard the door open, footsteps coming. In the lobby, tuxedo and gown adorned guests and others mingled or moved or waited for the elevators. A sign directed some to the Charles View Ballroom for the McPhee/Ida wedding reception, which I'd found on the Internet earlier. I walked up the escalator to the second floor. In a bathroom off the hallway, I took my tuxedo from my backpack, unrolled it, and changed. If I was uncovered as the DV, it might be my last chance to wear it for a while—the journalism award banquet would be off, and orange prison garb would be in.

I smiled. In a tux, I was a true dandy now. They could call me the Vigilante Dandy instead of the Dandy Vigilante. I combed down my gray wig with water, but it still resembled Einstein's hair, and being nestled among MIT properties here, it made me feel conspicuous. This was risky.

If a detective spotted me wearing a gray wig, it was evidence that I was the D.V.

While descending the escalator, I saw that the lobby crowd was laughing and milling about. I made my way through them, blending in with other tuxes. Let the detectives try to pick out the right penguin.

At the concierge desk, I took the sealed envelope by the edges and laid it down on the desk with fifty bucks. The concierge stepped over and greeted me.

"Hi, could you call a delivery service and have this sent confidentially, please?"

He glanced at the address, the A-1 Police station in Boston. "Certainly, sir. My pleasure."

"Great, that should cover it," I said, "and keep the change." I nodded a goodbye.

The formatting and font would match the DV letter that I'd sent to the police about the hit-and-run. It must have some credibility to help exculpate Debbie. Again, I felt vulnerable. Without Debbie, who could the murderer be; the jealous husband? *No, not him.*

I squeezed between guests and noticed one detective checking a hallway off the lobby. I exited the revolving front door, but to my surprise, the other detective approached me. I angled my face away from the overhead lighting and adjusted my bow tie.

A taxi pulled up. The valet opened the door. I slipped him a five and whispered a thank you to God.

"Central Square, please hurry." I took out Debbie's spare car keys. "Green Street Garage. Know where it is?"

"Sure do," he said.

I got Debbie's car from the lot and drove to the Mass Pike, then to I-93 South. How was I going to get information from a law firm in freaking Rhode Island? The client file had to contain the deeds, the trust document, and, importantly, the schedule of beneficiaries. Telltale notes would be a bonus. The entire series of transactions was suspicious; and a murder victim, Swanson, was at the heart of it, at least the visible part. The hidden parts were the client and beneficiary, who could be the same person, an excellent candidate for Swanson's murderer.

But first, I had a date with Swanson's ex-girlfriend in the suburbs, only she didn't know it. I took the Braintree exit and, after a mile and several turns in, I found Karen Hickey's house on Elmlawn Road and parked around the corner. A black RAV-4 was in the driveway.

I knocked on the door of the split-ranch house. As far as I knew she was single. I heard footsteps pad down stairs. The porch light came on. A button-nosed woman in her thirties opened the door and opened her eyes wide. She wasn't expecting prince charming in a tux. And I wasn't expecting to be him. This might go bad, in fact.

"Hello, can I help you?" She was short and thin, mousy.

"Yes, please. Sorry to bother you. Our limo broke down, and the driver's cell phone is dead. We left our stuff when we changed. Do you have a phone I can use, or could you call triple-A for us?"

"Oh." she paused. "Sure, of course." She went up the stairs.

I held the storm door open. "Thank you so much. Uh, sorry, may I use the bathroom? Do you mind?"

"Um—"

"Champagne goes right through me." I shifted my body like I had to go.

"Well, okay." She hesitated before pointing down the hall. "On the left."

Apparently, tuxedos could suspend suspicions. This would never happen in the city. I walked up the blue-carpeted stairs and turned into the living room instead. The place was clean. Family photos, none with her, dotted the walls. I sat on the couch; weird, but not an overt threat.

She pointed to the hall. "It's—"

"I know, sorry, just a sec. I'm confused about this." I took deeds from under my coat and spread them on the coffee table. "I'm actually here because of Bradley Swanson."

She stepped back, clutching her hands to her chest. "What? Bradley Swanson? You know Brad?"

"Yes. Sorry for the pretext."

She stepped back farther and eyed her cordless phone. "Who the hell are you? Is Brad in the limo or something?"

"I'm not here to cause trouble. I'm sitting by the big bay window where anyone can see us, and I left the front door open. You can also get your phone so you can feel secure. I just want to speak with you for a minute. One minute, that's all. It's just that I'm in a hurry and didn't really plan this out, how to approach you." I smiled. "I'm just someone in a hurry who needs a minute of your time. Is this okay?"

Her mouth hung open for a moment. "Ah, so, you don't want triple-A, right?"

*Duh.* I shook my head gently. "A quick question about these real estate deeds. They're in your name."

"What? In my name?" She tapped her chest. "Are you sure?"

"Positive. Unless you don't know him, and it's a fraud," I said.

"Look, my big brother is on his way over," she said. "And I have security cameras," she tacked on, true or not. "So you better be legit." She picked up a deed off the table, watching me. "Wow. No, this is—well, I guess it's some kind of fraud. I don't know, but not Brad. He and I used to hang out, for a few months."

"A romantic relationship? Or did it involve real estate?"

"Real estate? No," she said.

"When did you break up?"

"Months ago."

"Are you angry with him?"

"Well, no." She shrugged. "We were kind of good for a while. But he—I don't know."

"What? Was he with another woman, a Debra or Debbie perhaps?"

"I don't know about any woman or real estate, but, he talked about some district attorney as a sexy guy one time. Kind of put me off, and you know how it goes. One person gets put off, then the other's put off by the first one being put off, and so on. So he's history."

"More than you know," I muttered. My cell phone rang.

She tilted her head. "What do you mean?"

I checked the number. Debbie's lawyer. "Oh, excuse me. This is important."

"Who are you?" She shook her head, her mouth agape.

Attorney DeLay told me we could arrange Debbie's bail tomorrow, but the house would have to be put up for security. I agreed. He said it might have been an upward thrust that killed Swanson, but we'd have to wait for the autopsy results.

I asked, "When's the autopsy?"

Karen backed into the dining room. I waved and shook my head to reassure her. She raised her phone.

DeLay told me that the texts Debbie got from Swanson said to meet him at that house and to cut the cake and pour the champagne for them to celebrate, that he'd be right there, if not arrive before her. The police verified that from Swanson's phone.

Karen punched two numbers on her cordless phone. One more and I was up the creek with the local police. I mouthed *please* and put my index finger over my lips. Besides, how many tuxedoed, stalker-murderers took telephone calls on the job?

"Debbie cut the cake," DeLay said, "but hadn't opened the champagne, preferring to wait for him. Her prints were on the knife, but not on the bottle. Unfortunately, her prints were also on the counter, so that places her there."

That was it, so I hung up.

"Karen, please. The property isn't in your name anymore. So he must have just used your name, right? I mean, forty-two parcels of real estate; that's a lot."

I didn't tell her that if merged with small, adjacent lots previously acquired, they formed forty-two larger and, more important, buildable lots in the city—a contractor's wet dream that could net millions.

"Well, I'm not saying I know anything, 'cause I don't, but he works for Boston, on the mayor's staff. He did paperwork, which I think included real estate, but I didn't get into his business, ya know?" She sighed. "Look, are you a cop or something?" She folded her arms. "I'm not talking anymore until I know what's going on. Maybe I better talk to a lawyer."

"I'm something, not a cop, which I can't disclose right now."

She checked her phone again.

I held my breath a moment. "Okay, I'm a private investigator."

Too late—she'd pressed the last number, and someone answered. She hung up. "I don't know much about real estate. I'm a nurse. I didn't even buy this house. I inherited it." Her phone rang. "Whose autopsy were you talking about?"

I was out of time. She'd hung up on 911. They'd send a cruiser over. "Do you know anything about a trust? The Good House Trust?"

She shook her head. "Never heard of it. Now let me see some I.D."

"I see. Well, thanks for your time." I hopped up, but paused at the door. "Say, did he talk with you about friends or business associates or anything?"

"Not really. Why don't you just ask him anyway?" she said.

"Have you seen Bradley lately or heard from him?"

"No, but I didn't expect to, you know. After a certain point in time, a girl knows. And I'm not one to wait forever on a guy anyway."

"Right, never wait forever on a guy. So, you didn't love him, right?"

"Of course I didn't love him. Like I said, it was casual, but what kind of—"

"Good, because he was killed yesterday."

She sucked in her breath, looking frightened.

I peered at her. "Where were you last night?"

"Me?" The same chest-clutching gesture. "I was home. I was home last night, and the night before. I—"

"Someone can verify this?"

She said, "No, I mean—"

"I don't know what happened, Miss Hickey. I'm investigating these real estate transactions, see who was connected." I squinted and pursed my lips. "Is there anything you're not telling me?"

"No, I swear." She wiped a strand of hair from her face. "Who hired you anyway?"

"Sorry if all this is a shock to you. Good night." I hustled to the street.

She called out, "Wait, what's your name?"

I thought to call out, *the shadow knows*, but I'd just freak her out. I kept going to one murder suspect's Lexus around the corner. I needed more suspects. As I hopped inside, blue lights flashed on the houses opposite hers.

# CHAPTER 22

# Saturday, 6:24 a.m.

*What if Debbie had stabbed him?*

In bed, the thought bobbed up again, tossing me into a wave of anxiety. Though chilled, I kicked off the sheets. If she'd killed him, an affair was probably the root cause. The possibilities played out as I stared at the ceiling. The pressure in my chest squeezed up into my throat.

I had returned Debbie's car to her office and rode the Red Line home to Braintree and slept off and on. I hoped that Karen Hickey had simply told the Braintree police she'd misdialed 911. And I prayed that the Boston police would find evidence pointing to Ms. Hickey or someone else. After all, Karen didn't have an alibi witness, and she'd stopped dating Swanson mere months ago. The deeds were in her name, too, so it wasn't far-fetched, but she didn't look guilty. If proved that she'd signed the deeds out of her name, it would mean she'd lied; and that would be a different ball game.

Another possibility struck me. Ms. Hickey might not be the only straw person receiving deeds without their knowledge. This could be bigger than I'd thought. After hundreds of years, there must be many hundreds of miscellaneous little parcels all over Boston. As it grew, the city had incorporated neighboring towns, and real estate got repeatedly carved up. Now we're talking multiple millions of dollars profit.

The glow outside my bedroom window grew as the sun breached the horizon. By the subtle way Ms. Hickey reacted, and didn't react, I thought she was telling the truth. If I got stuck, I could try her again, but for now, her street was a dead end. Dead end. I went to the kitchen and left the lights off while getting a glass of water. I checked the window for cops—none in sight.

Reporting was a challenging job when you had to investigate a murder, but add personal consequences, and it was hell. So I had to get back on Kravitz's good side to keep investigating under the guise of reporting, perhaps regain my professional flexibility. If I found the murderer, maybe Kravitz wouldn't let me write the story under my byline, but I'd be in kudos heaven, and more importantly, Debbie would be free.

If I tipped off the police about Karen's involvement with Swanson, the police could speculate that Debbie had found out about Karen and became jealous, which would be motive for Debbie to murder. Conversely, speculation of Karen's jealousy could implicate Karen, so it was a double-edged sword.

But it came down to simple math. Adding one viable suspect to Debbie divided the suspicion in two. And if I was a suspect as well, it'd divide suspicion in three. So I'd tip them off, just not by a letter from the DV, but by the anonymous crime-tip hotline. You could text tips, too, but that seemed absurd, being traceable. In fact, it was Swanson's text that had started Debbie's trouble.

Maybe once Karen was involved, she could add District Attorney Cohoon as a suspect, making it a four-way tie for a life sentence. After all, Swanson had commented to Karen that the D.A. was sexy. It was theoretically possible that the D.A. had a secret relationship with Swanson. Taking it a step further, that the D.A. killed Swanson to keep the secret or because they'd a fight over something.

Creative theory wasn't evidence, though, but I was getting desperate.

The sun hit the tree tips in my back yard. Poor Debbie, s second night in jail; surely she hadn't slept. DeLay had all day yesterday to get her bailed out, but failed to do so, and he hadn't responded to my angry messages. He had time to do interviews with the press, though. *Dickhead.*

Exhausted, I stumbled into the shower and soaked under the steaming water. I dressed, got a cup of coffee, and checked email. Jimmy confirmed with the police Office of Media Relations that a press conference about the Swanson homicide was at 9:00 a.m. at headquarters, now only three hours away.

I pictured Debbie with a blanket on a thin mattress in a cell, an austere, depressing space. The very idea clashed with every sense of rectitude I had. Again, I went over the tasks to get Debbie out, like researching Attorney DeLay and finding good reason to keep him. I'd also called the bondsman before, but DeLay had told me to let him handle it.

In the barn, I wrapped my fists and hit the speed bag. My timing floundered. I cursed those who said you to exercise the body when the mind was tired and exercise the mind when the body was tired; they didn't say what to do when both mind and body were tapped out. I headed for the couch.

*** 

I woke with a start at 8:00 a.m. I got my gear on and sped by motorcycle from Braintree to Roxbury and reached the Boston Police headquarters at Schroeder Plaza. At the corner of Ruggles and Tremont Streets, I parked at a meter, took off my helmet, and put on my baseball cap.

At the front desk, a cop checked my ID and let me through. I took the elevator up to the press room and slinked into the back corner, cap tugged low. After a minute, I spotted Jimmy. He was sitting up front. Someone had given him a good seat again, and it wasn't Swanson. It reminded me that Kravitz's crony, the mayor, had the police department under his thumb.

Before I could duck, Jimmy waved me over. He looked surprised to see me. I didn't move, so he came over.

"Hey, I have a seat for you, if you want it."

"Great. Save it for now," I said, keeping my head down. "I'm trying to find a cop to talk to me. You know, off the record."

"Right. Hey, crazy times, huh? Hope you're doing okay, Dax. Oh, guess what. Swanson got hold of a still-shot from the video showing the Dandy Vigilante. He was supposed to email it to me, but I didn't get it. And they haven't released anything. A technician's trying to clear it up."

"Oh yeah?" I swallowed, praying for low pixels. "Great."

Jimmy nodded. "There's a lot of buzz about, you know. Your wife getting arrested. And Kravitz said you're not answering his calls. Wanna talk afterward?"

"Why don't you first go back and make sure no one gets our seats."

He nodded and left. Good. It was now fortunate that Debbie had kept her own last name instead of taking mine, but I still felt like slipping out of the press conference. That'd be all I'd need here, a projected photo of Debbie's mug shot, captioned as "Grantham's spouse," or a photo of the DV.

At the elevator, I kept my eyes lowered to my notepad.

"Hey, Grantham," someone shouted.

Several officers looked toward me. Sergeant Detective Flaherty, who was assigned to investigate Swanson's homicide, strutted over.

"Detective." I nodded. "Hey, how's Debbie's doing? Is she all right?"

He stepped close, face skewed. "Nice to see you, too, slick. But it doesn't look good for Debbie—or for you."

"Me? What?"

"We interviewed a restaurant manager who saw Debbie with Bradley Swanson."

"Yeah?"

"I showed him your photo, and he thought it was an 'older' you who'd asked him who Swanson was."

"An older me?" Brian hadn't recognized me the second time we met, so the detective must have pushed him on this point. "Well, I'd interviewed the manager about the DV."

"Come on, Dax. You interviewed him about the DV later. So what were you doing there, asking about Swanson?"

I thumbed my chest. "You think it was me? You'd better check with this manager and ask him how old that guy was, what he actually looked like, and without your enthusiastic suggestions. Besides, the manager was a little unstable when we met. Sneaking booze from the bar, I'd say. It had to be someone else that night. In fact, he'd even confused me with a guy who'd left his glasses there."

"Is that so?" He nodded, unconvinced.

A few cops looked on, whispering.

"Yeah, so ask him," I said. "Show him the Dandy Vigilante photo you guys are sitting on. Meanwhile, could you find the killer, so I can have my wife back?"

"Your loving wife, huh?"

"That's right. They were trying to create a youth center, and I believe her. So unless you got something I don't, don't accuse my wife of fucking around—and I'll do you the same favor."

My face was hot. I turned around and took the stairs down. The anger and pain were real, though the detective didn't know why.

# CHAPTER 23

# Saturday, 9:10 a.m.

On the Harley, the best defense was using my eyes, which now targeted a laundry truck rolling down a side street, timed to kill me if it failed to stop at the stop sign, which it did. I swerved, skidded out, but regained control and swore at the driver, which for a motorcyclist is safer than flipping the bird. The adrenaline surge ended with the thought that a collision would have delivered me from many problems. But, hell, as my friend Sunny said at times, you had to be alive to complain.

And you had to be alive to get your spouse out of jail. My throat tightened, thinking of Debbie locked up, but at least I was doing something about it. I entered the brick building of the D.A.'s office. Debbie's lawyer had arranged to put up our house for bail. I had signed the deed, which was to be held in escrow. Debbie would sign, too, at the bail hearing. I was buzzed in and asked for District Attorney Cohoon.

"Is he expecting you?" asked the receptionist.

"He's expecting this." I dropped the envelope onto the counter and left, rather than see his bleak, lumpy face.

Next, brain spinning, heart cracking, I drove to the *Boston Times*, parked, and snuck in through the loading dock. At my desk, I called Sunny, my police informant friend. She agreed to retrieve from the Registry of Motor Vehicles an image of Karen Hickey's driver's license and send it to a bogus email I used. When I got it, the signature obviously did not match the deeds, which killed off that optional Swanson murder suspect—*fuck!*

\*\*\*

At Jimmy's cubicle, I scanned his yellow sticky notes and checked his email. Nothing from Swanson with a still shot from video of the DV. Was Swanson murdered before he could email it to Jimmy? That would look bad for the DV, actually. Next, I checked his junk email folder. Bingo. I opened the attachment; the photo wasn't great, but BPD's Identification/ Photography Unit was using software to clarify it. The image might look like me if compared side-by-side. Jimmy might recognize me. Delete it?

Oh yeah.

I stood. No one hovered around, but I needed to leave to avoid questions about Debbie. I also needed a large cluster of aspirin and acid reducer pills. Back in my cubicle, I pressed my eyes shut and lowered my head. There wasn't a single, visible opponent. Dangers included many people, facts, places, legalities, and emotions.

I checked online for a bio piece on Swanson.

"Dax Grantham?" a man said.

I spun around on my chair.

"Yes, who's—"

"Sergeant Detective Montes, CID." Badge in one hand, he reached to shake with the other, and I obliged. His tie was knotted fat and loose between lapels of a navy blazer.

"This is Detective Carmel." Montes nodded toward the brown-suited guy behind him. I nodded. He nodded. So we'd all nodded; now what?

"I like your articles," Montes said. Despite his Hispanic name, he appeared Italian with his straight nose and Stalone-shaped eyes.

I stood. "Sure, thanks."

"And I don't mean to be sarcastic," Montes said, "but I'm here about one of them, ironically enough."

"Oh yeah?" I swallowed. Peripherally, I noticed Jimmy enter his cubicle.

"You had details in your story about the so-called Dandy Vigilante that the victims didn't give." He let that comment sit.

I knew where they were going with this, but had I slipped up? "And?"

"So, you were on scene, right?" he said.

"Yes," I said.

They look at each other, surprised at my admission.

"After the fact," I added, "as usual. We seldom get lucky enough to witness the events we cover."

"Well," Montes said, "then you weren't there before it happened."

"Correctomundo."

"Hold on," Montes said. "We wondered enough that we came down here and interviewed Mr. Kravitz."

Jimmy's head popped up over the cubicle.

I said, "Mr. Kravitz?"

"Yes. And we told him we were assigned to investigate this odd vigilante, and that you could be that vigilante. He was shaken up when we mentioned we were considering arresting you."

"What? Me? So you're going to add false arrest to your defamation of my character?" I shook my head. "Have you run down any real leads? Did you consider there could be copycats out there?"

He signaled for me to wait. "We—"

Kravitz came around the corner.

"We said we'd like his cooperation," Detective Montes said, "just to rule you out. Or else we'd get a warrant. So he agreed."

Kravitz added, "On condition that they don't arrest you, Dax. Or not here and now. Give us time to check things out, get them straight. I tried reaching you again."

Montes faced me. "He showed us a draft of your article. You mention the Dandy Vigilante got a license plate number."

"And?"

"And that draft was dated before the police went public with the fact that we had a plate number, which was supplied by the professed DV."

I froze, but then panicked about showing it. "So?"

"So? So you were there on scene, right? Maybe you were the DV, at least that night? Why else did the Dandy Vigilante stick up for your wife?"

"Whoa," I said. "He stuck up for Debbie? How, when?"

"Nice." Detective Carmel pointed at me and turned to Montes. "See how natural he looks, saying that, fully expecting we'd believe him?"

Sergeant Detective Montes said, "The DV was kind enough to mail a letter in support of your wife, unless it's a forgery," he paused." Did you forge a note to help your wife?"

"No," I said coolly. "That's interference with a criminal investigation." Beat him to the punch. "Besides, if it is from DV, whoever he may be, then it's not a forgery, is it?"

"Dax," Kravitz said, "under these circumstances, I had to speak with"—he finger-quoted—"'the bosses.'" He paused. "They pressured me to fire you immediately."

The detectives smirked.

"Leo," I said.

Kravitz eyed each detective in turn. "But I don't see enough evidence for a civil firing, let alone a criminal beyond-a-reasonable-doubt standard."

Detective Carmel frowned and finger-quoted, "'Just for the record,' we only need probable cause. Nothing explains how he got the license plate."

"Also true," Kravitz said, "but have you considered other sources of information he has and used? Sources protected under the U.S. Constitution?"

The detectives exchanged a glance. They'd have to get a subpoena to force the newspaper/me to divulge confidential news sources. If they got it, and a court order to enforce it, what could I say?

"We'll be in touch." Carmel nodded toward the elevator, and they left. Looking back, their expressions and body language said everything— we'll get you soon enough.

And they just might.

"Leo, I—"

"Save it, Dax. You're not fired. But you are suspended."

"What? Suspended?"

"Yes, with pay. For now. There's a little circumstantial evidence against you, so who knows who the hell the DV is?" He shook his head. "I don't care right now. The *Boston Times'* integrity is paramount. If you're suspected of being the DV, there's a conflict. And, I'm sorry, but your *own wife* is being held for the murder of the mayor's chief of staff. It's too much."

Even the best story possible on the DV wouldn't help me now. In fact, the better the story, the worse it would look for me, the opposite of what I was trying to achieve.

"Check the ethical guidelines we all sign every year," he said. "Even the appearance of violations can harm the image and integrity of the paper."

I nodded, shoulders slumped. "I'm aware."

"I'll be in touch, Dax." Kravitz grabbed my shoulder. "And if you want to talk." He nodded then walked away.

Jimmy bounded over. "Wow, yeah. If you want to talk—"

"Jimmy," I said. "Sure, I'll talk. Here's a hypothetical for you. Maybe you'll get the inside scoop, if you listen carefully."

He leaned in.

"The DV acts, yet 'victims' don't all report it," I said. "Why?"

Jimmy shrugged. "Do you know anything that could help me?"

"Yeah, they're not victims. Get going. I'm suspended." He wanted insider information for his big break, but I pointed outside. "The story is out there. Let me know what you find out and maybe we can help each other."

At that instant, I noticed building security approaching. It seemed the "bosses" had exerted their power after all and had turned this into a firing. I'd grab all my belongings at my cubicle, supervised by the uniformed guards, who would then escort me off the property.

But no, that wasn't it. That wasn't it at all; someone right behind them in a dark suit and red tie glared at me. My mouth hung open. Of all people.

Mayor Paul Grasso.

# CHAPTER 24

# Saturday, 10:05 a.m.

Grasso's eyes burned into mine. Jimmy eased back into his cubicle.

"Grantham." His voice was gravely.

"Mr. Mayor." I suppressed my shock. "It's nice to see you."

Ten yards away Grasso held out his arm to stop the guards, but he kept coming. "You son of a bitch."

"Excuse me?" I said.

He poked my chest. "Did you kill Bradley Swanson?"

"What? Of course not," I said indignantly.

"Just look me in the eye. Did you?"

"No." I resisted the urge to step back.

"The detectives said you're probably that vigilante guy, what, dressed up as an old man? What the hell is wrong with you?"

"Excuse me. I don't know what kind of evidence you're speaking of, but I didn't do anything wrong."

"Anything wrong? You're being overly broad, Grantham. Brad emailed the photo of you or the vigilante; we're still not sure which one; to your colleague, who was going to publish it. But you tried to stop that from happening, didn't you?"

"That's bull. My colleague received a photo from Swanson?"

I made eye contact with Jimmy, who shook his head no and dipped below the partition.

Grasso straightened. "Bradley Swanson was a good man. As good a public servant as you'd ever find."

"I'm sure he was. And I'm sorry he died," I said.

"Killed. And you'll be more than sorry. I bet you did it. If it wasn't for my stand against taking the law into one's own hands..." He thudded his fist against his chest, then whispered, "I'd put you down myself."

"That's absurd," I said evenly, meaning his accusation and his threat. I took a small step back, just in case.

"And I'll tell you something else." Grasso put his hands on his hips. "Debra Stapleton is an old friend, and I aim to help her."

"What the—Are you serious?" I said.

"You'd let her take the fall for you? Despicable," Grasso said. "The

D.A. will see to it that there's no revolving door of justice." He stormed off.

*What the hell? What just happened?*

"Dax." Jimmy held his forehead and staggered closer. "Dax. I can't believe it. The mayor just— He accused you of—"

Recap: I got suspended, my wife is in jail, the mayor is about to sic the police chief and the district attorney on me for murder. Time to go. Rhode Island sounded good about now; Tahiti, too.

I grabbed my backpack and headed to the rear exit, Jimmy calling after me, my cell phone ringing, brain swirling.

***

On Morrissey Boulevard, it was hard to focus on riding, or anything. I pulled over to check voicemail. Debbie's lawyer said she'd be bailed out by lunch time. I called her numbers and his; no answers. Via email, a news bulletin: police updated the D.V.'s description to include the possibility that he was younger but had dyed his hair gray or wore a wig. I hoped Debbie and her lawyer, if she told him, wouldn't divulge my jealous suggestion that I had a right to hurt Swanson.

My right mirror revealed an unmarked police car. Before blue lights flashed, with the freaking mayor riding shotgun, I shot off and rode and rode, leveraging my motorcycle's agility in the traffic, and lost my tail. A block away from Debbie's office, I parked; no sign of police. She knew *the mayor*? From sometime in her past? A family connection? School?

At the front door, I buzzed her office several times. Someone exited the building, so I grabbed the door before it closed.

Upstairs, her office was locked. Glass panels framed the door, the inside was dark. At the end of the hall, I grabbed a throw rug. I covered the glass panel closest to the handle and gave it a short, sharp punch. Nothing; punched it harder. Glass tinkled to the floor. I stuck my arm in, unlocked the door, and entered the reception room. Practice for Rhode Island, I supposed, if ever I get there to "investigate" the real estate lawyer's office.

In a vase on the coffee table were roses; ugly pink roses. On the credenza was a 5 x 7 photograph of her and me, arms linked, ankle-deep in Miami Beach. I hadn't known she had this here. We appeared rewarded to be next to each other; hot love. Half-dozen years later, I turned on her computer in the semi-darkness seeking photos and correspondence for telltale signs of adultery, duplicity, or connection to Swanson or the mayor. I opened her email software, which downloaded the latest mail.

Then a footstep crunched glass. I checked the reception area—a pistol, uniform. Halfway through the doorway, the cop's eyes locked with mine.

His posture tensed. "Don't move."

I didn't. The pistol was aimed at me, dead center.

"Hands on your head, feet apart." Overweight, short, he inched toward me.

I obeyed. "But officer, I'm not—"

"Turn around," he shouted.

I heard cuff's clinking. "Lean forward against the desk." He pushed my back.

"Officer?" A voice from the hallway.

"I said wait outside the building, ma'am." He cuffed one wrist and grabbed the other. "Got a burglar here."

A police siren sounded outside. I looked over my shoulder. I saw someone peek in. "Debbie?"

"Eyes front," the cop yelled, snapping the other cuff.

"Dax?" she said. "What're you doing here?"

I turned my face. The cop eyed me and her in turn. "You know this guy?"

"He's my husband." She stepped in.

"Oh," he said. "Well, is there a restraining order or something?"

"No. We're not estranged or anything."

The cop looked at me. "What're you doing here?"

"I was, I was, looking for keys. I locked them in here."

"What keys?" he said. "When did you lock them in here?"

I turned around. "Debbie?"

She appeared unable to offer an explanation.

"My car keys," I said to him. "I left them here before, and I have her car now."

He asked her, "Is that true? Is everything okay here?"

She said, "Yes."

"Nothing wrong, no charges?"

"No, Officer. Of course no charges. We're fine. And I'm exhausted."

The policeman shrugged. "Okay then."

He spun his finger in the air for me. I turned around, and he unlocked the cuffs. As Debbie came in, the cop stepped aside. She met my eyes, hugged me, and let out a long breath.

The cop edged toward the hallway. "If you're all right, ma'am, I'll be going."

"Thank you, Officer. Very much."

He tipped his cap and, as he left, shook his head. I heard him going down the stairs, using his radio to cancel backup.

Debbie turned to me, looking angry, and glanced at the glass panel. "Dax? Did you break my window?"

"Yeah, I did. Sorry."

Face flushed, she shook her head. "Why?"

"I'm sorry, hon. I knew you were getting out, and I couldn't reach you, so I thought I'd check here. With a killer out there, you know? You never know." I felt bad, but what else could I tell her? "I'll get it fixed, don't worry. Are you all right? Why didn't someone call and tell me when you got out?"

She shrugged. "I— I got out of jail. I couldn't find my car. My phone was dead. That officer saw how distraught I was—my God—and he gave me a ride."

"Come on," I said. "Let's get out of here."

I escorted Debbie to her car, and we left Central Square via Western Avenue. I had an urge to continue driving west until reaching the cliffs of California. By then, I should know whether or not to jump off.

Instead, I turned left at Memorial and rode along the river. She lay her head on my lap and fell asleep, her hot breath, penetrating, arousing. It had been a while. She appeared so sweet, and innocent.

Innocent of murder? I thought so, despite her prints. The medical examiner should pin down the time of death, which should help rule her out. Logistically, too, it was unlikely she could have killed him. Perhaps CSI could come up with something I'd never find, like fibers, DNA, electronic data, and so on, but they'd still have to get around my reasonable doubt.

Unfortunately, trust breaks at a lower threshold than "beyond a reasonable doubt." That was generally true, and why should I be any different? If the cops found more evidence, convincing evidence, I'd have to see Debbie in a new light. Wouldn't I? She'd remarked earlier in our relationship about how mysteriously our brains and emotions worked, so it should apply to her, too. I thought I knew her, believed I knew her, but a bit of doubt existed in most circumstances. That was the nature of reality and our inability to know. Add human nature to her suspicious behavior and whatever CSI came up with, and what would we have?

*No way.* I still couldn't believe it. I didn't want to believe it. I thought of all the times we'd had; images of us together, the places we shared, the feelings; the way we were; the tender moments she'd touch my face; her eyes, on mine, gentle or impassioned or full of myriad thoughts and feelings for me to read.

Inside the Hyatt garage, I parked her car one level above where I'd left my Jeep. I let her sleep, stroked her hair. Her blouse and skirt were tailored. I recalled seeing on her bureau a plastic surgeon's brochure on breast operations. Couldn't imagine she'd want to augment them. She opened her hazel eyes, which were smokier than ever, and she turned them on me.

"Dax." She sighed.

"My Jeep's here, but I'm going to get a room. Let's both go. We can relax and talk and avoid police and reporters. They're all bastards anyway, especially the reporters." I tried a smile.

She sat up, but then reclined her seat. "Let me rest here. And think."

I registered for a room inside, thinking of questions to ask her. I returned, and she came, linking my arm with hers as we headed to the front entrance. I'd never seen her look so vulnerable. I pushed the revolving glass door, and she entered ahead of me, disappearing briefly behind my reflection. Mayor Grasso's words haunted me, "no revolving door of justice." Well then, time to take a well-deserved time out.

Inside our tenth floor room, I slid the deadbolt. She spread out languidly on the bed. Her fatigue, from a frazzling time in jail, almost came off as coy or sexy. We were supposed to resolve issues, yet her body was coming to mind, and her mind grasped my empathy, and it was all connected and whirling.

She sat up abruptly and stared, but then kicked off her shoes and cast her heavy-lidded eyes up at me again. She lay back on the bed and stretched. The mattress sank under my knees. I hesitated, and then lay beside her. A feeling came over me, easily at first, then hard; we needed each other.

I pulled her toward me and kissed her firmly. The tense separation collapsed. We stripped away our clothes and pulled down the covers. We kissed over and over, desperate, eyes wet, touching our cheeks. Our thirsty mouths and hands went on to explore and return, explore and return, in splendid reunion. We made love passionately and completely. The strain of our existence, the compulsion to satiate raw emotion, all culminated in a soft fall back into the bedding, wrapped up in each other, and into the deepest of dreams.

# CHAPTER 25

# Saturday, 12:30 p.m.

Debbie woke, disoriented.

"Shhh." I caressed her cheek.

She sat up and stretched.

Scanning through TV channels, I skipped news stations and watched vacantly until the food arrived. We took the miso soup and deli sandwiches on the room's balcony in the atrium. The table overlooked the lobby, ten floors below. After eating, I pushed back from the table, wanting to savor our relaxation. But I needed to know how Debbie got into this trouble. I'd give her a chance to talk. Meanwhile, other questions needed to be asked.

"Know who accused me of murder today?" I said.

"Excuse me?" She wiped her lips on a napkin. "Someone accused you of murder? My God, who?"

I was unsure how to say it.

"Who accused you of murdering who?"

I said, "Mayor Grasso."

She sucked in her breath. It seemed unclear to her if I'd meant Grasso was the accuser or the victim. Her hands came to her face. "Where, how?"

"At work, by my cubicle. Stood point blank in front of me and accused me of killing Swanson."

She sucked in her breath again.

"Yeah. And he accused me of being the Dandy Vigilante. A doubleheader."

"You can't be serious." She stared, openmouthed.

"Wish I were. Jimmy saw the whole thing. The building security saw it. Might end up on the news."

"Dear God, that's…incredible." She lowered her eyes solemnly before glancing at the atrium. "Let's go inside."

"Not yet. What else is incredible is, not only did he highly regard Swanson, he has another friend he esteems." This lobbed the next logical question to her.

She placed her napkin on the table. "Who?"

I pointed at her.

"Me?" she said, not really a question.

I nodded.

She stood. "Yes, once. A long, long time ago."

I glimpsed the atrium's glass roof. "How long?"

She said, "Mmm, maybe ten years."

I stood and glanced at the lobby below. "Yeah?'

"And Dax. Sorry, I didn't tell you, but—"

I swallowed. "What?"

"We were more than friends." She glanced behind me.

I stepped closer, feeling a wave of anger rise. "More than friends? Dating? What are you talking about?"

"No, not exactly dating. Let's— Come on, let's go in. Someone could hear us out here." She reached for the handle.

"No." I threw my napkin onto the table. "No one's around. Tell me now."

She dropped her hand. "It was more than that. Remember that old boyfriend who was a grad student, in business school? That was him."

"Are you kidding me?" My heart plunged into jealousy. "That's just great." I leaned on the railing. "Holy shit," I whispered.

"I'm sorry, hon. I didn't tell you because I thought you might be bothered by it." She held the back of her chair. "Besides, he and I don't have anything to do with each other, so it's been irrelevant. Back then he'd been in the Marines already, before college. He had family money. He seemed, you know." She sat. "Of course, it never worked out, because... Different reasons. He was ambitious, would 'kick himself in the ass' to get things done."

"So what happened to Mr. Wonderful? Mr. Mayor of Boston, for crying out loud." I bit my lip, hating how I sounded.

"Well, he, he never married, and—"

"So what?" I said, but then asked, "Why?"

"I asked him. He just shrugged it off. Nothing to do with me."

"Who ended it?"

"I did. We were different. He'd be upset at me for being late, even a minute, yet he could be late if he was busy. Rigid, you know? People looked up to him, except those he ostracized. Just too possessive and controlling at times, disinterested others, be—" She stopped.

"Because?"

She fingered the tablecloth. "Because he was indulging in another relationship."

"Cheating," I said. "The thing you hate so much."

She nodded, looking down. "I saw it as pretty much black and white." She raised her eyes. "Even with us, remember? When you told me you were still married? We broke up."

"You wouldn't even talk about it," I said. "And it was just a technicality."

"True. I thought it was too much, even if you weren't cheating on her. For you not to tell me something so important. But back then I didn't know you had already been separated. Then we didn't talk."

"Of course, you had a point. But that's old territory. What about him? Grasso."

Her cell phone inside the room rang.

"Nothing," she said. "I met Bradley Swanson before I saw Paul again after all these years. And when I did meet him, with Bradley there, I told him—"

"Where did you meet Grasso?"

"In his office. First, Bradley said there was a legal matter he had to deal with. Later we met with Paul, and I told him not do me any favors. He agreed and told Bradley to help me out, but to make sure the youth counseling center plan I had in mind was a good idea and in the right location. Bradley was already on that issue. So, it was a tentative go from the beginning."

Her phone rang again. She gazed at the balcony door.

I nodded. "And now?"

"And now?" She bobbed her head. "Now? Now we find out how to get me out of this mess. You, too. Do you have any ideas? I've got to go home. And are you the—"

Her phone started again. She opened the door and went inside. "It's Attorney DeLay. I should take it." She answered and sat on the bed as I came into the room. "Dear God." She looked at me.

I held out my hands and silently mouthed, "What?"

"No, he never told me that." She shook her head. "I think, yes."

Lips parted, staring, she hung up. "The police found a witness."

"A witness? That's great," I said. "Isn't it?"

"No. Not a witness to the murder. A witness to you confronting Bradley Swanson. And you were both visibly upset."

More on motive for murder, by me; enough to arrest me, and they would, when they added everything together. I turned, faced all that atrium air, and felt as if my feet were coming out from under me.

***

I parked my Jeep behind Debbie's office and took my Harley to Roxbury via a circuitous route. I was determined to get to Rhode Island, to that law firm. It was my best hope to avoid a life of paying for another's crime. But if I'm lucky enough to successfully break in, find something helpful to identify a likely murderer, and get away, then what?

On Intervale Street I set my kickstand and walked up to Terry Mc-Call's triple-decker. Blue-gray paint curls speckled the siding. The long porch was lined with old recliners and chairs. By the time I reached the walkway, the porch creaked and several guys stood from their chairs to watch me.

Truth was, guns made me nervous; in other peoples' hands, that is, and Terry McCall, the subject of my article long ago, who'd since made good, had been around them. Reportedly, and not reported by me, he once led a local gang. Even if he was clear of that part of life, guns were still around. Two guys shuffled toward the staircase, pants hanging down, which, I noted, was not good for fighting.

The heavyset guy nodded his shaved head at me. "What up?"

"Hey," I said, affecting casual. "Terry around?"

"Terry who?" He said it like I shouldn't know.

"Terry McCall, Terrence, T-bone, FT." FT was for Father Time. Maybe no one had used that abbreviation, but it was logical, and it could put a question into this guy's mind; does this white dude know something I don't?

"You know Terry?"

I nodded. "And he knows me."

He gestured to a teenager in the doorway. The kid disappeared into the house. Seconds later, Terry came out, wiping his long hands on a dish towel.

"Dax? Yo, thought that might be you." Terry pointed his thumb at the kid in the doorway. "The way he described you. Butt-ugly, driving a shit bike, chalky scalp."

"Hey," I yelled.

His guys tensed; another one stood.

"My bike ain't that bad," I said easily.

Terry grinned.

Their eyes darted around, and they laughed as if reluctant to let go the tension.

"Come on up here, man," he said. "Let's go inside."

"That your posse now?" I pointed my thumb behind us.

"Friends." His smile faded. "The lucky ones."

I patted his back. We sat at the kitchen table in metal framed chairs. Shiny copper pots and pans hung over the counter with dingy, flower-patterned wallpaper behind.

"Summer jobs are over," he said. "And the city cut youth jobs from 9,000 to 6,000. The kids talk tough, but most know if they work it's a good thing, with other youth and adults who don't dis them. It's going all right. From a community point of view, I mean. Keeps 'em busy."

"Right. That's good."

I bet Terry still knew who had guns in this neighborhood and others. Gangs were different than in the early nineties. More youth felt the danger around them as a constant, something to be vigilant about, as Terry had once described. They formed groups for protection and finding a gun had become easier.

Terry had argued that gun laws were elitist, letting wealthy buy aesthetically elite guns, but depriving poor people access to firearms within their economic means, or even outright deprive them. There was one attempt to take away public housing tenants of their right to possess firearms, as if equating them with felons and lunatics. He had a point. But whether or not they were true gangs, they kept the killing culture going. Violence did beget violence; Debbie was right about that.

Terry's head was almost clean-shaved, which I hadn't noticed under the beret he wore at the march. I sketched out roughly what I'd been doing since back-in-the-day, and he did the same. His grandmother had died, and the house was left to him. It had been difficult keeping himself on course, especially when people looked to him for help. When it required his going up against old enemies, he tried to work through others to resolve things. Fortunately, with all his community activities, he did have others to work through, like community leaders he knew. All in all, he said, he was happy enough trying to use the old world while making a new one.

"Yeah, good for you then," I said. "You know. I got two worlds of my own. In a way."

He leaned back, his chair creaking, and interlaced his fingers behind his head. "Oh yeah?"

"You know the DV?"

"The DV? You mean, like, the D.M.V. or R.M.V. or something?"

"No." I smiled. "No. I mean the Dandy Vigilante."

"Oh, yeah, yeah." He pointed at me. "That dude is righteous. They try to fuck with him, and he's crazy; he don't care. He'll waste ya."

Seemed the D.V.'s reputation had grown out of proportion. I should have anticipated that. "Well, let me tell you something." I stared at him.

He waited. "Yeah?" he said. "What?"

I still stared.

After a long moment, he sat back. Then he understood my silence. "You mean— You—" He pointed to me.

I remained silent. He stood and waved his arms at me. "Naw. Get the fuck out of here."

One of his posse stepped in. "He gotta go?"

"No, man, you do. Leave us alone." He leaned in. "Dax, you? This is beautiful. This is a beautiful thing. How? Why?"

"Well, it's a long story. I'll give you that version someday. Right now, I need help."

"Ahh," he said, with a nod; another person needing him, a conditioned response. "What the hell you need from me? You want to start another Guardian Angels or something? What, the Guardian Spooks?" He laughed.

I smiled a bit, but didn't laugh. He could have meant spooks like spies or like an older connotation of spooks. I stay away from using the "N" word. Let those who could own it have it. "No, man," I said. "I'm in trouble. Personally, and the DV. What I need is—"

"Yeah?"

I leaned closer. "I need someone who knows burglary."

He sat back, the humor drained from his face. Maybe I was about to get kicked out after all. Then his posture settled, and he let out a low whistle.

"I've heard everything now," he said. "Look, I guess you don't want to tell me, and I don't want to know anyway. I run straight now. Well, almost." He squinted and nodded on a tilt. "Very close."

"By any means necessary?" It was a reference to a conversation we once had about the methods of Malcolm X versus M.L.K., Jr.

"You know how it is." He shrugged. "So let's say you want to interview someone for a job. I set up the contact. Nothing else. The rest is up to you. I promise he ain't gonna turn on you, but that's it." He waved his hands palm-down across his front like a baseball "safe" signal, ironically. Louder, he said, "And you gotta get back to me someday, man, before I end up on a rocking chair out here. Tell me that long story. A'ite?"

"All right," I said, relieved. "And for the record, this thing is 'necessary.'"

"Of course it is, my man." He made a fist and raised it. "Fight the power."

"Damn straight." I matched his gesture. Maybe my urban dictionary wasn't up to date, but if it amused him, fine by me.

He shook his head, holding a mild smile. "So, 'Dax X.' Ha—kind of redundant."

I laughed, making sure gratitude showed on my face.

"Inez is here," someone called out from the porch.

Terry glanced toward the front. "Look, Dax, I gotta make it plain. I got a new life. One with no problems—of the old kind, I mean. I have a son."

I sat up. "What? Congratulations, Terry!"

"Yeah." His smile grew. "It's amazing. He's three already. His mother and I knew each other back then, somewhat. I didn't follow through, you know? Until recently. Gotta walk the talk."

"Yeah. So you're back together?"

"Not really, but we're like a team. I don't know what will happen, but we know what's important. Ian's early years are critical, especially learning to read, then reading to learn."

I nodded. "Takes a village."

"Well, yeah, that, too, but parents first. And I mean mothers and fathers involved for real. I'm no Cosby or Obama, but I'm doing my part. It all starts there."

"I hear a Michael Jackson quote coming, 'if you want to make the world a better place, you'—"

His smile flickered as he smacked my shoulder. "Seriously, though, you're on your own. This is the last time for anyone. I'm just scared of making more exceptions, I just gotta draw a line, you know? I got to."

Inez came in holding Ian by the hand. He had bright brown eyes; Inez's were cautious. Terry introduced us. After a bit of small talk—Inez was going for her GED before going to Roxbury Community College—they went out into the back yard, and Terry made phone calls in his bedroom.

Within an hour, two guys showed up in muscle shirts and dark tattoos that I didn't try to decipher. Terry joined Inez and Ian outside. We sat in the living room. I told these guys the job. They liked the guarantee—$5,000 cash up front; better than the average take after fencing goods.

"Don't like the rush though," one said.

"Yeah," the other added, and lawyers work late, weekends, and security could be tough."

They agreed to check out the site tonight and if it would take more planning or effort, we'd discuss the deal further. At least, they seemed to trust me enough with Terry vouching for me.

As I left, it occurred to me that this operation was across state lines. I assumed federal crimes would be added to my list of real and supposed state crimes. *Yes, well, jolly good, no turning back now, is there, old boy? Full throttle ahead and all that rot.* In other words, I was probably screwed if I did and screwed if I didn't; time to do something desperate.

# CHAPTER 26

## Saturday, 2:35 p.m.

I rode the Route 1 center lane and watched for blind spots. Most accidents happened in intersections with little time for a driver to spot the motorcycle's small profile. It would be a shame to die with my life in such a mess—now that'd be a good bumper sticker: "It'd be a shame to die with my life in such a mess!"

Double-checked my mirrors.

At the Salvation Army, I parked in the rear and went inside. Dark clothes were required; nothing stuffed into an old bin, though. Even a slight, musty smell in clothes, closets, and basements put me off.

Debbie had asked if I was the Dandy Vigilante. By now, the accusation was likely spreading, probably on the news along with the detectives' and mayor's accusations. The press would be all over that story, having no other DV candidates. I'd told her she couldn't believe everything she heard on the news and said that my investigations were complicated, but that she need not worry, and that I had to leave right away to find exculpatory evidence. She left thinking God knows what.

At a pile of sock rejects, I picked out a pair and moved on to jersey bins.

"You never know what good deal you're gonna get, unless you plea."

The man's unfamiliar voice was close and spoken in my direction. I turned. I didn't like his suit or his partner's suit; or their badges.

He said, "You have a right to remain silent, but you don't have to be. So tell us what kind of deal you're looking for?"

The second detective moved around to my other side, boxing me between bins. I fought panic and held out my hands. I didn't recognize them. Somehow they'd tailed me. "I'll ask my lawyer."

"Put your hands down. Cooperate and we'll talk to the D.A., work it out, you know. Cohoon's a good guy. I mean, you can talk to him."

I looked at each detective in turn.

"It's true," the second detective said. "I played racquetball with him the other day. He kicked my ass, but got my informant a real good deal on a murder rap. Pled to manslaughter; easy."

I continued to exercise my right to remain silent.

Then I was handcuffed in the back of their unmarked vehicle. They drove to the shore and took Route 1A to Boston. Inside the Area 1 police station, I was booked for assault and battery against Swanson, though I doubted their witness saw any physical contact during my confrontation with Swanson in City Hall Plaza. I wondered whether or when they'd add charges for my DV activities. Then it was only a matter of time before I'd be indicted for murder; time I wouldn't have to prove my innocence. My throat tightened and my eyes watered, but I pushed back any emotion.

Cops came by the fingerprinting and interrogation to see me, the man on deck as the killer of Swanson, who'd just been here at the station; killed by the DV, an apparently jealous husband who'd gone over the edge. I requested a lawyer and shut up, so they put me in a cell.

I lay on the bed against the painted cinderblock wall, which was cool and smooth under the touch of my fingers. My plan was so close to happening, last chance to save myself. The real estate trust had to be closely connected to Swanson's murder, but I'd gained false hope.

I could tell them what I knew about the suspicious real estate transactions, but the connection was too thin, especially when they had a prime suspect and a backup, Debbie and me. By itself, my theory wasn't enough for these detectives to really go after it—in Rhode Island, and in a law firm, no less. Transactions weren't murderers. They'd lose focus on other suspects, too, like Karen or anyone else, whoever the true murderer was.

The cell door opened. Another arrestee joined me. I gave a nod, faced the wall, and cradled my head on my arms. Tears leaked at last, but silently, and I stilled my shoulders. Misery loves company, but not mine; I kept it locked up inside.

\*\*\*

From the preferred side of the bars, Attorney DeLay appeared grim. They wouldn't be transferring me to the county jail, he said, and he was in an ethical quandary, representing me and her both. "Even potential conflicts of interest with Debra are trouble."

My nod was minimal.

"Unless they drop the charges against her." He shrugged. "But I don't think they will," he said. "I mean, her fingerprints are on the murder weapon."

I hoped that wasn't his closing argument for her trial.

He'd have a lawyer from his office do this hearing, but then I'd have to get someone else. The hearing in district court was set at 5:30 p.m. The D.A. had implored the on-call judge to come in for this because of the critical nature of the case. DeLay knew the D.A. had called in a favor because the on-call judge was strict on bail compared to the regular one.

The guard let DeLay out. Over and over I stared at each plane of the cell, trapped inside a colorless Rubik's Cube. I knew so well that there was no place like home—if only I could click my shoelace-less shoes and awaken there. But this wasn't Kansas; it was more Alcatraz than Oz.

I'd have plenty of time to think how screwed I was. An angry confrontation with Swanson, witnessed in public. Now they had motives for murder; first, my jealousy of Swanson's relationship with my wife; and second, Swanson's role in pushing the hunt for the DV, if the cops could prove that I was the DV.

Beyond that, charges related to my actions as the DV would seem to nitpick compared to capital murder of a high-profile public figure. Would those charges reinforce my guilt on murder or make sentencing tougher? These questions kept circling inside my skull like sharks looking for brain food. I needed a really good lawyer.

No lawyer could stop the pain in my chest, though, which started when Debbie got arrested and had grown since. I felt isolation and terror. It felt like when I'd seen my brother Tommy for the last time in some government corridor, before our family disintegrated. Tommy tried to be strong, but I'd cried. I was crying still, I supposed, for something perpetually negative on the emotional balance sheet.

I jumped at the heavy clank of metal doors. They transported me by van to district court and into its secure garage. I shuffled into the holding cell. After a while, a gangly guy came and said he was my lawyer. Fluffy hair and eyeglasses.

"Max Garfunkel," he mumbled and extended his hand.

What if he'd earned the moniker "Max" for the lengthy sentences his clients received? I shook his hand, imagining "Max and Dax" in the tabloids.

He told me it'd be a plea of not guilty, assuming there'd be an arraignment later in Superior Court, and that today he'd ask for low or no bail. He didn't present well, but they must've hired him for some good reason.

In the modern courtroom upstairs, the clerk called my case. I stood with Attorney Garfunkel. A court officer stood behind me. Without the large windows, wooden paneling, and benches of Suffolk's old courtrooms, it seemed cold here.

"All rise!"

Enter the district court judge, Reginald Newsome, a rugged looking man in his sixties who seemed set to turn the wheels of justice, and he didn't look like the revolving door type. He loomed over the elevated bench, scanned the courtroom, and sat.

"Be seated." The white-uniformed court officer announced that court was in session. "Cell phones off or they'll be confiscated."

The juror box was empty, as was most of the courtroom, except some press I recognized. The judge nodded. The clerk, a clean-cut man at a table below the judge, read the case number and the charge, Assault and Battery. Judge Newsome greeted counsel.

"Your Honor, the Commonwealth suggests that this is a case of no bail," said Assistant District Attorney Kelly. She was chief of homicide for the Suffolk County D.A.'s office, and known as the biggest counter to dumb-blonde jokes in this millennium.

"Your Honor, respectfully, I say that that is entirely unnecessary," Attorney Max said, mispronouncing the last word. "Personal recognizance should be sufficient."

"Entirely what?" the judge said.

"Not necessary, uh," Max said, then more carefully, "unnecessary."

Great. Perry Mason he was not.

Through the blonde locks hanging by ADA Kelly's cheek, I detected a suppressed smirk.

"Oh." The judge darted his eyes around. "I read your papers, of both counsel. Bail is set at sixty-thousand."

I stepped behind Max as he packed his briefcase, anxious to talk to him. Then the courtroom doors swung open with a loud bang. I moved into the aisle beside the defense table and watched District Attorney Cohoon stride into the courtroom. Everyone turned to see him.

"Your honor, if I may," Cohoon called out, raising his hand, frowning.

"You may not jar my door, councilor!" The judge scowled. "You're late. Make it brief."

Cohoon was probably late from arranging for the press to come. *Asshole.* He pushed the swinging door in the bar rail.

"Excuse me," he said indignantly, brushing by me in the aisle. He plopped his briefcase on the prosecutor's table.

"Judge, given the severity of the likely forthcoming charges and the high status of the victim—chief of staff for the City of Boston, sadly, murdered—the accused is a flight risk. In fact," Cohoon said, "when he was arrested, Mr. Grantham was shopping, we believe, for clothes to flee in, obviously having caught word of his imminent arrest."

"Where was he arrested?" the judge asked.

"Um, says here... Salvation Army, in Saugus," Cohoon said.

I didn't like Cohoon's face, his lumpy tapioca complexion.

The judge sat back and renewed his scowl. "That's not exactly the airport."

"Your Honor," he said.

Attorney Garfunkel tilted his head toward the judge. "If it please the court?"

The judge nodded at Garfunkel.

"The place of his arrest is more like a flea market, Your Honor. That's all." He smiled. "My client, Mr. Grantham, is not a wealthy man with multiple and ready means of escaping the Commonwealth. Moreover, he's always been a law-abiding citizen. Always. In his life, he's never been charged with a crime, and this is the first such accusation, of any kind. For nearly a decade, he's been an esteemed Boston journalist. In fact, crime and justice weigh heavily on his mind, as demonstrated by the content of his many articles.

"He asks no quarter in regard to the charges; those will be challenged at the appropriate time. This is just a bail issue, and we request that reason, not publicity and 'potential charges,' be the benchmark. Besides, there's no evidence that Mr. Grantham was anywhere near the scene of the other crime, with which he is not even charged." He glanced at the prosecutor. "A symbolic bail for a man of modest means, a comparatively minor offense, an entrenched community member without real means of fleeing—in fact, he's intent on vigorously fighting these allegations and innuendos to clear his good name, Your Honor."

Wow. So, that's what they pay him for.

Cohoon lifted his finger to speak, but the judge smacked his gavel. "Fifty-thousand. Stay in the Commonwealth or you go back in," he said, directing the last part at me.

"All rise," the court officer announced.

Cohoon glared at me. If looks could kill, he wouldn't look away.

I thanked Attorney Garfunkel, shook his hand. Then I turned around to a friendly face. Debbie. She came to the rail and said she'd put up the money.

I walked out of the courtroom, free for now. Bail conditions included not breaking the law and staying in Massachusetts, two conditions I might have to violate to get us out of this mess. Cohoon was planning to crucify me more than ever, surely, and was probably signing autographs in his head already. This would become the kind of case that made legal careers, and particularly ended a journalistic one—mine.

Pushing open the heavy courthouse doors, I saw news crews hastily setting up equipment being pulled from several vans. Klieg lights were being positioned. Marguerite Ordonez stood in front of a news camera, microphone in hand. She was checking her notes, awaiting her cue. Debbie spotted her.

We took a hard right. Of all reporters, Marguerite saw me. She and her camera man soon caught up with us across the street, microphone close to her ruby lips, lights blazing. I noticed her look at Debbie, but I was afraid to see Debbie's face. I wanted out of here.

"No comment," I said as Marguerite opened her mouth to speak.

Peripherally, I saw them stare at each other. Debbie stopped. I thought she might say something. Marguerite opened her mouth to ask her a question, but then seemed to notice the quality of Debbie's gaze.

"I have a comment," Debbie said.

I took Debbie's arm. She looked at me.

"Mrs. Grantham?" Marguerite said.

Debbie pulled back. "No, it's Mrs. Stapleton."

"I-" Marguerite recognized her gaff. "Of course, I mean-"

"But I am married. You knew that, didn't you?"

"Come on, hon." I tugged Debbie's arm.

We broke away and hustled toward Cambridge Street. Surprisingly, Marguerite didn't call out any questions, as a courtesy, I supposed. Debbie dropped me at her office to get my Jeep. Then we met at our house. From there, she gave me a ride to the Salvation Army to retrieve my Harley.

# CHAPTER 27

# Saturday, 7:45 p.m.

I'd never been so glad to get home, despite Debbie's suspicion of what I'd been doing and my suspicion of her. She was the one who met, or was supposed to meet, Swanson. Her fingerprints were on the knife. And I was still toying with denial? The voice inside my head said to analyze this like a reporter.

I emptied the mailbox and picked up newspapers from the stoop. Inside, Debbie played the answering machine: her sister in Florida, to call her; several of my friends asking about the mayor's accusations, one sounding annoyed—"What's up with these people, Dax?"; reporters, some I knew, wanting an interview; an agent talking about a possible book deal, probably hoping for a public, close trial.

The self-important looking junk mail I tossed into the trash. A regular letter, from the adoption locator registry; my heart fluttered—had they found my brother? I opened it. It was only a confirmation of my registration from months ago; great. Years from now, if ever, maybe he could visit me in jail and talk over old times, the only times I'd have left by then. Earlier this year, I saw a political advertisement in favor of a bill making adoption privacy stricter; if it became law, it could be even harder for me to find him.

In one of my first memories, at three-years-old I found a metal square with rounded corners on the floor under our basement stairs. With bronze color and words and shapes, it could have been a dog tag. I'd asked Tommy if it was money. He said yes, took me to the corner store, and, surely with a wink to the owner, let me "buy" some candy.

Debbie opened mail and tossed some onto the counter. With few clients, she had a lot of free time, although she'd work on professional development and networking. She mentioned volunteering her services, once, but I didn't know if she had or hadn't. I should know, and not as a future investigative journalist, but as her present husband.

She might be napping upstairs. I should join her so we could talk later, rested. But a stubborn thought returned; I hadn't murdered Swanson, so if Debbie couldn't convince me otherwise, perhaps I should assume she'd done so. Just in case. "Who could truly fathom the depths of another's heart to see the hidden darkness?" she'd said to me in the past. Could she answer that question now? There were numerous examples of killers who had appeared beyond suspicion. But even with her prints on the knife, it was difficult to imagine Debbie stabbing someone, actually *stabbing* another human being.

My cell phone showed a dozen missed calls. On voicemail, Attorney Garfunkel said District Attorney Cohoon was furious that I was released and was reportedly preparing to present to a Grand Jury for indictments on multiple counts, including murder, and to revoke my bail. Bringing charges by indictment prevented my getting a probable cause hearing, at which I could test their case or develop an argument for bail.

If life was a bowl of cherries, I was toothless and gumming the pits. The "good news" was that they probably wanted to solidify the murder rap on me before dropping the charges against Debbie. That gave me a little time.

Blue splashes on the wall had me looking out the window. Two police cars pulled into the driveway and killed their lights. I needed a break, but it seemed like it was over for me. Unless they were here for Debbie. Exhausted, I almost didn't care, for a moment.

I opened the door and said loudly, "S.D. Flaherty."

"Mr. Grantham. You know what this is." He handed me the paper and walked around me. Three uniformed cops followed him into the house.

"Hey, hold on," I said.

They turned around.

I pointed upstairs. "My wife is asleep."

"Sorry," Sergeant Detective Flaherty said. "The search warrant includes her stuff, too. Frankly, she could be hiding or destroying evidence against you or her at this very moment."

I walked to the stairs and called out, "Debbie. We've got company."

Two cops started upstairs, but passed my bedroom, a modicum of courtesy.

Inside the barn, I slid the door closed and went to the back. I lifted a floorboard and grabbed my stash. After sliding the door open, I donned my helmet, mounted my motorcycle, and started it.

Detective Flaherty blocked the barn opening.

I said, "Shall I put on coffee before I go?"

"Thanks, why don't you stick around?" the detective said.

"People to see, things to do." My smile was patently false. "Debbie will be here. Give the D.A. my regards."

Being a smart aleck wasn't exactly smart, but... I twisted the throttle. In front of me, Flaherty didn't move. I revved the engine higher. Flaherty eyeballed me, but turned aside. I sped past him, down the driveway.

Within seconds, a cop followed me with its lights off. I had to reach those two guys Terry set me up with. I sped between cars in a line of traffic, beat the light, and lost the cop. Later, I stopped in Cambridge at Lindell's, my alternative to the alternative-styled coffee shop. Guess I'd have coffee after all.

I called Debbie from the payphone to explain why I'd left, see how she was. I had to leave a message, which should be okay on her cell phone, that I didn't want to risk arrest again, that the police and the D.A. could use any little thing they'd find to file additional charges against me. Then I'd never get out, never find the real killer. I hung up, believing that the message wasn't incriminating.

An issue leaped into my mind. The police shouldn't find anything on me for killing Swanson, but if, on the long shot that Debbie did it, the search yielded incriminating evidence, what would distinguish between her and me as the possible murderer? It reminded me to watch out for my own ass, too. I wasn't going to take the rap for someone else, not even, God forbid, for Debbie.

My cell ringing phone startled me. No caller ID, but I answered.

"What's up, Dax?" a male voice said.

"I don't know. What's up with you?" I said.

"You don't know who this is. Huh. Well, you do. We were supposed to meet last night. You weren't there."

"Barry?"

"Who the fuck else were you supposed to meet?"

"Elliot," I acknowledged. They didn't want to give me their real names, so they came up with Barry and Elliot, like the furniture store commercials.

"That's right, dawg. We checked it out. We go. You in?"

I'd about given up, I realized, but here was an iota of hope. "Yes, go."

"Same place, same time," he said. "Don't be late. Another thing. 'Appropriate dress required'."

\*\*\*

I passed along the cracked cement path into a shadowy park. Standing by the opposite gates were the B & E guys, as I'd dubbed them. They seemed like brothers, come to think of it. I'd suggested calling them Robin and Hood, but they'd declined.

We got in a van, me in back. From under my shirt, I took the large envelope and, from that, removed the two envelopes of cash. They didn't know that I'd been arrested, bailed, and couldn't leave the state. I needn't spook them with that detail. But if we got pulled over after crossing the state line, I was a goner.

"Five thousand, boys," I said. "That should get you some nice furniture."

They exchanged a look. In the passenger seat, Elliot checked the envelopes, then lifted the rug at my feet and dropped it into a custom compartment. This van was decidedly better than the Sheriff's van.

"Just so you know," Barry said, "we planned it. And part of that plan is not having the file traced to you, which could lead to us, right?"

I nodded.

"Good, we're gonna make sure it looks like a random burglary," Elliot said, then in a raised voice added, "And we know just how to do that, don't we, Barry."

"That's right, Elliot," Barry said with a smile, also sounding like a commercial or a game-show host.

"Shit, what is it, guys?"

"Just that we'll make a little mess—just a little. Snag any art and stuff that looks good. Nothing serious."

"Oh, fine," I said, glad they hadn't proposed arson. "What the hell do I care?" They laughed.

My phone vibrated—Debbie. I didn't want the cops to trace my phone, so I shut it off. Thanks for the reminder honey. We pulled out, on our way to commit a felony. But it was a necessary felony, despite my bail conditions. Later, I turned on my phone and retrieved Debbie's voicemail. It looked like they were going to drop the murder charge against her. That was news. Why were they doing that? I was surprised and happy for her, but the police would zero in on me now. Worse, she added that in executing the search warrant, police had discovered evidence possibly relating to Swanson's murder or the DV. She didn't know what it was.

I shut off my cell phone and slumped in my seat. What did they have? My latest disguise was in my motorcycle saddlebags, so the police didn't have that. The blanket was nondescript, and my other clothes used were ordinary. But they have something. They wanted me to meet them at the police station, she'd said. Yeah, right. They'd bring additional charges and revoke bail immediately. Sorry, honey, I'm a little busy breaking the law at the moment.

We crossed into Rhode Island. My actions, now inter-state, broke a federal law or two, as well. But so what? You don't worry about the lake getting wet when it rains.

Then it hit me, and hit hard—the worst of the worst possible scenarios. What if Debbie had planted evidence tailored to incriminate me in a crime? Like murder.

# CHAPTER 28

# Saturday, 11:50 p.m.

A patina trimmed the tall, arched windows of the turn-of-the-century building in downtown Providence. Once we entered, we had a good chance of ending up behind bars, and probably not for the first time for each of us. My days were numbered; my hours might be, too. I could be on my way to Canada, which was a backup plan that I couldn't believe I had to have, but there was growing news coverage outside Massachusetts of the DV and Swanson's murder.

Barry and Elliot briefed me on the way. The firm was on the fourth floor. They'd scrutinized the setting with a telescope. The slightly open window, perhaps not alarmed, was on an alley. And it was a commercial area devoid of nosy neighbors. I was glad it was simple. Simple was good. I was beginning to think I could've done this on my own, perhaps climbing the copper drain pipe. Perhaps killing myself, too—not the best way to avoid long term confinement, swapping metal bars for a wooden box.

Elliot backed the van into the alley. Barry got the extension ladder off the van's roof and set it up. We put on rubber medical gloves. At the top, Barry discovered that the window had a limiter; it only opened six inches. He used a screwdriver and in minutes the three of us landed on the plush, tan carpet. Barry handed us medical masks to cover our faces, too, in case of security cameras.

"Stay here," Elliot said. "Gotta check for motion detectors."

He poked an instrument around the doorway. We waited. Finally, he walked into the hallway, and I moved, but Barry grabbed my shoulder, shaking his head angrily.

Elliot came back. "Stay out of the reception area. Motion detector there."

We stepped into the dark hallway. In each direction were a half-dozen offices. I got to the first computer where the hallway widened. I touched the mouse, and the computer came out of sleep mode. The screen's haunting glare lit our faces like an electronic campfire. They moved off, penlights in hand.

I couldn't get past the screen password. I swore.

Elliot came back. "What's up?"

"Can't get in."

"Serious? Dog, move aside."

Elliot worked on the computer for a few minutes; he tried two others at other desks.

"You're in. The password was taped under the keyboard. No inter-account restrictions either. Ha, lawyers. Too arrogant to think someone couldn't get past their security guards and alarm."

"Damn." I felt like a stupid, lucky bastard. "Thanks, man."

I got into the hard drive. It took a while, but I found the firm's client list. My search inside for "Good House" bore no results, and the database info showed it was up to date. Next, I searched with different combinations and abbreviations, and tried "Swanson." No match in word processing doc or pdf files, so no schedule of beneficiaries or other lead.

A sound, maybe on another floor, froze me. Barry and Elliot were checking under desks, in draws, in the baseboards—any place cash or valuables could be stashed.

I'd have to search each attorney's hard drive through the network until I found it. After several hard drives and no luck, I reached one I couldn't access through the server. I found that attorney's computer, turned it on, and tried my searches—nothing. The file, if it existed it could be hidden anywhere on the hard drive. Combing through it would take too much time, so I moved on.

Next one, I typed a broader search as "Good" and "House." Many hits, but no match. I took out the penlight they gave me and wiped it down with my shirt as I thought.

Creeping by, Barry whispered, "Is that how you 'shine' the light?"

"Funny," I said. "I'm wiping off any prints I may have put on it. In case I leave it behind or drop it running."

Eyebrows arched, he down wiped his, too, and moved on to the next office.

Results—no documents fit my query; next hard drive. I heard movement on another floor, below us. It could be security or a cleaner. At the next hard drive, I killed the monitor to keep the light level down while waiting for results and massaged my temples. Computers too slow.

A loud tumbling noise came from inside the suite. I rushed over to another office. Barry shrugged amid a huge pile of files that had obviously been stacked atop a cabinet.

"The noise ain't gonna carry," he whispered. "It's just paper,"

I said, "Don't mess up files until I find mine."

He gave me the okay sign. Back at the computer, there was a single result. It wasn't the trust or a legal document; it was a telephone list.

Keys rattled against the suite's front door.

We killed our penlights, turned the monitors off, and dashed to hide. Someone entered the reception area. The overhead lights came on. Someone approached the hallway. From under the desk, I could see into the office we'd come through. Elliot's feet stuck out from under the desk. By the open window, paper moved. Several pages blew off, and one landed in the hallway.

"What the—" A man's voice, footsteps approaching.

Elliot got out from under the desk and climbed out the window. The footsteps ended by the desk I was beneath. The man picked up the paper from the floor. I heard him breathing. He walked into the office, and I peeked—striped black pants, white shirt. I backed out from under the desk, but stayed down in case he turned around. The guard, short, blond hair, leaned toward the window.

"I heard there was a break-in." Barry's baritone.

The guard jerked back as Barry rose from the ladder.

"I- I didn't, I didn't hear anything," the guard said, which was absurd because Barry also had the medical mask on his face.

"You have a radio to call it in?" Barry stepped inside.

"No, I, I'll run it in, right away or—" The guard backed up and turned quickly.

Then Elliot stepped into his path from the hallway and loomed over him. "Before you run it in, we got to finish here. Sit down. Over there."

The young guard, unarmed, nodded and entered an office across the hall, backwards.

Barry followed him in, knife in hand.

"Take it easy," I said, grabbing his arm.

Barry shook off my hand and pointed the knife at me. "You shut your mouth or I'll make another one in your neck."

I put my hands up and stepped back, wondering how bad this might go.

The guard crouched. "Look, I'm sorry, I won't say a thing."

"Sit down and calm down," Barry said. "No need to apologize. You doing your job, dawg. But you're right about not saying a thing; not yet anyway."

I moved closer to them.

Barry pulled up the phone line for that office and cut it. He backed out and pointed the knife at the guard. "Give me your cell phone." The guard fumbled for it and complied. "Keep your mouth shut. My colleague ain't so nice. Stay until we say you come out."

Barry shut the door. "My partner will be right outside the door. We gonna have a problem with you?"

"No, sir." The guard's voice was muffled by the door.

Barry winked at me. I shook my head and got back to work.

Bingo. Word-search located the telephone entry: "The Good House Trust." It was listed under... What? Charles Cohoon.

This was insane. I sat back and reconstructed my actions. Had I subconsciously typed that information somehow?

Definitely not. I sat up. Charles Cohoon. It had to be the Suffolk County D.A. I pictured his large, lumpy face. He was prosecuting Debbie and me. *Small world, asshole.* Unbelievable. I searched his name, located the client file, and wrote the file number on my hand.

I found that attorney's office, but searching his file cabinets bore no result. I examined photos and plaques. Nothing jumped out at me. Then I realized that the deeds had transferred the real estate mere days ago. The file could still be out. I rifled the stacks on his desk. Nothing. I spotted legal-sized files stacked on a wing-back chair. Yes! I grabbed it.

In another office, I told Elliot I had the file.

"Just a minute," he said. "Still shopping."

From the adjacent office, Barry popped out, a black laundry bag in hand. He had a Cheshire cat smile. "Beats the Home Shopping Channel."

"Hurry." By the monitor's illumination, I skimmed through the file. The Good House Trust was established by a non-profit Rhode Island corporation, although I couldn't find the name of it. I assumed that establishing all this fishy business out of state reduced the risk.

Barry tapped me on the shoulder and pointed for us to leave. I tucked the file in my waist, under my shirt, as Elliot went out the window.

Barry stepped near the door that the guard was behind. He whispered loudly, "Drew, stay right fucking here, dawg, ten minutes. We gonna check out the next office. Guard makes a move? Do him. Otherwise, we'll tie him before we go back to Hartford."

I got on the ladder, into the breeze, and climbed down. Barry followed, scanning for cops. Elliot was in the driver's seat. Barry loaded the ladder, and we got in through the side door.

Slumped in my seat, I blurted, "Un-fucking-believable."

They glanced at me, then at each other, grinning. We pulled out and made every stop legal, and used blinkers every time between here and I-93 North. In a few minutes, we were on it. At fifty-five miles per hour, Elliot put it in cruise and leaned back. "Ahhh."

Barry pulled out the loot and made two piles. When he made a third, I said, "No, I'm good."

He looked dead at me. "You may be good, but this isn't for you. It's for—"

I shrugged. "For what?"

From the front, Elliot said, "It's for a fund. You don't need to know more than that."

Barry looked back at me, considering, then he sighed. "Community chest, man. My brother-in-law was shot. A good preschool needs electrical work to meet code. A man needs donations to get votes to do something for the community, so—"

I held up my hand. He nodded.

The tires' whirr droned as the van headed into Massachusetts. Exhausted, I pondered the ethics of fundraising, political, charitable, and otherwise. I thought of community, of crime.

I laid my head back; drastic measures for drastic times. Malcolm X meets Robin Hood. I wondered if Terry would accept loot from Barry and Elliot, directly and knowingly. Slipping into slumber, part of me couldn't help dreaming for the downfall of the Sheriff of Nottingham, Prince John, and Charles Cohoon, Esquire.

# CHAPTER 29

# Sunday, 7:10 a.m.

In second gear, I passed through Central Square peering out of a new, dragon-emblazoned helmet. Yellow lightning stickers graced my gas tank. My camouflage was conspicuousness. For my plate number, blue sticker pieces altered them.

The Cambridge streets were deserted. Past the YMCA, I pulled over into building shadows just as clouds covered the sun. The combined effect startled like an unexpected eclipse. I got another chill looking up at Debbie's office building ahead. It could be staked out. A Crown Vic on Mass Avenue had no one inside. Debbie's car was out of sight.

After parking my Harley in a nearby condo development lot, I walked past her office building's brick and cement stairs, returned a block later, and went out back. Households nearby would be waking.

I shook my head, lips pursed. After the break-in last night, the file revealed a setback. In a Dorchester hotel, I'd paid cash and instructed the clerk not to charge the credit card. My trust in the clerk enabled a proportionate amount of sleep; practically none. The attorney's file contained a letter to Cohoon enclosing the Schedule of Beneficiaries. Only Cohoon had the name of the beneficiary, my best prospect for Swanson's killer.

It was a tough night in a musty hotel room. The sheets were tight, and I was too tired to adjust them, falling in and out of evaporating dreams. One claustrophobic nightmare seemed to repeat, as if I were trying to make it turn out differently. Security guards trapped me under the lawyer's desk with heavy boxes, and the mayor of Providence was on his way to kill me. Only a long hot shower followed by a brief cold shower brought me back enough to snap some mental cobwebs.

I snagged a landscaping stone and climbed the outside rear steps. With my coat over the door's window, I broke it with the stone. My heart thumped away as I pushed in jagged glass, stuck my arm in, felt the lock, and opened it. Inside, down the hall, cardboard covered the glass panel I'd broken before. I pushed it in, unlocked Debbie's door, and pressed the cardboard back in place.

Ringing. My cell phone scared the hell out of me. Stupid mistakes like that, not silencing a phone, could be costly. It was my lawyer.

"Yes, Max," I said softly, entering.

"Hey, where are you? I've been calling."

I locked the door behind me. "You don't wanna know."

He paused. "Okay, whatever. Look, an indictment for your alleged vigilantism and Swanson's homicide is supposedly coming out in record time. At least Debbie won't testify against you."

"What do you mean?"

"She's your spouse," he said.

For now, I thought, booting up her computer.

"It's a rule of evidence," he said.

"Okay, got it. And I gotta call you later."

I hung up, realizing I hadn't asked if the charges against Debbie were being dropped, and if so, when? I had to find out why, too, but needed to get out of here as quickly as possible.

I searched the Registry of Deeds website for the source of the properties deeded to Karen Hickey. I brought them up. Next, I checked their history. The deeds to Karen all came from the City of Boston and third parties, one parcel from each to form contiguous pairs around the city.

From Karen Hickey, or whoever signed the deeds in her name, they were deeded to the Good House Trust, of which Charles Cohoon, a/k/a District Attorney Charles J. Cohoon III, incredibly, was connected. This could be leverage against him, provided it was true and I could find some way to use it.

I checked for other properties granted to or from the Good House Trust. Others who received the combined parcels from the trust were diverse, so I didn't think they were co-conspirators. They apparently paid market price, which meant enormous profits for the trust.

The trust had to be for elections, for victory and power to come; in short, a slush fund. If so, Swanson surely had a part, except that none of the properties were in his name. Community Improvement Corporation was the trustee. So who could be the beneficiary? Cohoon was the best candidate, so far. But that was almost beyond comprehension.

A door closed downstairs.

Did Mayor Grasso know about any of this? I could dream of freedom and of the Pulitzer Prize, couldn't I? Maybe Debbie knew some facts about the trust activities, even if she didn't know their importance. I would search under Grasso's and Cohoon's names, although I couldn't believe Grasso would risk having his name on anything, if he was involved.

Footsteps padded up the stairs. I felt around the monitor for the button, but couldn't find it, and ducked under the desk. I pulled a plug, but monitor-shine still lit the wall. I pulled another; the monitor turned off. A cell phone rang. I heard Debbie answer as she unlocked the door. What was she doing here? Police with her again?

"It's not a good idea, Paul," Debbie said.

Paul? Paul Dever? Paul Grasso? Paul Mall? Who the hell?

"No, I don't think so," she said. "All right, Castle Island... Yes, I'll get it."

I heard her snap her cell phone into her purse and walk into her office. Under her desk, I didn't dare peek until I knew she was alone. She approached, but then I heard her open a filing cabinet. She closed the outer office door. Her footsteps receded. What? I flew out the back door and got to my bike. I couldn't see her. However, I knew where Castle Island was.

Soon I was riding Day Boulevard, which connected South Boston to Castle Island. Rain threatened. I kept glancing at the beachfront, wondering what was ahead. I entered the parking lot. Granite-block walls enclosed the revolution-era fort, which jutted out hundreds of yards into Boston Harbor. No one in sight. Several vehicles might belong to people fishing around here.

This was the best and likely last opportunity to find out what was going on with Debbie. I parked my Harley behind Sullivan's food shack and walked toward the Pleasure Bay side. Minutes later, her car approached.

I jumped down beside the sea wall and peeked through weeds at the top. She got out. Hair billowed across her shoulders. She glanced my way, and I ducked. Slowly, I checked. She'd veered off to a picnic table, thirty yards away.

A dark sedan came down the boulevard into the parking area. Raindrops dotted the car. It stopped near Debbie. A broad-shouldered man got out wearing a gray hat and trench coat, collar up. He reached into the back seat for an umbrella. When he turned around, I recognized him.

Good God, what was going on?

He went to her and took her arm. "You get away okay?"

She looked up at him. "Yes. No one followed. And you?"

Their voices were faint.

"No problem. The security unit keeps their distance when I tell them." He said something else muffled by wind, then, "You have it?"

Debbie handed Grasso a manila file. He rolled it up and tucked it into his coat pocket.

They walked toward the playground beside the fort. Instead of going left, to circle the fortification, I watched them bear right onto the causeway enclosing Pleasure Bay.

What would I say to them? "Why, if it isn't Debbie's old boyfriend,

Mayor Grasso. *Guten tag! Buongierno!"*

What type of file had she given him? Was she seeking information, or was Grasso going through her to find me? Perhaps she was convincing Grasso to help her with the police investigation, like getting the detectives to go after the "real" killer—but even if it pointed to me?

I knew her better than her lawyer and Grasso did, though. I prayed she was asking him to help me, like in Casablanca; Ilsa asking her former lover, Rick, to help her hunted husband, Victor Laszlo. Was this a painful, noble thing she was doing for me? Or was she doing this for herself? Grasso wouldn't want political trouble, but he would help her, yet he wanted to hang me. He'd told me so.

Light rain continued. They turned around, sharing the umbrella. Mild gusts flapped their long coats, and she squeezed her hair together and tucked it into her collar. Grasso stopped and held her upper arms, looking into her face. Then, one arm on her low back, he pulled her up while leaning into her. The umbrella tilted away as he kissed her, encompassed her.

Thank God I didn't have a gun.

There was tension between them, but she didn't fight. Soon she relaxed. His arms wrapped behind her body, her frizzy hair freed to undulate in the wind and rain.

*Fuck.*

I felt like dissolving into the earth. Was this a rekindling of their relationship? Did he want her again, as a lay or as a love? How fast could I run? I crouched down on the sand beside the seawall, squeezing my eyes shut, shaking my fists.

*No, Debbie. No.*

I stood. Answers flitted in and out. I couldn't solve anything in jail. Messing him up wouldn't get me out of trouble. I'd like to ask questions; questions he'd try not to answer but would. My anger at her was formless, flaring pain, but then it suddenly burned the fight right out of me. I slid my back down the stone wall.

I heard them walking past and sneaked a look. He continued to his car and drove away. She went to her car. I approached Debbie from behind. She opened her door and got inside. I could knock on her window and ask for directions, a knowing smile on my face, the snide gotcha approach. Or my tears could flow, which she could recognize instantly. My reflection showed anger and stress on a stubbly face. Instead, I popped open the passenger-side door.

She screamed. I stared. Her expression was shock and horror, but in which sense, and as applied to what, I could not ascribe.

"I've told you never to unlock all doors," I said with unnatural calm, "without keeping an eye out for danger."

She squirmed in her seat. "Dax?"

"That's right."

"Oh my God. What are you doing here?" Her eyes darted about. "Is there— Is there danger?"

"Explain, Debbie."

She froze, wide-eyed.

I got in and shut the door. "You must recognize the pointlessness of my speaking again before you do."

She swallowed, cleared her throat. After an eternal-feeling wait, she said. "First, I apologize. Now here it is. Ready? I wasn't having an affair with Bradley Swanson." She lowered her eyes and picked at her nail. "It was with Paul, kind of."

My mouth opened to say something, but nothing came out.

"In the back of my mind, at one point, I imagined maybe Bradley was to be a sort of beard, a cover, and I was flattered, but Bradley ended up hitting on me. Then Paul noticed my subtle change, especially in my being resolute that this would be all business—this we pieced together later, after Bradley was murdered. But before that, Paul had been trying to rekindle our relationship. Or, I should say, we'd let it rekindle."

*Mea culpa.* I shook my head slightly.

"I realized it was such a long time ago, in college, but it was serious," she said. "I didn't tell you before that it was him, because you might feel jealous or uncomfortable. Which sounds completely ridiculous now, I know. However, I wonder if I had preserved dormant feelings for him, too. I guess breakups can leave hanging threads there to pull on, and for me, I believe in second chances—generally, I mean."

My eyes popped. "Second chances, what the— How?"

"Believe me, I didn't mean for anything to happen. I didn't consciously give him a second chance. We saw that with you and me, and in our second chance, we got married. I even gave you a third chance, in a way, last year. And I'm sorry. It felt—I don't know—familiar, with Paul, too. We picked it up again, stupidly, like a bubble of time we knew would burst. And it didn't last long at all. It's already *been* over. Honestly." She rubbed her thighs. "That's it."

Heart in my throat, I nodded, unsure whether to breathe or vomit.

"With you, though," she added, "it was a conscious decision to give us another chance. And I'm happy we did, Dax. Another thing, if it's any consolation—"

"Nothing is." I pounded the dashboard.

She flinched and shut her mouth. I faced away.

We sat in silence.

"A contributing fact," she whispered, "was our troubles. I mean, back then, even though you didn't know that I knew about your meeting... her. It festered. This isn't an excuse, and it didn't start this, but it seemed to create a crack. And all the stress I've been undergoing lately. I don't even understand what I've gone through, and am still going through. It's going to take time." She sighed. "But it's up to you, ultimately."

I stared at her until I couldn't any longer, then I faced the choppy bay.

"Dax, so you know, I wanted to make it right with you, but my lawyer said not to tell you about Paul because you could turn on me. That's why he was adamant that you get another lawyer, too."

I nodded, mentally. I felt numb.

"It's in your hands, Dax. Do what you want. Whatever you want."

"It ain't over 'til it's over," I said, not at all knowing what I meant.

I thought about it. It could have a double meaning, like our marriage wasn't over now, or that it was over when the criminal matters were over. I guessed that left me with options and time to figure out what to do.

But I knew what I wanted. I knew right now, I believed. "Now it's over." I pulled off my wedding band. "That kiss." I shook my head. I jumped out of the car. Seagulls nearby lifted off.

"Dax, wait." She leaned toward me. "That was a kiss good—"

I slammed the door. Bye—that was a kiss goodbye, she'd said. So what?

Accelerating on my bike, in the rain, I knew it was a pitiable sight. She didn't deserve to feel pity, though, as it would only serve to convince herself that she was a decent human being. My heart was breaking, and I couldn't stop it. My stomach quivered to the point my knees were involuntarily lifting. I couldn't stop anything. I was a thought away from steering into the harbor. This was the end of something, my life or a part of it.

I headed north along the coast. There was one thing left for me to do, while I could. Get the Schedule of Beneficiaries from District Attorney Cohoon, by force if necessary. Yes, I still had a murderer to find.

# CHAPTER 30

## Sunday, 9:11 a.m.

A speed bump jangled my saddle bag, which was packed with a chisel, a 4-lb. crack hammer, and a reciprocating saw with blades for wood and for metal. Operation Save My Ass was now the D.V. vs. the D.A.

Cohoon's Revere neighborhood consisted of larger, modern homes, made by razing ranch-style houses and merging lots. On a side road near the beach, I parked my bike between addresses, hoping each neighbor might assume the bike belonged to a visitor for the other. I left my helmet on my sissy bar and took out the canvass bag. No disguise this time.

It could be a small safe, for a man of words and documents like the D.A., but I couldn't count on it being portable. If attached or built-in, I'd cut it or bust it free. Barry and Elliot could help me open it later, I hoped. The likelihood that the documents I needed were simply on his desk or in a briefcase was infinitesimal.

*Debbie.* I took a deep breath and exhaled fully. My head was ready to explode if my heart didn't first.

When I'd arranged to pick up the tools from Terry's house, he sounded irritated, but had left the tools on his porch. They'd been wiped clean.

If Cohoon ever had a spouse or kids, none lived here so far as I knew. Maybe he wasn't the family type. Or not the hetero type? Per Debbie, Swanson had a boyfriend he wouldn't discuss. Per Karen Hickey, Swanson had commented that Cohoon was sexy. Theoretically, then, they could be connected to each other beyond the shady real estate transactions. I'd have to look for telltale signs of relationships inside, the one place Cohoon had a solid expectation of privacy. A photo of Swanson and Cohoon entangled on the seashore of Provincetown would do nicely.

I crossed to the beach and dug into the sand with each step to the high-tide line. A few people walked along the water. The white caps were up; the breeze was cool. I inhaled the salt-scented air, preparing myself for what was next, as if I'd never feel that sea air in my chest again. I headed back toward the street. A Mustang with dark windows slowed. There was something about it. It stopped at the sidewalk fifty yards farther along. I watched it for a minute, but no one got out.

I crossed and walked toward Cohoon's neighborhood to access his house from an adjoining street. If someone asked, I'd say I was doing renovation work. I cut through a yard, squeezed through a gap in the fence, and from behind a shed, checked out the stand of pine trees by his kidney-shaped in-ground pool. His house had two upper floors, two large decks, and many windows. No easy floor plan here.

I sauntered to the basement door. After looking for signs of an alarm system, I put on rubber medical gloves. I covered the window with my coat and broke it with a front elbow strike, tearing a small hole in my coat. I opened the door; no alarm—no *audible* alarm.

The basement was unfinished. Of two stairways, I took the far one and ended up in a garage; no cars inside. Through the row of garage windows, I saw a pig-tailed girl riding a bicycle in circles in the street and a girl sitting on a lawn. A boy in a billowy Celtics jersey was shooting hoops. A woman watered plants four houses away.

I crept up the stairs to the interior door. No sound for a minute. The door creaked as I pushed it, then it beeped. *Oh no*—on the wall, an alarm console. Silent? I was totally going to jail if caught burglarizing, regardless of the other decades of imprisonment hanging guillotine-like above my neck. I wished Barry and Elliot hadn't refused the job. They only gave me tips like places to find a safe. Only one red console light was on. I got some *cojones* and moved closer. It wasn't activated, thank God, but Cohoon could return soon. Hell, he or who-knows-who could be home right now.

I crept around the first floor—kitchen, dining room, living room, den, and another living room. I stepped up the stairs to the upper floor rooms. No one was here. No sign of a safe. In this huge house, the safe could be well hidden. If I didn't find it soon, I'd have to risk smashing around. Ah, the den; that was the place. I went downstairs.

The vibration startled me—my lawyer again. At least I'd turned the ring off this time. I answered quietly.

"Dax, where are you now?"

"Ha, you *definitely* don't want to know. By the way, I doubt that Debbie did it. She wasn't romantically involved with Swanson. Call you later."

"Wait, listen, I got a list of items seized in executing the search warrant."

"Tell me quickly."

"Kitchen knives, various. Have you or Debra noticed any knives missing?"

"No. Debbie said she checked."

"Two things concern me. They got your shoe, and apparently it matches a footprint in the dirt in the alley beside Swanson's condo. But it's a common shoe," he said.

I glanced around. "Look, let's do this later. I gotta go—"

"But the key thing was a note from Debra."

The room seemed to tilt.

"Dax? Want me to read it to you?"

I didn't answer.

"It says: 'You don't think I listened, but I did. If this is what I have to do to save our marriage, then so be it. Bradley is history, and we can move on.' Ah, sorry, Dax, the news gets worse."

"Worse? Is that even possible?"

"A witness saw a Jeep parked near the vacant house, and a gray-haired man near the vacant lot. The Neighborhood Crime Watch hadn't called it in because whoever that was had left. Could've been some homeless person. So is there something you need to tell me, Dax? Keep in mind we haven't even discussed potential testimony from you someday."

"Nope," I said, recognizing that he couldn't knowingly let me perjure myself.

"Anyone who serves as look-out or stands by ready to aid would also be liable for the homicide. And conspiracy is a separate charge, and a co-conspirator's extra-judicial statement in furtherance of the conspiracy is admissible."

"What?"

"The note could implicate you in a conspiracy, by implying that the idea was yours. And even if Debbie killed him, your presence on scene could make you directly liable. That is, if a jury believes you participated somehow."

I paused. "Oh, is that all?" I powered down my phone and stared at the floor.

It felt like a void had opened, and I leaned over. My breathing, shallower, felt like waste in my throat, and I wanted to stop it all—the air—my life. I held my breath; thoughts of death, by hanging, somewhere, simply cutting off the air supply, the blood, somehow... A minute later, I sucked in lungfuls of air, hyperventilating, then stopped.

My breathing calmed. My center settled. Life seemed to seep through pores into my body and, surprisingly, I felt alive again, felt the contrast, and savored it. My will to live seemed to return with an astounding vengeance.

*Catch me if you can, bastards.*

Two den walls were wallboard; one was plaster. I checked under the picture frame on the plaster wall—nothing. I checked under a desk against that wall—nothing. Above the desk, papers were pinned to a hanging cork board. The desk was deep, so I had to lean in and lift the board. Behind, a wooden door was built into the wall. *That was it?*

I plugged in the reciprocating saw. As I knelt on the creaky desk, I took up the saw and calculated an angle of attack. I pushed the woodcutting blade into the saw until it clicked, but as I lifted it the blade fell out. I realized that a lever had to be lifted before inserting the blade.

"So what the hell clicked?" I mumbled.

"Me," someone said.

I spun around, holding the saw like an Uzi.

# CHAPTER 31

## Sunday, 10:04 a.m.

There was a silhouette in the hallway of a man crouching with a glint in his hand. "Drop it, I'll shoot!"

The saw thudded to the desk as I raised my hands.

He flicked the light switch. "*You.*"

It was Cohoon, sneering, in sweatpants, running shoes, and some 5-K run T-shirt. "Grantham. Unbelievable." He shook his large head, ashen-faced.

I bit my lip. I could just die—literally.

"Unbelievable," he repeated. "What the hell are you doing in my house?" His squash racquet clattered to the floor as he grasped the revolver in both hands. Maybe he'd accommodate my death wish.

The intensity of his posture abated, but not his deep-set eyes, glaring like musket balls in a tree trunk. "Don't move. You stay right there. I'll shoot you in a second. Don't think I won't," he said. "I'm a 'law and order' D.A., remember? That's how your article described me."

"True." I had to think of a way out, quickly—test him. "Still, it probably wouldn't be good for votes to shoot me."

"Don't give me ideas," Cohoon said, but an expression crossed his face. "No wig this time? I know you're the vigilante. I can't believe no one saw through that old-man costume of yours."

Words wouldn't convince this guy to let me go, but could elicit information, maybe give me a chance to escape. I shook my head. "Speaking of heat of the moment, from what I hear, you'd probably like it with the wig on."

He drew his head back. "What? What in the hell are you babbling about?"

"Your wild bi-gone days. Or do you still swing both ways?"

He tilted his hands out; revolver, too. "Who the fuck said that?"

"Swanson," I said, fishing.

"Swanson? Yeah, he'd know. And he knew I was straight, so—"

"Oh, I understand. Your generation had a harder time coming out."

"Who cares anyway? What are you trying to pull?"

"What are you trying to pull—wool over the public's eyes? You know

I didn't kill Swanson."

He shrugged. "We have motive, opportunity, and method. That's all you need."

"And you needed a slush fund."

Cohoon paused. "What?"

"You heard me," I said.

"I'm going to call the cops. You move, and you'll end up a bigger tragedy than you already are. I don't need the votes." He reached for the phone on the desk, revolver still aimed at me.

If I got arrested, there'd be no getting out on bail this time. "So, got the votes already? That's what a nice little real estate trust will do for you."

He hung up. "What are you saying?"

"You heard me," I said.

"I know I heard you!" He straightened his posture.

I nodded. "Fucker."

"You really are a lunatic."

"And you're a terrible beneficiary," I said.

"So, that's it. You're here because you *think* you know something. Well, let me tell you something. You don't know jack shit."

That was my invitation to tell him what I knew. Fine, the price for the time I was buying. "I know about the contiguous land parcels and the non-profit you find profitable, as the trust funds it."

"Sure it is." He tensed as he checked the revolver's safety. My heart pounded as I calculated distance and timing. But the safety was already off—glad I hadn't jumped him. "Well, it's not how you think it is." He squinted, tilted his head. "How'd you—what did you find out?"

"Was it to protect your slush fund? It's never too early to get a slush fund to help you get reelected."

"D.A.?" He laughed. "I'm already the fucking D.A., with the incumbent's advantage. Try mayor of Boston."

I wondered, their initial plans versus new plans. "Grasso's re-election?"

"I knew you were going to say that." He shook his head. "No, dummy. Grasso bids for governor, as he now is, as you know." He jeered. "He's got plenty of support lined up, some for me. I set up non-profit activity, some for him."

"And it's illegal as hell," I said, "if that's the technical description. You're supposed to uphold the law, not—"

"Spare me, will you? Liberal press, you make me sick."

"Descending to *ad hominem* attacks, are we, counselor? Well, how about the word 'corrupt?' Who're the corrupt ones?"

"Screw you. I'm going to be mayor. I earned it and no God-dammed note taker is going to ruin that. I'll take your life before I let that happen." His eyes darted around, probably calculating blood spatter from a shot this close with that caliber, something he'd be familiar with as the county's crime-fighting leader.

"What, the salary sucks?" I said. "You wanted more perks?"

He sighed and waved his revolver. "You've got to go, Mr. Grantham."

I raised my head. "What happened to the cops?"

"What? You've never heard of vigilantism?" The wicked look in his eyes, to me, confirmed my fear.

"Gonna take care of this one yourself, huh?" I nodded. "Come on, what can I possibly do to you?" Basement, I thought, was the best place for noise retention and a messy body.

"No, I'm not like that. I'm turning you in. How did you get in, by the way?"

"Through the basement door. Why?" He'd kick me down the stairs, hope to break my neck. A shot could follow, if necessary.

He stepped back. "Security, of course."

"So you killed Swanson?" I glanced around for something to throw.

"No, you did," he said calmly.

Did he actually believe I'd done it or did pegging me as Swanson's killer fit his plans? He wasn't explaining or talking a plea deal with me. Maybe killing the "murderer," me, would be more heroic for his mayoral bid. Cohoon was weighing options, and I bet none included me being in police custody where I could talk about his corruption.

"Fine, I'm glad it's over, I'm tired. I can adapt in jail, still write." I looked at my lap. "Just tell me one thing. Did you know about Debbie and Grasso?"

"Did you break in alone? Who knows you're here?"

I said, "No one."

"Slide off the desk, slowly. Wrong move will be your last, and I don't want a mess in here." He motioned with the revolver. "Self-defense against a psycho; can you see the headlines?"

*He's going to kill me.* I put up my hands. "Okay, okay."

"Move it. The cops will be here soon," he said.

"But you didn't call—"

"You tripped the silent alarm."

No, I thought, the alarm console hadn't been activated. And if it had, the cops would have arrived already. Only one explanation—Cohoon was lying.

A cord on the desk, from the saw; I could snag it and swing for his head.

No, wouldn't be fast enough.

*Is he really going to kill me?* I wiped my forehead with my sleeve.

"All right, all right," I said. Something hard and thin was under my leg; a letter opener. I dragged my right hand on the desk as I slid off and caught the opener. I slipped it into my back pocket as I stood. I had only moments left; in the basement, in the last seconds, he'd be most wary.

"Wow." I took two steps. "You guys got it all worked out. I don't care, but, seriously, did you know about Debbie and Grasso, their fling?" *Another step, any means, self-defense.* "And where did she fit in?"

"Sorry. I don't give a shit. Walk this way." He curled his index finger several times. I pictured the other one doing the same, pulling the trigger. He stepped back. I heard the gun cock.

I stepped forward, smelling his sweat, focusing on his ugly mug. "Where are you taking me?"

"Basement. Hold you there until the police arrive."

*That's it; last chance.*

"By the way, my lawyer has all this information," I said, wishing like hell I had the foresight to have made that devastating of a revelation true. I stepped my left foot closer to him. My right hand eased back to the letter opener.

# CHAPTER 32

## Sunday, 10:24 p.m.

Cohoon read my face for a bluff. His gun hand dipped. *Last chance.* I lunged, fencer-like, thrusting far and upward, but his gun— I braced for the shot.

Then he screamed and crumpled, emitting a guttural moan as the letter opener slid from his eyelid. On his side, his legs moved; his hand twitched, and the revolver fell.

The letter opener hit deep into his eye socket. It apparently jammed laterally into his brain, too, as I'd jerked away to avoid the bullet, which never came.

Then I looked at the letter opener. It was slimy, red-streaked. I dropped it. Nausea quashed my relief as I collapsed to the floor, eyes shut, then open.

Blood pulsed under and through his eyelid. I looked away. He stirred, groaned. I leaned closer. He turned his head. The bloody mix ran down his temple and pooled. I held down my howl to a growling moan.

He convulsed, startling me.

I kicked the gun away. Even if he lived, the brain trauma could be serious. I hustled to the desk and lined up the saw with the safe, hands shaking badly. The wooden door's old-fashioned keyhole was only decorative. I opened it. A black safe about eighteen-inches had a digital push button combination and a five-prong turnstile.

I checked Cohoon. He was still.

A gap down the side—was the safe attached to the wall? Then from that angle, I saw the gap in the door itself; it wasn't fully closed. I couldn't believe it. Apparently, he'd never guessed how much I knew or that I'd break into his castle.

I pulled my rubber medical gloves tighter, opened the safe, and removed legal-sized papers, wads of cash, a passport, and files. I heard a scuff and whipped my head around. His left leg slid along the floor. I bit my lip, unsure if I hoped he'd die or not.

Yet his survival could mean life in prison for me.

I returned the cash, the passport, and irrelevant papers. If something were discovered missing, it would alert them to burglary and make homicide seem more likely. I double-checked everything, locked the safe, and tossed everything else into my bag, including the letter opener. Why make it easier for them? Besides, I didn't think they'd let me keep it in prison to open my fan mail.

I stood over Cohoon.

*Fuck.* My stomach quivered. Why did this have to happen? I knelt to check his carotid artery. It pulsed. "Just trying to save myself," I said, breathing deeply. "Besides, you were going to kill me, admit it." After a moment, I spotted the phone.

I had to call 911.

He was incapacitated, and I had the evidence I'd come for. Sure, if they caught me for this, it'd verify every bad thing the public or government thought about me or the vigilante. They'd crucify me. I committed burglary here, too, a felony, and a man may die. Asserting self-defense in this situation would be self-deception.

Terry probably knew I'd come here. Barry and Elliot did know; they'd realize it was me. I could get caught a thousand ways. I was the one who put Cohoon in this position. And what if he wasn't going to kill me?

No, he was. I *knew* he was.

But still.

I put the letter opener into his hand and pressed his fist closed. Plausible deniability; he tripped and fell on it, tired from his work out. I checked around for loose hairs, fibers, or telltale signs of my presence, as if I could succeed.

I tucked the gun, a five-shot revolver, into the front of my pants, then found an envelope on his desk that'd been opened. It must have his prints on it, so I put it on the floor by his other hand. Using his cordless phone, I dialed 911, hung up, and left the phone on the floor, a simple hang-up to be checked out.

I flew down to the basement. I spotted a baseball and dropped it outside the broken window as I closed the door. I peeled off my medical gloves, pulled my shirt over the gun, and crossed the lawn, looking down. *Shit.* I hadn't un-cocked the gun in my waist or put the safety on. I tried like hell to keep down my pace.

I packed my bike and drove in first gear. At the intersection with the beachfront road, a man to the left turned around. His gaze at me lingered. About my age, he was a little heavier, with medium brown hair blowing in the wind. I turned right, popped into second gear, and in my mirror saw him jogging to a car, *that blue Mustang.* He pulled out and banged a U-turn.

My mind went spastic. I just killed the district attorney, probably. How was I going to get out of all this? Kill this guy, too? Well, the gun was ready if I was. I turned right, accelerated down a straightaway, and took more turns. Through a stand of elm trees, I saw a police car on a parallel street speeding toward the D.A.'s house. No lights, no siren. No ambulance either. And no medical examiner, yet.

*Go home.* I likely killed a man. Another man, that is, in cold blood.

I lost that guy in the Mustang, perhaps a goon with an axe to grind and a neck to find. I pulled over at a car dealership. In the lot, a half-dozen people inspected cars. I wasn't sure if I was going to puke as I nudged my bike into the lot with a little clutch release. I put on my hazards, got off, and squatted by my rear wheel as if checking something. I didn't know where to go. I wanted to put on the gun's safety, but couldn't risk it here.

I had to talk to Max. Cohoon could've been dead and Swanson was dead, and Debbie. At least one of them would be put on trial for it. Could they try us together for Swanson's murder or drop the charges against one of us? With a viable case against each of us, how could the prosecution reconcile them? Allege conspiracy, like Max had mentioned.

Max also said the police department's Major Crimes Unit, at the direction of the D.A.'s Office, was digging hard. It certainly wouldn't be Charles Cohoon III prosecuting, though. With Debbie's note, and that witness to a Jeep and an old man at the scene, it didn't look good. Maybe a witness was coached to say "old man," because I hadn't been wearing the wig then.

The pressure inside my head was unbearable. I prayed Cohoon wouldn't die. My life force felt diminished the moment I'd stabbed him. A James Bond video game came to mind; a kill-shot generated the sound of a weakened gasp, like a dying scuba diver, or like Jedi in *Star Wars*, when "the Force" was disturbed by another's death; silly, but not when considering the feeling they were trying to convey. I got it, more than ever. *God.* Giving a deadly blow made me feel humanity more keenly. What choice had I? He was going to kill me. Sure, it was convenient that killing worked in favor of my freedom, but that little doubt was ridiculous; it had to be.

Cohoon was not just a lawyer, but a gun-toting, corrupt, would-be killer. He'd probably have favored the twentieth century Sullivan Law in New York, where guns were made off limits to African-Americans, Italians, and other "undesirables." I'm sure he'd put me in that last category.

Back on Route 1A, I rode on. In Revere I'd worn a different helmet and had an altered license plate, if anyone noticed. If caught with these trust documents, though, it would directly implicate me. The police could discover that Cohoon had them in his home via his lawyer. I needed a place to examine these documents and set the damn gun to safety so as not to accidentally shoot myself in the crotch.

# CHAPTER 33

## Sunday, 11:31 a.m.

Few customers were in the 1369 Café. I rubbed my temples. I dumped the tools in a Somerville dumpster. The un-cocked handgun, put on safety, I tucked into the backpack. Even if the schedule of beneficiaries led to Swanson's murderer, could I go to the police with it? Hide behind First Amendment freedom of the press, citing a confidential source as how I'd received it? As backup, hide behind the Fifth Amendment right against self-incrimination, so I don't get nailed for Cohoon's injury? I'd have to ask Max about this.

I pushed aside my latte and donned medical gloves. In my open backpack, I thumbed through the folder; copies of the trust, deeds, and related documents. I didn't spot the schedule of beneficiaries yet, but the letter in the Rhode Island lawyer's file indicated it had been mailed to Cohoon, so it had to be here. I kept searching.

But no, of course it wasn't here. That'd save my life. And there were no other documents in the safe? I punched my thigh. I'd screened out papers there, but didn't consciously screen in the schedule of beneficiaries.

My phone buzzed with a breaking news alert: The District Attorney for Suffolk County was rushed to Mass General Hospital, unspecified wounds, more information later. *Fuck.* Who the hell wrote the copy with the word "wounds"? Should have said "injuries," unless there was already talk of suspicious means, which you'd think they'd come right out with, being more sensational. It was either an off-the-record comment or poor diction for news copy. The papers in my hands trembled. I returned them to my backpack.

If Cohoon died, the mayor would probably press to have me charged with Cohoon's murder if the cops ruled it a homicide. Blame the fugitive, the one already being prosecuted—persecuted—for Swanson's murder. The acting D.A. would try to convict me for killing Swanson, whom I didn't kill, and convict me for killing Cohoon, whom I did kill, but in self-defense. *I shot the Sheriff, but I did not shoot the Deputy,* it could be my prison anthem.

I prayed it wouldn't come to that. And while praying, I added one for Cohoon. If he was incapacitated rather than dead, it would be easier for me to live with. What the hell would my life be like when this was over? Imprisoned? Still married to Debbie? Divorced? Dead?

A Cambridge cop entered the café and surveyed the customers. I got ready to run—Cohoon's gun would land my ass in prison for life. The cop moved toward me, then to the side by the counter. He talked to someone. A kid brought the cop a coffee, and my panic diminished from Defcon 2 to Defcon 3. The cop left and I could breathe again.

But then I leaned over and gasped like I'd been punched in the belly. Heat seared my face. I realized where the schedule of beneficiaries listing the beneficial owners of the trust property—the evidence that could lead to the killer and save me--must be.

*In that file.*

The file that Debbie gave Grasso.

***

At the Garment District in East Cambridge, the store radio was playing rock music, but a newsbreak came: Cohoon was pronounced dead at Mass General Hospital. Circumstances were being investigated. My face flushed. I felt weak, sad, and sick, and stumbled outside with my purchase.

"Are you all right, mister?"

The clerk followed me out. I straightened, nodded, and stepped away.

I texted Debbie—"must talk, call if u can." I packed my saddlebag and took Memorial Drive to a park on the Charles River, near the BU Bridge. At the brick utility building, I sat on the granite wall, observing wind patterns on the dark water. My future was a big blank, as plain as a prison wall. Twenty minutes later she called. I asked if she was okay. She was, she said, and asked how I was.

"I don't know. I just don't know," I replied. "We haven't talked about what happened to him, Debbie. Happened to—you know."

"I know. There's been little opportunity."

That was true because her attorney had distanced her from me.

She said, "I told you the truth. I didn't do it, Dax. You can know that."

Across the river, a locomotive chugged under the elevated Mass Pike.

"Okay, but who did?"

"Well. I've thought about it, but it only raises more questions."

"That can be good, actually. Asking questions leads to answers."

She said, "Someone could have taken advantage of the situation. If they knew I was going to be at the vacant house or knew I handled the knife, you know? Alternatively, maybe the killer wore gloves and got lucky because someone else's prints—mine—were on the knife already."

"What did the knife look like?"

"A regular kitchen knife, I guess," she said. "Big enough to cut cake."

"Any knife missing from our kitchen?"

"No, not that I could see," she said. "I checked, several times."

"Did Swanson say or do anything to make you think something was wrong?"

"No. And Bradley's phone was on him when he died, or at least when they found him, right? He could have sent the text the message or—"

"Or someone set you up," I said.

She remained silent.

"Meet me," I said.

"What?"

"Meet me. Somewhere safe. We need to talk this out, carefully."

"There is no place safe," she said. "I'm sure I'm being followed."

"Go to a supermarket and leave through a back door. They wouldn't expect it from you. Then get your car. Meet me on George's Island."

"What?" she said loudly. "Dax. You're talking non-sense. This isn't going to work."

"Do it, Debbie. Trust me. George's Island. Take the ferry from Long Wharf. I'll meet you there in an hour. No, an hour and a half."

Silent, she was thinking.

"Okay," I said, "George's Island?"

She agreed.

"Be careful." A pro forma thing to say, but then I realized that a particular danger could apply to her, too. "There's a killer out there."

# CHAPTER 34

# Sunday, 1:55 p.m.

The passengers came seven miles to George's Island. Some gazed back at the Boston skyline, but most crowded the front, looking toward the island. Debbie had to be among this smorgasbord of tourists. On this island were picnicking areas, a visitor's center, and Fort Warren, the 1840s fortress.

In the cool breeze, I zipped my leather jacket, which I'd taken out of my side saddle to better cover Cohoon's gun. The jacket didn't help that shivery feeling, though. I wondered whether or not Debbie had unintentionally brought the police, or had intentionally done so, either to help Grasso or because she thought I'd be safer not being a fugitive. She might have even thought that I'd killed Swanson out of jealousy. The one possibility I tried not to think about was that she'd brought them because *she* had killed him.

The wind made my eyes water. Debbie had said it was over with Grasso, but hadn't expressly said that she wanted me. Maybe it was implied. She hadn't told me anything about their relationship or what was going on from Grasso's perspective. She was having an affair with the mayor of Boston. *How to End a Marriage 101.* When and how did it start? I didn't know how much detail I wanted to know. Some questions were touchy, but I'd ask them anyway; some I probably wouldn't ask—probably.

I was lost.

The bow wave receded as the ferry slowed, then maneuvered to the dock, churning the water.

I had to escape the horror that had become my life, and there was only one way out—find out more. What the hell was the mayor's involvement? His chief of staff and the D.A. had worked out their plan, but had they carried it out all on their own? The D.A. said the benefits were to enable him to run for mayor, and what better way than to time it with the mayor's run for governor? In fact, was this connected to Governor Leno's run for President, too?

As for Mayor Grasso, it proved he could benefit, but it wasn't evident that he was involved. Presumably, Swanson was to fit into the administration of "Governor Grasso." Grasso would deny it all if I went public, of course—Paul the politician. But was he innocent? To my thinking, he had an unfaithful streak and a big ego, so he was likely a risk taker.

Shivering, I went to the concession stand to get us coffee. I needed to eat something, too. In line, several children and a woman were ahead of me. A small TV was attached to the back wall. Then a name caught my eye—my name, on a banner under a TV reporter's face. It was a report of my bail revocation and additional charges, then it switched to a picture of my face which filled the screen.

I turned around, heart thudding away like I'd sucked down the coffees and ran up the Prudential Building. What a way to lose the last of your appetite. It had to end. Something had to happen before I got sent to jail, and I knew there'd be no second chance.

I spotted Debbie on the upper level, leaning on the rail, looking for me. Looking for a future, too? Or maybe to play me for information, set me up to get her out of trouble? I could be trapped here already. If Grasso was corrupt, what did Debbie know? I'd guilt information out of her to help keep me from becoming guilty of murder. After all, she'd crossed the adultery line, too, so maybe she murdered Swanson, according to the same analysis I applied to Grasso. But all this theorizing left a glaring question—why would she do it? If Swanson wasn't her lover, she wouldn't develop a murderous passion against him, so why?

Maybe Karen Hickey was the murderer, or some other lover, after all. I'd investigate Karen more, if I could. Ultimately, though, it could all lead to a dead end if a stranger had murdered Swanson. The police investigation could break any day, especially if it was something clear cut.

Debbie made her way down the ferry stairs.

My working theory was that someone else involved in the corruption had killed him. After all, the D.A. was apparently ready to kill me to save his own ass. And he hadn't actually denied killing Swanson. He'd said I did it, which sounded like a taunt, a cover story for after he killed me, which could imply that he'd murdered Swanson. I'd have to ask Debbie about the relationship between Swanson and the D.A.

God, I could still see Cohoon's face, his body. Prone, his face seeping ooze that I was careful not to step in. I still couldn't believe that had happened. I'd killed a man, again.

Debbie approached the gangplank. She waved walking ashore. No smile, but there was nothing to smile about. They probably weren't dropping the charges against her, not yet, given that enigmatic note she'd written to give me. They'd probably use the charges to pressure her for information against me. With both of us charged with murder, there was a good chance we'd never be together again. One of us would likely be imprisoned soon, likely me, and for many years.

Eye contact again; I tried a smile, but it faltered. Her smile vaporized, leaving hurt in her eyes. I turned and walked. She fell into step with me on the path. Passing a DCR park ranger, I overheard the ghost story of the Lady in Black being told to the tourists. Minutes later, Debbie and I stopped at a bench with a view and few people around. We sat with a foot of space between us. Where to start? She was trained to be mute long enough to compel the other person to speak, then she'd listen. I'd start it easy.

Looking off shore, I said, "So, How are you?"

She faced me long enough to answer, "All right."

"Debbie."

"Yes?" Her hazel eyes flitted to me momentarily.

It would be difficult to talk about us directly. I had to be careful. She brought to bear tremendous training in the human mind, but I knew language well, nuance and semantics, so we were competitive in this little dance. Starting smack in the middle had its own appeal, I supposed. "What does the—? What does Grasso have to do with the real estate?"

"The real estate?" She lowered her eyes.

"The" real estate, she'd repeated. Maybe she wasn't stonewalling, denying connections, yet.

"Yes." I faced her.

She gazed into the offing, then closer to shore, where a yacht with a faltering spinnaker passed the rocks. "Like I was saying before" She pivoted on the bench. "Someone could have taken advantage of the situation, if they knew I was going to be there or I handled the knife. I told the police I had shut the front door, but they said it didn't mean much because it had been jimmied several times before and didn't always stay shut."

I nodded. "Go on."

"Bradley didn't indicate anything was wrong. And it must have been him who texted me. Or—"

"Or someone set you up. I know. "

"Right," she said. "That's logical. And that's..."

I turned my palms up. "But who would set you up, Debbie?"

She shrugged. "That's where it stops—nobody. Nobody I can think of. A disgruntled patient? I don't think so, but you know how it is. Patients will hold things in, pretend they don't exist, hide, deceive. Possibly someone close to a patient who believes I gave bad counseling, Or even the jilted lover who was bad for my client. It could be anyone who refused to accept reality, or their responsibility for it."

Her words seemed to be sucking me down into a whirlpool of possibilities, "Is that what you believe?"

"No." She tilted her head and scraped her toe across the ground. "I don't know."

"Well?"

"I think the killer wore gloves and simply got lucky. My prints cover ..ticleisitors who'. or Dayy earlyed to the regular one. were on the knife. So the killer got away." She shifted to face me squarely. "Someone either wanted to kill Bradley, for whatever motive, or it was incidental. It's a tragedy, either way."

"Of course," I said, the sarcastic tone reluctantly skimmed out. "So, if intentional, why would someone want to kill him?"

"The police need to look into that." She breathed a deep sigh. "We need to tell them, as much as we know." She put her hand on top mine on the bench. "Both of us."

"You want me to talk to them?" I pulled my hand away. "I'm not turning myself in."

I held her eyes a moment, then cast mine to a seagull scooting away from an incoming wave. "I could call them, maybe."

"We should go together," she said, nodding. "To appear sincere, united, participatory in resolving this tragedy."

"Sounds naïve. They don't care. They just want their man." I leaned back against the bench. "Or their woman."

"Don't think I did it, Dax," she blurted, sitting ramrod straight. "And don't think I'm trying to save myself at your expense, don't you dare." She looked hurt.

"Let's just say I don't trust the judicial system, the police, or the prosecution."

She sighed. "We can get you another lawyer, the best. I mean, my prints are on the knife, Dax, not yours. Do you know how that makes me feel?" Tears welled between her eyelashes.

*So, tell me how that makes you feel?* "Back to Grasso," I said.

She sat back, and after a moment said, "Ahh."

I waited, curious.

"I don't believe he did it."

"Did it?" I said.

"Murdered Bradley."

"And why do you say that?"

"Well," she said, "when you asked about him, I figured you might think he was involved in the real estate. And maybe he got into a fight with Swanson, who threatened to go public, ruin Paul."

"True," I said.

"But he was in a conference that night."

"How do you know?"

"He called me from it," she said.

"So, he told you, that's it? No corroboration. And you trust him? We don't even have a time of death, so who knows about the timeline?"

She paused. "That's true. But he just wouldn't," she said. "He couldn't."

Her defending him felt like a kick in the chest, especially based on personal knowledge. "But he was involved in the real estate?"

"He never had problems with Bradley, who was good at it and loyal."

"So far as you know," I said. "And Grasso, he knew what was going on with Swanson?"

She tilted her head. "Hmm."

"I'm sure he had at least 'plausible deniability,' even with you," I said. She had no idea how many properties were involved and how systematized Swanson and Cohoon's scheme was. "I mean, he is a politician. The survival instinct and the ego are too powerful."

"You have a point." She glanced at the ground. "But I didn't know Paul to get involved in the city real estate. It was always Bradley, and maybe colleagues. I thought the goal was just a single lot for the youth center. Bradley's plan was to get a stray parcel that was too small to legally build on at rock-bottom price and get the adjacent parcel from the city to form a buildable lot and resell it for profit. I just needed one, but if we—they—did that several times, then—"

"A dream comes true. Land and money to build, develop an independent program."

She nodded, doe-eyed. "Buy the cheap neighboring parcels of land first, then open the little city parcels for a low bid."

"An insider bid," I said. "Or even just skip the bidding?"

Debbie shook her head. "I don't know anything about that." She leaned back. "But I don't suppose it would shock me. Anyway, it helps develop downtrodden areas, you know? It's urban renewal. They even have a neighborhood development division or something that does that kind of stuff, too."

"Are you saying you didn't suspect anything wrong?"

She picked at a manicured nail. "It's just the way things work, Dax, politics, I guess." Her forehead creased. She looked up. "Isn't it? Someone was helping me, but it helped the city, too. What's wrong with that? Otherwise, those little city parcels are left vacant, eyesores in the community if no one takes care of them."

"Uh-huh."

"Although," she said, "I do recall Paul saying something about it being 'off the grid' or something. I don't know if that meant the parcels themselves or the point system for selecting from among bidders or what."

"Okay." I wanted the $64,000 question answered. "Now, tell me. What was in the file you handed Grasso at Castle Island?"

# CHAPTER 35

# Sunday, 2:26 p.m.

The sunlight was fading. Debbie lowered her eyes to the band of light skin on my ring finger. She shifted on the bench.

"Well. I wanted no part of it, the real estate," she said. "Not since Bradley was murdered." She pursed her lips. "That's why we met. Paul asked for all documents back, whatever Bradley gave me. Copies of prospective lots, city papers, something about city real estate procedures."

I nodded. "What else?"

"I don't know what else." She turned away. Her hands were shaking. "Well, perhaps some trust papers, non-profit papers."

*Trust.*

Leaning against the bench, I scanned the horizon. My eyes landed on a cargo ship. "The trust is for his slush fund."

"No. It's—"

"It's his slush fund," I said. "I know."

"How?" she said.

*The D.A. told me just before he died.* "I just know," I said. "What was the name of the trust?"

"The Good House Trust or something like that."

"And the non-profit corporation?"

"Well, I suppose there were corporate papers of some kind, but I don't know if I even looked at them."

"What's the name of it?" I said.

She shook her head. "I don't remember. They handled the paperwork."

"Swanson and Grasso."

"No, Dax, I told you. Bradley or his colleagues, or maybe a city division that could deal with these matters? But certainly Bradley."

"Why do you keep—"

She said, "What?"

I had no chance to clarify with Cohoon, now dead, whether Grasso was a participant in the slush fund or just stood to benefit from it. "I thought Grasso was controlling?"

"He was."

"Well, who was listed in the trust as the beneficiary?" I said, exasperated.

"I—I don't know." She did look stumped. "I didn't think about a list of beneficiaries. I suppose there should be one. Wouldn't there be? I don't know about these things. If I saw one, I don't remember it."

I stood. "Are you, or were you ever, part of the non-profit?"

"No." She stared at me, brow furrowed. "No. I mean, not knowingly. I hadn't a final plan to get everything off the ground." Her shoulders slumped. "I should have consulted an attorney in the beginning."

That was an understatement.

If I told her about the fund for Cohoon's mayoral run, timed with Grasso's gubernatorial run, she might reveal information, maybe even her loyalty. Unfortunately, it would also implicate me in Cohoon's death. How else would I know that information other than from him? My fists clenched. If she was fishing for a way out by implicating me, though, all bets were off.

I checked the dock for the next ferry. Georges Island was the transportation hub for the thirty-two islands and two peninsulas in the Boston Harbor National Park.

"What about Cohoon?"

"The District Attorney, involved in this?" She shook her head. "No, not that I know of, although I know Bradley met him weeks ago. Him kill Bradley? That's out of this world. It's all hypothetical." She stared at her leather pumps. She obviously hadn't heard about Cohoon's death.

"Perhaps he set you up."

Her head jerked up. "Him? Why? That's infuriating to even consider."

"I don't know." I checked the dock again. "He didn't like you involved, you getting the benefits."

"I doubt it, Dax. It could just as easily have been Bradley's lover's spat with who-knows-who, a past or present lover. And murderers, burglars, robbers; they do wear gloves, as you know."

"Hey. Are they sure there wasn't another weapon? Has your lawyer looked into that?"

She nodded. "Attorney DeLay said the medical examiner confirmed he died of a knife wound. And they found only one knife there."

"But have they confirmed that the wounds were consistent with that particular knife?"

She looked off to the side, then back at me. "A mismatch would get me off, probably, wouldn't it?"

I nodded, watching another ferry approach. "Probably."

"But now, now they're not dropping the charges against me because of my stupid note." She sighed. "I only meant that once I got the property, I wouldn't work with Bradley anymore. Nothing else, for God's sake. Obviously, we didn't conspire to kill him. And I didn't even give you the note yet." Debbie stood. "I'm cold."

I rose from the bench. "Let's walk."

As we went uphill, I checked behind. A green uniformed man debarking concerned me a moment, but he wasn't a cop.

"Dax?" Debbie said softly.

I touched her back. "Yeah?"

"I'm scared."

We stopped and faced each other, close. Looking up at me, she appeared petrified. Thank God, a normal reaction. It could indicate anything, but I hoped it was innocence. Even if that made me more vulnerable to unearned guilt, it made me feel better. I put my arms around her and hugged.

"Me, too." I let go. "But—"

What else was there to say, but we're innocent? Maybe she was, but maybe she wasn't. And me, guilty? Ultimately, yes, I was—and no, I wasn't.

I continued uphill. Debbie followed.

"Dax?"

"Yes, hon?"

"There's another—" She cleared her throat. "There's another reason I didn't tell you I was once in a relationship with Paul."

I stopped, our hug's warmth blown away by the chill of her words.

# CHAPTER 36

# Sunday, 2:50 p.m.

What came next was bad. In the normal course of conversation, I'd ask what was her other reason for not telling me Grasso was her ex-boyfriend. But this wasn't normal.

I started walking again. "What?"

She followed. "Because he said not to."

Relief and confusion mixed inside. I looked at her. "That's it? Of course he'd say that."

"No, it's more than that," she said.

*Here we go.*

"You two apparently had some history together," she said, "in high school."

"What? What the—" I squinted. "In high school? No."

"He said you guys got into a scuffle or something."

"Paul Grasso? I don't think so," I said. "What are you talking about?"

"Apparently, he was a year or two older. And on the wrestling team?"

Breath caught in my throat. Something clicked. I stopped. "No."

They were older now, heavier, showing their age. They'd be hard to recognize. Still, I remembered their names. I would always remember their names.

"He was new that year," she said. "He'd moved to Braintree from Andover when his parents separated. Apparently, there was a lot of domestic violence. In fact, he said that's one reason he supports my youth project. Many are victims of violence inside the home."

Or victims outside the home. "But—"

"He and his mother used his mother's maiden name after they moved. She never legally changed it while he was in high school," she said. "The administration was sympathetic. When he applied to college, though, they couldn't avoid all that documentation. He had to use his legal name. Paul Grasso."

"Shit." I closed my eyes.

She put her hand on my arm. "What's the matter?"

I turned away, feeling my center soften into a glob. One question— the answer to one question could fracture my reality. "His mother's maiden name?"

"Arena," she said.

My head felt unbalanced on my neck. Sharp pains hit my stomach, like a crazed crow was trying to escape it.

"Do you remember him? What happened, anyway?" she said. "Was it that bad? Dax?"

I coughed. "Ah, did anyone follow you?"

"No, I don't think so."

I pulled at my chin. *Paul Arena.* It must be him.

I tried to picture his face as Grasso's face, but it was difficult. I couldn't see them as the same. Grasso was bigger now, which was to be expected over the years since high school. Also, his receded hair line and crew cut changed the shape of his face, which was fuller. And the different last name and completely different context threw me off.

I pictured the first incident, when Paul Arena chased me, which ended by my climbing an electrical tower. He didn't follow, and I'd wondered if he was afraid of heights or had lost interest in bullying me. He hadn't.

I started walking. "My family went through worse than a divorce, as you know. Even though you got me to talk about it, some of it." I kept looking straight ahead. "One thing I didn't detail was how I got taunted about it. Some creeps saw my sensitivity and responded like the masochistic dentist in *Marathon Man*, or whatever." I shrugged. "At one point, I was pushed around by a bad segment of the wrestling team. Just a couple of them, actually. That was one thing."

But not the worst thing. That happened later, and I became suicidal. Debbie knew nothing about all that.

"Why would they do that?" she said. "Are you saying Paul—?"

"You're asking me why? You know kids, first of all. And second of all, they're in high school. They had more capacities for cruelty, especially when feeling their power. Some found out my brother got adopted out, then me, which happened years before, by the way. My family broke up when I was about seven and my brother ten." I looked at her. "My mom called us her Irish twins because he was older, but small for his age. Did I tell you that?"

"You didn't mention it," she said.

"I never knew where my brother ended up, not even the state he went to." I looked down. "That's just not right."

She squeezed my shoulder, her brows pulled together in the middle. "I'm sorry, hon."

"Tommy was always getting in trouble. He went to a foster family. When they came for him, the man was huge, scary looking. I felt bad for Tommy. Soon after, my dad died. Then my mom was hospitalized. Definitely alcohol. She died while I lived with my grandmother. Later, I went with foster families until adopted. I didn't—" I checked Debbie.

She nodded for me to continue.

My vision blurred. "I heard about the adoptee-parent registry, you know, to re-connect with my biological mother. In case she's alive. I doubt she is; I mean, she isn't, I know that. But if—if she had ever registered to express interest, or if my brother had. I'd hate to think that could happen, and that I wouldn't at least know about it. That's one reason I reverted back to my original last name as an adult. You know?"

"Of course." She nodded. "So maybe they could find you more easily."

I checked the dock. We hadn't walked far, and the ferry was set to leave. Most people disbursed. One man broke into a jog alongside the ferry.

I sighed. "So, I finally signed up for a chance to find my brother." I fixed my eyes on the point where the bay opened.

She leaned in. "And?"

"Never heard anything. I did it when the law changed, you know, to make finding your birth family easier. I haven't done anything since. Let fate take its course, I suppose."

A deckhand shouted down to the jogging man, who shook his head. The ropes were thrown off, and the boat maneuvered out.

"It's not too late," she said.

I faced her. "Well, I don't know what else to do."

"Something. Anything might help, whether or not you ever succeed. It can give you a sense of control." She pursed her lips.

I looked at the fields and trees on the other island and then checked the man looking at the ferry. He wore a sports coat, unlike a picnicker or typical tourists.

"You know," I said, "that could be Detective Flaherty. It's far away, but his shape, his clothes?"

"Really? I didn't think I was followed. I sure as hell hope not."

Her rare curse, the expression; it irked me. Did Grasso use it in private?

"Where?" she said.

I pointed him out. "Let's go this way."

"I don't know." She looked up at me. "What should we do?"

"We have to go," I said.

The next ferry to Boston was due in a while; not that I'd take it. Escalating my worry, a helicopter approached the island head-on. Could be tourists, could be police. I couldn't see its markings at this angle. Did they have unmarked helicopters?

The man started walking uphill toward us, a few hundred yards away.

Others closer to him diverted his attention, but he'd see us soon, and we fit the profile. The helicopter veered right, elevated, and slowed before reaching the island. It hovered off the coast, diagonal from the dock.

I patted the revolver tucked into my waist, but knew I wouldn't use it on a cop; on a District Attorney, sure, but not a cop. *Yeah, right.* I'd already proved that I would do what I had to do, to survive. That, itself, was scary.

I took Debbie's arm and walked at a healthy clip. "You need to go the other way. If we're together, that increases his chances. Walk north, I'll go east. I'll call you, okay? Don't wait for me when the ferry comes."

"Are you sure?" She tied a kerchief around her head, looking scared though she wasn't the one on the lam. Charged with murder, yes; but not on the lam presently.

I let go her arm. "I'm sure."

The helicopter moved southeast along the coast, slow enough to see the sights, or sight a man. To get away, I had to slip onto the next water taxi.

"Bloody hell." Her eyebrows slanted steeply. Her lip quivered. "Dax, Dax, I want this to all be over. I really do. It's too much. I can't stand it," she said in a torrent.

Her eyes welled up. I felt that she wanted to bury her face on my shoulder. Her hands came to her chest and bobbled as if they might reach for me. I'd never seen her like this before. It broke my heart.

I could fight for what was mine and escape with her; I should, even, but then what? Still, I felt a flicker of hope. On Castle Island by Fort Independence, fittingly enough, I'd discovered that I'd lost her. Was I now finding her by Fort Warren on George's Island? Part of timeless battles, I supposed, for your mate, for your life. We touched hands, and then I stepped off, out of time.

# CHAPTER 37

# Sunday, 3:40 p.m.

Bundles of clouds catching the sun scudded east toward open-ocean skies. I leaned on the rail, staring at the dark water, as the ferry whipped us south toward the Hingham Ship Yard. A wave bounced the ferry and sprayed my face, which I wiped with my shirt. An image of Debbie's wet-rimmed eyes came to mind. Beneath the ferry's bridge, a thin woman in her thirties looked at me.

In high school, when I'd dressed as a girl for that news article, one of the school's wrestlers, Paul Arena, and his teammate went after me. I didn't tell Debbie that part. Testosterone ran rampant in the locker room—run afoul. Too embarrassing, too painful. Now I knew his real last name, Grasso. Seemed I wasn't the only one going around incognito; his disguise was as a public-serving, law-abiding man. He obviously became aware of who I was at some point, despite my adoptive last name used in high school, Buckley.

Grasso was a self-server, breaking laws with his body and mind. My anger pushed the thought further—even if Grasso had to kill someone. It was crazy, but I shouldn't put it past him. Maybe he killed Swanson, despite their supposed good working relationship. And the lack of any evidence, or motive.

That was the problem with nice theories; they could let you down.

In Hingham Bay, motorboats and sailboats bobbed or bounded over waves. I scanned for police vehicles on shore or on water.

Debbie answered on the second ring. "Can you talk?"

"Yes," she said. "It is Detective Flaherty. I put on big sunglasses and a kerchief around my head, you know, like a blonde Jackie O'. He walked past as I was squatting by children at the beach, looking at sea shells."

"What about Grasso?"

"Oh, wait, here comes the detective again."

"All right," I said, "but tell me about Grasso."

She hesitated. "What do you mean, what about him?"

I said, "Are you two—?"

"Oh, that, no. That is a no. That's not going to happen, Dax. What-ever happens with us, that's not going to happen. That's over."

I stared ahead.

"Dax? What are we going to do?"

I couldn't absorb that yet, the part about us.

"I mean what are we going to do to get you and me out of trouble?"

"Oh," I said. "I'm not sure."

"Well, what are you going to do? You're a fugitive," she said. "I don't know the law, but you're in a lot of trouble. You need a top lawyer, hon—Dax."

I looked back at the ferry's wake, then noticed the thin woman looking at me again. I said, "What I need is trust."

"Trust. How so?"

"I need you to trust me," I said. "Trust that I need everything you can tell me about Grasso. I need a lead. He was close to Swanson. There's got to be something. I'm not asking for a confession, any kind of confession. I just need to know how he operated. I need evidence, direct or indirect, and I need you to give it to me." I checked for anyone within hearing distance. "I deserve it. And so do you."

She paused. "I see."

"If you remember anything else, about him or Swanson or anyone, anything that might help, I need you to tell me. Especially anything about the documents you returned to him. Or other papers, even if you don't know what they were or what they mean. Like, where does he have them?"

She cleared her throat. "Where? At his home, I—I guess."

"At his home."

"Yes. But no, or not just there. He did say he was going to put them away, like hide them away."

"Yeah? How?"

"Wait. Flaherty's coming closer. I should go," she said.

"Just walk and talk," I said, pacing on the deck. "It looks natural."

"Okay, okay. He had this jar, a glass jar." She sighed. "I, ah—"

"What?" I asked. "Oh, I see. So you've seen this glass jar, at his house."

"Mmm hmm." She sounded uncomfortable.

"And?"

"And he had mementoes in it, but dumped them out and said he was going to put his papers in there and bury it. Bradley had been killed. Paul didn't want the police to get into his business or bother me, and he said he wanted to avoid a scandal."

"Of course."

"Like a treasure he had to tuck away, with everything going on, but, but he had had some wine by then, so I don't know how serious he was, how literal."

"But what was it? Just papers, keys, cash, jewels?"

"Just papers."

"What about the non-profit, too? Anyone involved with Swanson could have evidence to get us off or lead to the killer. It's all I have to go on. But it makes sense."

"Yes. I think. He did talk about keeping his distance. A pragmatic matter, he said. Keeping his name off things for political reasons—oh, and he said something about taking his name off something, too. Maybe that document is in there, with his name on it."

Bingo. "Okay," I said. "But the thing is, did he actually bury it and where?"

She coughed. "I haven't a clue."

"Uh-huh."

"But if he does bury it," she said, "it might be inside a metal box. He had that out, too."

"To protect that jar," I said, "which protects the paper."

"Logical," she said.

What a shot in the dark, buried treasure. *How poetic, Mr. Grasso.*

"Well, that's something," I said. "So let's assume he did that. Again, where?"

A long, heavy pause; what was she thinking?

"Honestly, his behavior worried me," she said. "Something wasn't right."

"In his yard?" I prompted her. "A favorite spot? A vacation home?"

"I don't know." She sounded frustrated or pressured.

"Okay, Debbie." Maybe she needed time to remember; remember where it would be buried or remember "us" and give it up. She could also fear implicating herself in fraud, although I was sure she didn't knowingly do any such thing.

"Thanks," I said. "Let me know if you think of anything else."

"Uh, I will."

I hung up, wondering if she felt a conflicting loyalty to him and to me, which inflamed my anger, like when I'd first discovered that Debbie had betrayed me, and I thought for a moment that I could kill her. Only figuratively, of course, but nevertheless, some things should never be said aloud, especially by a murder fugitive.

# CHAPTER 38

## Sunday, 3:55 p.m.

The ferry docked at the Hingham Ship Yard. I shuffled down the gang-way in a daze. In the lot off Route 3A, I straddled my Harley and strapped on my helmet, ready to go.

I stared, breathing heavily, tightness in my chest. My visor fogged. My eyes closed.

*No one else in the locker room... Two grab me. Paul, yelling about me wear-ing a dress before, when I wore that dress... and wanting something. "You know what that means, Miss Grantham? We'll teach you a lesson." I back up, away from my locker. He ignores my explanation that it's for the school newspaper. I'm scared. With his teammate, Paul wrestles me down next to the shower. A trash barrel tips over. I yell to leave me alone. He pulls off my gym shorts—what the hell? He's going to take my clothes and push me into the hall!*

But it wasn't that; it was something else. Something I'd never imag-ined.

*"I'll show you what you need!" Paul visibly responds to me, probably with more conflicting feelings than he knows what to do with, and pulls it from his sweatpants. I try fighting them off, but they're too big. I can't get him off my back. I'm younger, afraid, shocked. The friend is laughing, pinning my arms, shoulders, egging on Paul, sexually assaulting me. I scream, "No!"*

*The pain, the disbelief.*

*Then he finished. I know I'll never tell a soul—and pray those bastards don't either.*

My chest vibrated, startling me. I opened my eyes, flipped up the vi-sor, and gulped fresh air.

I took my other hand off the revolver under my shirt and grabbed my cell phone. It was Debbie. What would that do to her perception of him? Or of me? Did it matter anymore? Now, again, it felt as if it had happened to someone else, and I pushed back from the memory.

I removed my helmet. "What?"

"Dax, it's in the Blue Hills."

"It is?" Blue Hills was a woody reserve just south of Boston.

"The proof of land deals. 'Beyond subpoena and treachery,' that was the phrase. It must be incriminating. I should've paid more attention. But the way he talks sometimes, I don't know. He hinted that he'd take his money, start a new life, after his term ended, and he'd be governor. It was never definite, just talk, you know."

Had she held this back or had something jogged her memory? Had Grasso really said that to her, and did she believe him?

"I wasn't ever going to join him, though. I was confused and didn't know what I was going to do, but it wasn't that."

"Where?" I said.

"I don't know exactly. That's all I know."

Was she fooling herself then, or now, or trying to fool me? Grasso lived in Dorchester, beside Milton, which bordered the reserve. I said bye, hung up, and started my bike, an idea forming.

Blue lights flashed in the area where the boat taxis dock. A policewoman hopped out. My image was in the news, online, and on TV, so maybe the woman from the ferry had reported me, or maybe they'd used my cell phone signal to locate me.

I looked in the mirror. The cop approached with a hunting stare, then jumped into the police car. It was on. I punched the gas and clutched. The cop spun around and accelerated. I worked up to fourth gear, maxing rpm's, going way too fast. I skidded before the main road, checked traffic in a blink, and turned right, fast, the turn wide.

I crossed the yellow line into the path of an oncoming car. Its horn blared as it swerved away and sideswiped my leg. I caught my balance. I heard a screech and crash behind.

I'd escape or die trying. Ignoring the pain in my leg, I torqued the throttle. My heart galloped as I rode faster and faster. Bumps jolted my frame. My clothes fluttered violently. In the right lanes, I wove around cars and trucks. My left leg was numb. I couldn't check it. My foot barely worked the gearshift. I had to lay off the gas at a left curve, but I tried not to brake.

I hit a pothole. It pointed me toward a telephone pole. I braked madly. Before impact, the bike fishtailed right. I leaned with it. The tires hit the rounded curb. The bike launched over the sidewalk and spun over a bush.

I landed hard on a front yard and rolled. My bike landed, flipped, and landed flat. I saw stars, then nothing.

I came to. My shoulder was numb, my back hurt; much of my body did. A car squealed to a stop behind the bushes, then accelerated up the driveway behind the tall fence. The cop had probably called for an ambulance. I hobbled to my Harley, lifted, and pressed the ignition, which turned and turned. Clumps of soil and grass fell off.

She kicked the gate open. "Stop, police!"

The engine kicked in. I got on, accelerated, and crashed a white gate into the neighboring property, nearly spilling the bike. Up that driveway, I turned right onto the main road.

The bike had wobbled. If I got any dizzier, I'd have to stop.

Two cop cars passed me. One skidded into a U-turn. After a mile, I braked hard. The rear wobbled. The cop was gaining. I turned left into a neighborhood. I rounded a short block in two right turns. I pulled the clutch, shut off the engine, and lifted my face shield to listen as I coasted silently. A siren sounded closer, then the rapid acceleration of an engine. Through the back-to-back yards, I saw the cop car fly up the parallel street I'd just been on.

I started up and sped away. Back on the main road, no cops were in sight. My leg throbbed, my chest was sore, and my shoulder hurt. After a minute, I turned right and resumed a moderate speed on the back roads north, along the coast, hoping I wasn't injured worse than I realized.

\*\*\*

My leg pain increased as I limped into the Cambridge Public Library, desperate for painkillers. I heard a scuffling sound behind me and felt a sharp pain in my leg. I whipped around. A thin, dark-haired boy had tripped. He looked Indian, about ten years old. He looked at his hand, wet with blood; mine, apparently.

I leaned down. "You okay?"

The boy nodded, looking back and forth to his hand and to me. "Mister, you're bleeding."

I glanced around. "Ah, it's nothing."

As I walked away, I heard him call for his mother.

In the quiet brownstone section, I moaned involuntarily while sitting at an Internet portal. A young woman stocking a shelf gave me a look. I signed onto my personal email account to write the most important article I'd ever written, for all the beans in Beantown, for my life; specifically, an article for the *Boston Times*. Getting it in would be another matter.

I wrote about things I'd done. I outlined my theory about the corruption, the mayor, the D.A., and Swanson; swindling away city parcels too small to be built on, to an illicit real estate trust. Each of those parcels was merged with other non-buildable parcels picked up cheap. The resulting lots were large enough to be built on under zoning laws. With the exponentially increased value, they sold and reaped huge profits that went into a "non-profit" corporation bank account, but were actually used for their political campaigns and more.

A woman hovered nearby. The boy behind her leaned to peek at me. "Excuse me," she said. "Are you bleeding from your leg?" She pulled her headscarf tighter to her chin.

"I, ah—just a bit. I'm okay, thank you." I faced my computer.

"No, you must clean that up," she said louder, shaking her head. "You got blood on my son."

The employee stopped stocking shelves and approached. "Please, no talking in this room. Is there a problem?"

"No, no problem," I said softly.

"Yes," the mother said, "he got blood on my son's hand. I scrubbed it, but—"

"Actually, the boy tripped and landed with his hand on my lower leg, which I'd cut before. I'm fine, he's fine."

The employee bent forward to inspect. "I think you'd better get that checked out."

"The bandage must've come loose, that's all. I'll check it in a minute. Just have to finish this email," I said.

She frowned and went back to her cart of books. The woman led her son away. A couple of nearby patrons glanced furtively my way.

In my email, I left out the high school sexual assault. I left out the affair with my wife. As for D.A. Cohoon, I mentioned his plans to run for mayor and the mayor's run for governor, with Swanson on the coattails, bolstering motive.

I couldn't name the beneficiary, whether an entity or an individual, but I labeled it as a shell for the slush fund. I also didn't mention how I knew about this slush fund, which would implicate me in the D.A.'s death. And I didn't reveal that I was the DV.

I rushed to add that Governor Leno, as a Grasso supporter, could benefit from the slush fund, too, especially since Leno's Presidential run was arguably timed with the election campaigns of Grasso and, formerly, of D.A. Cohoon.

The employee left her book cart.

I reviewed what I'd written. It could convince readers that there was something to all this. In turn, it could convince authorities to focus not just on me, but on finding evidence of Swanson's killer from other sources. I was desperate for the alleged non-profit corporate info and proof of the mayor's direct involvement; otherwise, my theory would fall apart and I'd be the laughing stock of the city and permanent guest of a correctional institute of the Commonwealth's selection.

Over the intercom, the library announced closing time.

In my article, I "deputized" every citizen whose ear responded to the notion of "I'm fed up and I'm not going to take it anymore," a reference to quintessential public outrage, *Citizen Kane*. In my view, I wrote, effective vigilantism was diffused, not necessarily organized like the Guardian

Angels. Therefore, it wasn't a threat; not a threat to society, that is. It was community activism with teeth. Individual responsibility, executed all over. If grown, it was a permeating threat to violent criminals to supplant the fear they'd sown among us for too long.

Criminals would fear the unknown, the real chance of getting caught in the "city-wide web" of cell phones, cell cameras, new surveillance cameras, and an army of self-empowered citizens, some of whom were willing to step it up.

"It takes a village," yes—and in a real village, offenders get dealt with quickly and in no uncertain terms. No small benefit was the fact that the city-wide web would also be a check on police abuse. I'd made this point in an article the year before, but now it was all part of my manifesto.

The deterrent effect would steer future criminals into using their efforts and talents in legitimate ways. The expression, "If only he only used his efforts for good, not evil," sounds corny, but not to the parents of jailed or dead kids, and not to victims. I hoped Debbie would appreciate that.

I added details about the jar with documentary evidence inside, maybe protected by a metal container, and pleaded with people to find it. There'd be a reward, I added, without specifying it.

The library lights flicked off and on. I did a quick search on the Blue Hills Reservation: "[o]ver 7,000 acres from Quincy to Dedham, Milton to Randolph, a green oasis in an urban environment." I certainly wouldn't see an oasis when searching there to save my butt. Twenty-two hills in the Blue Hills had varied terrain. Great.

I printed a map. I'd look for roads from Grasso's house convenient to the reserve as a start. Maybe I'd discover another hint by pursuing Grasso or Debbie or by some other way, but it'd be a miracle and a half for me to find the box and jar alone. And if I got the article published and nobody showed up in response to it—disregarding the police, who'd search for me there—I'd never find it. It was crazy, but I was beyond desperate, with no more options.

I saved my article in a draft email. One small problem was actually getting it published. I couldn't show my face at the *Boston Times*. I wouldn't be able to get it through editorial anyway. And another reporter would care more about the story than the message or helping me, and could even set up my capture. Kravitz would surely kill the story, even if it wasn't slanderous and inflammatory. However, where there's a will there's a way. And I knew of only one possible way; I didn't have a choice on the "will" part of the equation.

# CHAPTER 39

## Sunday, 9:45 p.m.

The contiguous sports fields of Thayer Academy were expansive. I hadn't seen this much sky in a long while. Out on the water today, the horizontal views were distant, but the night sky stretched into infinity. And I really didn't want to be here.

The house was dark. Behind it, the gibbous moon was pasted low in the sky. I pulled up the chain-link fence, slipped under, and squatted behind the parallel stonewall. Neighbor's windows overlooked his back yard. The house was dark. Kravitz might be asleep, since he always arrived at the office by 6:00 a.m.

I jumped over the wall and dashed to the screen door. It was open, but the wooden porch door was locked. I checked the basement windows, but no luck. Near a back window was a bench that I stood on. The den was in here, if I remembered correctly. Kravitz had people back to his house after his wife's funeral several years ago.

I felt bad, but he could probably prove that it wasn't him who did it; that is, what I was about to do. I hoped he wouldn't play hero by fighting me or calling the cops. I was too close to the truth to let him get in my way. I patted my gun; it was my gun now. I'd adopted that power, the threat of which would keep him in check. I pushed on the locked window screen until it popped, banging the frame. I froze, listening. No lights came on. A minute later, I pushed up the window and crawled inside, wincing when my bruised, cut leg scraped over the sill—wincing greater when the gun slipped from my waist and smacked the wood floor loudly.

I waited. No sign of life. I picked up the gun and tucked it into my back waistband.

Kravitz's computer would give me access to the *Boston Times'* intranet. He viewed final production before printing and approved all articles for the City and Region section. Tomorrow was Labor Day, so articles—and advertisers—would get a lot of exposure. A surge of despair hit; he'd have done it by this hour for the edition. I might be too late, but the only shot I had to get around Kravitz was to fake his approval. From there, who knew?

I angled the desk lamp and switched it on. Framed Marvel Comics covers hung on the wall, and a couple from DC Comics; Kravitz's collection, which I'd never seen. I saw the corporate-issued computer key card needed for access. I touched the keyboard and the computer revived, but the light from the screen made me uncomfortable. I stood in front of it and looked behind me to check the light level. My shadow on the wall extended to the ceiling, huge and distorted.

He was still signed on; a huge break.

I signed onto my email account. One email caught my interest, from the journalism award committee. They'd retracted my award pending determination of events. No surprise there. Next, I downloaded my article to Kravitz's hard drive. I set it up for transfer to incorporate into the final layout of the *Boston Times*. The accompanying message I wrote had to convince the production supervisor to insert it for publishing without calling here to verify it.

The large circulation of this story would generate repercussions in Boston and beyond. I hoped something would break through somewhere to help me. Finger poised to hit send, I hesitated. I double-checked that everything was in order.

Then, to my right, a tall crack of light. To the left, the door opened wider. A pistol in the gap pointed at me. "You shouldn't have broken in."

Kravitz entered. He sat me in the corner with a jab of his pistol, probably a 9-millimeter Glock. Too late to grab my revolver, for now.

He stepped to the computer. I could see the hatred in his eyes.

"Legs crossed. Fingers interlocked behind your head."

I hesitated, but obeyed. It also lifted the bottom of my leather coat off my revolver.

Without his glasses, he leaned toward the screen. I thought to grab the gun, but he checked his aim on me. An option was gaining his interest or sympathy, but that was unlikely, especially after breaking into his house.

He read in silence, probably amused, then it popped into my head—what if Kravitz had something to do with this political conspiracy? He was in tight with some politicians, like the mayor, apparently.

"We've got a problem here, Dax."

"I know," I said. "I'm sorry."

"No." He looked at me. "I don't think you do know."

I stared, calculating the timing to draw my gun. "Well, that's it then? You're calling the cops?"

"No," he said, a smile pulled to one side.

I didn't feel relief; I felt afraid. Where did he connect to in this mess?

"First, I can't believe you had the gall to break into my house. But the article; you can't file it."

"Excuse me?" Shoot to disable, get his pistol. "What?"

He took a deep breath. "What I mean is you can't file it like this."

"Why not?" I knew why not, of course, but not what he meant.

He smiled, sadly. "I told you, you must submit your articles to me first."

"Ah, okay." He was playing games. Why?

"And your syntax in the last paragraph needs work."

Now I gaped, confused.

He leaned back. "Like I said, Dax. The story is still the story."

Kravitz lowered the pistol and, after a pause, smiled and put the safety on. Strangely, he appeared more relaxed than ever. I lowered my arms. He put the pistol down on the desk.

"I know you thought I'd sold out somewhat," he said, "but I hadn't. I want you to know that. I admit I played the line too close at times, but..." He pursed his lips. "Maybe I can make up for it."

He shrugged, then frowned as he stood and reached for a photograph on the wall, a yacht with billowing sails in an azure sea. He looked it over, tossed it into the trash bucket, and turned his eyes on me. "Don't ask."

I had the feeling Kravitz was risking legal trouble, but that there was a good chance now that either way he'd be "retired," perhaps without enough funds to sail into the sunset. "Leo?"

"Never mind." Kravitz typed fast for a minute, sat back and read, then clicked send. "There. I also took the article out, to place it on the front page with your byline."

"Thank—" I shook my head, choked up. "Thank you." I rubbed my hands together, hard, eyes watering. Relief flooded through me chased by excitement. I had a chance.

"Don't thank me too soon. If this doesn't work, I'm going to have to report the break-in to my house to pile onto your charges. I can't admit authorizing this, of course."

"Yes, yes, of course."

"And I removed Governor Leno from the article. First, you don't want to stir up more confusion when trying to make your case. Second, you lack the proof. Third, more opposition you don't need right now."

I shrugged. I nodded.

He typed away. "There. I emailed a message that I edited it personally so it doesn't get rerouted to the copy desk, to wring the life out of the story or red-flag it. Of course, I'll deny writing the email, too."

"Of course," I said.

"I told the layout editor to put it above the fold if he could. Okay, Underdog?" He smiled, closed-mouthed, arms folded. "Besides, this is as close to being the Green Hornet as I'll ever get."

I followed his eyes to a framed, autographed photo hanging on the wall, the Green Hornet—the daring vigilante and newspaper publisher character posing in front of his well-armed car, Black Beauty. In the driver's seat was his faithful valet, Kato—Bruce Lee—kung fu expert and driver of the sleek car. I'd trade my Harley for that car any day, especially today.

Today was live or die day.

\*\*\*

The Victorian house in the Savin Hill section of Dorchester was surrounded by large homes. Grasso's lot was larger. Being on a hill, the three-story house probably had a harbor view. A Cadillac Escalade stood behind the driveway gates. I strolled past, watching for Grasso through the few windows that weren't blinded.

When I left Kravitz's house, my full respect for him was realized. Although I had doubts before, the man proved himself tonight. The story was still the story, i.e., integrity before politics. Sure, he procured and protected sources, but he didn't let them control his journalistic mores; he just pushed the limit and led them on. His wife would have been proud.

I entered the gate, feeling shaky; no sign of his protection unit or security, but I wasn't surprised. His tough-guy ego was big enough to feel he'd scare trouble away. And he'd need privacy to carry on with his lovers, male or female—or both, I should say, as I'd painfully become aware in more ways than one.

I pressed the door bell, and it gonged. I put a note on the ground and ducked behind a bush.

After the assault in the locker room, Grasso had told his teammate to stuff me into the towel bin. I sobbed as he closed the lid and put weights on top of it. The darkness and diminishing air, that abuse; it made me freak out, and I passed out. I didn't come to until some kid opened the bin. I didn't know how much time passed, and I didn't know why the kid opened it.

I pushed the doorbell again and hid. I didn't favor guns, but at times they could prevent harm more than martial arts could. A gun would stop them from attacking you, but they'd be apt to say, "Yeah, right," if you warn that you're trained in karate. They'd seen the likes of Chris Tucker alongside Jackie Chan.

The door whipped open. I hadn't heard anyone approach. A footstep sounded outside, then the paper rustled. I peeked out; it was him. My heart beat madly. *Him*—after all the years, the trauma. My head seemed to tilt inside. He looked up from the paper, right at me.

"Well, I'll be damned," he said.

I stifled my nerves. "Yes, you will be."

# CHAPTER 40

## Sunday, 11:18 p.m.

"Well." Grasso spotted the revolver in my hand. "Nice of you to visit, Grantham. Won't you come in?"

He turned inside. I leapt out, gun leveled.

"Stop," I said. "Move slowly. Don't try anything that's going to end with holes in your body."

"Careful, Grantham. You might be the one with holes *filled* in your body."

My jaw fell. *I'll kill him.*

He laughed quietly. "Sorry about that. Where are my manners? Enter." He waved his hand for me to step through. "We're expecting company."

He was lying.

"You first," I said.

He entered, then moved back. I followed and kicked the door shut. His security detail was handy at the push of a button and routed to the closest police station, I bet.

"What kind of company are you expecting?" I said.

"The men in blue," he said. "Friends of yours that are anxious to see you. You've become quite popular recently."

"Thanks to you. And I suppose you invited them when you heard the doorbell. Or maybe the scary note on the ground made you push the remote hanging on your neck, like a sick old lady. I doubt it. Go sit down."

"Now you're playing host? How rude," he said. "Don't blame me for your troubles."

"What, like the scars of high school? I should fill your hole with this gun, except I think you'd like it."

"Still the poet? It was a long time ago, Dax. Get over it."

It took a moment to process. He meant it. That shouldn't be a surprise. "Tell me about it," I said. "What was a long time ago?"

Grasso eyed me. "I'm not saying anything."

"What, asking for your lawyer already?"

"Not that," he said. "Let me see you're not wired."

"Huh," I said. "You don't think I'd violate the wire-tapping law, now, do you? Sit." I pointed to the white leather sofa.

He sat, a safe ten yards away. I lifted my shirt, pant legs, and patted myself down, showing him no recording devices. "It's a good idea, except that isn't why I came here."

Worry crossed his face. I was here to kill him; why else would I show up?

"I don't know what to say," Grasso said. "Why are you here?"

I shrugged. "Where do I start? Violence? Dishonesty? Treachery? Criminality? Fraud? Adultery?"

"I didn't know it was you, Grantham. I didn't know Debra was your wife."

"*Is* my wife!"

"Okay, okay. *Is* your wife," he said, holding his palms out. "I just meant past tense, when it happened. That's over. And I didn't know you were…

His hand came up. "*Are* her husband."

"When did you find out?"

"I'm not sure. She didn't want to tell me, and I was okay with that. We weren't planning on anything, so didn't expect it to last. It seemed unimportant."

"It seemed unimportant? It's important now, isn't it?" One-armed, I raised the revolver to point at his head. "Stand up."

Fear seeped deep into his eyes and glowed there.

And it soothed my soul.

Grasso stood. "Of course, it's important. Later on, I had you investigated, reconnaissance. Found out you were adopted, went to high school in Braintree. I thought, I thought your name sounded familiar. It might have been around when I found out she was arrested."

"Not sooner?" I said.

"I don't think so. I remember thinking that I—"

I bobbed the gun at him. "What?"

"That I… I finally realized my fear. That we, ah, know each other from way back when."

"Know each other? If you're speaking in the biblical sense, I don't think people will understand."

"I know. And that's precisely the point. I'm a politician. It's easy to get destroyed in the press. And the incident in high school, it would do just that."

"I think you recognized who I was sooner. When Bradley hit on Debbie."

His face belied his shock, maybe from the fact that I knew about it, not the fact that it had happened. He dropped into his seat.

"It's a twisted world," I said, "isn't it?"

"Twisted?" He squinted. "What about you? Practically prancing around in your underwear like a little boy playing Superman."

"I suppose you'd like to see that."

"Oh, don't flatter yourself," he said. "Besides, you need a shave and fresh clothes."

"Bastard," I said softly. "I know you tried to derail me as the Dandy Vigilante. I had a negative influence on your perceived performance—as mayor, that is, right? Sensitive about your performance?"

His pissed-off expression evolved into a false smile. "I think you enjoyed it."

His performance or being the DV? Was he doubling my double-entendre?

"And I think you enjoyed it," I said, "sticking it in—"

He arched his eyebrows.

"—to Bradley; the knife."

"Fuck you," he shouted, standing from the couch.

I stepped closer, jutted my face, and jabbed the gun center mass. "No, fuck you, man. You got rid of Swanson. Dumped him for political ambition, that's all. Because of your run for governor."

His face was ashen.

"In fact, with Governor Leno's run for President and the D.A.'s run for mayor, it's all connected, and you didn't want anything loose in your little machine, did you?"

"That's it. You killed Cohoon, didn't you?"

The D.A. had given me that info. "Hell, no," I said. "He killed himself. He fell down."

"Sure, just like Bradley fell down."

I said softly, "And all the mayor's men couldn't put him back together again."

Grasso lowered his eyes.

"A knife, a letter opener, what's the difference?" I said. "It's all part of your sphere, if not your plan. Swanson knew too much. You had a spat. He threatened to disclose."

From Grasso's expression, I'd hit the spot. Mixed with admission was guilt, regret, sadness. He sat and leaned his face into his hands.

"He had the papers to prove it?" I said softly. "You fought over them?"

Grasso didn't respond. Police could be on the way. He was biding his time. I stepped into his line of view. "He didn't tell you what he did with them, did he?"

Grasso remained silent.

I said, "The deeds, the copies of the trust, the non-profit papers."

He looked up. Could he read my bluff, or was he thinking that only

Debbie would have that information? He could believe that she'd made copies. Some people habitually document, especially to retain power. *If only.*

"And the schedule of beneficiaries," I added.

Grasso cupped his face again. Grief or regret? Hiding or faking? Whatever it was, it didn't help me. He wasn't volunteering and wasn't falling for it.

Well, there was another way. "Give them to me."

"What?"

"Give them to me. The original papers. The corporate papers you have, with your name on them, and the schedule of beneficiaries connecting them."

"I don't know what in hell you're talking about." He attempted to look annoyed, but he was full of it.

"I'm going to count to ten. One..."

Savin Hill was isolated by water and the highway. Only one street at each end allowed egress. If I didn't get out of here fast, I'd be trapped.

Grasso shrugged.

I stepped toward him. "Ten," I said right away, trying to startle him.

His eye twitched, but he didn't move or say anything.

I aimed at his head again.

Nothing.

I pulled on the trigger. A little more. A little more and I'd be done with him.

Sweat beaded on his brow. Seemed he'd rather die or take his chances than give in to me and give up everything he had.

I released the pressure on the trigger and smiled. "I just wanted you to know how screwed you are," I said. "It's in all the papers tomorrow, except the *Boston Times*, which turned its back on me. Thanks to you, I suppose. Well, fuck with my career, and my wife, for that matter, and I fuck with your life."

I waited for a response, a reason to pump him for information or an excuse to pistol-whip him. He remained still, maybe lulling until he would lunge for me or an alarm. I should knock him out with the gun or tie him up. After a quarter minute, I turned and walked out, leaving the front door open.

As I passed through the gate, I heard him shout. "No!" Through the window, I saw him running. A klaxon alarm sounded.

Seemed his guilt expired or was trumped by survival instinct. I sprinted down the street, around the corner, and cut through a yard that I thought was my escape route. I turned down a side street toward Savin Hill Avenue. Blue lights already flashed here and there across house-tops, street poles, and foliage. Despite the revs of accelerating engines, I couldn't tell where they were going.

Running across a street near an intersection, I saw a cop car fly around the corner. It skidded. I ran into a back yard. I heard a car door slam shut. As I hopped a fence, my gun dropped—couldn't leave it. I hopped back, jammed it into my pants, and went back over. Sprinting away, I saw a cop round the corner of the house behind me.

A cop car accelerated, probably to cut me off. Others had to be on their way to Grasso's house and the surrounding area. I zigzagged around houses and shifted direction.

A few blocks down, winded from the sprint, I ducked behind a building with a fenced-in lot. This was it. From my backpack, I took a new disguise, one that should throw them off. I changed fast, secured the new wig, and checked myself over. I left and walked straight toward Dorchester Avenue, the main thoroughfare, catching my breath.

The taxi gods were with me. One approached. I flagged it down and got in. As it pulled away, I checked my phone; a text message from Debbie. "Box located on Big Blue!" That helped; only one hill to search. Wish I knew that when I'd sent the article to the newspaper, so any others looking could focus on that hill, too.

The old driver set his meter and eyed me in the rearview mirror. A police car approached. I heaved a sigh as it passed. The driver gave me a wink and a nod. It seemed odd, until I realized why.

The driver said, "Where to, Miss?"

# CHAPTER 41

# Monday, 10:37 a.m.

My body, sunk into the feather mattress. Sunbeams energized my damp skin, which tingled. The dreaminess faded as body aches surfaced. I felt rested and unconcerned with time like a boy on a summer morning, or maybe a man on vacation...

*Or a man in prison*—my eyes sprung open as I recalled everything. Grasso, the police, Debbie. I checked the time. *Late.* I threw off the comforter, leapt out of bed.

*The article.* What happened? Maybe they hadn't published it, but plastered my face all over the news to capture me. I couldn't fly out the door without a plan. My left knee and calf felt bludgeoned by Thor's hammer. I noted the claw-foot bathtub, deep and inviting.

Paul Grasso would try to preempt the story with his cronies by contacting newspapers and news stations, but in reality, he'd be helping me to, as Sinatra had sung, "start spreading the news," because I hadn't, in fact, contacted any other press as I'd said to him. I should have added to my article "I'm leaving today," as in leaving Massachusetts, to take the heat off me here.

*A Bed and Breakfast* was an inn near the Cambridge Rindge and Latin High School. I had registered under a false name and paid the owners, Doane and Karen, cash for two nights. Instead of setting the alarm clock, I'd opened the curtains on the east-facing window; stupid, but I'd been incredibly exhausted. The sun would've woken me hours ago, normally.

I stripped and examined the dark scrapes and bruises all over my body. They varied in size, shape, depth, and angle, like my body had been painted by a caveman on amphetamines. In the shower, I wondered if there was an article about a break-in at the mayor's house. Would Grasso claim an assault, a burglary, by a stranger or would he name me? Any statements would help me guess what he was thinking. I scrubbed hard and fast, painfully, with a soapy cloth, and then dressed.

Limping in the hallway, I saw my face in a mirror, dark, puffy circles under my eyes, and facial stubble that looked Rogaine-enhanced. I powered up my cell phone. Sixty-two missed calls and eighteen text messages from various friends, Debbie, unrecognizable numbers, Max, the *Boston*

*Times,* and Kravitz. A friend's text about the mayor and my article—so it *did* get published. *Hallelujah.*

My phone slipped. Trying to catch it, I knocked it against the wall. It fell apart. *Damn it, not now.* I pieced it together but kept it off. I used the room telephone to retrieve messages. Several friends expressed disbelief and support. Jimmy offered to help and requested an interview with laughable politeness. He said the mayor relocated his press conference to police headquarters, time to be determined. Debbie said to call her; Kravitz said the same, several times each. Other messages were news reporters I knew, some I didn't know, and hang-ups.

My friend Sunny on the BPD left a message, too. "I need to speak with you. Call me on my cell phone," she'd said, without identifying herself. She must have information.

I called. "Sunny, it's me."

"Hey, baby, you hanging in there?"

"Yeah, thanks." Our banter was gone. This was serious.

"Listen, a little blue bird tweeted. And it went like this. She got a text to meet him at 8:00 p m. at that address. That was definitely from his phone. But an hour earlier, he got a text to meet her at 7:00 p.m. for a surprise, but not to call. No number associated with the text, so maybe sent to him from a website, you know? It might not actually be from her. You get it?"

I thought about it. So it had to be a set up. Swanson must have been murdered before she got there, probably lured upstairs where it was dark. "Yeah. I think I do."

"And get this, his cell phone wasn't found on him, but it was found."

That was why Debbie couldn't reach Swanson or hear his cell phone ringing when she was waiting for him. She'd assumed that the phone was found on his body, but it wasn't. And I'd assumed that she got that assumption from her lawyer—I knew what they said about assumptions, but what could you say about making an assumption about an assumption?

I said, "Where?"

"You're gonna love this—at the A-1 police station. He'd left it behind at the meeting there. That would be watcha call unexpected."

Of course it was; otherwise, the murderer would've tried to destroy his phone to cover his or her tracks.

I gave Sunny my heartfelt thanks and limped downstairs, holding the rail. I passed through a living room where plaques and world artifacts were displayed. In the kitchen, no newspaper was in sight.

"There he is," Doane said. His silver-blond hair, too short for a pony-tail, stayed tucked behind the left ear. He was once a Peace Corps volunteer in the late sixties, which I'd gleaned from framed photos and documents in the hallway.

"So he's alive," Karen said, gleaming. She glided through the kitchen to the counter by the table. Green patterned China and cotton napkins matched the thriving potted plants. "Great. I'd hate to see these fresh muffins wasted on a goner."

"Good morning." I wondered about the "goner" comment.

"I'm sure you needed your rest," Doane said. "Take your time."

Karen was tall and subtly vibrant. She pointed out the coffee, eggs, and bacon under ceramic covers, and the condiments and fresh fruit. I dug into each and carried my plate to a table by the window overlooking a cherry tree. I got second helpings as they went about their business elsewhere. I tried not to think of this as a last meal before a life of prison food.

I brought a refreshed coffee mug outside. In the Japanese garden, I sat on a stone bench. Looming over me were old trees, spread by long experience with the sun. Their limbs won competitions below, so the trunk elevated them, their foliage blazing victoriously. Dogs barked in the distance. Sparrow chatter came from the arborvitae. Crows called out, lonely-like, though not alone; they flapped and called until repositioned, yards away. *Peaceful.*

I took out Cohoon's revolver and removed the bullets from the cylinder. I stepped over to a huge garden boulder, lifted it, and shoved the gun underneath; ashes to ashes, guns to rust. Despite the danger of entering the Blue Hills, I didn't want to be caught there with Cohoon's gun.

Beside the garage, I dropped the bullets into the garbage bin. I returned to the room and grabbed my stuff. At the front door, Karen and Doane stood from the stoop.

Doane said, "So, you're off?"

"Yeah," I said. "Going for a ride, do some exploring."

Karen nodded. "Yup. New territory, I'm sure."

I thanked them and made for the back yard.

"Good luck," he said.

I glanced back, wondering. "Thanks."

"We're behind you all the way."

It stopped me in my tracks. I scanned the area for police.

Karen waved the *Boston Times* at me. I went back and took it; on the front page, above the fold, my article.

"So you guys knew?" I said.

They grinned at each other. "Of course," they said, nodding at me.

"Recognized you last night, too, old man," Doane said. "Your face has been on our TV Your license photo and newspaper photo. The video images were grainy."

"Wow."

"It's been all over the news today," he said, "Stations breaking into scheduled programming with bulletins. It's just so different, so big. Thousands of people collected in front of TVs and radios listening, not just us."

"And not just local," Karen said. "CNN has a correspondent on it."

"Well. I guess it's all I'd hoped for. What are they saying?"

"Well, first of all," Doane said, "it's great you're doing something. Although we believe words are a form of action, and non-violence is the way to go. Sometimes it has to be this way to spur change."

"By any means necessary?" I said.

"Something like that." Doane said.

"But not quite," Karen said, checking a potted plant beside her. "By the way, Mayor Grasso denies your allegations and claims you're dangerous, mentally unstable, and all that jazz. A *mur*derer."

I shook my head. "I'm not, by the way."

They nodded affirmatively, Karen with a gentle blink that said she believed me. I was touched. I nodded and tipped an imaginary hat. Down the driveway, I straddled the bike. I had such a pleasant stay, but time to ramble on.

# CHAPTER 42

# Monday, 11:49 a.m.

After a nervous ride, I parked in the nook of a garage with the apparent grace of the God of Motorcycle Cloaking. Inside the South Shore Plaza, I opened a pre-paid cell phone account and forwarded calls to my new number.

In a public restroom, I shaved and, in a stall, changed into my new disguise again. I don't think anyone noticed a "woman" in white sneakers and mauve sweat suit exit the men's room. The suit was loose, and the auburn wig looked fitting. I took smaller steps and held one arm by my stomach and swung the other.

It had been a long time.

Walking by shoppers, I wondered at just how unaware they were of who passed them and what I was about to do. Exiting the mall, I passed a Braintree cop with a German Shepard Dog. My heart started pounding as if I were at the edge of a tall cliff with a short future ahead. The Shepard didn't seem to pick up on my fear. Then I tripped on my sneaker lace. The dog dodged and growled. The cop choked up on the leash. I wanted to squeal an "ooo" or something but feared my voice would croak.

"You okay, M—?"

He was going to say *Miss*, surely, but stopped because I looked like a Mrs. or perhaps a Mr.

I nodded and started to walk.

"Hold on," he said.

No way could I escape the dog or the cop's semiautomatic. I stopped. He came closer, bent down, and picked up a paper. "You dropped this."

"Thanks," I whispered, taking it.

His eyes widened. I didn't think it was my voice as much as proximity. Perhaps I missed a spot shaving. I froze. But then I smiled wide realizing there was only one good way out of this.

I winked at him, spun away, and, adding a feminine sway, hummed my way into a Veteran's Taxi. I handed the driver the paper with the address and nodded when he verified my destination and pulled away.

The driver turned on WBZ news radio: ". . . that Grantham has no evidence of this fantasy story he came up with and needs an evaluation before standing trial. The sooner he's caught, the Acting District Attorney stated, the safer he and the public will be."

Bad sign; the new D.A. sided with Grasso. The weather report began. The driver checked me in the rearview mirror. Did I look familiar or masculine? We ascended the long road of Chickataubut Hill into the wooded reservation. I hoped for a strong Labor Day presence of visitors to the reservation, particularly visitors who read my article. I opened the window and the warm wind flowed over my face. People rode bicycles and hiked paths. Sunlit leaves on the trees were scarlet, tan, and lemon, a picture-perfect New England day.

But a unique storm was coming.

I should have grabbed something to eat. I'd lost more weight and felt weak. I checked voicemail. Messages from Kravitz and friends said to watch out; everyone in eastern Massachusetts was looking for me. A message from Lieutenant Detective Reynolds said for us to meet and work it out.

A co-worker's voicemail mentioned Grasso's statement that he was staying at city hall to get city business done. Grasso denied any part of any real estate conspiracy, and he said people should stay out of Blue Hills to let police do their job.

A message from Jenna, an intern at my office, quoted Grasso, "There's no place for vigilantism." She ended with "Yada, yada, yada, it's not his jurisdiction anyway." I took that as a sign of support.

Yet I worried more than ever. They'd be looking for me, collectively and individually. *Shit.* If that Braintree cop or taxi driver realized who I was, they'd know my starting point and time. The public would keep their eyes wide for me as if for a burglar in an Easter Bunny suit, quirky but interesting, dangerous but maybe not to them. In fact, they'd actively seek me, a weekend treasure hunt on steroids—catch the Dandy Vigilante, catch the murderer, spot the crazed journalist, hit that clown, ring that bell!

*Oh shit, I'm losing it.*

My phone rang. I should shut it off, but I answered because it was Terry.

"Yo, good luck, dawg," he said.

"Thank you, Mr. T."

"Ha, bet you never expected to be where you are, did you? Neither did I, ya know."

"What do you mean?"

"My path changed big time once, starting with a counselor at a youth center when I was fifteen," he said. "Helped my self-esteem, trust of others. If it wasn't for that foundation, don't know where I'd be. Maybe six down, but not where I am now," he said. "So, just a word of support for you. Paying it forward."

I thanked him and shut off my phone. My thoughts settled. It was full circle. His success was exactly what Debbie was advocating by starting her version of a youth center. We weren't far apart on this issue after all. Minds were won more often with hearts than with fists, something martial arts taught me long ago, but a lesson I'd let dissipate. The prime problem wasn't crime; it was whatever created criminals. "An ounce of prevention is worth a pound of cure;" so true, so basic. I was startled at my emotion-driven ignorance of late.

At the top of Chickataubut Hill, the taxi slowed. I'd never seen so many people here. I hoped they'd concentrate on searching for the documents, not me. Half-dozen print, TV and radio reporters, and a couple of network affiliates were in the parking spaces, using the distant Boston skyline as a backdrop. A helicopter swooped in from the north, over the taxi. Policemen cordoned off the path leading to the viewing tower, but people entered the woods from other points.

I caught the driver's look in the mirror again. Was he going to ask me for a date or report me to the police? A mile farther, the Houghton's Pond lot was jammed. Cars were parking alongside the road. A news van sped in the other direction. We turned right on Route 138, but traffic was backed up.

"Almost there."

"Here's fine," I blurted.

I paid and hopped out. A few minutes walking brought me to the ski hill, a grassy, open section of Big Blue. Nothing else accounted for this many people here. Ascending, I watched for cops.

Then my heart filled with pride. Passing Chickataubut Hill, I'd noticed individuals with cell phones or cameras taking photos and videos, and now many on Big Blue had their various cameras out. They wielded them in their First Amendment freedom, freely expressing and even participating in the press upon the invitation of a particular, and peculiar, Boston journalist.

I turned on my phone, and it rang immediately—Jimmy.

"Make it quick," I said.

"Dax. Did you get my messages? Around 1,500 people descended upon Blue Hills. The TV and cable stations picked it up. Dude, you've got to give me an interview. I mean, an exclusive. You can even edit. I mean, you can't write it, right? You need a third-person perspective, independent view. Dax? Dax, hello?"

"Okay, Jimmy. You and Oprah, a joint exclusive in my jail cell." Assuming some cop in Grasso's pocket didn't kill me. "Now, do you have anything to help me?"

"What can I do?" he said.

"Tell me what's going on."

"You've set off a tsunami, that's what." He laughed, giddy. "Sorry. Anyway, thousands of eyes scour the hills as we speak. I'm by the Chickataubut tower. Where are you? People are probing with sticks and metal detectors, even groups like softball teams, college students, high schools; I don't know, whatever. So many human-interest stories there, too, it's like a feeding frenzy for the press. Even a few Boy Scouts. Some think this thing is a promotional activity, like a hoax or scavenger hunt. I mean, it's freaking wild, man."

A slight Vietnamese accent emerged for the first time that I'd noticed. Jimmy had never been this close to a major news story. This was also the closest I'd been to a story this big, too, but I *was* the story. Well, the mayor and dead officials were, too.

"I hope they find something," I said. "Interview lots of people over there. Get their views published."

"The mayor's calling in favors to reign in the press and suppress this groundswell of people."

"But he can't shut this down. This isn't like the manhunt after the Boston Bombing."

Grasso would try to isolate me then hunt me down. "Yeah, but the cat's out of the bag and all that. Report whatever you want on that, but it doesn't do anyone any good, especially me, if we can't find that evidence. And let me tell you something, he mur—"

Jimmy paused for me to continue. "What? What? Murdered? Murdered who?"

What the hell. Jimmy would do the story right. And he'd helped. "Swanson. He murdered Swanson."

"The mayor? *The mayor?* How do you know that? Can I quote you on that? Wow, I've got to get out of print and get this story onto the radio or TV news."

"Calm down," I said sharply, though I smiled, imagining him tugging his hair into black spikes. "I'll tell you when you can quote me, and I'll tell you how I know that, if you can help me find that jar in that metal box. Deal?"

"I'll do everything I can, Dax, anything, so—"

"I know you will." I hung up.

I continued up the steep ski run with small, sideways steps, and the pain in my calf and knee excruciating now. At the top, I took a path to the tower at the peak of Great Blue Hill, 635 feet high. The tower was a good landmark to bury something near. I didn't have the benefit of metal detectors, like some. If something was found, I wanted first crack at checking it out. I'd flash my *Boston Times* ID and hope they wouldn't notice it was a man in the photo and that I was in drag.

Before leaving the clearing, I turned my face to the sky and sent out a mental, spiritual signal requesting help, while trying to accept whatever was to be.

In the woods, clusters of colored clothing drifted here and there, people on foot. One group, spread in a line, poked leaves with their feet or sticks. My heart dropped at the sight of one person at the end, in blue—a cop, watching. There were probably plain-clothed cops, too. I considered slipping in near others.

Debbie texted that she had a definite clue. At the South Shore Plaza, I'd forwarded my cell phone calls to this pre-paid phone, but hadn't realized that texts could be forwarded to, which worried me. With all this technology, could they track me down to this new phone? I called despite the risk, which would be even greater if she was deceiving me or cooperating with the police.

"The documents," she said breathlessly, "they must be at or near Patriot Printers. I checked my caller ID from when he called. It's supposedly a family-connected business. I remember he used it for election printing. Placards, signs, stickers. It's in Milton right on the edge of Blue Hills. Not on Big Blue, but down from it."

"Wow. Great." From ridiculously impossible, it was now a mere impossible.

"Look, it's a hunch, but he didn't say bury the documents. He said 'sink' them where no one would find them, something like that. 'Dunk them' maybe? It was weird."

The sun had passed its peak. I scanned the area. "So, a swamp or stream or something?"

"I guess so. You can dunk or sink things in any liquid, but other than bodies of water, nothing comes to mind. Sand? Just think about it. I'll let you know if I think of anything else."

"Thanks, Deb." I considered other questions and their answers, unrelated to finding evidence.

"So what are you going to do?" she said.

Good question. "Where are you?"

"At home. I've been watching the news. My sister is coming to visit. Do you know what you've started? You'd better be right about him, Dax. Because if you can't prove it... My God."

"I know. There goes my life," I said, "or whatever's left of it."

"Good luck, hon," she said. "Tell me if I can do anything else."

"I will, Debbie." I scratched my head. "Did you talk to him?"

"What? Ah, yes."

Her hesitancy set off a surge of panic, and my breath caught. She could be setting me up—Grasso kills the documents; the cops kill me. I hung up.

Then her help felt like she was making up for what she'd done, but perhaps that was a mind trick not even she could fully accomplish. I was grasping at straws.

Swamp; maybe he'd sunk the jar of papers in a swampy area. On my cell, I voice-searched "Patriot Printers" and selected the GPS map. I limped onward. Maybe Grasso would host me one last time.

# CHAPTER 43

# Monday, 1:33 p.m.

A crag loomed ahead. I scanned the terrain for the best way around, then checked my phone GPS. Not by road; I'd encounter police and, equally dangerous, news vans. I went as the crow flies—or as the GPS arrow pointed. My wig slipped and I repositioned it. After passing the crag, I entered a stand of trees on a southern slope. The sun barely penetrated the thickly scented pine.

*Debbie.* I yearned for her. But did I really trust that she was doing a good deed here? Between the dark and the light, an angel who was a little both, and she was more angel than I. I had to find the printing company. Maybe it was blind faith; if not faith in her present honesty, then faith in me.

It was my only choice in any case. I spotted the Skyline Trail. Minutes later I couldn't believe what was on it—a dozen pink-faced and tan-faced cheerleaders, chattering, moving up a path. Several glanced over and one waved, so I waved back. Some had blue marker on their forehead or arms. "Facts for Dax" and "Go Dax". I felt like a star at the freak show. I hoped they'd actually scour the ground and find something. It was no picnic for me, whatever others searching the woods felt, the pressure was all mine.

At about fifty yards, they appeared to be high school age. As they leaned into the hill and climbed, from the rear, the white underlining of their skirts penetrated the gloom like the patterns of so many woodland doe. Attractive girls, but they didn't want to attract unwanted or insincere attention. The first time this hit me about young women, I was dressed as one doing the article for my high school newspaper. I'd felt harassed. Now it felt like I'd attracted the whole state to oppress me.

The printing company was at the edge of Milton between Route 138 in Canton and Route 28 in Randolph. I'd try to avoid all people, supportive cheerleaders and non-cheerleaders alike. One slipped wig at the wrong moment and I'd end up in the wrong place—behind bars. Besides, I should keep a close eye out for water while nearing the company, about two miles northeast. A jar could also be sunk in sand, so I'd watch for it, too.

I continued off path. My cell phone vibrated. *Kravitz*. I answered.

"Don't worry," he said, "I'm not dead."

I said, "Why would I think that?"

"Because that's the line Grasso is feeding off-record to journalists to put the pressure on you. I'm at my cottage down the Cape. I left to avoid the chaos. This will have repercussions for years. The media are all over this, and national media, too, and all over the Internet news, all sorts of sites. They'll be interviewing you for a long time, that's a fact."

"Sure, from prison."

"Just stay alive. Other people or other evidence will come forward. Well, that's what I hope for you. Another thing, city councilor Groves is publicly suggesting an investigation into you but also into your allegations."

"Let's hope they do it."

"But Groves won't support you unless you're seen as Mr. Clean real soon. The police countered that the investigations are active. Maybe they are." He paused. "Look, Dax, it's a long shot, but I didn't do this on a lark. I think there's something to it. It's damaging to Grasso, but it's not necessarily going to put him behind bars or prevent you from being put there. Find those documents and whatever else you need. If you can't tie him into the corruption you've written about—"

"Aye aye, captain." My heart plunged. It was even more of a long shot than he knew. I took a deep breath. The sweet-scented woods here were a stark contrast with my reality.

"Last thing. You know Grasso has friends and contacts galore. He's got the mounted state police looking for you. Park Rangers, too. Good luck."

After descending a couple of hundred feet, I arrived at an area of sharp decline, exhausted and hurting. I kept an eye out for timber rattlesnakes. I checked the terrain map I'd printed, so I didn't walk down just to walk up again. I must be at Wildcat Notch. I could veer east to cut across Hemenway Hill, but a lone man was hiking there. Instead, I'd stay north of it and skirt Breakneck Ledge. The Massachusett, "people of the great hills," were the natives; seemed none of these hills were named for them, though.

I might see Grasso within the hour, either because Debbie had set me up, or she'd let slip, somehow, that I would be going after the papers. Perhaps because, as planned, I had spooked him at his house by demanding the incriminating papers, which he could've received from Debbie, Swanson, Cohoon, or all the above. "Beyond treachery or subpoena," he'd said to Debbie. He probably also thought "beyond search warrant." I was betting that he'd destroy or—more likely, given his controlling nature-

-hide the documents today in these hills or at the printing company. I bet my life on it, which was, in fact, all I really had left.

It took a half-hour for Breakneck Ledge to be on my right. I passed the ledge and descended a quick hundred feet or so. It was cloudy and cooler, but I was hot, and unzipped my sweatshirt, showing a flatter, broader chest. I'd zip up if I came across anyone. Loose sweatpants were more gender neutral, at least.

After a while, I adjusted east to keep a hill and several border residences on my left. On my right was Unquity Road. I listened for traffic. By way of a downed tree, I crossed a winding brook, looking up and down for signs of a hidden box or jar or a disturbance in the water or the bank. I moved on.

After a quarter mile, paths diverged around a cascade of small hills. The sun was getting lower. A turkey vulture wheeled above. I was in and out of shadow. The woods were thick, but I was closer. I followed the sound of cars until spotting a building, and then a second building. The sign on the smaller one: *Patriot Press*.

A state police car turned on its lights and sped toward the short access road to the building. After it passed, the wave of fear inside subsided. The buildings appeared deserted. They were the only structures around, and me the only human, so far. The printer building was nearer the woods. Behind it, two sections of wooden fence cordoned off a storage area.

Why would Grasso put the papers here? Why not inside his home where he could exercise more control, like in a secret safe, if he had one?

I entered the cordoned off storage area and walked up and down a line of plastic buckets stacked two or three high.

Because he was scared, that was why. Because I had pieced together so much on him, provided I could get the evidence. He wanted it all beyond the scope of a search warrant, beyond reach of any kind—except his own.

I looked at the back door within the fenced-in storage area. Nothing here. Nothing but buckets.

*Wait, buckets can hold fluids.*

Slower, I walked down the line along the wooden fence again. I had to find it. I had to. I was exhausted, weaker, injured, dehydrated—spent, emotionally and physically. If only...

I spotted a blotch of ink against the wall, shiny. Recent? I pulled the five-gallon commercial buckets to the front, trying to minimize the scraping sounds. One in the back was blue and partially wet. *Yes.* I had a dream, reasonable doubt—it might become real.

Grasso must have been here within the hour. No cars were in the marked parking spots that I'd seen, but he could return. *Damn*. He could be parked on the other side of the building right now. I whipped out the bucket and pried at the hard plastic tabs on the lid. It hurt my fingers, but I focused and jerked up with all my strength. Several tabs flew up with a sharp sound. Then I popped up one at a time. The cover came off.

The bucket was up to the rim in dark-blue ink, impervious to light. From a pallet, I pried off a two-foot piece of pine and used it to fish, spilling ink. I was more likely to find an octopus than the evidence I needed, but this was the only game in town.

I hit something, tried lower, and then caught the object. I lifted, holding it against the side, and it slowly rose. A container—*a glass jar.* A rag sticking out from under the pallet I grabbed to hold the jar, which dripped as I set it on the ground.

A noise inside; I strained to listen while the slick ink slid down. I wiped down the jar with the rag and then tried to open it. It was too slippery. I held the rag-covered jar between my feet and used my index fingers and thumbs to unscrew the top. After several tries, it opened. Folded papers were curved inside the jar. I wiped the ink from my hands onto my socks, then on the inside leg of my sweatpants.

Then I froze—a door clicked; a metal door ten feet away. Being locked or unlocked?

I screwed the lid onto the jar. *I hadn't brought the gun.* The mandatory sentence for possession didn't fucking matter now, did it? And you had to be alive to face life in prison.

To my horror, the brown door opened farther, slowly. I took a few steps to escape through the gap between the door and the storage enclosure, but had to freeze as a man came out, a big man.

I crouched. He was looking the other way, but he turned around, and I saw the gun—and the face of my enemy. He leered as his arm rose.

# CHAPTER 44

## Sunday, 3:16 p.m.

Grasso held the handgun straight out. He lined up its sights on me. I tossed the glass jar into the air, toward him. His eyes followed as he leaned back and reached up to catch it.

I charged and dove at him. The gun exploded.

The jar landed on his lap. I pushed him onto his gun-arm side, snatched the jar, and sprinted around the storage-area fence.

Two gunshots splintered fence pickets beside my shoulder. I ran for the woods at an angle, clutching the jar. Then I dodged among the trees like a fucking ADHD gazelle on coke. Fifty yards in, I peeked back. It was dark in here, overcast, late afternoon. He might be looking for the jar and documents, which I had, or adding bullets before hunting me down. My leg throbbed. Then I noticed my shirtsleeve was wet. It wasn't blue. It was red.

My arm was bleeding. Blood dotted the ground. I took off my sweat jacket and used my T-shirt to wipe my arm. The bullet had grazed me, leaving a divot three inches long in my upper arm's flesh. Half a hole was better than a whole one, but it hurt. I tore a strip from my T-shirt and wrapped my arm as I kept watch then put the sweat jacket on over it.

Heading deeper into the woods, I relived that first gunshot. I'd thrown the jar at Grasso, but he didn't know what else to do. Luckily, I'd made it to within two steps of him before he noticed my charge. My ears were still ringing. *I almost died, again.*

I wasn't ready for a trip downtown, whether to jail or to the morgue. Lost in the woods with Grasso on my tail was something to avoid. If I saw a cop, I could surrender with the documents and take my chances, especially if Grasso had me cornered. Could I trust the cops? Grasso could own some. I could hide or skirt around him to a main road to get a taxi or steal a car.

The State Police barracks were south on Unquity Road. Canton Avenue was closer. Yet those streets weren't my best bets precisely because they should be; Grasso would try to find me along there, maybe using his car. And he might have help.

Keeping low, I ran, hobbled, and walked. The longer I didn't appear the farther Grasso's net would have to stretch. The problem was that my limbs were sending amps of pain signals to my brain. I stopped and tried to stretch and massage my leg muscles and ligaments, but the shooting pains made my eyes water.

Several hundred yards farther into the woods, I stopped at the top of a small hill, a good distance from which to decide whether to run deeper or run for the road. I heard something…barking? Not too close. I couldn't tell the direction. Didn't sound like a German Sheppard, as in police dog; after a minute, I caught a glimpse of a small dog.

Then came Grasso, stepping carefully, watching his dog—no, two dogs. They were moving quicker than me. A three-foot diameter conduit ran up a slope behind me. The open end by me was a few feet off the ground. It led to a small factory that appeared abandoned last century. I couldn't outrun him and his dogs, not with my injuries.

I ran as best I could in a fifty yard loop around trees, then down a little path to an open dirt area, hoping to confuse the dogs. I rubbed my palms on several rocks and tossed them at a right angle to my travel at increasing distances, leaving a false scent-trail. I checked the conduit. If I crawled in head-first, I might see to avoid snakes, rats, or raccoons.

I hated confined spaces.

I tucked in my shirt to put the glass jar down the front, freeing my hands, despite a long crack in the jar. I put it inside my shirt anyway. Holding a fist-sized rock, I crawled into the cement conduit. At twenty yards, I regretted not backing in. And if a dog got inside, I'd have to fight it off. They were Terriers, but they could be vicious.

Thirty yards in, the damp smell hit me, making me more claustrophobic. My body blocked the light from the opening behind me. I paused, but forced myself to keep going.

At forty yards down the pipe, I choked down a sob. Then I checked my pocket. *Yes*. Vigilantism did pay. I pulled out the lighter the shopkeeper had given me and lit it.

But now I could see how confined I was, and the conduit split into two smaller branches. I could fit in either, barely. I was feeling seriously claustrophobic already, nauseous and shaky. *Visualize an open field*, Debbie would say.

I put the lighter into my pocket to try backing in. Crunching to bend my spine, I started to turn, but got my head and back jammed opposite my bent legs, which couldn't pass to make the turn around. The jar pressured my stomach.

My wig slid off. My compressed chest made it hard to breathe, so I tried harder, but it hurt and released a torrent of panic. If the glass jar broke, it'd puncture my stomach. *Focus*. I got my left leg passed to the split, but it didn't free me. Corroded conduit scraped my scalp. I let go the rock and tamped down the panic, marginally. My leg dangled, trembling, down the smaller conduit. I tugged the wig.

*Maybe it was a ruse, nothing incriminating in the ink-covered jar.*

I heard an animal in the conduit, coming toward me—*oh no.* A rat I could handle, but it didn't sound small. Even if I weren't stuck, a dog would be hard to deal with on elbows and knees. Grasso would be close behind.

Pushing harder at an angle with my shoulder hurt my head and neck, but then my shoulder slid past. It tore my sweat jacket, but I was able to bend my body to finish the turn around. *Thank God.*

I faced the opening, a small circle of dim light obscured by a swaying silhouette, the animal. If it couldn't see me, it could hear me or smell my blood. I spit down one smaller conduit and wiggled back into the other. The animal, shrouding the last of the light, growled.

Ten feet. That was it—my limit. I wanted to get out so badly. It was so completely dark; I was dying inside, sensing earth all around me, pushing in, pushing down ready to crush me. I couldn't breathe. The conduit was really shrinking.

The Terrier sniffed the intersection. I held my breath—*good doggy, good doggy.* It went down the other conduit. Bred to dig out animals from underground, it was a matter of seconds before it came for me. I counted five, then pushed with my elbows and wiggled to the larger conduit and speed-crawled toward the light. The dog's claws scratched as it scurried toward me from the dark, growling devilishly. *Teeth—gun—wife—career—prison—death.* A moan escaped, and I began to hyperventilate, crawling away.

A snarling lunge at my face—*the other Terrier.*

"Ahhhg." I raised my arm.

It snapped close to my face, and I swung to keep it back. It kept coming, barking, snapping. I screamed at it. The one behind bit into my bad calf, and I howled. It shook my leg and I cried out, the pain shocking.

I snapped my head to look back and kicked the dog off, then moved backward to kick again, but the front dog nipped at my cheek. My kick missed the dog behind. Their growls and barks were deafening. The front one passed my punch to nip at my forehead and darted back.

I moved back and kicked but the dog bit my leg again and wouldn't let go. The glass jar dug into my stomach. Sweat or blood came over my left brow. The front dog bit into my left hand and tugged. I yanked, but it held on and got near my neck. I screamed and pushed it.

At each end, they were ripping me apart.

I pulled in my left hand and smashed my right fist down. It released me. Crawling fast, I shoved it, and the Terrier backed up, but I wouldn't stop. It barked and feigned attack, but I wouldn't stop. The Terrier behind bit at my legs and feet, so I pulled them up for an instant, counting on another lunge, then kicked. *Got it!* The dog yelped and I crawled forward rapidly. *Almost there.*

The front dog's rear feet slid off the conduit's end. I shoved it off. I pulled out the glass jar and left it behind as I slid my torso free and bent at the waist. My head dangled near the ground. The Terrier hobbled toward my face, snarling.

"Heel!"

I tried to see who commanded the dog. But in my adrenalin-drenched heart, I already knew.

# CHAPTER 45

## Sunday, 3:59 p.m.

From tree shadow, Paul Grasso stepped forward, smiling. "Hey, tunnel rat. Like my Terriers, Jack and Russell?"

My arms shook, my chest heaved. "Fucking dogs are great," I said, falling out.

Grasso aimed his pistol at me while making a call on his cell phone. "All set," he said, then pocketed his phone.

"I see you kept in good shape," he said. "That's good." He chuckled.

"Screw you." I stood.

"Really?" he said.

Grasso stuck the pistol into his waistband, but kept it outside his sweatshirt. He stepped back as if to give me a sporting chance against a quick draw, or to validate a self-defense excuse. "Despite what you might think," he said, "you're not my type."

The Terrier charged, but then backed off.

Grasso put his finger to his lips. "Shhhh. I know his wig is loose." He gazed at me, smirking. "Long time no see, eh? Wow, what a splendid outfit. I can't believe you're back to your old tricks."

I whipped off the wig and glared. "So much for remorse."

"Well, anyway, Dax, as they say, 'You don't get to choose how you're going to die. Or when.' Isn't that right?"

I nodded slowly, trying to figure out what to do. "Did Debbie know?"

His eyes got a cautious look. "About what?"

I dusted off my hands. "Couldn't keep them both, could you? So you killed Bradley." Swanson's first name, emotionally provocative, perhaps a stepping-stone to information or time.

After a moment, he looked at the ground. "No, maybe I couldn't. In theory, it could have been utopia, Brad and I. And Debbie." He sighed, and I couldn't tell if he was sincere. "But reality is different."

I shifted my head side to side, weighing his response. "Like the stereotypical saying about having two wives, I suppose. So you killed him."

He raised his head. "No. *You* killed him, for the record. And me? I'll act in self-defense."

"How'd you do it?"

Grasso looked at me askew. "Don't you know curiosity killed the cat?"

I eyed the woods and the pistol. It looked like a .45 caliber. "Seems like it might be kinda redundant now, don't you think?"

He shrugged. "So inquiring minds want to know, huh?" He nodded. "Okay. I used an unmarked city vehicle, tinted glass. One's kept at my disposal. No one would check the log. So right now, your 'news article' is simply from a raving fugitive who killed Swanson."

"But why did you set up Debbie? I don't understand that, Paul."

"Huh, yeah. Well." He tapped his foot. "Look, let me make it easy for you; numbers."

"What do you mean?"

"Numbers," he said. "I kill many birds with one stone—too hard to resist. Bradley is gone. He knew too much, *and* he threatened me—an unhealthy combination, it turns out." Grasso shook his head. "After all I did for him. Then he developed a thing for Debra."

"Sure. But nothing happened between them."

"Is that so?"

"Yes." Let guilt seep in. "I know for a fact."

"Well." He looked away, then down at the ground. "That's something."

"Debra left me, too," I added. "For you."

Then it hit me that she'd left Grasso, again, and that she'd come back to me, again.

"Anyway," he said, "setting her up forced me to detach from her. Having her would only guarantee you'd eventually know of the affair."

I nodded.

"You'd be likely to allege adultery. More likely allege the incident with you in high school. I avoid all that now, don't I? I don't know how many birds per stone that is, actually, and there's more. It preempts your corruption allegations in case you discovered my role. And I live to tell about it."

I said, "The best defense—"

"Is a good offense. It's true," he said. "I explained that I'm only friends with Debbie, which is believable. I openly came to her defense."

"So it all fits together," I said.

"All but one last piece," he said.

I nodded, reluctant to get to the inevitable.

He pulled the pistol from his waistband and held it by his leg. "I'd prefer it if you jump off that cliff, but do you want to choose?"

I followed his line of sight to a deep gap between trees. He knew this area. I nodded.

"So it's the cliff? That should do it, and if not, I'll come down and give you a break. What are friends for? After all, you gave me back Debbie, even if that was temporary."

"Are you taunting me or do you mean it, that you don't even want her?" I couldn't hit him from here. "After everything."

"Well, I didn't say that." He circled me to the conduit and whistled. The dog inside whimpered. "He'd better be all right or I'm gonna shoot your damn knees and stomach and give them the final go at you."

"Hey, I like dogs, too," I said. "I only kicked him. What the hell did you expect?"

Grasso held his palms up. "Sure. It's only business. Which reminds me, give me the documents."

I leaned over to wipe the blood off my face with my shirt and caught my breath. Every time I moved my swollen knee, it seared my nerves.

Grasso bent to pat the dog and peeked inside the conduit. I calculated the rush to the gun and moved toward him, but he turned back to me.

"Thought you'd have run at me by now. Too late. Now give me the documents." He tapped the pistol against his thigh.

There must be incriminating information in them, or he worried that he hadn't wiped all his prints off the jar. "Okay."

He stood and bobbed the gun at me. "Move it."

I held up my finger and hobbled toward him. He moved away. I leaned into the conduit. He moved behind me. I walked my hands in, feet still on the ground. The dog inside growled. I stretched to the jar, wincing, and retrieved it.

Grasso backed up and grinned eerily as I placed it on the ground between us. Papers showed through the ink-smeared glass.

"Step away," he said.

I did.

Grasso knelt to open the lid, which was still slippery, but he managed. He put the jar down and took out the documents. He checked them before replacing them into the jar. He stepped back. I had the feeling this was terminal distance. He might just shoot me right here. He wasn't going to give me any chances now that he had everything lined up.

*Could I have done anything differently?* I stepped closer.

He stood. "So the cliff?

"Well, definitely not the gun," I said. "I wouldn't want the other people to hear you shoot me."

He pointed the steel barrel at my head. "Don't be a wise ass! Just 'cause someone might hear it doesn't mean you're rescued. I'll shoot you first and come up with a decent excuse after. I'm the mayor and you're a God-dammed psycho; that's front page news. If I'd even have to do that. Because I could have an alibi—your wife. If you're gone, she'll back me because I'll deny it to her. And, you have to admit this is poetic, it might save her from legal trouble, too."

"Grasso—"

"Hey, I know," he said breathlessly, "my dog can chase you off the cliff, and I can rename him Clifford in your honor. Get it? Cliff for short?" He tilted back with laughter, then checked around; not another soul in sight. He peeked into the conduit again and whistled again.

I examined the ground, gauging the traction. "Well."

All amusement drained from his face. "So. I got what I needed from Debbie, she'll get what she needs, I guess. And you? Which will it be? Cliff or dogs? Last chance to decide."

"You know, Paul. What you said, 'You don't get to choose how you're going to die. Or when.'"

"Yeah?"

"It's a quote from Joan Baez," I said softly.

"Hey, that's right. You would know that. She's one of Debbie's favorite singers."

I edged sideways toward him as I folded my arms and looked off through the branches. "You didn't finish the quote."

"No? What is it?"

I dropped my arms and gazed at him. I was tired.

"Well?" he said.

"It ends with this. 'You can only decide how you're going to live'."

"Those are your last words?" he said.

"No, but it reminds me, one last request." I looked him dead in the eyes, peripherally lining up the jar, less like karate, more like soccer. I only had one chance only, I knew.

To cover my slight bend forward, I coughed, eyes lowered. I kept the target in my mental-physical scope.

"What is it?"

"Eat shit." I half-stepped fast and punted the glass jar toward him. Leg pain flared through my body, and I saw white light as I collapsed.

# CHAPTER 46

# Sunday, 4:11

Grasso ducked and raised his hand—too late; the jar smashed into his nose and shattered. I forced myself to stand. He clawed at the glass before the larger shards fell away. He raised his arm.

I was staring down the barrel's black hole. I dove right, blasted with sound, maybe a bullet. I somersaulted and came up facing him, but collapsed again with knee pain, unable to suppress a grunt. A Terrier barked.

Slivers of glass were in Grasso's face. He growled and waved the gun as he squinted hard, trying to brush them out with his other hand. He pulled at his face frantically, cutting more. He crouched, screeching in agony, and staggered backward.

My leg was bleeding. I was shot there, too. If the femoral artery, I'd be dizzy soon. *Now or never, run or get the gun.* Then I saw it; it wasn't merely his face—the glass was in his eyes. Pieces had cut deeper during his pain and panic.

I picked up a thick stick, threw it to his right. He spun and fired there. I charged, but hobbled with an involuntary grunt that warned him. He turned his gun on me. My left hand grabbed the gun, but his arm and grip were strong—stronger than mine.

He pulled it away, turned toward me, and fired.

Shifting right, I grabbed his wrist, but he raised the gun over his head. We staggered backward, but he wouldn't go down or let go of the gun. I tried sweeping his leg, but he was too heavy; not enough leverage at this angle, and I couldn't shift without risking another knee collapse. He had to catch his balance, though, and I smashed my right palm into his chin, knocking his head back. He kept staggering.

A Terrier chomped into my bloody leg and hung on. Grasso elbowed me, cracking my ribs, knocking air from my lungs. I kept pushing my chest against his to keep him off balance. The Terrier fell off.

I jerked Grasso's wrist down behind his back. He spun little, but fell onto his back. Using all my strength, I yanked, rolled him onto his stomach. I knelt, got his wrist to my hip, and wedged his shoulder into the ground, arm straight. With my weight and torso power, I smashed my forearm onto the back of his elbow.

I heard it crack. He roared.

I did it again, and his arm bent to an unnatural angle. The gun fell.

I picked it up and staggered away. The Terrier snarled as it ran at me and made a flying leap. I slapped underhand at its torso, mid-air, and it cart-wheeled onward. It landed in a furry heap, rolled, and spun to growl.

Grasso sat up and held his bent arm. Small pieces of glass were still in his face. The larger ones caused the most damage. He shook his head and grunted in pain. His lids were cut. His eyeballs were sliced and bloody, one looking smaller already. It all happened so fast. Fluid globs and blood streaks reached his chest. Well. That was three eyeballs damaged in two days, counting Cohoon's.

"Looks like you won't be seeing me again," I said, catching my breath. "Get it? Looks, see?" I should have felt bad. But I didn't. I liked people, and I liked dogs, but this was personal.

"Goddamn," he said, breathing heavily, grimacing. "Goddamn." He moaned. He looked sick. The documents were on the ground behind him. "I'm fucking broken up."

After a long moment, he inhaled deeply and held it in. His exhale broke out, and he groaned, which turned into a growl. It seemed to control his pain, and he stood, unsteady. He winced as he dangled his bent arm. "Congratulations," he said and coughed. "Looks like you won, Dax. Congratulations."

I reached for the documents, impressed that he seemed to regain his composure. "Thank you."

Grasso lunged at the direction of my voice, a primal shout coming from him. "Arrghh!"

His good arm came at my neck. I ducked. It slid off my head, and he thudded to the ground.

He sat up, wincing, and hung his head low. "Shit."

"I could have shot you," I said.

"You'd miss, asshole." He growled in pain and shouted, "You're fucking lucky, Grantham, that's all, fucking lucky! I can't believe this!"

Eyes on him, I moved back and clamped the loose papers between fallen leaves to avoid leaving my prints over his.

Grasso heaved a sigh. "Dax," he said after a moment. "Look." Breathing heavily, the pain seemed to be getting to him. "Look, your joke about seeing. After my joke at you about going off the cliff. I get it. Well, seriously."

"What?"

"Give me a choice, too."

"What choice?" I said.

"Gunshot or cliff. I'm not fucking going to jail, especially blind.

That's for damn sure."

"What?" I considered his request and the ramifications of granting it. "I don't know."

"Dax? Let me make this easier. If I go to prison, so will Debbie."

Wow. He could have evidence, like other documents, other witnesses, or something. Hell, his own testimony. If I chose to let Grasso live, there'd be the risk that he'd take Debbie down with him.

"Why should I care?" I said.

But I believed that I did care. It had all come down to this, after all these years; everything that had happened in the last year, and in recent weeks. I sensed abandonment, mortality, anguish. That was what my gut said, but what did it mean? So many conflicting facts, conflicting feelings, tossed in the air.

"You know, you have no idea what you've stumbled upon," he said, sounding strange, amused.

I didn't reply.

"It's deeper than you'd ever imagine." He sounded matter of fact, which made me curious. Was he trying to distract me?

What was important? My dreams, like family? My brother Tommy popped into my mind. I felt guilty even though there was nothing I could've done. In a sense, my brother didn't leave me; I left my brother. I was younger, easier to place, the first to get adopted. The guy who took Tommy looked like a wrestler, with a thick neck and muscles, but he'd supposedly adopted him. I could tell Tommy was scared of him, too. A lady holding papers was with that man; his wife, I hoped, although she looked cold, too. I think she had an accent, but I wasn't sure if my memory was faulty or fantastic.

"Dax?" he said from the ground. "Come on. You there?"

"I'm thinking."

Tommy had been in trouble often. The last thing was stealing a school bus. The juvenile court judge was displeased to see him again, although Tommy had told me they'd baked him a cake; not true, I was sure even then. He had the capacity to be a joker or a wise ass, but in a likeable way. I always wondered why the school bus? His way of taking control of the world that hurt him?

Then there was Debra; my Debbie. Reluctantly, I searched back and saw a time when she kind of saved my life, when every wound inside me seemed to surface and push me to the edge, but she was there, over time, instead of a path to possible suicide.

I stared at Grasso, Paul Grasso, wondering if this was another bluff for a chance to get me or escape. "Okay. You got a choice."

He nodded sharply. "Sidearm. In the heart. From the front." He pointed to his chest.

That seemed honorable, in some sense, a Marine kind of thing. And it could get me in trouble. Murder, murder weapon. The police weren't predisposed to believe me. "No," I said. "Your choice is cliff or dogs."

He shook his head, ran at me, and stumbled. "You fucking bastard!"

I hobbled around him, toward the cliff. It was his only real option, if he didn't want to be disgraced and go to prison for life, disabled and beaten into submission daily. No, that wasn't for anyone, of course, but especially not for him. I could threaten to blow out his knees or something to make his prison experience worse, but he knew that. "This way."

After a long moment, he followed my voice and stumbled over brush and roots, good arm out in front. The dogs followed. The sound of my progress led him. I couldn't tell if he was shedding tears. His face was a mess, and he grimaced in pain. He tripped and fell, but got up.

"Just tell me when we get there." He grunted as he tugged off his sweatshirt and dropped it.

After a quarter mile or more, we made it to the cliff. Looking out, the foliage continued across the contour of the hills, but down below was out of view.

"Five feet, straight ahead," I said.

Grasso stopped. He called to his dogs. He patted them but pushed them away when they started licking him, whimpering.

"Out!" He chased them off with the wave of his arm.

I worried suddenly that I wasn't doing the right thing. I should turn him and the evidence over to the police; let him suffer all the consequences. After all, he hadn't given me a choice when he abused me in high school and stuffed me into the bin, and everything else he did to me since. Still.

He nodded, inched forward, angling his head several ways as if trying to use some remaining vision. He sucked in his breath when he felt the hard cliff edge with his foot and pulled it back. I actually had an iota of compassion at that moment. I put the pistol into my waistband and continued along the cliff thirty yards. I scanned the area, but didn't see anyone else. I was far enough away not to be accused of pushing him or forcing him.

"Dax?" he said.

Using my shirtsleeves, I unfolded a document. Incorporation papers for a non-profit that named Debbie as president and unknown others as treasurer and clerk. Youth United, Inc. They weren't signed or stamped, so probably weren't filed with the state yet, but if disclosed, it could hurt her position.

Another document was a copy of the trust on legal-sized paper. Underneath was an unattached sheet of paper, the Schedule of Beneficiaries. Only one beneficiary was declared, a non-profit corporation under a different name, the Morehouse Trust Co. Additional paper I scanned, related corporate documents. Then I found its original incorporator and past CEO—"P. Delahunt Grasso," a relative?

"Dax," Grasso called out nervously.

"I'm here."

No, it was Paul Delahunt Grasso. It was the Mayor of Boston. And fingerprints in fresh blue ink were all over them, how apropos—*gotcha*. My dream was realized; reasonable doubt.

"Dax. About the choice."

I looked up.

He hung his head onto his chest. After a moment, he nodded, then straightened his shoulders and held his head up high. He said, "Thanks."

I said, "You're—"

Grasso leaned and jumped out, feet first. He fell through the air. The flapping clothes fell quiet after a few seconds, until he was too close to the cliff edge below to see him. I heard branches snap and crash, then his body impact, the final sound.

"-welcome," I said, finishing the sentence.

# CHAPTER 47

# Tuesday, 6:15 a.m.

The sun's red-orange arc, rising over the ocean water, fulfilled dawn's promise. Its flickering sheen stretched across the water's surface. Its beams continued onto the deserted beach, making the wavy sand resemble miniature tan hills with westward shadows. Even the residual clouds from the overnight thunderstorms moved behind me, toward Blue Hills, about eighty miles away.

But all was not clear. A Chinese proverb says that success in the end erases all mistakes. Unfortunately, this wasn't China, and this wasn't the end. The fallout from Grasso's death I couldn't fathom yet. The investigations would continue. Autopsy results and forensic testing results would come back, tests that I hoped I'd "pass."

The onshore breeze was cool. I kicked a hollow crab shell, winced, and then limped along. It was funny how much pain you could ignore when fighting for your life. Since injuring my leg and knee on my motorcycle, my knee had swelled. The ace bandage made it extra-large. Add the scrapes and cuts all over and, well, let's just say I wasn't ready to shake my tush on the catwalk. But a gunshot to the thigh wasn't something to shake off. Luckily, it was to the same leg, so my good leg could bear most of the weight.

The five-minute walk back to Kravitz Chatham cottage was a ten minute limp. At the patio table set for two, he poured coffee. Laid out was a spread of Eggs Benedict, toast, and fruit. My mouth watered.

I was so thankful that Kravitz had offered refuge when I called last night. I drove my Harley. He simply said to come inside, take a shower, and get rest. I relaxed some, but felt mentally numb and physically exhausted. I also dressed up the hole in my leg, which hurt like hell despite the ibuprofen. At least, no artery was hit. There was an exit wound, too. I patched up both sides, but it killed. I disinfected and bandaged the scrape on my head and elsewhere, like the Terrier bites on my legs. I couldn't go to the hospital with a gunshot wound and dog bites, especially since Grasso would be found with gunpowder residue on his hand and his dogs nearby.

"So, the police located me," Kravitz said, sitting at the table. "A Braintree detective, Michael Donovan, asked if my house was broken into up there." He bit his toast.

I nodded, fixing my coffee, then sat gingerly, extending my left leg.

Last night I'd washed my hands several times with different soaps and repeated it until my skin was raw, so there'd be no gunpowder or other residue on my hand or body. I rubbed moisturizer all over, wiped it off with a towel, and repeated. When I left the woods yesterday, I'd wiped down Grasso's gun, smeared it in mud, and tossed it off the cliff after him. There'd be no prints or residue on it, but that was for the police to speculate about.

Kravitz turned to gaze at the sliver of ocean in view, stirring his coffee. "And Boston Police called, Sergeant Detective Montes. 'How'd the article get published, and on the front page?' he'd asked. And so on."

I sipped from the steaming mug. "And?"

Kravitz looked at me like I was a dummy. "I told him to talk to my lawyer."

I smiled. Sometimes a straight shooter must let his lawyer do the shooting.

"They know I'm alive." Kravitz appeared annoyed. "That's enough for now. They can't charge me with anything. Obstruction of justice? It's facilitation of justice—I couldn't say that, you understand."

"Of course," I said. "And thank you."

He smiled. "Did you hear the news about Debra?"

"What?" I sat up. Coffee slid over the rim, and I put down the mug. "What happened?"

"This just in. It's not just what happened; it's what's not going to happen."

"What?"

He tilted his mug slowly, smirking over the rim.

I reached my hands over as if to strangle him. "Don't do this to me!"

"Hey, keeping you in suspense is your payment for such a delicious breakfast. You ready, slick? The acting Suffolk D.A. is dropping the case against her."

"That's great."

"Because of forensics," he added. "She's a straight-up gal, this D.A., not a complete political animal. Not yet, anyway."

"Forensics," I said.

"The blood on the knife was Swanson's, true. And Debbie's fingerprints were on the knife, but the police' Latent Print Unit re-examined it. Apparently the size and angle of the prints indicate it couldn't have been from the person who stabbed Swanson," he said. "In fact, the prints were consistent with someone holding it easily, not with pressure, as if to cut cake, as Debra had claimed."

"Wow. Of course."

"Of course it's 'of course.' The killer was strong, and wiped down the knife, ready for Debra's prints. And I think the cops decided, at some level, to hold back on this stuff when they realized it, to pressure you."

"I hadn't thought of that." Add Swanson's cell phone text to Debbie, and the web text to Swanson to go to the vacant house earlier, which Sunny told me about, and Debbie was in the clear. She was set up by Grasso.

"You haven't had time to think of that, Dax. Don't feel bad," he said. "Feel good."

"I do." I wanted to ask about other forensic results, but I'd better review that with Max, not Kravitz.

"I heard the mayor's body was found." He sipped his coffee.

I opened my mouth to speak, but shut it.

"Suicide," he said. "Unofficially. According to one source, they can't explain broken glass on his body."

"Maybe he landed on it." *Better shut my mouth.*

"Well, there's a lot of scrutiny, especially under the circumstances. It's from a glass or jar or bottle, but it's not all there. They're searching the area, but—"

*Damn.* In my article, I'd mentioned the possibility of the documents being in a jar. Investigators could make that connection. "What?"

"You know. The leaves, the wind, the rain."

So I hoped. During our fight, my DNA had probably rubbed off on Grass's sweatshirt. I shivered. What if I hadn't remembered to retrieve it? After I left the cliff, I walked by a gutter drain, kicked his sweatshirt inside, and then flagged down a taxi to get my Harley.

"The rain, alas, will likely wash away certain evidence." He sipped. "But we'll see what they come up with. Hey, you know what I have? An advance copy of an esteemed daily newspaper. I have connections, you might know."

I nodded, worried. There'd surely be ink residue on the jar fragments that would match Grasso's inked fingerprints on the corporate documents. How could I get the documents to the police without implicating myself?

Kravitz pulled out the *Boston Times*, Monday edition.

"It seems that the land search in Blue Hills turned up a lot of other things. Like two bodies, one is male, possibly Jimmy Hoffa."

"The missing union organizer? Get the hell out of town," I said.

"It's not him." He grinned. "Preliminary comparison is said to rule him out, but it could be the body of the guy who killed Hoffa, who then got snuffed himself. Hoffa's ID was buried there in a canvas pouch." He shrugged. "But who knows, maybe it's a hoax. We haven't printed the story yet, actually. The details are sketchy."

"Amazing, though. Even if it's just his ID," I said.

"Yeah, you know that's all over the news. And there's a silver lining."

"What?"

"They found a silver urn by Paul Revere that lore had as long-buried hard by the Charles River."

I arched my brows. "What?"

Kravitz waved his hand at me, smirking. "Never mind. I *will* get the hell out of town this time."

His cell phone rang. "It's Jimmy," he said. "Oh—not Hoffa." He winked, then picked up and asked Jimmy what he'd found out.

After the phone call, Kravitz updated me. The D.A.'s office, off the record, may have found evidence pointing to city hall corruption. "They won't go public until they investigate more. They found papers on Grasso and something else they won't disclose."

I nodded, hoping nothing would implicate me. "Well, that's good."

"It is," he said.

Kravitz gave me the eye, but didn't comment or question. Maybe he wanted information directly from me to scoop the story. I certainly owed him, but from here on I'd clear everything through legal first—Maximilian, worth the max, worth a million. I'd probably have to send the corporate documents with Grasso's prints on them to Kravitz or the D.A.; anonymously, of course.

Kravitz' land line rang. He answered, then told the caller to wait and covered the mouthpiece. "You here? It's Debbie's lawyer, DeLay, looking for you."

I nodded, surprised, and took the call. DeLay told me he got word that the police had received an anonymous report of Grasso taking a city vehicle the night of Swanson's murder. The mileage difference from prior and subsequent log entries matched exactly the distance to the site of Swanson's murder and back.

*How nice.*

DeLay had scheduled a hearing to rescind the bail revocation. It would keep me out of jail, for now, he said, but he was unsure about the chances. The charge against Debbie was dropped, so there'd no longer be a direct conflict of interest. Plus, he said, their case against me was weaker now.

Apparently, he thought he was taking charge of this case, too.

I elected not to tell DeLay about the corporate documents with Grasso's fingerprints. I'd save that for Max Garfunkel, whom I insisted to be my lawyer. DeLay relented and said he'd keep Garfunkel on my case. I'd tell Garfunkel everything in person and keep him working hard. I was just relieved that I wasn't going to be on *America's Most Wanted* tonight.

My cell phone was dead, but I remembered Terry's number and called from Kravitz's landline.

"Thanks," I said.

"Excuse me?" Terry said. "I don't know who this is. Furthermore, I don't know what you're talking about, my honkey homey."

I pictured his smile. "A'ite." I hung up

I owed him more than tools and a Pabst; I owed him a truck full of Guinness or whatever. Actually, he was a wine aficionado, since he'd gotten into cooking. I'd give him a case of something top shelf or top wine rack or whatever.

I iced my knee and popped aspirin this time instead of Ibuprofen, analogous to cross-training, then I limped back to the beach. Something kept bothering me and I couldn't ignore it. It was muddled, but at the heart of it was Paul Grasso. I'd effectively killed him.

I pressed my hands against my face, pushed them over my head, down my neck. And because of Grasso, I'd killed another man earlier, Charles Cohoon. I didn't know either one or much of what they'd done in their lives, not enough to be their *de-facto* executioner. I suffered an intense guilt, not of getting away with it, but of doubt and angst in taking the lives of others. That was it. Even though I had good cause to do what I did, it hurt me deeply, unexpectedly. I just didn't know how to live with it.

I saw a more human side of Grasso regarding his loss of Swanson, even though Grasso killed him; and regarding his apparent love for Debbie, even though he was willing to sacrifice that love so selfishly. Finally, his apology to me, though late and small, had some genuine element of remorse for an act so long ago. Grasso was a criminal and a bastard, but he ceased being an undiminished monster. He became more human, the death of which couldn't be so tidily swept out to sea.

I thought back to Terry. Father Time, a nickname ostensible earned for killing someone. He must have felt remorse, whether he admitted it or not. However, he turned his life around, redeemed. And if he could be, why couldn't Grasso, me, anyone? There was the rub, though. Grasso had chosen not to be redeemed, but to pay a price for what he'd done, or for some of it. That I had let him choose his price instead of him suffering injured pride and imprisonment? I didn't know what to think of that. It would take time.

I turned my back to the salty onshore wind. Good and evil were society-defined controls of people by branding them or their behavior; by admonishing them, fining them, giving second chances, imprisoning them, or ultimately executing them. But I defined Grasso as an outlaw, outside the laws of society, without its protections, and had my way with him.

*Vengeance is mine, sayeth the Lord.*

Yeah, but I was just helping out.

# CHAPTER 48

## Tuesday, 8:45 a.m.

**M**y Harley Davidson wheels rode the white line on the Sagamore Bridge at a comfortable distance from the double-height granite curb. I thought back to the people I helped as the Dandy Vigilante. It felt good in a civic, spiritual way. I'd been too inwardly focused for too long. That was part of the surprise for me, that I could do all that.

To my right was the Cape Cod Canal, and beyond was the Atlantic Ocean, all shimmering. The panorama was beautiful at the apex of this convex bridge, which mimicked the earth's curvature beneath me, and I felt high.

Yet I might fall.

Kravitz had offered to let me stay on at his cottage, but I had places to go and people to see, and places and people to avoid. When I reached Plymouth, I exited the highway and got a shock; Governor Leno, his face right in front of me, about ten feet tall. The billboard announced his candidacy in the primaries for his party's nomination to be U.S. President.

I found a payphone near the Mayflower II, not far from my old apartment. I retrieved messages, skipping many. Debbie said I should call her, if not meet her. We had decisions to make, I knew. Who stayed, who went? What stayed, what went? Maybe I should just go to our house. Then again, it was probably thick with the press, and maybe the police. I was still a fugitive.

Attorney Garfunkel said to call him back. Twice. I guessed "no news is good news" didn't apply if the news was merely avoided, so I plugged more coins into the phone. Garfunkel answered.

"Dax, I've new information," he said. "Cohoon's death hasn't been ruled a homicide, yet. It's likely, but first they have to get beyond the appearance of it being an accident. It's possible that Grasso could have had something to do with it, but they're looking into you, too."

"Oh?" I tried sounding surprised. Maybe I should have taken a shot at indignation.

"First, Cohoon was trying to convict you," he said, "which could be a basis for motive."

"Sure, me and thousands of others."

"Second," he said, "they still suspect you of being the vigilante, and that profile makes you someone more likely to act out. Third, an unknown motorcycle was seen in the neighborhood."

"Any description?"

"No, not of the motorcycle or the driver. Not yet, anyway. And I don't have to advise you. You should—"

"No, you don't have to advise me," I said.

I had to get those bright stickers off my motorcycle and dump the new helmet. Not that Garfunkel knew I was the one, but I assumed that he had to assume the worst-case scenario. He likely dealt with clients whose common denominator was guilty until proven innocent.

"Dax. There's more," he said solemnly.

I swallowed, not ready for more. "Yes?"

"The letter opener could have ended up in his eye and brain by accident. However, if they place you there, at his house—and I'm not assuming you were there or that they could prove it—you're looking at being charged with manslaughter, at least. I don't know what else they found onsite, but in the best-case scenario, they'll say you pushed him, or worse, that you two got into a struggle."

I said, "That's not good."

"What's more, there's the broken window in the basement door, which could be accidental, but it could also be tentative evidence of burglary, a felony charge itself, which also means felony murder. They'd have to put it together, and Cohoon's involvement in corruption is possible, but don't count on his misbehavior to get you out of another murder charge."

"Oh, *damn.*"

"Hold on a second. I got—hold on." After a half minute, he got back. "Dax, well, my contact said Grasso's whereabouts are apparently accounted for elsewhere. So, they've no one else to look at right now but you, it seems."

"Oh, come *on,*" I said. "Attorney Garfunkel, this is ridiculous. Dig around; they'll find others who had bigger beefs with him than I did. Why would I kill him for doing his job? I'm not some drug-induced maniac or a gangster offing a guy to get off a prior murder charge. That's insane."

"What you say makes sense, Dax," he said. "Let's hope they see it, too."

"They will," I said. "Because you'll help them see it."

"Okay, but they'll request a DNA sample, so—"

"Can we talk? Can I tell you what happened?"

"You shouldn't on a cell phone."

"It's a pay phone. Listen." I outlined in vague, hypothetical terms what had happened at Cohoon's house—a "Good House" gone bad.

"Wow. Breaking and entering. Even if one didn't intend a homicide, it happened during the commission of an inherently dangerous felony, which B&E is, by statutory definition. See, intent of the felony substitutes for intent to murder. To avoid it, maybe one can prove one abandoned the burglary and gave up, and claim deadly force was necessary, but I gotta say—"

"I know," I said flatly. "Fat chance of a jury believing that."

"Insanity?" Max said.

"True," I said, "but no."

"Well, we can maybe show lack of malice or intent on the B&E, so no felony murder. Just second degree murder, but I'd have to research that angle. It depends."

I coughed.

"I don't know," he said. "Maybe plea bargain?"

"Don't think so."

"A bail hearing for the assault and battery is set for this afternoon. I was hoping to get your bail reinstated, but then a source inside the D.A.'s office said that may rush them into new charges regarding Cohoon's death, whatever the charges would be, to keep your bail revoked. Sorry. They'll wait until after the hearing to dismiss the Swanson murder charge against you, if they do. You're kind of stuck for right now."

"So it seems," I said.

"Actually, think about it; you haven't even been arraigned on the Dandy Vigilante charges. The new D.A. might pick that up."

"Well, isn't that nice."

"At least, the article didn't identify you as the DV. That would have sealed your fate."

"And my jail cell." *Thanks for the editing, Kravitz.*

"You're in a pickle," he said. "Unless you have an alibi."

That was his invitation, I supposed. "I see."

"That's key. We'll discuss that later."

Right. Give me time to get my story straight. This guy was deceptively smooth. I hung up and noted the yellow lightning stripes on my gas tank.

On the way back to the highway, I pulled behind a school to peel off the stickers from my gas tank, but then kept going instead. It was the kind of scene the police would stop for. I got off the highway in Weymouth and rode back roads to Braintree. I passed a cop parked road side. I was full of hope—hope that I was also full of luck and wouldn't get caught.

After another couple of miles, I turned onto Tremont Street and parked at the rear entrance to French's Common, where they'd put in a small lot. I peeled off the stickers and wiped it down. Now, if the police got a good description of the motorcycle near the D.A.'s house, at least it wouldn't match mine.

As I remounted my Harley, a shiny blue car came, a Mustang. I felt like I was supposed to remember something. The car stopped in the drive, blocking my egress. *Shit.* No space to squeeze through at the corner, either, because of a concrete column.

A man got out and walked toward me, instead of into the tennis court or the common. My pulse started banging away. He was about my age and height, but heavier. I couldn't read his face and didn't recognize him as law enforcement.

He looked familiar. I pointed to his car. *Oh no.* I'd seen his face before, in Revere, after leaving Cohoon's house, the man getting into the blue Mustang. I eyed the tennis court gates.

He looked behind at his car then he faced me again. "Dax Grantham?"

# CHAPTER 49

# Tuesday, 11:50 a.m.

"**A**re you Dax Grantham?" the man said.

I squinted at the maple trees that edged the street. "I don't want any."

He looked confused. "Any what?"

"Insurance or whatever you're selling." I was tired, pissed off. "Now move your car, please. I have an appointment." *Yeah, right—with a jail cell.* I was at the end of my rope, which would surely be used to hang me.

"Sure," he said. "But wait a second, I just want to know. Are you?"

"No comment." He could be a reporter, but not one I recognized. No, wait. The sharp-featured face, the wavy brown hair. He was definitely the guy in Revere, but maybe I'd seen him elsewhere, too.

He said, "You are, aren't you?"

I exercised my desire to remain silent.

"Well, I have a comment, Dax. My name is Thomas."

"You're not a cop, right?" I said hopefully. "A reporter?"

"Nope, sorry." He looked me over. "I'm here to help you."

"What? Help me? Do you know what a monumental task that is?"

He smiled. I didn't.

"You're going to be charged with manslaughter," he said. "And possibly murder, of District Attorney Cohoon."

*Fuck.* "And that's something to smile at? What are you, court-appointed counsel or something? I already have a lawyer."

"No," he said seriously. "I'm a publisher, a small independent press in Western Mass. My name is Thomas."

"Yeah, you said that already, Thomas. I think you left a message on my answering machine, too. So who the hell are you?"

He shrugged, and his smile reappeared; indecipherable but genuine, a curiously big smile. "I'm Thomas...or Tommy."

I froze. I stepped closer and looked him over. "What? What are you saying?"

"My last name used to be Grantham," he said.

*Grantham? Used to be?* He did look familiar. An old cousin?

"Before I was adopted," he said.

I stared at him, floored. "This is a hoax, isn't it?"

He shook his head. "No, it's not," he said evenly.

"Yes, it is."

"I'm your brother, Dax."

I stepped up to him and grabbed his shirtfront, my eyes digging into his. I lifted him onto his toes. *"Who put you up to this?"*

He pushed back gently. "Whoa. I understand you're upset, but hands off, bro. We haven't gotten in a fight in a long time."

"How the hell do I know you're my brother?"

"How? Because—" He looked off as if searching his mind. "Because I lied to you."

"What the—? So you're lying to me?" I released him.

"No. In the past. Dad didn't die from a grizzly bear attack. It was a car accident."

I didn't want to believe it. I was too beat up lately, for a lifetime. I was so unprepared.

But I also wanted to believe it. And for a second, I forced my defenses down, and the years peeled away briefly, and I caught a glimpse of him underneath. *My God.* It was him, my brother; my older brother, Tommy. What a terribly sad and joyous feeling.

"The registry contacted me a while ago, but I don't know. I didn't know what to do. I was dealing with other things and I wasn't ready." I could see grief linger in his tentative eyes, slate-blue like mine. What scars did he have? All I'd thought about, at least lately, was my own.

"Oh my God." I grabbed his shoulders.

He grinned, warmly. "I've been following your story."

*This person was my brother.* I kept saying it inside my head, waiting for the meaning to sift down into my heart. "Really?"

"Yup." He mock punched my shoulder. "And you were with me the night of Cohoon's death," he said firmly. "Now let's get the hell out of here, bro."

***

Blowing on my latte, I gazed out the large café window from half-dozen tables away. Rain fell steadily, a gray screen to the black night.

Mentally, these last few weeks had been an undulating, winding path, leading me through a staggering range of emotions. The deepest root of my recent actions was Grasso, his attacking me with his accomplice because of his own sexuality, cruelly confining me in that tight, airless bin, and me screaming until I'd lost consciousness. It affected my psyche deeper than I'd known. It led me in different directions.

The foam suppressed the latte's steam, and the first sip scalded the roof of my mouth. I was alone, for the moment.

Ultimately, the attack was a major cause for me choosing a journalism career despite the bad experience, and eventually to embrace the chance to play the superhero as an adult. It was a catharsis—to vindicate myself and free myself within. In the end, Grasso's sentence—his free fall in all that open-air space to his death—was fitting and just. I realized it was sad on both sides, too. Nothing excused his behavior, of course, but this series of events formed a greater tragedy.

Now my brother Tommy showed up, like the cavalry, like a big brother. It salved even older wounds, and he saved me with an alibi for Cohoon's homicide. He'd tell everyone that I was with him elsewhere at the time of Cohoon's death. Then the acting D.A. would have a hard time charging me. There were no fingerprints because I'd worn gloves. Even if there was DNA evidence, it would be minimal and explained away as my having brushed against Cohoon in court. The courtroom audio system had recorded him rudely saying "excuse me" as he arrived at the prosecutor's table, which was when he'd brushed past me. That could establish reasonable doubt.

I didn't get away with murder. I wasn't a murderer. But unless I was missing something, it seemed that I'd gotten away from a lot, and gained much more.

Tommy and I had spent over an hour together. We found that we both grew up to make a living off the printed word. He printed a variety of material at his independent publishing house. So many questions remained, factual, chronological, and emotional. If only we could see either of our parents...but the time for that had long passed. Tommy, or Tom now, said he'd locate our parents' graves.

I hadn't sought Tommy sooner, but I'd felt isolation in being adopted, and Grasso only deepened that feeling. Tommy hadn't looked for me sooner either, for whatever reason. In fact, I was still having a hard time believing it had happened, that he was my brother and he had found me. We used to be closer in size, but I hadn't even seen him enter adolescence. Compared to me now, he was taller and bulkier. The face, too, I had to strive to see the resemblance to the boy's face, but that was to be expected, especially without the benefit of old photos.

Alone, I can remember some of my childhood, and by trying together, I thought more of the past would come back for Tommy and me to reclaim. But he seemed reluctant, like it brought back too many bad memories, but not all memories were bad. Still, I had no idea what he'd been through. I thought I had it bad growing up. My childhood therapist, Tricia Overton, sympathized, but I always suspected that Tommy had it worse.

The adoption record was sealed, and the authorities had no reason to suspect Tommy of being related to me, thus biased. Maybe we could safely reveal it someday, which depended on how everything turned out in the police investigations.

Tommy was like Racer X, the mysterious brother of animated character Speed Racer. Behind the scenes, he helped save Speed on racetracks and mountain roads around the world, except that I knew now that Tommy was my brother. Speed never knew Racer X was his brother.

Now what about "Trixie"? She should be here any second and I was unsure how this was going to go down.

Despite the joy of finding Tommy, though, something bugged me. It was too convenient that he'd shown up just in time to save me and be willing and able to provide an alibi for me. I thought he was a lefty, but when we were going over the alibi, I'd noticed that he was writing notes with his right hand. I had to be either remembering wrong or mistaken, surely. I supposed I was still learning to trust; trust the world and trust individuals. But I still had to ask questions, like how he'd known that the acting D.A. would be bringing charges for manslaughter or murder.

I could breathe again, and if I could do that, I could fight. It wasn't over yet, of course, but I also had the feeling that there was more to it. Grasso had said that I had no idea what I'd stumbled upon, that it was deeper than I'd imagined. Was he bluffing? Well, we'd see—or at least, I would.

With progress on the severest of my legal troubles, it had finally sunk in that I could hope to move on; hope for my own redemption in the face of where I'd been, what I'd done, like my faith in Terry's redemption even before he changed his ways and went to college. If he could do it in his situation, so could I in mine. If I could have faith in him, I could have faith in me. It was a lot better than jumping off a cliff, certainly. I guessed I believed in second chances; *now that sounds familiar.*

Debbie arrived at the cafe. She came to me. We greeted politely, not touching, and sat at the table, silent for a minute.

I went to the counter to get her favorite tea and brought it to her. She thanked me and sipped a few times. On the table was a paper bag, small and white, with red print illegible because the bag was rolled at the top.

"What's this?" I said.

She smiled, but seemed scared and pushed it toward me. I opened it and was surprised, confused. It was a package of pills.

"What's this?"

She shifted back and forth in her seat and moved her mouth to speak, but didn't. That was rare.

*Birth control pills.* I said, "It's yours?"

She nodded.

"And, you— You're…going to take these?"

She shook her head, her eyes watering. She couldn't speak. That was definitely a first.

*Wow.* I nodded, realizing what she meant. "So. You used to take these."

Debbie pursed her lips, and the tears rolled out. She nodded and bowed her head.

This was her confession. She'd started birth control at some point when she had doubts about us. That was why we couldn't conceive a child. It hurt all over again; the frustrating inability to conceive, the affair later. But I wasn't expecting this, not at all; furthest thing from my mind.

I put the pills down. She opened my hand, put the pills in, and pressed my fingers closed around them.

"Please," she said, her voice soft, deeply emotional.

I didn't know what to do. I assumed she wanted me to throw them away and take her back. Try again? Have kids? Why should I, God damn it? I wanted to swear at her, curse the hell out of her and walk out.

Instead, quietly, I got up and walked to the front.

I looked back at her, then looked at I didn't know what, not focusing. Time seemed to freeze. But my mind kept moving, with pieces coming together, some peeling away.

She was sitting up straight, watching me. Hope and doubt fluttered across her face like a subtle wind on a sail. Where did this vessel take us? Did we sail away? Or did I leave her behind in port?

I threw the pills into the trash barrel. Her eyes relaxed, her smile eased warmly onto her face as she leaned back. The relief and genuine feelings were touching.

But I turned to leave. I glanced back once more. She sat up again, anxious, lips slightly parted, about to call out and about to cry.

I kept going, out of the coffee shop.

At my Jeep, I unlocked the door and got in. I opened my glove compartment and took out something. I brought it back inside. At the table, her head was down. She was sobbing quietly. The table was wet beneath her face.

"Excuse me, is this seat taken?"

Debbie sniffled and looked up, surprised. Her eyes were wide and glassy. "No. No, it's— She wiped her cheeks with her hands and reached for a napkin. "No, it isn't taken."

"May I sit down?"

"Oh, yes. Yes. Please do," she said, her voice strained. She tried to sit straighter. She brushed her face with her wrists and glanced to each side, unsure of herself or what I was doing.

"Here. I believe this is for you." I handed her a fist-sized box wrapped in brown paper.

She touched her chest. "Me?"

I nodded solemnly.

She opened the package, then her jaw dropped and eyebrows leapt in surprise. Her smile reminded me of a child's Christmas smile.

It was a desk bell, the kind that used to be taped to my dashboard when we were dating in college. We used to hit it whenever one of us said something funny or had a fun idea. It was a symbol, a promise.

"Oh Dax," she cried.

*Every Saint has a past, and every sinner has a future.* You got that right, Oscar Wilde. It applied to all of us to some degree.

As she leaned toward me, another tear rolled down her cheek and splashed into her cup. She brought her chair closer and threw a knee over mine, then flung her arms around my neck. She pressed her face to mine, kissed me, then tucked her wet face into my neck, and cried, and she laughed. Her laugh was beautiful.

I couldn't laugh, though, not yet, but I knew what to do. I leaned into her, held onto her, and reached one hand behind her back. I raised my hand. *Ding!*

## THE END

# OTHER ANAPHORA LITERARY PRESS TITLES

*PLJ: Interviews with Best-Selling YA Writers*
Editor: Anna Faktorovich

*East of Los Angeles*
By: John Brantingham

*Notes on the Road to Now*
By: Paul Bellerive

*Folk Concert*
By: Janet Ruth Heller

*100 Years of the Federal Reserve*
By: Marie Bussing-Burks

*River Bends in Time*
By: Glen A. Mazis

*Interviews with BFF Winners*
Editor: Anna Faktorovich

*An Adventurous Life*
By: Robert Hauptman

CPSIA information can be obtained at www.ICGtesting.com
Printed in the USA
LVOW08s1639280714

396370LV00006B/981/P